# MERGERS &
# ACQUISITIONS

# MERGERS & ACQUISITIONS

## DANA VACHON

RIVERHEAD BOOKS

a member of Penguin Group (USA) Inc.

*New York*    *2007*

RIVERHEAD BOOKS
Published by the Penguin Group
Penguin Group (USA) Inc., 375 Hudson Street, New York, New York 10014, USA • Penguin
Group (Canada), 90 Eglinton Avenue East, Suite 700, Toronto, Ontario M4P 2Y3, Canada (a division
of Pearson Penguin Canada Inc.) • Penguin Books Ltd, 80 Strand, London WC2R 0RL, England •
Penguin Ireland, 25 St Stephen's Green, Dublin 2, Ireland (a division of Penguin Books Ltd) • Penguin
Group (Australia), 250 Camberwell Road, Camberwell, Victoria 3124, Australia (a division of Pearson
Australia Group Pty Ltd) • Penguin Books India Pvt Ltd, 11 Community Centre, Panchsheel Park,
New Delhi–110 017, India • Penguin Group (NZ), 67 Apollo Drive, Mairangi Bay,
Auckland 1311, New Zealand (a division of Pearson New Zealand Ltd) • Penguin Books
(South Africa) (Pty) Ltd, 24 Sturdee Avenue, Rosebank, Johannesburg 2196, South Africa

Penguin Books Ltd, Registered Offices:
80 Strand, London WC2R 0RL, England

Library of Congress Cataloging-in-Publication Data

Vachon, Dana.
Mergers & acquisitions / Dana Vachon.
p.      cm.
ISBN 978-1-59448-934-1
1. Bankers—Fiction.   2. Dating (Social customs)—Fiction.   3. Manhattan (New York, N.Y.)—Fiction.
4. Wall Street (New York, N.Y.)—Fiction.   I. Title.   II. Title: Mergers & acquisitions.
PS3622.A33M47      2007                    2006101559
813'.6—dc22

Printed in the United States of America
1   3   5   7   9   10   8   6   4   2

BOOK DESIGN BY MEIGHAN CAVANAUGH

This is a work of fiction. Names, characters, places, and incidents either are the product of the author's imagination or are used fictitiously, and any resemblance to actual persons, living or dead, businesses, companies, events, or locales is entirely coincidental.

While the author has made every effort to provide accurate telephone numbers and Internet addresses at the time of publication, neither the publisher nor the author assumes any responsibility for errors, or for changes that occur after publication. Further, the publisher does not have any control over and does not assume any responsibility for author or third-party websites or their content.

*For Thalia, Elizabeth*

# MERGERS &
# ACQUISITIONS

# The New York Racquet & Tennis Club

The bride-to-be needed to change the dressing on her wound, and her black-suited mother let her know it by pointing to her shoulder, then raising her Botoxed brow as best she could. Lauren Schuyler had been born wealthy and healthy and beautiful and she was right to view herself as entirely blessed, save for the dozen or so moles splattered across her arms and chest. Not even the city's best plastic surgeons would touch them for fear of scars, so she tanned the rest of herself to a darkened umber, and in this way kept the moles from standing out. No one wore costumes on the night of her engagement party at the Racquet & Tennis Club, but in the ballroom of that club, that limestone manse sitting like a sphinx on Park Avenue, the most prosperous street in the most prosperous city in the most prosperous nation that ever lived, you didn't need costumes to have a masque ball. Everyone knew their role, and played it. The members of the Racquet & Tennis Club—which had nothing to do with Racquetball and less to do with

Tennis—walked about like reborn Roman senators, which is not too far from what they were. Their names were written in gold leaf on mahogany plaques across the walls of the changing rooms, Whitneys, Phippses, Rockefellers, and they bathed naked together in the Turkish bath and played obscure racquet sports passed down from Bourbon kings and sealed billion-dollar deals with clinks of glasses over lunch. And at these parties, if you were not a member, you were a guest and set your face stern to conceal your awe. You were solemn to foil discovery of the wonder that mugged you of your confidence as you came up the old staircase lined with oil paintings of old men and horses, then into the grand ballroom that invited you to look down on who you had been just moments before, on the street below. You hated loving being there, and you struggled to conceal yourself, and all of a sudden, you were in costume. Just like Lauren Schuyler, whose dark tan made it impossible for anyone to see that she was bleeding. As the bandage turned dark brown with Lauren's stale blood, it disappeared entirely against her flesh. I might have missed it like everyone else, but before I had been the worst young investment banker on Wall Street, I had aspired to be a doctor, and had seen bloodied bandages. From my place beneath an oil painting of a polo pony, I noticed the girl and her wound. I drank gin and wondered how, as a premed with a C minus in organic chemistry, I had ever expected to get into a good medical school in the first place. I guess the thing was that I had seen a documentary on CNN while I was at Georgetown, about all of these poor Liberian child soldiers. I had thought then that even if you went to the worst medical school in the world, you could probably do some good.

Lauren Schuyler was no Liberian child soldier, but I thought of those poor little guys, all brainwashed and bullet riddled, as I watched her bleed in her party dress. I thought that the doctor must have cut right down to the muscle, and that beneath her bandage things probably didn't look all that different from one of those Liberian bullet wounds.

I was right. Lauren would confide all of this to a friend in confidence much later, and the friend would violate her confidence, and everyone would know that she had pressured Roger Thorne into proposing to her after learning of the little cancer and feeling inexplicably diminished. All around me people spoke of bonuses and booze and drugs and sex and cheating and having. The ballroom ebbed and flowed, a rolling wash of brightly colored pastels and silks. The young men and women spoke in refined and civilized tones as, smiling, they savaged one another. Only the waiters were separate from it, grave and dark and discarded beneath their silver trays of appetizers. Not even Lauren's fiancé noticed as she orphaned her drink and rushed to mop the drainage from her wound.

"Did you know that Lilliana and Silvana are bisexual, but only with each other?" Thorne asked, as he handed me my third gin and tonic and pointed to a pair of Hermès-clad Latin women just across the room.

We had met Lilliana and Silvana in Cabo San Lucas, just after Thorne asked Lauren to marry him. Roger had fallen in love in Cabo, and then had his heart broken, and in the end became something of a Mexican national hero, at least to the upper classes; Mexico City society glossies still ran pictures of him fighting off kidnappers, and hailed him as "El Gringo Misterioso." Of course Lilliana and Silvana had come to celebrate his engagement. Roger had, after all, saved their lives.

"They flew in from Marbella yesterday," said Thorne, plucking a very small piece of toast with an even smaller piece of salmon atop it from a passing waiter's silver tray.

"It's good to see that they've gotten over the loss of Manuel," I said, because both women had seemed very much in love the last time I had seen them.

"They are just two very resilient babes," said Thorne. "They were pretty sad, sure. But the human spirit is inspiring. We had cocktails at the Carlyle, then went up to their suite, poured chocolate syrup all over each other, and made a flesh sundae."

"A flesh sundae?"

"Big time. It was highly sexual, Quinn. I mean, yeah, I was busy getting ready for the party, but I figured it was the least I could do to help those stone foxes out. Especially after all they've been through. You know, the grieving process can take months . . ."

Across the ballroom the two women fed each another pieces of smoked salmon, then licked each other's fingers.

"They really do seem distraught," I observed.

"They're totally shaved," Thorne informed.

"Are you at all excited to be getting married, Roger?" I asked him.

"Big time," he replied.

ROGER THORNE AND I HAD SPENT THE ENTIRE YEAR WORKING together in the Mergers & Acquisitions group at J. S. Spenser. Thorne had saved my career, and I had saved his life, and in this way we had become friends. He proposed to Lauren Schuyler just before our doomed business trip to Cabo San Lucas, from which we had returned only by a miracle, and one that I now sometimes regretted. I had never told Thorne that I had applied to medical schools, and even gotten accepted at one, El Universidad de Medicina de Santa Filomena, in Costa Rica. He was always open with me, and often said that he would have liked to have been an explorer. Roger's only problem was that, as we had both shown up a bit late in the human drama, there was not a whole lot left to discover. The odd mountaintop here or there, perhaps a swamp or two, but none of the real majestic stuff. Thorne said he wished he had been born in a different era, but I always thought his arrival in the course of human events had been timed perfectly, right down to the second. To my eyes the nation had been working toward the creation of a Roger Thorne from its very start: His great-grandfather had been ambassador to England; his grandfather had worked with Prescott Bush at Brown Brothers Harriman; his father had been a partner at Morgan Stanley. I always pictured Roger standing triumphantly at the end of their line, a dazzling Late American, his roots so firmly planted in the past that he saw no reason to bother with it at all. Decades of prosperity had lifted him from base human concerns, and freed him to pursue other, higher interests.

"Did you see that shot of Lindsay Lohan on *The Superficial* today?" He asked, as if the up-skirt shot of the young actress had run on the cover of the *Times*.

I had spent the morning packing for a flight to Costa Rica, because my younger brother was down there, and because the Universidad was there too, and by that point I just wanted to get away. I had meant to tell this to Thorne, but couldn't bear to stop him in mid-reverie.

"You could see right under her hood! Her *poussoise*! Freckles like crazy! Full-on commando! So, I got all pumped, and then, dude, it turned out it was Photoshopped! What kind of pervert does something like that? They had a Kate Bosworth nip-slip, though. Totally real too, and I can always tell, because nipples are so unique to a woman that . . ."

I too followed the era's nip-slips, but only through Roger, who always had someone's nipples on his mind: Janet Jackson, Tara Reid, Paris Hilton, Keira Knightley, Lindsay Lohan, Jessica Simpson, Angelina Jolie. Each woman had escaped her blouse before a large bank of cameras, and turned an otherwise bland afternoon into a space of joy for Roger Thorne. He began to enumerate his favorite areolas, but stopped speaking altogether and passed into a state of shocked ecstasy when, by the staircase where his fiancée's mother now stood alone greeting guests, a full set of breasts came into view, their olive skin buoyant and hypnotizing with the full promise of sex.

Sophie Dvornik's father had won two Academy Awards, and somewhere along the way she had begun to think they were her own. We had been in the same class at Georgetown, and I had always liked her. No one else in Manhattan would ever think to enter the Racquet & Tennis Club in a sheer black lace top and matching skirt. Any normal woman would fear expulsion from charity boards and the wrecking ball of gossip far too much to ever consider it. Sophie, however, was confident that because the outfit was Dior, and her breasts were fantastic, no one could object. Of course she was wrong, and all with eyes were scandalized. Lauren Schuyler's mother stared at Sophie's chest as it bounced up the stairs, paralyzed by Sophie's dark olive skin and plum-sized nipples, almost as if it were not a girl approaching, but a horde of rampaging Huns. The Botox kept her face from registering any shock, though. Sophie was welcomed to the engagement party as though she were just another Chapin girl.

Still, even the polo ponies in the oil paintings seemed a bit offended as Sophie entered the ballroom, glorying in the stares of young men and the ghastly glares of their girlfriends. But she had spent the year working at the PaceWildenstein gallery for the most famous artist of our time, had grown up next to Steven Spielberg, and been thanked in two Best Picture acceptance speeches, and had no real use for any of these people. Except for Roger Thorne, in whom she found something new. Their relationship had begun that fall, when Sophie had invited Roger to her apartment in the Time Warner Center. Thorne had wanted to be an explorer, and with Sophie as his navigator, he had found his way to a new world of sexual wonder. I had to believe that she bared her breasts for him on this night, and indeed, for Roger the sight of Sophie *au savage* ignited a great many old passions. He gazed at her as she scanned the room for him. He followed her chest with his eyes when finally she found him and strode over on her pagan bonfire legs.

Sophie kissed us both hello, then pulled a large PaceWildenstein envelope from her bag and gave it to Thorne. Roger opened it to find a glossy digital image of Sophie in a latex bodysuit, whipping a man who looked very much like . . . Roger Thorne.

"This is from the first night we met!" he said.

"I know, it's just a little engagement gift," replied Sophie, then flipped the picture over. "I had Yves Grandchatte autograph it on the back. It's in French, but it says 'To Roger Thorne, who embodies the spirit of his age, and inspired my *Amazing Machine*.'"

The unveiling of Grandchatte's sculpture, *The Amazing Machine,* had been the most eagerly anticipated cultural event of that past year. Grandchatte himself was still, by many accounts, the most celebrated artist in Manhattan, and had grown only more famous in the wake of the personal-injury lawsuits, the arson charges, and his ten-year banishment from MoMA. Sophie told us that even the smallest pieces from his last work were selling for hundreds of thousands of dollars, and that Grandchatte was going to put the money toward an even more ambitious work. Frances Sloan, the woman I'd spent the better part of the past year with, had always thought of Sophie Dvornik as a pimp and Yves Grandchatte a fraud. I tried to imagine her reaction as Sophie described her work on the noted artist's next affront to American sensibilities.

"You wouldn't believe the permits you need just to have a few dozen orangutans in Central Park," she explained. "You would think that the fact that they are attached to helium balloons would get you around a lot of it, but it really just makes it worse. All of a sudden the FAA gets involved, and the Parks Commission is still in the picture, because obviously the monkeys are doing their business down into the park, you know, onto people. But that's the whole idea, and they just don't get it . . ."

"That's so wrong," said Thorne, nodding in agreement, though he was no longer listening. A woman in her mid-forties had just entered the ballroom, and from pictures I knew her to be Lauren Schuyler's aunt, Halsey Paulson. You may have heard of this woman, who just recently was involved in a Palm Beach sex scandal that made Jeffrey Epstein's most depraved dreams seem almost quaint. To look at her you might have thought that she spent every hour of every day with a physical trainer or a facialist or a masseuse, taking breaks from her pampering only to attend social functions or sleep. And you would have been right. What you would not have known, however, was that this woman had also played a significant role in Roger's sexual development, such that her presence affected him even now.

Thorne handed me the envelope for safekeeping, and as he did asked Sophie if she was free the next Thursday night. She said she was, and Thorne kissed her on the cheek, then went off to stand beside his fiancée and give kisses to Aunt Halsey.

"WHERE IS YOUR LOVELY GIRLFRIEND, FRANCES?" SOPHIE ASKED after Thorne had gone.

"She's been at a spa in Arizona for the past month," I lied. "She's coming tonight, but I don't think she's here just yet."

"Please, Tommy," she said. "No one could stay at Canyon Ranch for a month. You'd starve to death."

Everyone in the room believed this nonsense about Frances having disappeared to a spa, but Sophie was smarter than everyone, or perhaps her breasts acted as lie detectors. Either way, she knew I was lying. Through her gallery she had friends at the Institute of Fine Arts, and through them knew that Frances had stopped attending her classes months before. She didn't know about Oscar de la Hoya, or Frances's father's vasectomy, or the broken glass, or that awful cat, but I guess she didn't need to. She saw that I was protecting a lie, and that told her enough.

There is an odd thing about our truths and lies that I first suspected a long time ago. When I was six my older brother, Alastair, died. Alastair had inherited a great many superior traits from our many ancestors, and only one weakness, discerned too late—an allergy to peanuts. He went to boarding school at Portsmouth Abbey, where my parents later sent Mickey, and while there he made history as the only student ever to be sent into anaphylactic shock by a cafeteria egg roll, deep fried in peanut oil. I've been involved with a good many deaths since then, and even killed someone myself, but that was in self-defense, and even then I nearly died myself, so it doesn't really count. Anyway, with these other deaths I've always felt terribly sick, and in some sense, even responsible. But somehow not with Alastair. I remember being six and going to his funeral and just thinking that Alastair had really drawn a short straw, and crying, yes, but also realizing amid the tears that in his newly diminished state Alastair could no longer beat the crap out of me. He never really left us, though. From the way my parents carried on at his funeral you'd have thought it was the Dalai Lama who had died. They went on and on about how promising he had been, and how he would have gone to Princeton. They made up this whole fantasy obituary about the things he might have done. I had thought it pretty ridiculous then, but not said anything, because my mother had been crying, and my father wasn't talking to anyone, really.

Many years later, I realized that I had been right on that evening, and that the world in general had not really suffered much from the loss of my brother. He would have come to New York and worked in finance and made himself a fortune and said witty things to pretty people at cocktail parties in the hope that they might love him. And fine, maybe he *would* have gone to Princeton, but when was the last time anyone from Princeton really shook things up? Einstein, maybe, but nuclear fission has yet to make good on its promises to humanity. The thing is, everyone knew that Alastair was just another privileged jerk, of the sort that the nation's more elite institutions have been minting for as far back as anyone can remember, which is not very far. This was why it was so important for my parents to pretend that he was more. Otherwise his death wouldn't have been a tragedy at all, and to acknowledge that would have made it really unbearable. Our lies are more fragile than our truths, you see, and so we have no choice but to guard them closely. I thought of this as I lied to Sophie about Frances, and looked across the room, and realized that Alastair would have been awfully proud of me if he were still around. I thought of him, and how perfectly at home he'd be today in this room, and I felt almost as ill as I had been the last time I'd stood by his grave.

Sophie walked to a long oak table in the center of the room, and from its pile of cheese took a wet slip of Brie. It seemed that everyone present was afflicted by a rare strain of oscillating Stockholm syndrome that had you as a captor one moment and a captive the next. Frances's friend Phoebe had just arrived, and was forty-five minutes late because she worked at *Seventeen* magazine and had been editing an article about Ashlee Simpson's fabulous new look. Phoebe dated Laurance Whistlestopper, a fifth-generation Rockefeller who was oblivious to most things and didn't even seem to notice on the fairly frequent occasions when Phoebe introduced him as Laurance Rockefeller. He stood in the far corner of the ballroom and looked happily at an oil painting of a beagle as Phoebe blew by him to find her friend CeCe, who Phoebe thought was famous. The thing is that CeCe's picture often appeared in magazines and on websites, and as these magazines and websites constituted the entirety of Phoebe's media, well, it was hard to blame her for being such a fan of her friend. Phoebe found CeCe and they hugged. The entire engagement party paused to look in on them, and everyone knew that one girl was a senator's daughter, and the other the daughter of a successful financial criminal. Watching them together, you could not but be excited for their excitement. They sensed their audience, and though they had next to nothing to say to each other, rehashed an old conversation for the benefit of the many gazing eyes. There was only faith and envy for these girls, and the moment. It came from the same hopeful and empty place as the faith that we all placed in the post-post-postwar prosperity, that blessed, sourceless phenomenon whose trajectory, everyone agreed, extended into an infinite succession of tomorrows. Here Frances was different as well. She once took me to the Met and showed me an old Mayan calendar, and explained how it ends, abruptly and without apology, on December 21, 2012. I had found this frightening then. Looking around that room, though, I couldn't believe that the Mayans had not clocked us all out sooner.

"Did I ever tell you that I got into medical school?" I asked Sophie.

"I don't even want to consider which medical school would accept you," she replied, because she knew about my pi GPA and how I had failed to break 20 on the MCAT.

"El Universidad de Medicina de Santa Filomena," I told her, and for the first time didn't think to apologize for the institution's admittedly ludicrous name.

For all of her fraudulence and sadomasochism, Sophie was perceptive. I think she realized where my thoughts were, and that the room was getting the better of me, and that I couldn't bear to watch Lauren Schuyler's bandage fill up with discharge again. She took me by the hand, and led me through the crowded room, toward the French doors that opened out onto the terrace.


AS WE WENT WE PASSED TWO MEN IN BESPOKE SUITS TALKING politics. I had once thought golf the most extended form of masturbation available to modern man, but as of late have come to think that talking politics at a private club is the real prizewinner. It's not like there are any Marxists at these places. You know you're going to be squabbling over meaningless points at the outset, so why bother? You might as well play backgammon. Terence Mathers didn't feel that way, though. Mathers was the most powerful vice president in Mergers & Acquisitions at J. S. Spenser, and had been my boss for the better part of that year. He had also recently had his cellular phone stolen by a member of the Bloods, and listening to his thoughts on the Middle East, I saw that the experience had hardened him.

"We at least ought to *consider* using nuclear weapons against Iran," he began. "Or at the very least a good saturation bombing of their nuclear facilities. These Arabs only understand *force*."

"The Iranians aren't Arabs, they're Persians," countered Mathers's conversation partner, a blond Englishman named Ashley Aitken. Aitken had been the youngest managing director in the history of J. S. Spenser, and then gone on to found his own hedge fund. Mathers struggled to conceal the pain of having been found to confuse two major ethnic groups by a man more successful than he. Sensing his discomfort, Aitken took a turn for the pedantic.

"What you might consider, Terence, is that there is a war of civilizations that has been going on for literally *hundreds* of years. I read a fascinating piece in this month's *Foreign Affairs* about this very idea . . ."

Aitken offered no further explanation. In conversations like this one, the citing of a prestigious policy journal was generally enough to quiet your opponent. But Terence Mathers would not be defeated so easily.

"I think that's a terribly reductive approach," he said. "This is about broad *dialectics,* not cultures. And along those lines, you have to conclude that the Iranians are *dialectically* much further along than the Iraqis, and therefore are far more likely to be receptive to a bombing. Do you know that there are lots of young Iranians?" Mathers asked, eyebrows raised. "It's true. Iran had a baby boom just like ours. Only later."

Mathers was proud. He didn't even really know what a dialectic was, but had managed to use the word as both a noun and adverb. What's more, in doing so he had let Ashley Aitken know not to mess with a graduate of Harvard Business School. He pressed on for a full victory.

"So I don't believe that we are in the middle of any cultural war," he said. "This is about building democracies. We did it in Germany and Japan. We could do it for the Iraqis if only they would stop blowing themselves up . . ."

Mathers looked triumphant, but Ashley Aitken would not be so easily defeated.

"It's the Palestinians who blow themselves up," he said, with a wry smile. "The Iraqis just blow you Americans up."

Vanquished, Mathers found solace in Sophie Dvornik's chest. He stared at her like a hungry infant as she and I strolled outside to the terrace, and she smiled at him with exquisite cruelty. Outside Sophie leaned against the old concrete railing, entirely oblivious to the cars driving by on Park Avenue. The Racquet Club's terrace made you feel like you were flying. You stood there with your cocktail and quietly believed along with the others that for the time being you had been somehow exempted from the rules governing the cars and people and buildings all beyond and below. Heaven must be like this. The ambience was penetrated only by the flashing yellow of the taxis that sped down below as Sophie reached into her big pharmacy of a Fendi handbag, and from it pulled a small amber prescription bottle filled with the remnants of June's Xanax refill. She opened the cap and dropped a pill into my gin and tonic, and she laughed and I laughed after I took down drink and pill in the same swig. There was something of a disaster not too far behind me, you see, and I figured that if this little pill would make things better, just for a while, well, why not?

I sipped the Sapphire and Xanax and tonic and waited for it to slow the eddying of my assorted troubles: of Frances and her sister and Oscar de la Hoya; of the flower-strewn bedroom and the glass-covered floor; of that poor Mexican whom I had killed; of Jesus, who had promised salvation, then robbed us; of Mickey's escape; of Alastair's grave; of the two-hundred-million-dollar man choking on a fishbone; of the explosions! of the bleeding! Of the soggy bandage on Lauren Schuyler's arm and the rancid cells most likely still beneath it. These hauntings slowed and faded as I sipped that cocktail, and leaned back with Sophie in the reflection of the amber-pink American sun, which though fast falling still bathed us all.

I went to loosen my tie but spilled the drink all over my shirt. Sophie wiped me down with napkins, and amid the cocktail chatter a familiar voice called my name. At the far end of the terrace, sitting on a wicker chair, awkwardly smoking a cigarette, was Lauren's cousin, Lilly Schuyler. She had been Mickey's girlfriend at Portsmouth, where she transferred after getting bounced out of Hotchkiss. For a time I had been attracted to her, and felt sick about it, and realized only later that it was because she reminded me of how Frances must have been in the years before I knew her. She stood in her white party dress to say hello, and I began to regret my Xanax cocktail, and also to wish that Sophie's breasts had not been so much on display. I wore a smile for her benefit, but it was no use. Lilly approached, her happiness fading to confusion and then to concern. She looked quite curiously at Sophie's strange top, and the wet spot on my shirt, and the bottle of Xanax that had not yet been put back into the big Fendi bag. I orbited drunkenly in place, and tried to think of something to tell her, but what she saw was more or less the state of things.

"How have you been, Tommy?" she asked, and I could only shrug. Oh, I wanted to tell her everything. To tell her about all my dead: about Alastair and Makkesh and Manuel and Frances's mother. I wanted to tell her that she looked like Frances might have looked a while ago, and how it was only Frances I had come to see. The words wouldn't come. I tried for them, but they got redirected, and resulted only in another shrug.

"Well, it was good to see you," she said, with a touch of pity. She excused herself, and retreated into the ballroom, where there were presumably fewer bare-chested women and cocktails mixed with Xanax.

I watched her disappear into the shining mob and I thought back to the summer before, when everything had been well, and Frances had filled a room with flowers. I had lain with her, looking up at them all, thinking that I had a good name for a new species of gigantic flower, if there were any more to be discovered. I looked at the tall, beautiful people in the ballroom, and thought how with a bit of booze and Xanax they seemed to move quite a lot like flowers in a field. I thought that I had just the name for them, but the word would not be summoned. I looked deeper still, and strained for this word, and as I did I thought that I saw Lilly again, then realized that in truth it was Frances, who had come to Thorne's engagement party after all. She was greeted by CeCe and Phoebe, and their hugs drew new looks of interested excitement from the assembled guests, who asked her how Canyon Ranch had been, and were told that it was wonderful. And though I had seen her at her very worst, she still struck me as entirely perfect. I searched against the booze for the word that I had thought up that summer, the one for the giant flowers, the one that now reminded me of those people. It simply wouldn't come. Instead I remembered a quote that Frances had told me that summer.

"*Entre mon berceau et ma tombe, il y a un grand zéro,*" she had said, and though I speak no French, I had understood her.

"Between my cradle and my tomb is a big zero," I said now, because in that moment I grasped more fully what it meant.

You start your life with a baptism, end it with a funeral, and spend the intervening years evading the horror of the thought of the space between adding up to nothing. I watched Frances. I reached into my jacket and felt for my airline ticket. I pressed my skin against its sharp edges. They grated against my fingertips. I stared at this girl with whom everyone thought I still lived in total bliss, and tried to figure out just what to do, and where it had all gone so very wrong.

# 2

# PRINCETON

Like Roger Thorne, I wound up on Wall Street more through contacts than merit. An early admission: I got accepted into the training program at J. S. Spenser because of my father, Brian Quinn, a squat man with a broad, freckled, forever smiling face, who was not too many generations removed from his potato-farming Irish progenitors. He was fond of quoting Winston Churchill, and as Churchill said of the Germans, he was always either at my feet or at my throat. In three decades he had traveled from the lower-middle-class sprawl of Long Island to the lower upper-class ennui of Westchester (Rye, to be geographically exact). I grew up in a large white house on a large hill full of green oaks, silver Range Rovers, and chocolate Labradors. My father is a partner in a small law firm that you have never heard of, Tullis, Schacter & Scott. He ended up there after failing to make partner at a large law firm that you most likely *have* heard of, Cravath, Swaine & Moore. He was a litigator, and by most accounts a very good one. After eight years at Cravath he had been told by many that he was certain to make partner. But something went wrong, and of the four remaining associates from his class he was the only one to be politely asked to leave at age thirty-five, after giving eight years of his life to the most prestigious law firm in Manhattan. No matter how well he did after Cravath, it was never well enough, because his thirst for the trappings of success was always greater than any degree to which he had actually succeeded. He spends over sixty thousand dollars a year on memberships to the Union Club and Winged Foot and Westchester and Apawamis and Baltusrol and Sleepy Hollow and others, as if the letters of these names might magically rearrange to form Cravath, Swaine & Moore. I imagine that he will continue to skirt all mention of his beloved, betraying former employer until they do. So it was a selfless act bordering on love when, after all of the American medical schools rejected me, he mined his painfully buried Cravath connections to help me land at an institution whose name was so illustrious that for a time it seemed capable of redeeming both our failures.

J. S. Spenser's training program had for years been regarded as the best on Wall Street. The firm had hired the most promising liberal arts majors from the best colleges in America and then turned them into world-class bankers with a yearlong tour of the Spenser offices around the world. In that golden era, you could find yourself structuring M&A deals in Paris, issuing IPOs in London, or even being sent down to Lima to help the junta of the month sort out its national debt or, as was more often the case, just walk away from that debt altogether. By the beginning of his second year, a Spenser banker could issue bonds in Spanish on one phone and sell stocks in French on another, all the while offering an opinion on Chilean table wines and extracting escargots from their shells in deft motions with a tiny fork. Spenser's young spawn were so well trained that they were inevitably lured away by competitors with more lucrative offers within a few years of starting work, which made the whole thing a losing proposition for Spenser.

It all ended when the bank was sold to Chase Manhattan, a company that, for all of its flaws, at least had the good sense to avoid spending hundreds of thousands of dollars training employees for the benefit of its competitors. By the time I arrived, the legendary Spenser training program had been condensed into a six-week financial boot camp, with not an escargot in sight. There were two sessions, the first starting in early August and the second in late September, which was when I found myself seated at the back of the vast auditorium in the basement of J. S. Spenser's skyscraper at 277 Park Avenue. The building stretches forty-seven floors into the sky from one of the most expensive plots of real estate in the world, forty yards north of Grand Central Station. On each floor teams of men and women do everything possible to make money, and when they're done, they go on to do everything possible to take credit for the money made. This is how you prosper as a banker, and this is why a career in banking beats out even corporate law as the most risk-free way to make a fortune.

And this is precisely what the two-hundred-odd Ivy League graduates surrounding me in the airless auditorium had come for. The lure of easy money was enough to make even privileged young men and women afraid to complain as we sat, day after day, in the windowless basement, not far from the nuclear-bombproof vault where the bank's gold reserves had been kept in the sixties, spending our first fall after college graduation puzzling over financial equations and corporate earnings statements. There were two broad groups that nearly everyone was headed into: Corporate Finance and Sales & Trading. Working in Corporate Finance meant advising billion-dollar corporations as they bought other corporations, issued stocks, and borrowed money with bonds and loans. Sales & Trading was entirely different. Half of the people in the group would be given millions of the firm's dollars to actively trade in the hope of making a profit (they were computer-science PhDs and applied-mathematics majors—basically, MIT grads who would have been just as happy building missiles for the Pentagon), while the rest were salespeople of the sort you would find in any other field. It was the job of the salespeople to charm clients, working personal relationships to sell investors the stocks and bonds issued by the billion-dollar companies advised by the people in Corporate Finance. Salespeople had to be attractive, charming, and highly social. Since there is no PhD that confers these qualities, most openings on the sales desks were filled through back channels. The managing directors who ran things simply hired the children of friends for summer internships, and then, as long as these scions were not shown to have overt impairments or more than casual drug habits, took them on full time when they graduated. Mildly put, it was affirmative action for the already affirmed.

And as my own entry to J. S. Spenser had been less than meritocratic, I wasn't too surprised on the first day of training to see that more than half of the sales-traders were head-turning young women from Connecticut. They talked at length about nothing with the many male analysts who dropped by their desks to say hello, and were all very pleasant. Except for Loren from Geneva. Loren from Geneva had been Lauren from Greenwich until she spent a semester abroad in Paris and developed a love for all things European so intense that it caused her to recall her birth in a Swiss hospital and apply for dual citizenship. Loren's Swiss passport had magical properties, and once she received it she began to speak with a vaguely European accent, changed the spelling of her name, and in conversation made fond and frequent reference to her adopted homeland. Yet, to her great horror, J. S. Spenser had listed Loren as being from Greenwich on the analyst contact sheet. Determined to maintain her hard-won international status, she spent the first day of training shooting corrections and nasty looks at the many would-be friends who greeted her and asked if she knew friends of theirs in Greenwich. She was nasty, and worse, she was beautiful. She wore her black hair in a high bun and looked out on the room of mere Americans through prescriptionless Armani glasses, which enhanced her beauty and did nothing whatsoever for her sight.

The men all stared at Loren from Geneva, and though I resisted at first, I too found myself mesmerized when she got up to chat with another girl near the door of the auditorium. She dressed on the very edge of corporate decency, her long smooth legs jutting out from the bottom of a black miniskirt that ended four inches above the knee. I surfaced from my inspection of this girl's lower extremities to find that the guy sitting next to me was every bit as taken. He flashed the thumbs-up, as if to celebrate and confirm our shared interest in legs. This was Roger Thorne, the John Audubon of preppy flesh. He spent his undergraduate years as a legacy squash admit at Princeton making unique contributions to the study of all things nubile and feminine. His research had been exhaustive, though he was no academic snob, and he referred to the subjects of his study with a single, broad term that belied the depth of his analysis: "babes." In our first encounter he shared a term that he'd coined for the particular species of babe who chooses a career in finance: "That babe is a turned-out, java-hooked, bond-flipping machine!" Thorne declared. It was difficult not to be interested.

"Really?"

"Big time." Thorne then furrowed his brow, and seemed to be deciding on something. Finally he leaned over his accounting text, and after explaining how Lauren became Loren, offered a bit more information about her.

"Total Euro-fox. She hooked up with two dudes at once during a Cowboys and Indians party my junior year at Princeton. I walked into the room and saw her skiing with both their poles! We call her Poke-a-hontas. What a babe . . ."

He paused to let the pun sink in, and when it didn't, he set about animating it by poking the forefinger of one hand into a small cup formed by the other. I stared blankly at this man, my first friend at J. S. Spenser.

"Roger Thorne, man," he said, shaking my hand. "Dig your loafers. Also dig that watch." He pointed at the face of my Rolex, hesitating for a moment to study the movement of the mechanism—that is, to see if it moved slowly, and was real, or ticked, and was a fake. The watch had been won by Bo Sloan for claiming the first flight of a member-member golf tournament, and as he already had a great many watches he had sent it to Frances to give to me as a present for starting work. Thorne nodded to certify its authenticity, then held out his own for comparison.

Thorne stood over six feet tall, with a partially receded hairline; his skin looked a decade older than its years, like that of a man who had been left unattended on the beach during summers as a child and then gone through subsequent years with full faith in the ozone layer. He looked not a day younger than thirty-five. I wondered whether Roger Thorne was not in fact a managing director who had come here on his lunch hour to have a bit of fun with the new hires.

During the first five minutes of our conversation, Thorne revealed without apology that he had gotten his job at Spenser because his father had attended business school with a retired head of Investment Banking. Thorne's father also seemed to have access to deals on monogramming: Thorne *fils*'s initials, RPT, were everywhere. On his shirt. On his belt buckle. On his cuff links. On his pen. Even scribbled with his pen on his notebooks. If anyone was entitled to use the old-boy network to get his first job, it was this man. Thorne's hobbies, I soon learned, included sunbathing, squash, and the acquisition of luxury goods; he could spot a pair of fake Ferragamos from a hundred yards away. On that day it happened that we were both wearing Gucci loafers and Rolex watches, and in the world of investment banking, this is more than coincidence—it is fertile ground for friendship. I tried to return the compliment.

"Thanks, Roger. I dig your loafers and your watch too."

"Got 'em in Italy!" he boasted, raising his foot above chair level so that his shoe might be admired up close.

I had never struck a bond with another human being on the basis of purely material terms, but under the circumstances, I was happy to do so. After all, my options were limited. The man to my left had been sent over from the Tokyo office and communicated only with the aid of a Franklin Electronic Translator, into which he was constantly typing. Thorne and I would be sitting beside each other for the next six weeks, and so he was currently the best friend I had.

THE PROGRAM WAS DIVIDED INTO THREE UNITS OF TWO WEEKS each, with an exam at the end of each lesson. The first was taught by Stephen Hoarey, an older English banker from Spenser's London office, who liked to pound his fist into his palm as he rambled on about the many perils and pleasures of making loans. He was a pear-shaped man with a face made red by the decision to have just one more cocktail, repeated hundreds of times each year over four decades. Hoarey dressed immaculately, with big gold cuff links, red silk suspenders, and handmade suits from Savile Row. On the first day he told us to ask questions freely, and Paritosh Gupta, a summa cum laude graduate from Wharton, seized upon the invitation to distinguish himself as the smartest student in the class. Gupta knew the answers to all of

Hoarey's questions, sometimes even before he asked them. But there was one question that lingered. No one could understand why this man was teaching us, and not out making millions. We soon found out. On the third day of instruction, one of the girls in the row ahead of ours sought to challenge Paritosh Gupta for the distinction of star pupil. Apropos of nothing, she brought up the frenzy of overdevelopment presently going on in Florida's panhandle, known to real estate speculators as the Redneck Riviera, and asked if it presented any risk to J. S. Spenser. Before she even finished, Hoarey froze up completely and stood paralyzed before the class, save for a slight twitching of the shoulders. After a few seconds of beautifully accented stuttering he came clean.

"I'll have you know, young lady, that the head of J. S. Spenser in Europe, Robin Lord Peregrine, shifted me into an instructional role at Spenser after I lost many millions of Italian pension fund money to bad loans in, in, in . . ." It was hard for him to say it, but he finally managed the words "in Florida."

It was right then that I began to suspect that J. S. Spenser was not the firm it once had been. Who had sent an Englishman to go running around the Florida panhandle lending money? Was it any wonder that he had been taken? This man owned the failure as his own, though.

"So I'd rather not talk about Florida, or Robin Lord Peregrine, thank you very much," he concluded.

Hoarey hated our class after that. As the days went on he scribbled numbers across the blackboard that were large enough to see but too small to actually be understood. Every time someone tried to ask a question he would tell them not to make a fuss. "Don't make a fuss!" he'd say, and then, "Moving right along!" This was nothing at all like my last academic experience, a class at Georgetown called The Earth and the Planets Today, in which I had received one of only two undergraduate A's by watching Discovery Channel documentaries about life on Mars, and then staying after class to chat about them with my professor. He was a UFO enthusiast.

But the Discovery Channel has no programs about gold cuff links and gin cocktails, which seemed to be Hoarey's primary interests. I had no clue what the Englishman was talking about, or for that matter, what was going on in general. Wall Street was about making deals, right? Didn't that mean ringing phones, client golf outings, and steak dinners? So why all the algebra?

Every one of the ten days with Hoarey was virtually the same. After the first hourlong lecture, he would give us a ten-minute break, during which we all raced to the back of the room to descend on a Lilliputian buffet of small bagels and small muffins stacked on small platters. Small butters and jellies sat neatly tucked into small baskets for the small bagels and small muffins because small bagels and muffins don't need lots of butter or jelly. Just small amounts. Two weeks had never passed quite so slowly. Roger Thorne spent most of his time hunched over his laptop reading Page Six, chatting with friends on Instant Messenger, or sleeping behind whatever section of the *Wall Street Journal* happened to have the most numbers in its headline.

The Japanese banker, Yuki Hoku, passed the hours drawing anime sword fights in his accounting text and researching resorts in Thailand for a well-deserved break as soon as all of this nonsense was over. He shifted from these activities only once, during the last day of Hoarey's instruction, when he began pointing wildly at the two Indian girls sitting in the row in front of us. They had spent a good portion of their Spenser signing bonuses on Chanel pumps, and the rest on Fendi bags whose silver and gold hardware sparkled under the fluorescent lights. The two placards taped to the backs of their chairs said that their names were Vema and Vanita, and that they were graduates of the

Wharton School. Several empty little Ziploc bags on their desks and their frequent fidgeting, sniffing, and trips to the bathroom told the room that over the summer they must have gotten in touch with a dealer of medium-grade cocaine and were by now pretty much addicted to the stuff. Yuki could not believe the scandal, but Roger took it all in stride. He woke up long enough to share with us the scientific name for girls like Vema and Vanita, drawn from Thorne's Taxonomy: "Those babes are chatched-out, Riti-fiend maniacs," he said, after I nudged him and pointed out the Ziploc bags. He then went back to sleep.

Every bank on Wall Street has a Human Resources department filled with former field hockey and lacrosse players from the University of Virginia and UNC Chapel Hill. These women spend their undergraduate years building their calves to a point of hulking muscularity, and then spend their professional lives trying to conceal them. Some are successful. They marry bankers and go on to move to the suburbs, where they make their presence felt by supplying pastries for PTA meetings, arranging car pools for tennis lessons, and making felt costumes for school plays. Some accept their huge calves and move into finance themselves, where they prosper and amass small fortunes. A very small few are defeated. They never marry or leave HR, and understandably grow quite frigid in the cold wake of so many dreams left unfulfilled. Gwen Guthry, or as Thorne more affectionately called her, "that fucking bitch," was such a woman. She had calves the size of my thighs and stood five foot eleven, with short blond hair and a sandy complexion that was the product of a great many SPF-less summers on Nantucket. Her face was grainy even in comparison to the thick polyester weave of her Liz Claiborne suit, and she had never moved beyond the hairstyle of her sorority years. I later learned that she had attended Saint Lawrence University in the early 1980s, and that during those years she had been quite something to behold with a lacrosse stick. But entropy is the rule of the universe, and we cannot escape it: By the time I met her the muscles had turned to pudge, and her athletic aggression now found outlet only upon the classes of young J. S. Spenser analysts. Her one remaining power was the ability to fire you before you ever got to work. That power would disappear without a trace after the six weeks of training were over, so you really could not fault her for exercising it while she had the chance. She walked up to the front of the room, shook the hand of Stephen Hoarey, and thanked him for his time. Then she tapped on a microphone and began to speak.

"There is a man sleeping in the eleventh row."

The room emitted a great "oooh," and turned in a rippling wave of heads to see a puffy-eyed Roger Thorne emerge from between pages A17 and A18 of the September 15 edition of the *Wall Street Journal*. Thorne's first instinct was to delight in the attention, and he gave a frat boy smile to the class before realizing that charm would not work here. He then decided to do his best to look serious, and although Thorne was very good at looking serious, Gwen Guthry was having none of it.

"That is fine, but you should remember that there will be tests after each lesson," she said, in a stern, prison-guard voice, "and if you do not have an average of seventy-five or higher, you will not be accepted into the analyst program."

"Tom, that fucking bitch is going to ruin training!" Thorne said, after she had looked away from him.

As the days passed, his comment proved remarkably prescient. We managed only low seventies on the exam given after Stephen Hoarey's two weeks of instruction. Neither of us had a mind for numbers, so training would have been an uphill battle under any set of circumstances. But the prospect of firing made things a bit different, and since we were probably the most likely candidates in the class to meet early career ends on Wall Street, a sense of shared adversity deepened my nascent friendship with Thorne. When he learned that I was dating Frances Sloan, with whom he had attended Choate, our bond was sealed.

The following Monday, we met our new instructor, Suichi Ozaki, a Japanese foreign-currency expert rented at a rate of twenty thousand dollars a week from Harvard Business School. He was brilliant in all matters of finance, mathematics, and international trade. Ozaki's first book, *Pengoe Woe,* is to this day considered the authoritative text on hyperinflation in interwar Hungary. His second work, a collection of essays written during the tech boom, entitled *Told You So: Financial Bubbles Throughout History,* was a bestseller and launched his career as a speaker to corporations. Indeed, Ozaki's stature was such that the people at HBS had never had the courage to make him learn anything beyond the most basic English. He was teaching perhaps the most technical part of the program, and he did this in language that was only barely intelligible. He also suffered from stage fright, and dealt with it by fiddling with the volume control on his wireless microphone. The end result was two weeks of ululating static, thickly accented English phrases, and lots of equations.

Of course it all made sense to Suichi Ozaki himself.

"So it is just as I said!" he would say.

"Tom! What did he say?" Thorne would whisper.

"Something about something he already said."

And we would both curse.

The days passed with the Japanese foreign-currency expert going on in gibberish, Thorne and me totally clueless, and Vema and Vanita riding high on the white horse. We might have met our ends then and there, but salvation came from Yuki Hoku, who perfectly understood broken English spoken with a heavy Japanese accent. For the first time since his arrival in New York he comprehended everything that was going on around him. Yuki proved himself to be something of a humanitarian by staying after class to tutor Thorne and me in his own broken English. We became friends with him after that, and I think everyone benefited. Yuki stopped feeling so lonely and drawing anime sword fights during class, and we got invited to join him that fall on his carefully planned Thai vacation.

With Yuki's help Thorne and I both pulled high eighties on the next exam. We were beaten only by Vema, Vanita, and Paritosh Gupta, who, it seemed, knew everything. But not everyone survived to go on to unit three. Loren from Geneva completed only half of the exam and scored in the high thirties. This, coupled with a low score on the first test, mathematically eliminated her from employment at J. S. Spenser. Gwen Guthry escorted her from the room. Loren passed us on her way to the door, stunned and on the verge of tears. Thorne joked that she would probably be much happier with a Swiss bank anyway, but it could easily have been us leaving in disgrace, and it probably should have been.

The final unit in the training program focused on Mergers & Acquisitions and, thankfully, was taught by J. S. Spenser's own associates. Mergers & Acquisitions is a very simple business. Investment banks give advice to billion-dollar companies buying other billion-dollar companies, and they take around one half of one percent of the value of these multibillion dollar deals as a fee. One half of one percent on a twenty-billion-dollar merger is ten million dollars, made in a period of a few months without ever risking a cent. All you have to do is lots of math. The M&A instructors threw more formulae and facts at us in the two weeks of this last unit than I had seen during all of my premed work at Georgetown. Thorne had his mother FedEx him his Adderall prescription, and he shared the little orange thirty-milligram pills with Yuki and me each morning over little muffins, little juices, and little bagels.

By the end of that final unit, Vema and Vanita had rolled most of their accounting textbooks into small straws, yet somehow they had managed to maintain a 97 average. Perhaps Hadrian and the Stoics were right, and in the infinite variability of the universe Vema and Vanita had been born with an innate understanding of accounting that even heavy narcotics were powerless to destroy. Or perhaps the Wharton School really was America's preeminent institution of undergraduate business learning. Or perhaps they were just really good at guessing. In the end Roger and I decided that the act of snorting cocaine through the pages of the accounting text had somehow delivered the information on those pages to the appropriate parts of their brains.

Roger and I each pulled low nineties on the final exam, and ended with averages in the low eighties, making the cut along with the other one hundred and eighty remaining survivors of the originally two-hundred-person program. We would now be welcomed to suckle at the bosom of J. S. Spenser until our lips gave out. Those less fortunate were unceremoniously fired. Gwen Guthry handed out all of the graded tests from the M&A unit, then stood behind the podium that she so loved and told anyone who had not received a test to meet her outside the auditorium. Some had failed by wide margins, others by just a point or two. All packed their things and left the auditorium. Many later found jobs at Deutsche Bank, which for a brief period seemed intent on hiring every banker on Wall Street.

After dispatching her last batch of crying twenty-two-year-olds for the year, Gwen Guthry lost a bit of her brio. She returned to announce in a somber voice that at five o'clock the following day buses would arrive at the auditorium to take us to the Brooklyn Botanic Garden, where we'd have a party to celebrate the end of the training session, hear speeches from leaders in each division of J. S. Spenser's investment bank, and meet the people in charge of the different groups that we'd be hired into over the coming days. It had not ended a moment too soon: Thorne's Adderall supply was running low, Vema and Vanita were looking more like Pete Doherty every day, and Yuki Hoku was pining anxiously for his Thai getaway.

IT BECAME CLEAR TO ME UPON ARRIVAL THAT THE BOTANIC Garden party wasn't really a party. It was simply a way for the Spenser executives to put the incoming training class through one more filter, this time based not on test scores but on intangibles. The buses pulled up outside an immaculate white tent that the company had set up outside the garden's gray manse. There had been nervous chatter on the long ride from Manhattan, as all of the remaining analysts handicapped our odds of joining the various groups in the bank. I had attended several garden parties during college, and had mistaken the J. S. Spenser affair as being distantly related to them. Consequently, while my colleagues wore conservative wool suits and dark ties, I sported a pair of lime green pants, a navy blue blazer, and a white shirt sans tie. As it turned out this was not the evening to underdress, as your appearance had a frighteningly large impact on your career prospects. Starting out in a group like M&A could make you a banking Brahmin, just as a group like Internal Credit Portfolio Research could render you an untouchable. We all knew this, and it weighed heavily on our minds as we stepped inside the party.

Vice presidents and managing directors milled in cocktail clusters with Spenser's new analyst class across the big room. Waiters in tuxedos moved about with trays of chicken satay, as bartenders served up drinks to executives who were happy to be off work, and training-program graduates who were happy to be free of Gwen Guthry. Of course, I had traded the anxiety of Thorne's fucking bitch for that brought on by a pair of Day-Glo pants, which set Yuki Hoku into hysterics. He pointed to me from across the room as I entered, pathetically drunk from only two bottles of Amstel Lite, which he held to his stomach as he convulsed in laughter.

"Haro, Tommy Quinn! Got the berry bright pants! Berry bright!"

A few of the Spenser bankers noticed the red-faced Japanese man laughing at the lime green–pantsed man and began laughing themselves. I looked at them and laughed back, until I realized that I was at the very end of the laughter chain and would find myself making collateralized loans to sausage companies in Buffalo if this continued much longer. The Botanic Garden party was indeed so important that Paritosh Gupta had experimented with hair gel and brought out his four-button suit for the affair. Looking every bit the young Nehru, he hovered around the punch bowl with two friends from the Wharton Undergraduate Fixed Income Securities Society, of which he had been founder and president. They laughed uneasily at one another's jokes and discussed SEC regulations. Far more at ease were the Connecticut girls, who chatted happily with the very family friends who had hired them in the first place, all the while picking the bread off of hors d'oeuvres, nursing Cosmopolitans, comparing handbags, and talking about whatever it is that girls from Connecticut talk about while adhering to the Atkins diet, nursing Cosmopolitans, and comparing handbags. I walked over to the bar to order a Sapphire and tonic, which I finished just as Roger Thorne bounded in from the far end of the tent. Thorne looked far happier than anyone in the room; after a summer of cramming and playing catch-up, he now found himself at an advantage.

"Listen up, Stan, I've got a plan!" he said. Thornean rhyming was really quite charming, in its way. He pointed to two men in the corner of the tent who looked as though they had made good on a bet to dress as twins. Both had left the last buttons of their charcoal gray suit cuffs undone to show the world that the buttons actually worked, which could only mean that the suits were custom made and therefore cost more than three grand each. Whatever individuality was on display came in the form of their neckwear. Each wore a sinfully rich Hermès silk tie, one teeming with yellow ducks on a blue ocean, the other with pink whales on an aquamarine sea. Both were tied into Windsor knots over shirts that, though made of different fabrics, still looked very similar. Even their facial expressions matched, as each struggled to affect an aura of decision-making gravitas while selecting chicken satay from a plate that offered only chicken satay, and therefore little cause for consternation.

"Dude, that man on the left is Terence Mathers, vice president in M&A," Thorne instructed. "He's standing next to Dewey Ananias, who's in charge of all of Mergers and Acquisitions. He is also total fucking boys with William Cleveland, who runs the whole show."

Thorne paused to signal the bartender.

"GREY GOOSE on the ROCKS with a LIME!"

Then right back to the plan.

"Well, guess what, Tom?" He was so excited about his scheme that he didn't even wait for an answer.

"Terence Mathers used to dog my sister at Princeton."

"He used to what?" I asked.

"He used to take her down. They used to rock it!"

Dogging. Taking down. Rocking it. In the singular vocabulary of Roger Thorne, these things meant making love.

Thorne's sister Kara went to Princeton during the late eighties, and Thorne had told me a lot about her and her roommate Tara. Specifically about how Kara and Tara had dealt with the many uncertainties of mutually assured destruction in the cold war era by sleeping with the sons of as many powerful men as they could. Now that the cold war was over, and other wars were being fought, Kara Thorne's web of promiscuity had aged quite beautifully into a powerful network. Roger could now play squash with these guys. They could help him get jobs. They could teach him things. And why wouldn't they? They used to dog his sister.

Thorne was entirely unfazed by the idea of his sister having engaged in drunken, drugged, collegiate coitus with the man in the suit standing next to the man in an identical suit hovering over the tray of chicken satay across the room.

"If we get to be boys with Terence Mathers, then we will be down with Dewey Ananias, and then we'll be fucking pimps and it'll just be like . . ."

Roger searched for words.

"It'll be fucking awesome!"

So awesome that he made twin Satan signs with his hands.

Thorne loved his plan, and I did too. Not only because I was wearing fluorescent pants, and therefore feeling desperate, but also because it made sense. J. S. Spenser recruited so many accounting majors that fewer and fewer of its young bankers knew how to work politics. As the rest of the class had rested on their high GPAs and the CFA, Roger had been busy cataloguing the power players in Investment Banking at Spenser with the same frightening accuracy that he had used to study babes in college. It is a great elephant walk to the top on Wall Street, and it stood to reason that if we only put our noses firmly into the right ass that was connected to the right sequence of other asses, we would wind up very wealthy men.

Across the room Gwen Guthry set upon a tray of satay like a lion upon the carcass of a dead wildebeest. She had pretended for hours that she was not interested in the food, letting the hunger well up inside her like a great geyser before unleashing it when she thought no one was looking. The waiter tried to get away from her, but she motioned for him to stay for just one more minute. With great, greedy hands she plunged kebabs into a waiting dish of Thai peanut sauce. (The yet to be written definitive social history of the early twenty-first century will have to include a chapter on Thai peanut sauce, which for a brief period in the early years of the new millennium turned up at more Manhattan cocktail parties than a socialite with a publicist.) It can rightly be said that the satay never had a chance. Kebab after doomed kebab disappeared deep into the mouth of the woman who delighted in canning young men and women for scoring 74 on accounting exams, and who would have fired Roger Thorne, me, or any number of our peers had she only been given the chance. When she had met her own mysterious poultry quota, she clapped her hands, quieted the room, and made an announcement.

"People! People! It's been a great experience. You have learned a lot. We have had a lot of fun. Now it's time to hear from the professionals who run the various lines of businesses that you'll be assigned to in the coming days." She gave herself a bit of applause, then ushered our training class into the main reception hall. A podium with the J. S. Spenser logo stood at the front of the room, and rows of chairs filled the rest of the space. One by one the now-buzzed men and women who were the future of J. S. Spenser finished their drinks and found seats. Except for Thorne, who was so high on strategy and Grey Goose that he could not stop talking.

"What we need to do is introduce ourselves to Terence Mathers after this thing is over," Thorne said. "We need to let him know that we are all about working in the M&A group."

"Don't you think everyone will be doing that?" I said.

"That's why we let him know that we are super-intense. We tell him that we want to churn and burn, grip it and rip it, rock and roll. Plus, THIS GUY USED TO DOG MY SISTER!!!" Thorne's eyes lit up, and his voice became charged with energy as he concluded his pitch. Somehow his id was thrilled with the fact that he had to kiss the ass of a man who had, to borrow a Thorne-ism, tagged the ass of his sister. He folded his arms across his chest and grinned wildly. It was agreed that after the speeches we would put the full sale on the man who had administered so many spirited doggings to Kara Thorne at Princeton.

WE WALKED INTO THE MAIN AUDITORIUM TO FIND A BALD, round man with a thin mustache standing at the podium, speaking about Equity Capital Markets. He seemed to have recently attended a course in public speaking in which someone had told him to use his hands to make points and to involve his audience.

"All right, guys! Who in this room owns common stocks?" he said, in the manner of a game-show host. Nobody really felt like playing along with Public Speaking Guy, who had introduced himself as Gerry Jeffries. J. S. Spenser hadn't done any significant work in equities since Chase bought them. The Spenser people had all left or been fired, so that in the end Chase's billions had bought only a name, which was now used somewhat misleadingly for the entire corporation. Moreover, even assuming that through divine intervention—or, a more likely scenario, flagrant violation of securities laws—the firm did succeed in equities sometime in the future, the real money would be made by the bankers in the industry coverage groups. The guys in Equity Capital Markets spent most of their time just taking orders, and every man and woman seated in this room thought him- or herself far too hot a piece of shit for that. All of Wall Street can be understood in terms of shit. Young bankers and traders learn early on in their corporate lives to sniff an important man from an unimportant one, and to treat him accordingly. It goes like this: There are those that you can shit upon, those who can shit upon you, and those whose shit-on/shat-

upon ratio matches your own. This last group of people includes the
ones you must treat as colleagues. The guys in Equity Capital Markets
lived at the bottom of the corporate latrine and could be freely shat
upon. Thorne and I proved this to the room by lingering in the cocktail tent while the program was beginning in the main auditorium,
then making our way in and walking the full length of the floor, faces
red with booze. We were actually thanked for the interruption.

"Hey, guys. Thanks. Just find a seat there. Right, all right," Gerry
Jeffries said. Sometimes men are shit upon so often and consistently that
they lose their capacity to shit on others. They drown in shit. Gerry Jeffries was one such man. Still, he expected an answer to his question.

"So who here owns common stocks?" he repeated.

Sal Paglia had the face of a Sicilian boxer, and had not said one word
all fall. All anyone knew about him was that he had quietly passed all
of his tests, still lived at home in Brooklyn, had an extensive collection
of Versace, and had paid his way through NYU by playing in poker
tournaments and trading Beanie Babies on eBay. But for some reason
he chose this moment to make his presence known, to the great delight
and satisfaction of Gerry Jeffries.

"Right there, you! This gentleman. Would you mind standing up?"

Sal stood up, and Gerry asked him what stocks he owned.

"I own about twenty thousand shares of this very high-technology
company called Initech," Sal said.

Gerry Jeffries had a look of consternation on his face; he had never
heard of Initech, and was supposed to be an expert on U.S. equities.
Then someone laughed, and all at once there was a group realization—
Initech was the company in the movie *Office Space,* which almost all of
us had watched not six months earlier while drunk and high as college
seniors. The realization passed across the room in a wave of whispers
and giggles. Gerry Jeffries was the only one who didn't get it.

"So, how has Initech performed for you?"

Sal Paglia showed no mercy.

"Oh, strong. Strong to quite strong," Sal said, quoting Ben Stiller from *Meet the Parents*.

Poor Gerry Jeffries, who went on to have an earnest discussion with Sal Paglia about Initech's vaguely defined business model and the two outside consultants named Bob who had been working wonders at the company. Jeffries eventually began to sense that something was up, but he'd been so conditioned by his extended life as a vice president that he couldn't help but continue to be courteous and solicitous, even now when he suspected that somehow he was being ridiculed. At the end of his presentation, Jeffries told Sal Paglia that he would look into getting some research reports on Initech. The room exploded in laughter.


ONE AFTER THE OTHER, THE VICE PRESIDENTS AND MANAGING directors addressed the class, receiving respect in direct proportion to the degree of their perceived power. Everyone sat at attention and asked intelligent questions of Eric Gunther, from the Natural Resources Investment Banking group, after he announced that his group had made $103 million in the last twelve months off of America's gas and electric companies. Henry Wasserstein was in charge of Spenser Partners, the firm's private equity arm, which at one point in the late nineties had been regarded as the sexiest in the bank. Wasserstein would have been received like J. S. Spenser himself had his group not lost $2.4 billion in bad telecom investments over the past three years. There were rumors that Spenser Partners would be shut down, and we all knew that they wouldn't be hiring. Still, people respected Wasserstein, and we all pretended to believe him when he said that he looked forward to working with us. On the other hand, it was generally regarded as an opportune time to urinate when Mike Brennan of Internal Credit Portfolio Research ambled up to the podium to try against all odds to lure a few talented souls to the least prestigous group in the bank. ICPR had been created to audit the bad loans made by Spenser over the past decade. The group operated out of Jersey City.

Finally, Terence Mathers spoke. Mathers had all the forced affability of a first-term congressman campaigning for reelection, with a grin that wouldn't stop, and jet-black hair parted with extreme precision. Terence Mathers took Terence Mathers seriously to make sure that everyone else would take Terence Mathers seriously too. He stood before the podium and unhooked the microphone from its stand so that he could walk around the room holding it, Oprah style. Yet as he began speaking, all of the oratory flair in the world could not hide the basic truth that Terence Mathers was a man in great need of a visit to a psychiatrist of the highest caliber.

"Hi there. Welcome. Welcome to the House of Spenser," he said, in a calm monotone with just a hint of affected lockjaw. The House of Spenser was what they used to call J. S. Spenser before the Chase merger. Mathers was one of the people at Chase who had engineered the merger and afterward decided to take J. S. Spenser's name for the merged entity before firing most of the J. S. Spenser people. It was bizarre for him to present himself as the heir to a firm that he had played a significant role in destroying, but Mathers could have welcomed us to the Tenth Annual Conference of Gyroscope Manufacturers and Baptist Bishops and we would still have nodded politely and listened until he was finished. We were, after all, desperate young materialists.

"My wife hates me," began Mathers, as if it were normal to begin speeches with such revelations. The room braced itself and leaned forward to listen to whatever wisdom could possibly follow such an odd introduction.

"Do you know why she hates me?

"Let me tell you why, guys. She hates me because I am always canceling our reservations at Café Boulud."

Most of the people in the room came from very privileged backgrounds but had at that point lived in New York for only two months. And most of that time had been spent studying balance sheets and income statements in the basement of a skyscraper while hopped up on Adderall, cocaine, and little muffins. So our awareness of Manhattan's elite dining scene was dim at best. Mathers seemed disappointed when his mention of Café Boulud failed to impress. So he tried harder, and wound up constructing a series of very strange impromptu haiku.

*"You know, they know me*
*There, at Café Boulud, I*
*Eat there all the time.*

*"And I always get*
*A great table, but often*
*I have to cancel.*

*"Do you know why I*
*Am always canceling my*
*Reservations there?"*

Mathers looked out across the rows of young men and women, all of whom, to his mind, ought to have been deeply impressed by his dining habits. We were all just very puzzled, but over the course of the summer we had grown so accustomed to answering questions that the raising of hands at the conclusion of interrogatory statements had shifted to the Pavlovian regions of the brain. Paritosh Gupta was seated to Thorne's left and gestured that he had some hypothesis as to why Terence Mathers was unable to keep his many reservations at Café Boulud. Mathers was thrilled.

"You there in the front row. Why do you think I have to cancel?" Mathers happily asked Paritosh, who sat up straight in his four-button suit, and replied in his thick accent.

"Because you are always working?"

As had been the case throughout so much of his life and that summer, Paritosh Gupta was correct.

"Yes!" Mathers exclaimed. "I am working. I am working on deals. I work in Mergers and Acquisitions, ladies and gentlemen. In M&A, we only work on deals. We do deals all the time. We merge some of the biggest companies in the world with some of the other biggest companies in the world and when we are done they pay us millions of dollars in fees. You know what?"

No one knew what.

"Millions of dollars in fees will not always be there. But Café Boulud . . ."

He gazed out on the crowd, with whom he now shared a most profound epiphany.

"Café Boulud will always be there."

On this point, Terence Mathers rested his case. In his own mind he had just made a point of such dizzyingly revelatory logic that we would need a few moments to let it all sink in. The heliocentric universe, $E = MC^2$, and the Intermittent Need to Cancel on Daniel Boulud. You had everything worth knowing right there. There was silence in the room as some of the supposed best minds in America struggled to grasp the strange relationship between Café Boulud, Mergers & Acquisitions, Terence Mathers's wife who hated him, and their own career paths. I looked over at Thorne, who gazed up at Mathers in admiration. At that point I knew Roger well enough to tell that he was

wondering whether, perhaps tired of his repeated cancellations at Boulud, Mathers's wife would one day divorce him so that Mathers could
be reunited with his sister Kara, making Terence and Roger brothers-
in-law.

"This guy is a total fucking hitter. This guy is a rock star. Let's hook
it up. We've gotta get into the M&A group," Thorne said.

Someone began to clap, and before long the entire room offered its
applause for Daniel Boulud's most erratic diner. The applause was as
much a tribute to the stupidity of young men and women after four
years of elite education as it was to the success of Spenser's training
program. Six weeks of accounting tutorials had not done much to prepare us for work at the bank, but it had succeeded wildly at making us
desperate to start working. Terence Mathers could have said more or
less anything, and so long as we perceived him as representing the
wealth and power to which we aspired, we would have treated him
like a hero.

Mathers nodded politely and then walked over to Dewey Ananias.
It seemed safe to guess that Ananias had also been, in his day, a chronic
canceler of reservations at Café Boulud. It also seemed safe to guess
that with practice and a little ass-kissing, Roger Thorne and I might
live to cancel dinners at Café Boulud, merge big companies, get paid
big bonuses, and own fine homes in which to raise fine children with
wives who hated us just as Mathers's wife hated him. Thorne and I
could distinguish people with power from people without it, and it was
only rational to choose to work with an apparent narcissistic sociopath
over the far less auspicious Gerry Jeffries, or the man from Internal
Credit Portfolio Research.

Thorne and I walked outside and shook Mathers's hand, and as we
did we mentioned our connections to that prolific and flexible Princetonian, Kara Thorne. As the kids from Wharton prepared to send
their accolade-laden résumés to Human Resources, we arranged to

have a cocktail with Mathers the very next day at the River Club. He would have to cancel another reservation at Boulud to meet us, but he was more than willing to do so because he was, by his own account, "dedicated to developing the firm's junior resources."

At the club we ate tuna fish sandwiches and listened to Terence tell us about himself. He recalled his days on the Princeton tennis team; he expressed his excitement about recently joining the Racquet Club; he asked himself a great many questions about himself, and answered each in turn. Outside of the club we thanked Terence for the tuna fish, and he told us that he had greatly enjoyed getting to know us, and looked forward to working with us in the future.

A week later, the J. S. Spenser Analyst Class received its group assignments. Gupta was put to work making syndicated loans. Sal Paglia found his way to an equities desk. And Roger Thorne and I were selected by Mergers & Acquisitions, the most illustrious group in the bank. I had never known that tuna fish could be so powerful. We were joined by Vema and Vanita, whose 4.0 GPAs and perfect test scores throughout training all but guaranteed them a top choice. And we were happy to have them along, because we still didn't know very much, if anything, about finance, math, accounting, or banking.

# 3

# MASCARAS, BAHAMAS

My father always meant well, and over dinners at Christmas and Easter would tell my brother and me that he saw it as his personal duty to make sure that we both went to heaven upon our deaths. That he would be there waiting for us was always assumed. He was thrilled when they accepted me at Georgetown, a Jesuit school, unwavering as he was in the opinion that the Catholic Church, even as it played host to more pedophilia than Neverland Ranch, was mankind's best hope for redemption. I'll tell you plainly that, more than anyone I've known, my father had a vested interest in redemption, and not just for himself, but really for my older brother, who had died, and therefore had to be in heaven, or to not *be* at all. I've only recently stopped holding this heaven fixation against him. There are far worse religious obsessions at play in the world, and after spending a year watching the news of all these jihadists and born-agains and promised-landers, I've begun to see that man isn't likely to get over God anytime soon. We expect too much of God, and too little of ourselves.

I read in an article on the BBC website that God is more or less built into the genetic code, that we can't help ourselves, that if you put someone in a muddy gorge, you can be sure that he'll find something to worship, and with a little time, something to revile. So maybe my father can't be helped. I see that now, but didn't back then. Especially when he sent my younger brother Mickey away to boarding school with the Benedictines, and happily wired the Brothers twenty thousand dollars each September for all that they might do throughout the school year to minimize Mickey's future stay in purgatory, which, like man's need for redemption and my father's secure place in heaven, was never questioned. I felt terrible for Mickey when they took him out of the local high school and packed him off to Portsmouth Abbey. He didn't talk to Mom or Dad for his first two months up there, but he called me on Sundays when he was allowed to use the phone. I could hear his muffled sniffling as we hung up, but he said it wasn't so bad. At the very least it made our father feel as if he were doing his part as a spiritual guide, which was important. On a day-to-day basis things were difficult for him.

The years at Cravath were by far his best; in those days he would return home from work just as I went to sleep and bound into my bedroom, pick me up, and spin me around until I was dizzy. I would press my nose against his suits from Brooks Brothers, smell the city, think of how much I loved him, and listen to him tell me how much he loved me. Then it all went wrong. He left Cravath and started from scratch and began to stutter. *"Tyut, tyut, tyut!"* he would spit at strange places in his sentences, and then stretch his eyes in surprise at the strange virus that had infected his speech. The early career that had once been a lifetime's achievement became a reminder of promises unfulfilled, potential untapped. We never wanted for anything, but there was no more bounding through the door. He came home tired, and he would watch old broadcasts of the British Open in perfect silence for a few hours before really talking to anyone. He didn't want us to ask him about his day. He did well, as I said, but never well enough, and certainly never as well as he would have liked. He began to worry about money in the way that semi-wealthy people do. Sometimes he would bring it up out of nowhere.

"If I just had another two or three million, Tommy! Just another two or three! I'd buy tax exempts and that would be it . . ."

Just another few million would fix everything, because his aspirations generally exceeded our immediate means, and the difference between the two caused him great pain. (An economist would say that this is the case so that the aspirer will stop aspiring, and the pain will go away, but economists assume lots of things that don't always pan out, as I would later learn in Latin America.) Soon he was fully usurped by this new and unhappy self, so that by the time I graduated from Georgetown the entire family went to great lengths to salve his ego. It was hardest on my mother, whose own father had willed her a few million dollars a decade earlier. My mother's inheritance stalked my father as a personal phantom, whispering always and everywhere that the finer elements of our family's lifestyle were financed by her, not him.

After I graduated from Georgetown, Dad paid a hundred thousand dollars to join the Harbour Island Club near our beach house in Rhode Island. The club membership was his eighth, and brought our family's annual golf and tennis dues up just past the seventy-thousand-dollar mark and far past the point of affordability. My mother didn't have the energy to object. My father wouldn't have cared anyway. What really bothered him was the idea of playing golf as a guest, instead of as a member at this club. He had worked too damn hard, in his own words, not to have a golf club by his beach house. But selfishness is a sin, so he told Mom that he was joining as a gift for her—even though the woman plays no golf or tennis, to my knowledge—and wrote out the check. Mom loves Dad despite all of his flaws, and forgave him even this. People can become strangers to each other over time, and when she had married him he was full of optimistic ambition and prospering at Cravath and she was starting an English PhD at Columbia. My mother walks with a slight limp, the result of one leg receiving the signal to stop growing just a bit later than the other. My father had helped her to the subway one morning, and was quite taken with her, and they had fallen in love, or some approximation thereof. I've found that to really know someone by chance, just for a moment, is an incredibly lucky thing, but not all that strange. Sometimes you get thrown together with someone, and just because of the circumstances you know what's going on in their head, and they know what's going on in yours. To keep this going is the real feat. Because one morning you might have a thought that leads you one way, and they might have a thought that takes them in another. And words can only do so much. Sometimes I think you can become estranged from someone without ever leaving their side. As the years went on my father's dormant flaws became active and dominant. Mom dropped out of school after receiving her master's degree to have kids and raise us, and although she volunteered at the Rye Free Reading Room her life outside of this single activity was entirely a subset of my father's. She never told him that she was unhappy with their arrangement, but she did have a tendency to develop mysterious stomach ailments on the eves of parties and benefits, and she often sent him off to them alone, knowing that his rigid faith in the risen Christ would keep him from straying too far.

But she couldn't always bail out. So when Dad joined Harbour Island she strapped on a battered Gucci bag and navigated the welcoming parties for new members of the club. She stooped to chatting about nothing at all with women from Greenwich and Palm Beach, in whose graceful company she and her widely observed (never discussed) limp had never felt entirely at home. She cursed these damn meet-and-greets with such fervor that I almost thought she would say something to him when he vetoed her plans for a quiet Fourth of July in favor of an evening of cocktails and chatter at the club. Instead, she drank Chardonnay and polished her diamonds. She didn't have it in her to explain herself to him, and anyway, they had stopped speaking the same language years before.

It all made me consider myself quite lucky to have the job at J. S. Spenser, where I wouldn't be doing any great service to humanity but would at least gain financial independence and a little karmic distance from the old man. I privately fantasized about making so much money on Wall Street that my own life would be free of my family's strange, confused class identity. Dad acted like a new father when Spenser hired me. He took me to Brooks Brothers for new suits, and then to the Union Club for dinner, and that was where he told me how proud he was of me, and I thanked him, and we were both quiet and awfully disappointed. The exchange had been a letdown, and that was when I first suspected that words can sometimes fail us, that they can conscientiously object or simply desert if asked to bear a cargo of particularly noxious thought. So we sat in extended silence, my father looking into my eyes and around my face, like he was trying to find something. He's worn the same round, tortoiseshell eyeglass frames since 1968. Their succession of lenses had thickened over the years and that night I saw him only as two blurry puddles of color, amplified and distorted. As he squinted into me I didn't have to ask what he was looking for, or how the search had gone. The only one of us he ever took to the Union before that had been my older brother, Alastair.

Alastair is the Scottish variant of Alexander, which in Greek means king of the world, and in my father's view was just about where my brother fit. Of course Alastair's true destiny was far less exalted, but this was never held against him, and though I often thought about it, I would never have dared to bring it up. Rather than take issue with his absentee God, my father took Alastair's death as a divine trial, and wasted no time in channeling his grief downward onto Mickey and me, who never matched up. I don't hold this against him either. Alastair was in every way superlative, but even if he had just been above average, the grossness of Mickey's and my collective deficiencies would have made him seem so anyway. I really think that when my father looked at his sons he saw not a family portrait but an evolutionary chart, with Mickey leaping about on the far left as spastic Java Man, me in the middle as a passably competent but ultimately disappointing Neanderthal, and on the far right, tall and erect, spear in hand, forging ahead, Alastair.

He was named after a partner at Cravath, an Episcopalian whom my father somehow convinced the local priest to allow as a godfather. If there was an award for godfathering, this guy would have won it. He sent presents to my brother on his birthday and for Christmas and took him to Mets games and gave him all sorts of advice, but evidently he had nothing to say about the perils of Chinese food, which as it happened was the one area where Alastair genuinely needed warning. Like Mickey, he attended Portsmouth Abbey, but while there brought my parents significantly more pride and less panic. They sent him off when he was quite young, so I don't much recall him. He liked to watch WWF wrestling, and after watching the various suplexes and flying kicks and headlocks he would practice them on me. He loved me out of a sense of superiority, and perhaps that is a sort of love.

My father was closing in on partner at Cravath, and when we brought Alastair to Rhode Island you would have thought that he was sending himself off to prep school. He was so proud he bowed before each passing priest as if he were pontiff, and when Alastair made the football team he gave money to have the fields resurfaced. Alastair took the adulation as a matter of course. He seemed to sense that he was a natural aristocrat, and that all of this was due him. I suppose that he deserved it, because to be fair he really was exceptional: He played varsity football as a sophomore; scored 1,450 on the PSAT without tutoring; had a genuine interest in professional athletics; could tie a Windsor knot; attended Mass regularly and believed every word of it; was never once caught masturbating; dated the hottest girl in Rye, while still at Portsmouth; told insipidly self-aggrandizing stories at Christmas parties; was forgiven all of his assholery by people who wanted simply to be near someone so remarkably superior. Alastair was also remarkably allergic to nuts, and went into anaphylactic shock after dinner one evening when Portsmouth's new cafeteria service added Chinese food to a menu that had not been changed in decades.

My parents had never considered burial options for their sixteen-year-old son and decided to lay him to rest in the school's cemetery. When they interred him we saw that an error had been made in arranging his tombstone, which was supposed to have been white and marble, but arrived made of rough granite marred by varicose impurities. My mother pretended that it did not matter, but my father had a proper marker made in Florence and a switch was made six months later. After the ceremony the headmaster invited my parents over for tea and subtly inquired as to their tendencies toward litigation. My father had forgiven the Catholic Church its every crime from Emperor Julian to Galileo Galilei, and was not about to hold this latest incompetence against them. No lawsuit was filed; no money was exchanged. Me? I would have sued those bastards until they had to sell their vestments, a real modern-day defrocking, but I'm not sure what it would have accomplished. Even spiritually, no reparations could really have been paid. What prayer explains the mechanics whereby your strong and able son is felled by an egg roll? Christ did not get around to that one. Then again, Christ was probably more of a falafel man.

Alastair died, and his death, I came to grasp, was doubly awful. First there was the drawn-out pain of suffocation by the spasms of your own trachea. Then there was the added insult of reduction to such a state by a dollar-fifty item on a Chinese menu. Try to "Our Father" that sort of thing out of your system, and let me know how it goes. It has not worked for my father, this I can tell you. Though he can't. This I can also tell you: I received a great deal of attention in the wake of Alastair's passing, and I enjoyed every moment of it. As I've said, I was sad, it goes without saying, but in all my life no one has taken the initiative to beat the crap so thoroughly out of me as Alastair. So I guess you could say that I put him behind me, at least for a little while. My mother stopped working at the library and drove me to and from school. She wrote loving notes on colored napkins and put them in my Hulk Hogan lunchbox. My father read to me from Edmund Morris's biography of Theodore Roosevelt each night, and when the book was finished he took me to the city to visit Roosevelt's birthplace, then for lunch at the Union Club.

In presleep mumblings to my flannel-cloud pillows I sometimes declared him an idiot for eating the egg roll without first inspecting the school fryers to see whether they contained anything that might kill him. Soon my parents had Mickey, who was born early and spent two weeks in an incubator, and that more or less put the Quinn family out of the baby business. We rarely talked of Alastair after Mickey came, save for on his birthday, when my mother would make the carrot cake that he liked, and all would eat it in reverent silence to mark whatever age he might have attained in a world without peanuts. Everyone except for Mickey, who had never met the boy he replaced, and when sensing that he had been temporarily upstaged by the specter of the departed, complained audibly that the cake ought to be chocolate and decorated with sparklers and sugar-based dinosaurs. This always set my mother crying. My father never did, but I know for a fact that he has gone to Mass for my brother every day since his passing, praying for him to make it into heaven, since Princeton was, alas, no longer an option.

Between my father and me, Alastair was explicitly mentioned again only once, at the end of middle school. He drove me to visit Portsmouth Abbey, and our inspection of the campus began and ended at Alastair's plot in the graveyard overlooking Narragansett Bay, and this is where he broke down crying. I placed my hand on his shoulder. He swatted it away. The experience, combined with the school's many bleeding Christ sculptures, confirmed my desire to have nothing whatsoever to do with the place. We were silent on the drive back to Rye, and that night I announced that I didn't want to go away to school. My father grimaced and shook his head, as if to say, "I've got the good one in the ground, and the bastard at the table." He then treated me as the dead son for the better part of a month. A psychiatrist later required eight sessions and more than four thousand dollars to identify this as the advent of the common era of our difficulties. Perhaps I should have gone into psychiatry. Or maybe that shrink should have worked on Wall Street. I didn't go to Portsmouth Abbey, or any other such private institution. I went to Rye High School, which was decent, and in this way a good match for me: I made decent grades, dated decent girls, played decently at junior-varsity sports, and got into Georgetown, a decent school. My hiring at J. S. Spenser was my sole violation of this middle-of-the-road approach to living, and as my father happily signed the chit for our dinner at the Union and told me how beautiful the suits I had picked were, I noted how greatly just one departure from the average could change things for a young man. I have been noting it ever since.

———

SPENSER WAS THE OLDEST, PROUDEST BANK ON WALL STREET, but it had entered into the early stages of a slow decline around the time I was hired. It was in all honesty this trend toward mediocrity that best explains my hiring. I first sensed that the firm might be off its game when they sent me fifteen thousand dollars just for agreeing to work there. I had seriously considered only one other career option, medicine, but it had not gone well. My grades were weak, my MCAT atrocious, and I was rejected everywhere except for El Universidad de Medicina de Santa Filomena. I forgot about El Universidad altogether when the check arrived, and rushed to cash it before the people at J. S. Spenser regained their sanity. It would be the first summer on record during which I would not be completely broke, and I resolved to do whatever I pleased.

I spent the months immediately after graduation visiting college friends in Europe. In London I stayed with the son of a Moroccan arms dealer and tried cocaine for the first time. In Paris I stayed with a descendant of Madame de Staël and slept with a girl named Alexandrine. I thought it strange that with fifteen thousand dollars you could do all these things, and that without it, you could not. But in broad terms I did not think much about anything. I simply moved around, and saw, and consumed. This might have been a good reason to abandon the bank entirely, and to try to make medicine work through some post-baccalaureate program or other. But I felt farther from that sort of existence than ever. You don't realize how badly you need thousands of dollars in your checking account until you *have* thousands of dollars in your checking account, and looking back I have to believe that whichever person at J. S. Spenser came up with the idea for a signing bonus had been very much aware of this.

My father had wanted the entire family to spend the Fourth of July weekend at the beach, so after deplaning from London at JFK, I rode back to Westchester via Metro-North, and took the old silver Volvo 960 station wagon up I-95 to East Beach, Rhode Island.

It was there that I first met Frances Sloan. As a new member Dad felt quite understandably obligated to attend the club's Fourth of July cocktail party, Mom's lack of enthusiasm notwithstanding. I was a bit jetlagged, but gave in to my own curiosity to see just what sort of facilities awaited a man willing to spend more than my starting Wall Street salary on a country club. My brother Mickey loved the club, and had already spent the first couple of months of the summer (his seventeenth) there, golfing and masturbating, though one may argue that the former is simply an extended version of the latter. He reported that the place was nice enough. Though Mickey is not exactly a model student and suffers from every form of attention deficit disorder identified or invented in the last twenty years, he is a smart kid. He could have done better in school, but he lacked the hearty appetite for nonsense that is more or less required to withstand the SAT tutors, façade extracurriculars, and transcript-padding classes that line the mindnumbing road to the Ivy League. My father was hoping that a family friend could get him a spot at Holy Cross, and had excused him from working over the summer so he could prepare his college applications. He managed to finish only one paragraph of one essay, but even for this he was congratulated by my parents, so low was their general estimation of his abilities.

I have come to think of Mickey as the smartest in our family, Alastair be damned. In the seventh grade he realized that his French teacher was giving tests purchased from a publishing company, so he found out which one and ordered the exact same materials Madame Langlois had been using on her long coast into retirement. He proceeded to stun and amaze with a streak of perfect French grammar tests that lasted well into the semester. It would have been a perfect plan, but he threw off the curve for the entire class, and as Rye is a pretty competitive town, it was just a matter of time before the PTA mother-mafia found out, and put in a call to the principal. Dad, of course, took it all to mean that Mickey was hellbound. That's when he decided to ship him off to the same boarding school Alastair had attended, hoping that the Benedictines might right whatever was perceived to be wrong with him. It didn't work. Late one night, after the first snowfall of his sophomore year, Mickey and a friend populated the lawn of the main quad with a cast of life-size, anatomically correct snowpeople, each locked with a partner in some phase of the Kama Sutra. The monks and my mother decided to have him examined by a psychiatrist, who soon concluded that Mickey had an impulse disorder and Ritalined him to the gills. He was always a little checked out after that.

Mickey bitched and moaned about having to go to the July Fourth bash at the club, but in the end he threw on a pair of canary yellow pants with his Portsmouth Abbey school blazer and managed a sloppy part in his white-man's-Afro hair for cocktails. He even lent me one of his nice Hermès ties as a sort of welcome-back gesture. As usual Mom was a trooper, her fair Irish skin enjoying whatever color SPF 50 would allow, her face already placid with a Chardonnay smile. Dad was in rare form too. Bow-tied and buttoned, polished and shining, his tortoiseshell glasses firmly in place and his kinky red Irish hair forced straight and back, he was eager for an evening at the golf and tennis club, which he had joined as a gift for a wife who did not know how to putt or volley.

It was a nice place. If the world is just buildings and people, this was at least a pretty building full of pretty people. The clubhouse was done in new cedar shingles treated with chemicals so they would appear re-spectably weathered, and it gave onto a wraparound porch with tiers of steps leading down to a fertilizer-green lawn stretching up to the fairway of the first hole. Beyond the fairway was a great expanse of dessicated beach shrubs, beyond which lay the dark sapphire blue of the midsummer ocean. The porch was alive with the chatter and vapor of sweating men in blazers and pastel ties, their wives dressed up (by way of trying to appear dressed down) in linen and cotton of white and green and pink, their shoulders bare and tan, their necks and wrists aflame with gold and diamonds. They came from all over, and they were all somewhere near the peaks or ends of careers in finance, law, or racquet sports. My father ignited into a great sycophantic dynamo, greeting old friends and making new ones, my mother at his side in the role of conversational Sancho Panza. The shrink had told Mom to detox Mickey during the summer, which made him something like a cold-turkey Marlboro Man. The poor bastard was fidgety and miserable. "This scene is AARP! Can you hold my jacket? It's a locker room out here, Tom. Did you read my Boston College essay? Brian wrote it about me tutoring some kid, but I never actually went to tutor him. Or, is that okay?" Mickey said, grinding his molars. He always called our father by his first name when we talked, having never taken him half as seriously as I had. From Madame Langlois to Dad to the Benedictines, Mickey never took anyone seriously enough to let them break him down, except maybe Mom and the shrink. His eyes fluttered about the porch in search of entertainment, but instead found only the vaguely complementary browns of liver spots and loafers. Finally, he settled on something exciting, something so eye-catching that even his rattled synapses could pull it together for a fleeting moment of focus: the beautiful girl who hung on the arm of Dad's latest chat-up, and made you think that where the rest of the race had evolved slowly from muddy gorges over millions of years, her own line had sprung forth from a marble bath filled with Chardonnay and honey sometime just before the American Revolution.

"Who the fuck is she?" Mickey blurted out, spitting an ice cube back into his glass to make way for the question.

She was Frances Sloan, the first and only daughter of my father's old Cravath colleague, Robert "Bo" Sloan. If Dad's life had been a tribute to slow progress and rigid self-control, Bo had been born under an entirely inverted alignment of the heavens. I'd heard his sordid but golden career recounted by my father over countless dinners while growing up. The Sloans were an old American family that had made money on every feast or famine in the history of the republic, and had done especially well by marrying. Bo had quit Cravath to look after family interests after his fourth year, just after his second marriage to the model daughter of an old oil family whose name need not be sullied by inclusion in this story. He nearly lost both the woman and their entwined fortunes during the two-week bender that immediately followed his resignation. It started with the Mets winning the World Series and ended with one of the worst days in the history of the bond markets up until that point. By Tuesday morning, ten million dollars of trust funds, passed carefully down for generations, had vanished, and so had Bo Sloan. He woke up to find himself in the Bahamas, wearing a red leather miniskirt, his face full of mascara and his mind devoid of any clue as to how he had gotten there. But Bo had some of the great WASP traits: whereas a Catholic might have viewed the entire misadventure as a divine wake-up call, or even punishment for personal waywardness, Episcopalian Bo got right back in the saddle. With what money was left, he bought brownstones, options, art—anything that could be traded for a profit. And a decade later, just as my father was adjusting to his life as a middling corporate attorney, Bo Sloan had grown magnificently rich adding millions more to millions spawned from earlier millions.

Bo divorced Frances's mother and took half of her now greatly expanded treasure as his own. She went off to live in Maine; he stayed in New York and prospered. Just that spring he had been made a trustee

at the Met. Frances's mother never got over him. In Maine, she made
a pharmacy of herself, and in pictures aged twenty years in the space
of ten. She is still up there, just in the ground. Bo remarried, many
times. His marriages fell apart almost as quickly as anyone could keep
track of them, but even here he was undaunted. (My father sometimes
cited Bo's failed marriages as proof that money cannot buy happiness—
this, of course, despite my father's own frenetic pursuit of happiness
through money.) Bo had married again earlier in the year. The new
bride was a reporter for New York 1, and had met Bo while profiling
him for a segment about museum patrons. That night she was nowhere
to be found, and when I first saw Frances on his arm I figured her for
a spouse, not a daughter. Her skin was like alabaster dipped in sun.
Her hair was pulled back but coils of honeysuckle platinum had escaped, and now hung down her temples like laurels. The beauty had
not cost her anything, though. Sometimes it is so easy for beautiful girls
to get what they want by smiling that they forget what they are smiling
about altogether. Not with Frances. Humor and pain skipped around
the fire of her face as full partners, and spying upon their dance
through the human thicket of the patio I wanted only to move with her
in time. Looking back, I can see that I forgot myself quite fully. Perhaps it was an extension of the peculiar magic that followed her father,
the same stuff that so captivated my own father, who was waving furiously for me to come and say hello. Mickey was by then lost in a platter of finger foods even as he made a meal of his own fingernails. I
thought it best to simply let him be.

"Tom, this is Bo Sloan. We worked together years ago," my father
said, casting a look of full admiration at his prosperous former colleague.

I shook Bo's big hand and watched as the introduction soaked into
his booze-bathed neurons. As he presented my credentials, my father
forgot every disagreement that had passed between us.

"Tommy graduated Georgetown this spring and starts the training

program at old J. S. Spenser in a few weeks . . ." I tried to think of
something to say but could only picture this big WASP passed out at a
Bahamian Holiday Inn with a face covered in mascara.

"I've heard a lot about you from my father," I managed politely.

Bo jerked his big, bronzed, balding head up at a choppy angle and
cackled before regaining his composure.

"All lies! Except the good parts—which are all true," he said, shaking a few drops of spilled gimlet off of his necktie.

He emphasized the "true" by lazily raising his index finger, and
arching his eyebrows. The finger just sort of hovered there, stalling out
for a while, before he finally got going again. It took the elbow of his
daughter to kick him back into gear. Perhaps he really was magical;
there certainly seemed no other explanation for his success.

"Tom, this is my daughter, Frances . . ."

Frances nodded to acknowledge that she was in fact this man's
daughter, and I did my very best not to seem overly awed by the subtle
craning of her neck.

Bo and Dad went on about real estate and interest rates and war and
golf. Mom had already limped away from the porch with a pack of cigarettes. Doubly happy to have her nicotine and an excuse to stand still,
she gave me a knowing wink.

It turned out that Frances had just graduated from Trinity and was
also moving to Manhattan; she had been accepted into the master's in
art history program at NYU's Institute of Fine Arts. She seemed bored
as I told her of my vaunted career as a kindergarten finger painter, and
then she offered to show me around the club. With drinks in hand we
took off across the lawn to the fairway, then headed through the brush
and down to the beach, where she kicked off her shoes and ran atop a
boulder. She looked down at the sand for a bit before speaking.

"My dad is all to the wind tonight," she said. "But he means well. He
always means so well."

Little did she know that I knew he was a lush, but so much of being polite rests on minding the boundaries between what you know about other people and what other people know you know about them. At this moment, as far as I was concerned, Bo Sloan was a devout Mormon.

"It's a cocktail party. If you weren't drunk, it wouldn't be fun. You're his date? They call that filial piety, right?"

She laughed.

"No, his date is on her back at home in Aspen, racked up with the thing . . ."

Ebola? Tuberculosis? Gout? What was "the thing"? Frances grabbed me, pulled me up onto the boulder, and didn't let go of my hand once I was there. The little waves lapped against the rocks of the shore, and I could feel her breath on my neck. The last girl I had been with was Alexandrine in Paris, and of course her accent had done most of the work. I struggled to come up with a bit of small talk, and the thing seemed as good as any.

"What's the thing?" I asked.

"My stepmother is pregnant," she said, as if informing me that the woman had Parkinson's.

"Does the thing have a name yet?"

She looked out at the water and didn't reply. She didn't like talking about the thing. Time for new conversation. If only I was allowed to know about her father in women's clothing in the Bahamas! We could have laughed for hours. Instead I did just a little better than discussing the weather.

"Have you had a good Fourth?" I asked her.

"It's been beautifully brutal." She laughed. "Though at this point that can't be helped."

I didn't know what to say, but I didn't have to say a thing.

Pretty Frances got up on the tops of her toes, pressed her lips against mine, and all previous conversation was forgiven. I was so surprised that I didn't even immediately pick up on the trembling of her hands.

The biggest mistake that you might make on the porch of the Harbour Island Club would be to arrive, through your own democratic sensibilities, at the conclusion that because they all spoke of the same things, played golf on the same eighteen holes, and lived within three miles of one another, these people floated with equal access in the same cell of Late American social fat. This was not the case, though we were all neighbors. In fact, the entire community was nestled on a narrow isthmus with the Atlantic Ocean on one side and a curious inlet on the other, the result of a colossal tidal wave that had hit during some long-forgotten hurricane. You might think that the most desirable homes were on the beach, but here, again, you would be wrong. Save for a small stretch of sand owned by the club, the entire shoreline was the property of the state, and therefore open to any day-tripper with a cooler of Bud Light. And on that Fourth of July, even as they celebrated America and its noble, multihued masses, the members of my father's new club, like so many of the meritocratic oligarchy, had no desire to really come in close contact with these people. Like safe sex and business ethics, the nobility of the teeming masses is one of the great and lofty American ideals that people are happy to revere, but not necessarily endure. It is for this reason that it is so easy to get good dinner reservations in Manhattan on the weekend of the Puerto Rican Day parade, and also why the most valuable real estate in East Beach was located not on the ocean, that happy *mer des plebs,* but curled around the still-private water frontage of the inlet, a semicircle of prosperity whose curvature allowed God's glowing sun to rise and set each summer day upon his self-chosen people. It had to filter through the thick hedgerows and picture windows of a more successful neighbor to reach my family on the teakwood deck of our shingled abode, a modest million-dollar home across the street from the water. The birds on the water were more colorful, and majestic. At night the moon seemed bigger. The morning breeze carried in fresh scents of ocean, which did not make it to the homes inland. I did not know this until that summer, which I spent with Frances at her family's empty waterfront manse, alone but for her cat, a Siamese named Chairman Meow.

We were together for most of each day and every night. Frances would come over and my mother would make us lunch on the porch, and although she would leave to give us privacy Frances always asked her to stay. They would sit out on the small deck and talk about books and paintings and places they had loved. Frances never once paused to study my mother's uneven gait. I can still see them in the gray wood chairs beneath the leaf-filtered July sun, each finding something long missed. At the end of that summer my mother gave Frances a silver-framed picture of the two of them laughing at some joke. She kept it on her bookcase until the very end.

One night I told Frances about the Universidad. Frances wondered aloud why I had applied to such a place, and I had confessed my MCAT score to her, and we had both agreed that my avoidance of the medical field had been for the best. We spent nearly every minute together, because the girl had a leveling effect on time from the very beginning, and around her the days seemed very thin indeed. I know that we read books. I had to complete a report on Longus's *Daphnis and Chloe* for a Georgetown course whose professor had been kind enough not to hold my failure of his final exam against me. The book was about two young Greek lovers, a shepherd and a shepherdess, and how they spent their days kissing and eating berries until one day the boy was kidnapped by pirates. I read the abduction scene aloud to Frances, and she thought it was marvelous and told me that she hoped no one sailed up to the house and took me away in the night. Then we went to pick flowers.

There was a farm stand atop Frances's street. It was run by a local man with silver stubble who had fought in the Second World War, and after the liberation of Paris had fallen in love with a French girl. It was a small and beautifully inefficient farm, vaguely devoted to corn. But just off the road, in the shadow of a rusted tin silo, there grew lilacs and lavender and sunflowers and gladiola. We would walk to the farm, and to its faded shed in which sat the little French girl taken from Paris, now an old woman in Rhode Island. She would give us pairs of clippers and cardboard boxes, and we would go out into her field, and pick flowers. We would stand beneath the blue summer sky and watch our sweat fall into the dirt and take handfuls from the great swath of color, and the old Frenchwoman would watch to be sure that we didn't trample or steal. We knew she didn't like us, but by then it was always late afternoon, and the rest of the day had been too wondrous to let her get us down.

Each morning Frances and I would wake and have breakfast on the shingled balcony adjoining her bedroom and regale each other with tales of the great happenings of our lives prior to our meeting. In the sixth grade I read an illustrated book about Ulysses, and although I had no real idea who he was, I remember looking at the pictures of these amazing battles and triumphs, and feeling awfully left out. "Where was I during all this?" I had thought, then realized that it was worse than being left out, that I had simply not existed. And I felt this same way when we told each other where we had been before being with each other. She told me about living in Paris with her aunt every summer from the age of ten to sixteen, and how they had been neighbors with Jean-Luc Godard, and how he watched her some afternoons, and sat her on his couch, and showed her his films. I had no such brushes with genius, but had gone through first grade twice with Chaim Spero, a Tourette's syndrome sufferer with a tendency to emit loud *eep*ing noises whenever excited. Chaim's *eep*ing might have been the only thing that confounded our teacher more than my tendency to smuggle copies of *National Geographic* into the class, a habit that kept me from learning subtraction for several years. That year Chaim and I became best friends. He was loyal and kind, and his father was Italian and his mother was Jewish, and at his Bar Mitzvah lasagna was served and I was asked to light a candle. Frances loved him, and wished she had been in our class to join in the *eep*ing and distraction and avoidance of subtraction. I'm still unsure as to what draws people together, that is, beyond the really ugly things: money, beauty, family, desperation. But I suppose that if someone can make you feel like you are seeing a new world, or just an old one for the first time, you might decide that you love to be around them.

The farmer's French wife had been beautiful in youth, and a framed picture located behind the cash register proved it. Now she was wrinkled and stout and dyed her hair a stunning vermilion that made it seem to me like a flaming cannonball. She rarely spoke, and after giving us the clippers would walk with us to the flowers and in her muumuu supervise the picking. At times that summer she accused Frances of tomato molestation and me of insensitivity to corn, and as punishment for both crimes refused to sell us any of the swollen plums that grew just beyond the flowers. Still we went back each day, and each week we hung flowers in bunches and set them in crystal vases all across the house and Frances's bedroom. Then, one day in early August, the farmer's wife decided that she liked us. Perhaps we had misread her all along. Maybe she had grown to respect us as steady customers. But in light of what happened later that evening, I can only think that, as she had weathered a war, and crossed an ocean for the sake of eros, this woman knew a bit more about it than some other people and that, on that day, her two early afternoon flower gatherers perhaps made her recall the fleeing Germans, and ocean crossing.

"Iz zee luh-vahs!" she sang happily as we approached, and Frances understood her long before I did.

*"Oui, c'est vrai,"* she said, and kissed me on the cheek, and a second later, I realized what she had said. The old Parisian woman smiled broadly and adjusted her vermilion bouffant and did not watch or bark as we went into the sunflowers. Looking back, it was beautiful, but I was at that point beginning to grow used to beauty, which was suddenly everywhere. So I bent down to cut as always, and stopped only when I felt Frances's arms around my waist, and her lips on my ear, and her voice within it, speaking in French at first, *Je t'aime,* and then providing translation.

"I love you," she whispered, and immobilized my lips before any reply could come from them. The sunflowers blazed and the lilacs glowed purple on Frances's skirt, and we'd have stayed like that until it was dark were it not for an offering of plums.

"And today I have ze plums for you!" the cheery woman said as she giggled through the flowers. Flushed, we broke apart as she shuffled from the sea-battered shed, flip-flopping toward us in her dirt-stained muumuu. We met her at the edge of the patch, and there, with the same but different hands with which she steamed across the Atlantic, she made a gift of a green paper basket piled with plums.

That night Frances dressed in her cotton robe and opened the windows as always, but folded the louver doors as never before. She lay with her head resting on my shoulder, and I followed her eyes as they examined each of the dozen or so crystal vases, all filled with the flowers of the past month. Some very alive, some less so, some not so. But we had picked them and kept them and would not throw them away, because they were not so much our picked flowers as our passed days, and in this room were all that you could see, through Asprey glass, brightly. And then, darkly. Frances rose from the bed and switched off the lights, and when she came back her robe was gone, and though we had slept in the same bed for the last month, we had not yet slept together. I didn't want to ask for it, and get it out of pity. I didn't want to steal it with sudden suggestion in the midst of some lesser act. As she was the more beautiful between us, it simply seemed hers to give, I thought, and that night I was proved right.

"Will you make love to me?" she asked when she had come to the bed, and I was so excited that I almost *eep*ed.

"I do love you," I whispered.

She put her arms around my back, and ran them over the fine scars left from my not heeding my mother's advice against scratching at chicken pox years earlier. With her fingers she traced and accepted each dimpled imperfection. We rolled to our sides, and facing each other, interlaced our legs. The louver doors breathed seawater and night as amid the dying flowers of summer we tried again and again to climb into one another, at first in earnest, and then in ecstasy, and finally in vain.

We then lay still. Frances traced her finger over my nose, and as I watched her mother's pear-shaped diamond move in the pattern of my face she told me I looked like a baby bird, like an baby eagle, *l'aiglon*.

"*L'aiglon*," she said, and told me that her aunt taught her the word, and how it was the name given to Napoleon II.

"I didn't know there were multiple Napoleons. I thought just the little one, with the big hat . . . ," I said, honestly confused, and this made Frances smile.

"He had a son with an Austrian princess," she explained. "And after Waterloo Napoleon I made Napoleon II emperor, but he was only four, and his reign only lasted for about a day before he and his mother were taken back to Vienna to live with her father, the emperor of Austria. What makes it so interesting to me is that, yes, they were at home, but not because they wanted to be. Really, they were just hostages . . ."

"Hostages," I said, really because I had nothing more intelligent in mind.

When I heard the word, though, I thought of tall flowers, like giant tulips but with petals three feet long. I thought that just from its sound *hostages* would be a good word for a large flower species. I thought that it also sounded good for, well, hostages.

"He always loved his father though," Frances continued. "He slept with a portrait of him over his bed. Imagine that? Like a big middle finger. Then, when he was around our age, he just died. Bonapartists say his family killed him, to keep him from going back to France, from becoming emperor."

"Emperor," I repeated, and thought how this word would never do for a flower.

"Do you know what his last words were?" she asked, and holding her closely I shook my head.

*"Entre mon berceau et ma tombe, il y a un grand zéro,"* she whispered.

And in time I would grow to distrust words, to know that sometimes they do betray you. That night, however, they were well on Frances's side. Just to hear the sentence, whose every word sounded like what it meant, I had no need of translation. Napoleon Jr. was only letting everyone know that he didn't kid himself, and he knew that for him things hadn't gone quite as he planned, and that between his cradle and his grave, in the end, there was only a lot of nothing.

We told each other that we loved each other, and slept.

—————

WE MOVED TO THE CITY DURING THE LAST WEEK OF AUGUST,
after two months of lying in bed and on the beach up in Rhode Island.
She was very familiar with it all, having grown up on Sixty-fifth and
Park with her mother until she was twelve, then shuttling back and
forth between Hartford and Manhattan on weekends during her years
at Trinity. She took me through a succession of overpriced apartments
under the guidance of a broker from Richard Ellis, who for a two-
thousand-dollar fee found me a small one-bedroom on Seventy-third
and First Avenue, which I rented for twenty-three hundred dollars a
month. The deal delivered another blow to the fast-dwindling pile of
cash given to me by Spenser; I had never realized that fifteen thousand
dollars could disappear so quickly. The rent was at the high end of
what I could afford on my starting salary at the bank, and the apartment itself paled in comparison to Frances's arrangements. She moved
into her father's prewar duplex on Sixty-fifth and Park. Bo had just left
Manhattan to spend the fall and winter in Aspen, and would not return until April. He saw no reason for his daughter to live cheek by
jowl with roommates when there was a perfectly good apartment on a
nice block sitting empty.

On the night before my first day of training at J. S. Spenser, Frances
called me and, giggling, demanded that I come over, alluding to a surprise. When I arrived at the apartment, she disappeared up the staircase to the master bedroom on the second floor. I knew my way around
the apartment, since I spent most of my nights there with her in the big
canopy bed. I followed her up the stairs as she slipped into one of the
walk-in closets on the far side of the bedroom. The days were already
getting shorter, and the dressing room lights cast an orange glow
through the slats in the door. I sat on the bed for a few minutes, hear-

ing only the lazy honking of traffic headed across town on the big avenue below. Then came the flicking of a switch, on-off-on-off-on-off.
Frances liked to do it three times—she said she liked the sound. Three
chutes of dusty late-afternoon sunlight seeped in through the windows.
The dressing room door opened, slowly, and there she was, covered in
one of her mother's old kimonos that had been wrapped in tissue paper
in a box atop her dresser. Her mother had visited Tokyo with Bo on
a business trip, and bought them while there. He had divorced her
not long after their return. She evidently had known that she would
not have much use for them in Maine, and had left them behind. So
it seemed as if the kimonos had been waiting for Frances all along. The
yards of ancient red silk dripped down her body. The weight of
the garment pulled at the chest, so that her cleavage was exposed
and shifted with each step. We had been having all sorts of sex since
that first time, making love at times, fucking at others. But a Japanese
motif had yet to be explored. I got up off the bed and put my arms
around her. She unbuttoned my shirt and undid my belt, and soon I
found her full lips in a long kiss. I traced my hands down her sheer silk
silhouette, feeling her firm B-cup breasts and soft hips, which were
wonderfully curved for a girl who came from a line that could be
traced back to Puritans who were seriously intent on getting rid of
sex altogether. She began to massage me with her hand, and as much
as I enjoyed the whole Emperor Tokugawa fantasy, I found that I
couldn't stand it anymore. I worked my fingers into the knot of the
kimono's sash and wiggled it about until it became loose, and, finally,
undone. The thing melted off her body into a little silk puddle on the
floor.

Frances daintily raised a leg away from the sloughed skin and
pushed me back onto the bed. I held her thighs as she perched on top
of me, kissing my neck as I buried my face in her chest, and we rocked
back and forth quite pleasantly for a great while, until the enviable

soundproof qualities of the prewar building had been thoroughly tested and she lay beside me. She batted her eyes and smiled.

"Are you happy in the city?" I asked her.

"It's beautifully brutal," she whispered. "But I'm very happy with you, *mon aiglon*. Will you stay with me every night, like this?"

I told her that I would like nothing more.

"Want to fall asleep?" I asked.

*"Oui, mon cher enfant,"* she whispered to me, and kissed me on the neck, and we dozed off.

# 4

# BIG LARRY AND
# LITTLE JOHN

At the end of October Bo Sloan called to tell Frances that he and her stepmother, Wendy, had just bought a parcel of five hundred acres adjoining their ranch in Aspen, and that they would stay out West to raise the baby when it came. Wendy now knew that she was having a girl, and planned to name her Sunshine, in keeping with her Native American roots. Wendy was one-thirty-second Navajo.

Frances's immediate reaction to the news was to throw herself into her studies at the Institute of Fine Arts. I would come home from training to find huge books on topics so unrelated and scattered that it was strange to think that they could be required by any one course. I asked no questions, though, because she was full of passion for these big mysteries and ideas, and watching her go at them made me think her more perfect than ever. For a course at the Art Institute she undertook a study of paintings of the fall of Constantinople, in 1453. Somewhere in her research she decided that Genovese cannons had played a much larger role in siege in one city than was popularly thought. She corresponded over e-mail with Dr. Omer Babuga, a professor at the Istanbul University, and often called me during training to share whatever revelations had been made. Dr. Babuga invited Frances to write her theories up for formal consideration, but she lost interest in Constantinople and its fall altogether later the next week, upon receiving an auction catalog from the Howard Rose Gallery. Soon she was an expert on pre-Columbian pottery. At night we lay in bed, and she spoke to me like a favored pupil as she flipped through books with glossy pictures of fertility totems and rain-making wands and little jaguar warrior figurines. One day she bought a single clay fragment of a Mayan calendar from a dealer in San Francisco for nine thousand dollars. When it arrived she said it was the most beautiful thing she owned, and that she only wished she could afford a complete calendar. The fragment went on the mantel, where it was admired and then forgotten. The next week Frances read seven books about the 1883 eruption of Krakatoa.

"It still affects weather patterns today," she had said.

"I love you," I had replied.

Frances found something of interest in every artist who ever lived, except Yves Grandchatte.

I had first heard of Grandchatte from my Georgetown classmate Sophie Dvornik, who had called me one day at the beach that summer, thrilled to have been hired as an assistant to a dealer at the PaceWildenstein gallery. She was more excited, however, that her first and only duty at this job would be to act as personal handler to Yves Grandchatte. She said he was French, a genius, and a drug addict. Also a black belt in karate. He had achieved notoriety and then prominence during our senior year at Georgetown with a piece of performance art that still had many people afraid to fly. On three separate occasions he successfully boarded airliners at LaGuardia wearing a T-shirt that read I'LL BE YOUR SUICIDE BOMBER TODAY in Japanese, Russian, and German. He then returned a fourth time wearing a shirt that read I FUCK GOATS in Arabic, and was promptly taken into custody by Homeland Security, which held him without charges for a period of forty-eight hours. The entire thing was recorded and put on the Internet, where it was linked to the Drudge Report and a thousand other websites. Before Grandchatte knew it he was very hated and very loved and given a sixty-five-thousand-dollar grant by the Guggenheim Foundation.

Sophie had told me that he would unveil his next work at a gala in his honor to be held at MoMA that winter. I would have known this even without her, however, because during that fall in Manhattan Yves Grandchatte was inescapable. He had needle-scarred arms and tattooed fingers and he looked like he smelled very bad. With eyes like oil spills he stared down at you from billboards and up at you from the pages of discarded magazines. He popped up on your computer screen and he raced by you on buses. Sometimes he thrust his groin in your face. Other times he did roundhouse kicks in your general direction. Often he just seemed very bored. But people were fascinated by him, and could never get enough. There was one Sunday when he made it into no less than four sections of the *New York Times*: The Styles section profiled him on a night out with his rumored lover, Kate Moss; Arts and Leisure did a feature on his upcoming MoMA gala; and though few noticed, he was quoted in both the Health and Home sections as an authority on the topics of heroin abuse and topiary gardening, respectively. He seemed all things to everyone except to Frances, who insisted that he was a fraud. Still, she was curious to meet Sophie, and hear firsthand about Grandchatte. Thorne was excited too, and so we decided to plan a dinner where all of our friends could get together. Frances invited her two best friends from Choate, and on the last Saturday in October, the weekend before I was due to start at J. S. Spenser, we took a cab downtown to Cipriani in Soho.

———

WE MET ROGER THORNE AND LAUREN SCHUYLER OUTSIDE OF the restaurant, amid the tables that spilled out onto the sidewalk of West Broadway, all covered in white linen and teeming with long-limbed, listless models and the paunchy foreign playboys who date them. One Latin man punched a number into his Nokia. Five tables away another man's Motorola began playing the ringtone version of Enrique Iglesias's "Escape."

"Giacomo!" said the first man, throwing his arms into the air.

"Simone!" replied Giacomo, rushing over to greet his long-lost friend.

We walked inside, where Lisa Gastineau sat with two other older, attractive women at a table beyond the bar, and raised her neck to look at Thorne. Though aware of her admiration, Roger seemed somehow afraid to look at the woman for longer than an instant; Lauren Schuyler trained her eyes on him, at once daring and forbidding him to so much as acknowledge any of the would-be Mrs. Robinsons, though in the end it was not the divorcées who ought to have concerned her.

Thorne's gaze had been drawn to the bar, where stood all five feet and eight inches of Sophie Dvornik in the Dolce & Gabbana jeans that had so shocked the prep school girls during our first year in college, and fit her as though Dolce & Gabbana had conceived them with only her legs and ass in mind. Just as these jeans struggled to contain her sin-inspiring limbs, what seemed to be a vintage micro T-shirt contained her formidable chest. Silk-screened on this shirt was a nude woman, and upon closer inspection it became clear that the nude woman was in fact Sophie Dvornik. Beneath the picture was a statement in Arabic that was easily translatable to anyone familiar with the work of Sophie's star client.

"Yves Grandchatte made it for me," Sophie boasted as she approached, and joined us in walking to the table where Frances's friends were already seated. Everyone except for Frances looked at Sophie's chest with jealousy, and it wasn't only for her breasts. They had seen the videos and the billboards, and they too wanted a shirt made by Yves Grandchatte that read I FUCK GOATS, in Arabic. The interest in Sophie was writ so large that she had no choice but to address it.

"I work with him at PaceWildenstein," she said, and relished in explaining. "Did you know he's French-Algerian? And he's more than just a filmmaker. He's also a genius sculptor and painter. I've been working on his MoMA gala, and it is going to blow everyone away. He's totally self-taught. Totally *sui generis* . . ."

No one knew exactly what *sui generis* meant, only that they had heard the term on a few occasions, and on those occasions also not known what it meant. This didn't stop the table from nodding in agreement with Sophie, though. Frances alone seemed to know what she had said. Smiling mischievously, she broke the momentary silence.

"And, *impudens leno es,* at least that's what I think," she said.

"Absolutely," said Sophie, and again, everyone agreed with her.

"What did you say?" I whispered to Frances amid the nodding heads.

"That she is a shameless pimp," she replied, and burst into beautiful laughter.

Unaware of Frances's insult and content to have established herself as a cultural arbiter of some merit, Sophie smiled confidently and shifted into a seat. The table gave off light chatter, and Frances set about introducing me to her friends.

"Tommy, this is Phoebe . . ."

Phoebe had eyes like costume jewels, shiny and unconvincing. Her father was a senator from a flyover state, and you did not need to look beyond her intricately highlighted hair to see her Midwestern roots. Frances had said that she was the sweetest girl at Choate, back in the years when her father had been a mere state attorney general. She said that Phoebe had been different since his ascension to national politics, and indeed, the exfoliated, permatanned woman seated before me had little in common with the ponytailed girl I'd seen in old yearbooks. Phoebe leaned in for hello kisses, a kiss on the left cheek, another on the right. She had done a year studying in Florence before landing a job as an editorial assistant at *Seventeen* magazine, and demonstrated both her worldliness and world-weariness by kissing everyone twice. She introduced me to her boyfriend, who gave further testimony to her worldliness: He looked like a kindler, gentler Uday Hussein, and moved a green Lehman Brothers duffle bag from his lap before lifting his butt four inches off his chair to offer a lazy handshake.

"I'm Biglari," he said, before settling back down from his semi-standing position.

"Big Larry?" I was puzzled.

Frances had mentioned earlier that Phoebe had gushed that her boyfriend made a six-hundred-thousand-dollar bonus last year. That is a lot of money, it's true, but did it really entitle him to call himself Big Larry? To go from Larry to Lawrence for a bit of added prestige would be considered acceptable by most, but adding an adjective like Big was crass by any standard.

Phoebe giggled and rolled her head. "No. His name is Biglari! He's Purrrrsian."

"Biglari," he said again, emphasizing the first syllable this time, to make the point. "I work at Lehman Brothers."

I soon learned that Big Larry's family had been part of the exodus of wealthy Iranians who'd fled the country before the Ayatollah toppled the Shah in the late seventies. He seemed none the worse for wear and had clearly found a full, new identity working at Lehman. Way down in his Lehman Brothers duffle bag, Larry's Lehman Brothers Black-

berry vibrated with Larry's Lehman Brothers e-mail. He was a
Lehman Brothers bond trader, and he had no choice but to bend down
and dig around for it. Soon he was happily punching away, oblivious to
anything beyond the high-resolution screen of his little device, which
he spoke of only to praise.

"Lehman gives us these. They are not Blackberries, but Blueberries.
The new Blueberries, with color *and* Internet. Lehman is always at
the cutting edge, always the very best. Tommy. Roger. Tell me. Does
Spenser give you a Blueberry?"

Roger and I were silent, and taking this silence as a no, Biglari went
back to typing.

Next to Phoebe was Frances's other Choate friend, CeCe. With a
head of blond hair and a naturally golden complexion CeCe looked as
Phoebe wanted to look, and seemed to know it. She worked as a publicist for Carolina Herrera, but carried herself as if she guarded the
holy grail. Frances had told me that her father had gone to jail during
the eighties for illegal funding schemes, and joked that so far as she
could tell the experience had only made him more a more cunning and
successful financial criminal in the nineties. CeCe seemed quite right
as the daughter of such a figure. From the first she gave me the impres-
sion that all of Manhattan was a large soiree, and that she made the
guest list. She was a girl who knew fifteen hundred ways to say "fuck
you," and nodded to Frances that I passed muster, but perhaps only
barely. She didn't bother getting up for a formal hello, and it really was
just as well. I'd been lucky to guess Phoebe's greeting kissing ritual correctly, but could not be assured repeated success. Half of the young
women in New York think themselves European, and kiss on both
cheeks when you meet them. The other half live content in their
American identities and kiss only on one cheek, if at all. So you never
know where you are going to get kissed, or how many times. I've an-

ticipated second kisses that never came, and found myself with puckered lips staring at some bewildered girl like a senile pervert. Other times I've shifted my face after the first kiss, only to receive the second awkwardly on the lips. This is how disease is spread.

CeCe nursed a pink-orange Bellini and cooed to her date, who gave a wave and introduced himself as John. I immediately noted that he had strangely small shoulders and a remarkably large head.

"We miss you, Franny! Where've you been hiding?" CeCe asked, swishing her Bellini and playing with her hair. I felt Frances's legs bouncing beneath the table as she stared up at the big picture of Dizzy Gillespie hanging on the wall across from her.

"Here and there. Reading a lot, studying . . ."

"Well, seriously, you should come out more! We have all kinds of fun . . ." CeCe commenced to astonish me with a demonstration of a memory that, if not perfectly photographic, was frighteningly close. "Ungaro's party for his new thongs on the third! Cavalli's party for his new store on the sixth! Then the Met party at the Temple of Dendur on the twenty-first, and then the screening of John's new movie last night! And it's gonna be at Cannes!"

"Cannes is fabulous," said Sophie knowingly.

"Totally, babe," said Thorne, admiring Sophie's legs and access to the entertainment world.

"Yeah! Cannes!" Phoebe exclaimed. Big Larry looked up from his Blueberry. "Cannes?" he said, suddenly interested in the table conversation.

CeCe beamed and put her arm around John's little shoulders as she said it again, not only to make sure everyone knew, but also because she loved saying it. Just the word got her excited.

"Cannes!"

Lauren Schuyler was feeling left out and now provided the final chorus of the Cannes choir in an attempt to keep pace with Thorne and Sophie.

"Cannes . . ."

Some sociologists write that call-and-response is not a feature of modern societies, but they are wrong. Like fading verses of "Swing Low, Sweet Chariot," the echoes of Cannes rippled across the table. You could produce ninety minutes of rhesus monkeys playing Nerf football, and as long as you got the damn thing screened at Cannes people would want to know you for having done it.

John basked in the attention of the Cannes-obsessed table for several minutes before excusing himself to go to the bathroom. He pushed back his chair and hopped down to the floor, where he buttoned his tiny blazer and straightened his tiny khakis. And under the many bright lights of Cipriani's tremendous crystal chandelier, I realized all at once why his head had seemed so big, and his shoulders so small. The man was a midget. Frances's jaw dropped as she joined me in the revelation, but John didn't seem to notice. He strained to place his napkin on his plate, and marched off to the bathroom like Frodo Baggins off to defeat Sauron. The only sound at the table was Big Larry, clicking away on his Lehman Blueberry. The rest of us sat in silence, watching the top of John's big midget head bob and weave its way through the tables and chairs. Poor, beautiful, brilliant CeCe, who wanted only to date a star, no matter how small. She spoke. "Robert Redford is really short too, you know," she said, in a tone more apologetic than defensive. Yet CeCe wasn't sleeping with Robert Redford. She was sleeping with a midget. She was not a Robert Redford fucker. She was something else, something unplaceable. But what?

"Midgetfucker."

Yes, that was it. The word hopped out of Frances's mouth just as it came into my head, truthful and precise. Later that night, she would tell me that after saying it she appreciated just how tough things had been for Chaim Spero, and what a harsh place the world must be for all Tourette's sufferers. CeCe looked confused, then craned her neck in my direction. For a moment it seemed as though Sophie and I alone had heard Frances's outburst. Any differences between the girls over Yves Grandchatte were forgotten as, eyes and smiles wide with anticipation, we watched CeCe's face to see if she would decipher *midget-fucker* from the garbled tape of memory. It was not to be. In a few seconds she had forgotten what had confused her in the first place, and gone back to thinking of herself as dating a petite Redford. John returned from the bathroom, climbed back onto his chair, and grabbed CeCe's inner thigh, which caused her to exclaim a long "oooh!" and begin to giggle. He may have been a small man but seemed in possession of a giant libido. Still oblivious to being in the presence of a midget, Big Larry dropped an antacid tablet into his already sparkling water and took a big swig as he loosened his tie. Phoebe reached into her purse, tossed an invisible object into her mouth, and washed it down with a gulp of Big Larry's antacid water.

A waiter in a white tuxedo danced over to take our order. Phoebe rushed to go first. "I can't have any sugar or carbohydrates so I'm going to have the chef's salad without potatoes or croutons . . . ," she said, quite used to such culinary editing.

"The croutons and the potatoes. They are together in the salad," he said, turning his palms up in a gesture of helplessness. Then he adjusted his piqué bow tie and made a proclamation more grave than anything uttered by an Italian since Mussolini. "We no can take them apart!"

Phoebe would not be deterred. She slurred a bit while again attempting to compose a meal entirely bereft of at least two major nutritional building blocks. "So then I'm gonna have the clam soup? Does the clam soup have carbs?" She was saddened to learn that the clam soup was filled with as much pasta as clam. "Does all pasta have carbs?" she asked the table.

"Any pasta is going to have carbs, Pheebs," CeCe informed her.

CeCe stared at Phoebe. Phoebe stared at CeCe. They had been through this all before, and in a single voice placed their order.

"So then we'll just have the endive and avocado salad."

"I'll have the salmon with white wine and leeks," Big Larry said, looking up from his Blueberry again.

Frances asked for more bread and ordered risotto. The order was scribbled down next to the endive and avocado salad times two, and Big Larry seized upon the post-scriptum silence to discuss himself.

"I just worked on a very big financing for a group of Vietnamese fish farms over at Lehman. These guys raise salmon in buildings! Can you imagine a salmon living in a building? Great deal, though. The bonds traded up all afternoon, and I won't say how much, but . . ."

Sophie looked sadistically at Phoebe before ordering a large plate of spaghetti and one-upping Big Larry.

"My father is doing a movie in Vietnam with Russell Crowe right now," she said, taking a lazy sip of her third Bellini. "It's going to be like *Apocalypse Now,* only more apocalyptic, and more of the *now* . . ."

"Really?" said Thorne excitedly.

"Really," said Sophie coldly.

"Does he need any more young dudes to play soldiers?" asked Thorne, who had always believed that if given the chance he could be a movie star.

"I think he's got all the young dudes he needs," said Sophie.

"Maybe he could use, like, a young associate producer?" suggested Thorne, hopefully.

"No, he's all set," said Sophie, a bit surprised that Thorne would not be discouraged.

"Well then, do you think he could just use someone with serious muscles?" said Roger, flexing a bit. He was dead serious, which made Sophie break into laughter.

"Why would you want to leave Wall Street?" she asked upon recovery, after sipping one of a newly delivered round of Bellinis. "You're the quintessential J. S. Spenser banker. It's perfect for you."

Thorne nodded in knowing agreement, but looked bleak and bare as he leaned over to Sophie and revealed his soul.

"It's true, babe," he said. "But sometimes I don't know. Deep down, I just feel like I need to be out there, you know, interacting with celebrities."

Sophie looked into Thorne's eyes for some sign that he was joking. Roger took her stare as sign of true connection, and began to pitch her on the project that he knew could make him a star.

"I've got this idea for a movie called *Jugsaw,* about the ghost of this chainsaw killer who comes back from the dead, and cuts off babes' jugs. I mean, I think it could be a real franchise. T-shirts, coffee mugs, babes. Dig?"

Sophie took on a mischievous smile and told Thorne that she thought he had a future in film and that she would like to help him. The two then disappeared into one another in the way that people do over dinner. Sophie didn't even notice when John the midget took her Bellini and drained it in a single gulp. I looked around the table to see that we had three bottles of Sauvignon blanc and at least fifteen empty Bellini glasses, and even with my diminished mathematical abilities I realized that if none of the girls offered to pay, and they probably wouldn't, I would soon be out several hundred dollars. The worst part was that there was nothing to be done about it.

Phoebe and CeCe talked about their years at Choate with Frances as Big Larry read e-mail and Lauren Schuyler tried in vain to listen to Thorne's conversation with Sophie over the din of the packed restaurant. Though Frances kept her hand on my thigh, the midget and I were the only ones not actively engaged, and this proved grounds for an (appropriately) small friendship. John pointed at his empty Bellini glass and looked up to see if I would join in his drink reorder.

"Maybe something a bit less peachy?" I suggested, eyebrows raised.

"Fuck, yeah!" he replied, and roared with laughter at the sound of his own profanity.

"Johnny want a Johnnie Walker Black Label! Make it a double!" he barked to the waiter.

"Grey Goose on the rocks," I followed, not to be outdone by this little man and his little liver.

When our drinks arrived, Big Larry from Lehman offered a story about the time he made three hundred thousand dollars in a single afternoon. Soon he was recalling his recent move from London to New York.

"I kicked ass in London, now I'm gonna kick ass in New York," he said, to blank stares all around. John and I drank long and deep to all the ass that Big Larry had kicked in London and the many asses awaiting his kicking in New York.

Soon John was really opening up to me, and he began talking about the early days of his career.

"When I first started out I didn't know what sort of roles I would get . . ."

He was as sloppy as Phoebe, his consonants and vowels thick and rolling.

"I was thinking Willow? You know, *Willow*?"

I did know *Willow*. In fact, I loved *Willow,* and told him so, albeit at a volume that apparently seemed much louder to everyone else than it did to me.

Several diners turned their heads.

Big Larry, the ass-kicking bond king of Lehman Brothers, stopped in mid-conversation to shoot a disgusted look from across the table.

Once again Frances's heel hit my shin. But there was no going back. John scrambled on his chair to get up on his knees, and stretched a hand over the basket of Cipriani bread sticks for a high-five.

"Well, Willow sucks, man! So I played Puck!"

The midget was quite plastered. Big Larry lost his audience entirely as the girls turned to look at the more animated goings-on at the far end of the table. I had taken a drama course at Georgetown and knew of another midget who had once played Shakespeare's Puck.

"Didn't Webster once play Puck?" I asked.

"Emmanuel Lewis in the house!" he boomed, and I got a big red boozy smile and another high-five from my new friend John the midget before asking something I had always wondered.

"Is Webster a midget too?" I asked.

There, it was out. I said the *"m"* word. No more pretending. John and I had grown close, but this tested our bond. He paused for a brief, awkward moment, concluded that my inquiry was sincere, and gave an honest answer.

"No, not at all," said John, expertly. "He's just really short."

This observed difference between extreme shortness and actual midgetry set Frances into spasms of laughter, which caused me and John to recognize its absurdity, and begin laughing too. And when we were done laughing on the matter of midgetry versus shortness, we continued to laugh just at the sight of each other laughing. John tried to calm himself down with a long drink of whiskey, but somewhere deep in his big head he found a new lode of comedy and exploded anew, spraying the entire table with a mist of equal parts aged whiskey and saliva. He had just enough self-control to aim the spray, and it goes without saying that Big Larry got the worst of it. Mortified, CeCe flashed the waiter the international sign for more Bellinis, pointing in a circular motion at the empty glasses on the table. Frances leaned over and whispered confusedly in my ear.

"She was really very sweet in high school."

I felt the pear-shaped diamond of her mother's engagement ring sharp against my palm, and we held hands as CeCe rattled away about planning parties, doing seating arrangements, and answering phones. Soon the waiter brought our food. As John and I each confronted a large cut of meat, I wondered about the size of his internal organs. CeCe and Phoebe rearranged their salads while Frances ate her risotto, and poor Lauren Schuyler excused herself for a cigarette. Thorne didn't even acknowledge her exit and gestured excitedly as he explained to Sophie Dvornik the surprise ending he had planned for *Jugsaw III: The Reawakening*. Big Larry gingerly forked his salmon while describing the wonders of this summer's timeshare in Bridgehampton to CeCe in such vivid detail that no one noticed as Phoebe draped her tongue about the inner rim of her flute to get at the final drops of her fourth Bellini, smiled across the room in a big droopy arc, and then suddenly passed out into her endive and avocado salad with a plate-rattling thud. The impact sent silverware skittering to the floor and left avocado pasted in slick patches to her over-dyed thicket of hair. In day spas across town she might have paid in excess of three hundred dollars for such an experience and referred to it as a treatment. She remained unconscious for a few seconds, until the painkiller-and-Bellini bloodstream interactions that had knocked her out were undone, and she came to as if stirring from a long nap.

"That babe just totally peaced out," observed Thorne to Sophie, as Phoebe raked the lettuce from her tresses with long manicured nails that were almost too perfectly suited to the task.

Big Larry rubbed her back. CeCe gave her water. Frances offered risotto, which was declined with a weak hand for reasons already made clear. John struggled to maintain his composure at first, and distracted himself with a forced swig from his third double whiskey. But when Phoebe pulled an overlooked sprig of rosemary from her eyelashes the little man lost it and sprayed down the table for the second time, like a very tiny Old Faithful. Thorne and Sophie alone escaped the deluge, but the rest of us were soaked. Big Larry was rip-shit and CeCe was devastated. Phoebe was beside herself, and Lauren Schuyler embarrassed beyond belief. We sat at the whiskey-stained, avocado-strewn table, drying ourselves with napkins, waiting for the check.

"Did I tell you guys we hung out with Lauren Conrad at Bungalow last week?" asked CeCe, and Phoebe nodded that it was true, and the night was over.

## 5

# SHOOTING WITH
# DICK CHENEY

By the time Roger Thorne and I reached J. S. Spenser's two sky-scrapers on each side of Park Avenue at Forty-eighth Street, the classical font of the original J. S. Spenser logo had been transformed into an italicized NASCAR-like logo: *JSSPENSER*. Over the past several years of bad mergers and failed acquisitions there had been firings and resignations en masse, but the cadre of men who ran Spenser's Investment Banking business still made multimillion-dollar bonuses, sometimes without doing much at all. An investment banker who can play politics will thrive in even the most adverse business environments, and everyone agreed that Terence Mathers's future was regarded as very bright indeed.

The most highly regarded vice president of each group was given the job of staffer and charged with overseeing the development of all analysts and associates. Mathers was the staffer of the M&A group, which made him effectively the boss of everyone below VP. He welcomed us into his office, where we had been told to report on that first day. In an early move of career treachery, Vema and Vanita had beaten us inside the building, reneging on our earlier agreed-to promise that everyone would arrive at eight thirty. Wharton's finest sat attentively in Mathers's office with a pair of massive candy-colored Louis Vuitton tote bags, nicely blinged-out for the first day of work.

The M&A group was moved down to the second and third floors after 9/11 robbed skyline views of their status symbolism. The bulk of the bankers operated on the third floor, with the Latin America team on the second. The Latin America group was staffed almost exclusively with the sons and daughters of the presidents, prime ministers, and plutocrats who controlled the countries in which they transacted their business. Each was wealthy beyond belief, but as a group they were somehow incapable of making a dime. It wasn't that they didn't work hard. According to the agencies that rank such things, they had done more deals in nearly every area of their business than any other bank for a decade running. The problem was that for every dollar they earned they spent at least two on suites at the Copacabana, outings to Machu Picchu, and weekends in Buenos Aires, all in the name of entertaining their clients who were, in most cases, also their relatives. Yet their top ranking gave the firm the ability to claim excellence in at least one area, and that had a value all its own. So they came and went as they pleased in four-thousand-dollar suits and python-skin shoes. Not even Dewey Ananias would touch them, and he had fired more people than anyone could count. As the head of M&A, Ananias got the largest bonus in his group—fifteen million dollars last year—despite the firm's dire straits. His office was twice the size of anyone else's, with a sweeping view of Park Avenue, but this wasn't his greatest trophy. The rest of the managing directors were given mere *assistants* from the firm's permanent staff of disgruntled, options-rich, phone-non-answerers, but Ananias alone was allowed an *executive assistant*. He had hired Monica

Speer from the wreckage of the John Kerry campaign, paid her two hundred thousand dollars a year, and gloried in thinking that this woman who had once written speeches for a presidential candidate now carried out mundane tasks on his behalf. She was tall, he was short. She was skinny, he was fat. She was attractive, he was not. She did his planning and his calendar and his firing, which made her feared by analysts and associates and even a few vice presidents. Ananias sat her in a cubicle just off his office. However, it was Mathers who sat immediately next to him, with Tyler Russell and Peter Walker, his two favorite managing directors, nestled into the two smaller corner offices on the Park Avenue side of the building

Mathers had made his office a great tribute to himself. The oak shelves and desktops bristled with silver Tiffany frames, each holding a picture of Terence Mathers and someone more important than Terence Mathers. There was Terence Mathers on the seventh green at Shinnecock with Dewey Ananias. There he was again, having drinks at Seminole with Wayne Huizenga. There he was once more, hair slicked back in a Barbour jacket, shooting geese with Dick Cheney.

"Where did you go shooting with Dick Cheney?" clients and colleagues often asked.

"An undisclosed location!" Mathers loved to reply.

"Did he get you?" they sometimes quipped, and if they were more powerful than Terence Mathers he would laugh and say that he had narrowly escaped, and if they were less powerful he would say nothing at all.

The only framed picture not of an overprivileged white man was one of an underprivileged black boy, named Latrell Phelps. Latrell Phelps lived in a very bad area of the Bronx, and Mathers treated him to one-on-one basketball and hot dogs every third month as part of the firm's community outreach program, *SpenserCares*. The program had been established as part of a settlement for regulatory infractions in the

1980s, and participation was generally viewed as a good career move, especially as it required only about six hours a year. Mathers said that he found Latrell inspiring, and you'd have thought he was Mother Teresa from the way he discussed the four hours that they had spent together thus far.

Terence loved his picture of Latrell Phelps, but his favorite office item by far was his little silver Porsche. With the eight hundred thousand dollars he had made last year, he bought a real-life version of the model car, and kept it parked in a garage on Central Park South. He had a special love for the little model, though, and was spinning it in wheelies across the top of the desk as he welcomed us.

"You can go from analyst to managing director in this group," he began. "That is a huge opportunity. That is an opportunity not everyone has . . ."

He nodded toward the picture of little Latrell Phelps by way of explanation, and paused to let it all sink in. Then he talked about some of the deals that Spenser was working on and what was expected of analysts. We were to be detail-oriented, career-planning, all-giving, hard workers. The finger-fueled toy Porsche raced in laps on his mouse pad. I was mesmerized by the little car and realized that I had spaced out only when Mathers spoke directly to me.

"Tom, we have a big pitch to Robertson Energy Partners coming up. They are a seven-billion-dollar private equity fund. Spenser Partners owns a large stake in several Canadian oil fields. As you know, Spenser Partners has been . . ." Mathers struggled to hide his delight in the collapse of Spenser Partners, whose many talented employees might have rivaled him down the line had their investments not tanked. Soon he had his verbiage. "Spenser Partners has been *adjusting to new business realities,* and they want to sell. The good news is that they still have money to pay us fees, so Dewey and I are meeting with Robertson Partners next week. These guys are self-made billionaires, and they've just raised a seven-billion-dollar fund. Jack Robertson is the managing partner, and the guy owns so much coal and oil that he prays to Mecca. Makkesh Makker is our associate, and I've staffed you on the deal. Touch base with Makkesh and he'll loop you in."

Vema and Vanita were assigned to help Peter Walker handle General Electric. Mathers explained that as GE was such a large corporation it would be a full-time assignment, and that they would be reporting directly to another of Ananias's most senior vice presidents, Michael Fowler. The girls were immediately excited. Everything about them was ready for Wall Street—even their vocabularies.

"When will we get *looped in*?" asked Vema, with a look of grave sincerity.

"As soon as Peter and I *touch base,*" replied Terence, curtly.

"And then we'll all *circle up*?" asked Vanita, hopefully.

"Unless he *circles back* with you first. Either way, we'll *reach out to you.*"

What had they said? Something seemed to have been communicated and decided. Was I supposed to loop in or touch base or circle up with Makkesh? How exactly did you go about doing those things? I wasn't sure, but before I could ask, Mathers turned to Roger Thorne.

"Stick around afterwards, Roger," he said "I've got something special for you."

At that moment Thorne began what can only be described as the most remarkable rise toward early prominence in the long history of J. S. Spenser. Though he could tell Turnbull and Asser from Thomas Pink blindfolded—he really could—Thorne had no practical experience doing anything much beyond sailing. Mathers had taken him in as a social courtesy, but wouldn't turn Thorne loose on the group without some assurance of competence. He started him off with an internal assignment that, no matter how badly botched, could do no harm. He told Roger to compile a master list of all of the deals presently being worked on in the group. Meaningless work like this was referred to as shit work, and Mathers was giving Thorne a big pile of it until he had some idea of his capabilities. Of course Thorne didn't see it that way, and he approached the shit assignment as if it were the final negotiation of a forty-billion-dollar merger. Then Mathers got a phone call from someone more important than himself and dismissed us all with a quick thumbs-up. Vema and Vanita bounded off toward their cubicles, and Junior Titan Roger Thorne got right to work, marching proudly down the aisles of offices and cubicles, introducing himself to everyone as he went, the buckles on his Gucci loafers jingling to announce his arrival like miniature heralds.

I settled into the eight-by-eight cubicle whose carpet had once been gray, but over the years had been Jackson Pollocked with tumbling chunks of sesame chicken and spilled splashes of Starbucks lattes. The inside of the cubicle was effectively one big desk, with oak countertops and drawers on all sides. On the desk was a large flat-screen monitor, which glowed before the J. S. Spenser standard-issue Herman Miller Aeron chair. Panels of glass separated my cube from those surrounding me, but I realized right away that my neighbors would be able to see my every expression and hear my every conversation, and that at Spenser only the vice presidents and managing directors were entitled to privacy. To my right was Craig Snyder, the number-one analyst in the class before mine. Craig had never taken a vacation, and for this selflessness been rewarded with a sixty-thousand-dollar bonus in his first year after graduating from Columbia. The more constant reward for all of his hard work was more hard work, and the degree of his success was most fully observed in the razor-burned skin of his neck, and the bags of darkened capillaries sagging beneath his eyes. He looked away from his computer long enough to offer a short nod as I got settled, and then went right back to work.

My other neighbor was Alfred Chan, a twenty-seven-year-old computer programmer from China's Guangdong province, who by his own estimate had been smoking Marlboro Reds for two decades. All of us shared an assistant, a wonderful woman named Flora Fanatucci. I heard the whooshing of her Sergio Tachini running suit as she came over to introduce herself. Flora had worked at Chase Bank since the day she graduated from high school in 1982. In the more than two decades that followed she had gone from blonde to brunette to redhead, pioneered the running suit as an acceptable form of corporate attire, and accumulated more than two million dollars in exercisable stock options—all without doing a thing. Now a wealthy woman, Flora did not answer phones, did not send faxes, did not take messages, and did not label files. Indeed, to the candid observer her duties seemed limited to page-by-page reading of the *Daily News,* measured consumption of tropical-flavor Lifesavers, hourlong conversations about the Yankees, and domination of the online Tetris world. After a long day of these things she left work at three for spinning classes at the Staten Island Sports Club. The only area in which her life had not been somehow charmed was in love. Office gossip had it that there had once been a Mr. Fanatucci, but that after marrying Flora out of high school he had mistreated her, sometimes physically, and that the marriage had ended not long after it began. Flora never spoke of this, but I sensed that it had to be true halfway through my time at Spenser, when she told a young associate who was leaving the firm to get married to be sure she was treated right. The statement had left the girl puzzled, but it confirmed all I had heard. Flora loved Thorne, and after his remarkable rise would even arrange for him to move into an office overlooking Lexington. She was less enthusiastic about me, and as her first and last act as my assistant, handed me a box of green pens and an empty tape dispenser, then told me that my tie was sharp before swishing back from whence she came.

I swiveled back in my chair and found staring at me through the cubicle's glass an enormous Indian man in a custom-tailored shirt of purple and blue gingham, every square inch of which was flooded with the fleshy expanse of his cherubic figure. Makkesh Makker smiled widely, setting several of his more minor chins spreading into happy arcs beneath his face. His chair rose a few inches and squeaked in relief as he labored up to offer his hand over the glass. "Tom Quinn? You'll be working on the oil deal, man? Mathers says they are going to buy. But I don't think so, man. I say NFW, man!"

Makkesh Makker had never been able to lose his thick Indian accent, but seemed to have recently come to believe that if he simply used enough slang it would go away. "NFW" was his most recent acquisition—an abbreviation used by analysts and associates to express their doubts when the MDs and VPs sent them on wild-goose chases for deals that would never be done. It stood for "no fucking way."

"NFW, man! These oil fields have no oil! They are not oil fields! Just fields! NFW, man!"

Makkesh cleared a pair of empty Sunkist orange soda cans and a bag of stale Cheez-Its from his desk to reveal a sheaf of papers bound in plastic. He handed me the book, explaining that inside it I would find complete financial data for our bank's Canadian oil fields. The firm had paid a billion dollars for the fields in 1998, and was hoping that with the increase in global oil prices they might be unloaded for a profit. Spenser Partners might have sold the fields themselves, but Dewey Ananias was more powerful than Wasserstein, so it would be political suicide for the Spenser Partners to try to do a sale without going through the M&A group, and paying a fee. J. S. Spenser Partners was prepared to pay J. S. Spenser Investment Banking more than twenty million dollars for selling something that J. S. Spenser already owned. Bizarre, yes, but more bizarre still: In this particular transaction most of the financial opinions were to be generated by a young man with a hangover from binge drinking with a midget, and only the vaguest grasp of the difference between a U.S. dollar and a Canadian dollar.

I came to regard the book of financial data as devout Muslims regard the Koran, sure that if I simply meditated upon it for long enough all problems would be solved. I plugged away until well after midnight each day through the beginning of the following week, pausing only to eat lunch at my desk and to order dinner with Makkesh, who pressed the Shun Lee Palace Chinese menu against the glass dividing our cubes each night at a few minutes after seven.

"Fried dumplings, man? Moo shoo pancakes?"

Makkesh was going out of his way to get to know me, and he loved Shun Lee so much that I couldn't bear to disappoint him. He would lumber over to my desk like a triumphant hunter an hour later with two Happy Family specials. Over dinner I would ask him questions about our deal, then watch and listen as he chopsticked great knots of lo mein into his mouth and talked about what he viewed as the most fascinating thing happening in the world today: reality television.

"I cannot stand to wait for the next season of *Laguna Beach*! But there will never be another Kristin! Kristin was very mean, but very pretty! What lovely legs!"

He was right, and though I too appreciated Kristin and her legs, the intricacies of finance proved elusive. The numbers never spoke to me as they do to some people, and Makkesh found errors in everything I touched. He seemed to find my failures highly entertaining, though, and after a day of rejecting my awful work would sit at his desk before putting in our Chinese order and look at me with eyes that always seemed to say, "What in Shiva's name are you doing here?"

"What did you study at Georgetown?" he had asked me at the end of that first week, after I had failed to make even a basic model of our oil fields and their cash flows.

"I was premed," I told him.

"Why aren't you in medical school?" he asked.

"I'm not too sure," I told him, not wanting to further downgrade his opinion of me with a discussion of my failed premed coursework.

"Did you get into a medical program?" Makkesh asked in disbelief.

"Yes, I did," I said, and hoped he wouldn't ask me which one.

"Which one?" he asked.

"The Universidad de Medicina de Santa Filomena," I said, as if everyone had heard of it. From the smiling of his chins I knew he found the name of my would-be medical alma mater nearly as amusing as my error-ridden financial analysis.

"It's not an American school," I said, as if it were not evident. "But I never thought of myself as a heart-transplanting, broken-head-fixing sort of doctor. I saw myself more as a deliver-your-baby, fix-your-broken-arm kind of guy. You watch the news and think the world could use more of them, and you don't have to . . ."

"Oh, I do believe you!" said Makkesh, his many chins aflutter. "Knowing you just a week I will say that you do mean very, very well! What you are doing in this bank, I have no idea!"

On his desk was a picture of a very beautiful Indian woman, smiling with a red dot on her head, dressed in saffron and purple robes. Makkesh gazed at her, and his chins lost a bit of their bounce.

"Do you have a girlfriend?" he asked, and I told him that I did.

"Then go and spend this weekend with her!" he said. "Because this deal is shit, man! And everything you do is wrong anyway! So for now, we have no more work to do!"

Deciding that working for Makkesh Makker made me the luckiest young drone on Wall Street, I thanked him, went home, and spent forty-eight hours with Frances.

BY THE END OF MY THIRD WEEK IN THE GROUP I HAD TAUGHT myself enough about Excel to complete a basic financial model showing the sort of money that the billionaires down in Texas could expect to make after acquiring J. S. Spenser's Canadian oil fields. The other analysts were on to far more advanced things, but I was still quite proud of this little model. It had a little button that converted all of the Canadian dollars into U.S. dollars, and also several much larger buttons that didn't do anything at all, but which I couldn't figure out how to remove, and thought looked nice. I gave it to Makkesh in the morning, and he came by my desk late that afternoon.

"Congratulations!" he told me, with a printout of the multibuttoned masterpiece in his hand.

"Is it good?" I asked.

"Not at all!" he said. "It's very, very bad! But I see you work very, very hard. So tonight, we go to Smith & Wo's!"

We got our jackets and walked from Park over to Third, then inside Smith & Wollensky. I had a house salad and the petit filet. Makkesh had a porterhouse on a bed of blood and grease, which he used as gravy for his miniature buffet of sides, which included but was not limited to creamed spinach and fried potatoes. He ordered a bottle of Cabernet and toasted my first week at the firm.

At dinner, he talked about his mother back home in Jaipur, and told me that before he came to America she had arranged a marriage between him and the daughter of a wealthy rubber-manufacturing family. Makkesh explained that his family owned farmland, and that it was deemed a smart move to marry into a family that made rubber. He also said that he had loved this girl, and she had not much cared for him, but her family had spoken for her, and so she agreed to marry Makkesh. There had been two weeks of wedding celebrations, and even the beginning of the Hindu matrimonial rite, all against the advice of family astrologers, who advised that the heavens were well set against the union. There was great pressure from both sides, however, and so preparations continued, and the wedding would have happened, except that something went very wrong. To complete the ceremony Makkesh and his bride had to dance backward, eight times, around a fire. He grew dizzier by each lap, and on the seventh lost his balance entirely, then went crashing into a statue of Vishnu. The mishap was rightly taken as a terrible omen, and the girl's parents finally heeded her wishes to have the wedding cancelled.

"We have weak hearts in my family," he said with regret, still pained by his misstep. Makkesh told me this story and showed me the scar left on his forehead from his close encounter with the divine. He cringed as he passed his finger across it.

"Vishnu capped my ass!" he said in his strange Hindi locution, running his finger across his scar. "You see, he gave me this scar for playing hide-and-seek with myself!"

"Maybe you should have been more careful, and just taken it easy with the dancing," I suggested.

"No, it was simply not to be," he said. "We have weak hearts, and my own was broken for a very, very long time."

I had just suggested that Vishnu and Shiva might not be too thrilled with him for having eaten the better part of a cow when he looked straight at me, his scar now flushed.

"I had a very holy nephew, Tommy Quinn," he said, and motioned to the waiter for our check. "And it is said that when he died he was offered to come back as a very wealthy, beautiful man. Some people think that wealth and beauty are all that do really exist. Not this cousin! He decided to return as a brightly colored bird!"

When the bill arrived Makkesh took a pen from his pocket and on the back of the receipt wrote down the name of every banker who sat within twenty yards of us: Alfred Chan, Craig Snyder, Terence Mathers, and five others whom I had never even met. This allowed us to use their nightly dinner allowances, and in so doing to spend two hundred dollars on a meal that was only authorized to cost twenty. Only at J. S.

Spenser could you eat dinner with eight other colleagues without ever being on the same city block with them. In fact, Makkesh and I had probably enjoyed dinner at several other excellent restaurants on that very evening without even knowing it. The result of this—well, it was fraud, I guess—was poor, choppy earnings for J. S. Spenser's shareholders, and fine, eclectic dining for its bankers. Makkesh was pleasantly buzzed and in excellent spirits. As we left he patted me on the shoulder, and said that, Shiva notwithstanding, he was willing to cover for me at work, but could not do it forever. As we parted he told me to give his best to my girlfriend, and to enjoy the weekend.

THAT SUNDAY I TURNED TWENTY-FOUR, AND FOR A SURPRISE Frances had Bo arrange for us to receive a private tour of the Met. We ate a late brunch at Le Bilboquet, and took a slow walk up Fifth Avenue to the museum. It was after five and all the visitors were filing out, but the security guards waved us both in. The curator was waiting for us, and as soon as the lobby had fully cleared led us through the galleries, then back into the museum's storerooms. Frances had already told him what she wanted us to see, and the man seemed to know where everything was. He showed us vases painted with pictures of Bacchus and Dionysus, and explained how the two faces were identical to the early paintings of Christ. He showed us a medal with a small eaglet on it that had belonged to Napoleon II. Finally he took us to the pre-Columbian archives, where behind glass were three Mayan calendars, the sort of which Frances had long been dying to own. She asked the curator to remove the glass from the most intact of the set, and he agreed.

"See?" she said, and ran my fingers across the calendar's surface, which unlike her fragment, was pristine, and glazed in umber and turquoise. You would have thought it a beautiful ornament if you didn't know it kept track of time. This seemed to be why Frances loved it most.

"They saw time as a circle, not like a line," she said, running her finger in a concentric circle around the calendar. "There was none of this *end of the world* nonsense, just one cycle stopping and another starting. So this calendar *is* that idea. So is there any wonder that it's breathtaking?"

"But if *I* am part of the cycle that stops, isn't that more or less an end of *my world*?" I asked her.

"*I* is somebody else," she said with a smile.

"What about *we*?" I asked her.

"*We* is the best thing for *I* and *you*." She laughed.

The curator told us what he knew about the calendars: that they were more accurate even than those used by the Romans, and that they tracked dates thousands of years before and after the fall of the Maya. When Frances asked him when the calendar began, he told her only that it went back thousands of years. Then she asked when it ended, and he was a bit slower to respond.

"My specialty is classical art, not pre-Columbian," he said. "But it's my understanding that the Mayan calendar rather abruptly stops on December 21, 2012. Whoever made them seemed to think that a very significant cycle would end on that day, and they just lost interest after it. . . ."

We talked about the world ending on December 21, 2012, all the way home.

"I hope those Mayans got their calculations wrong," I said. "I hope that we catch Osama and fix Iraq and get all of the Muslims cross-addicted to online shopping and HBO."

"Isn't it a little too late for that, my love?" Frances laughed.

"It's never too late for online shopping and HBO," I advised.

"No," she said, slowing her walk. "I mean, doesn't the world feel like an awfully old place? It's as if you've walked into some play you've never seen before, but you can tell by the audience and the actors that it's almost over. You can tell that it's very late in the play."

"Well, if you feel that way we should leave," I said. "I call up the Universidad de Medicina and take my spot. We'll make a telephone out of coconuts, and train monkeys to sing us songs. We'll breed them in different colors, and call them iMonkeys. The really skinny ones will be iMonkey nanos."

Frances managed a laugh, but as we approached her apartment I began to appreciate that I was involved with a girl who took her endings very seriously.

"I think it's even too late for escapes," she said, as if she had already considered this. "And besides, I don't much care what happens in 2012, as long as I am with you."

She stood on her stoop, lifted the black pashmina from her neck, and kissed me. She took a small box from her pocket, wrapped in a scrap of newspaper bearing Iraq headlines, and gave it to me. I opened it and found a pair of cuff links made from gold Roman coins.

"They're minted in 362 by the Emperor Julian," she said, pointing to the bearded man on one of the coin's faces.

"They have eagles on the other side," she said, and gestured to the other cuff link, which showed an eagle. "I thought you'd like that, because you're my little eaglet."

I told her that I didn't know who the Emperor Julian was, but that I thought he had made lovely coins, and that I would treasure the gift. She told me that he had been the last of the great emperors, and that was why she had bought the cuff links for me.

"There were angry Persians and crazy Christians back then too," she told me, and I smiled broadly at my luck for finding a girl like this. We stood on the stoop amid the falling fiery leaves, kissing and laughing in the late evening.

———

THAT NIGHT I TOLD FRANCES A STORY ABOUT THE TIME IN FIRST grade, the second time around, when Chaim Spero came to school for Halloween dressed as Skeletor, then continued coming to school dressed like this until Thanksgiving. Frances said he seemed at home with himself. We laughed and made love and we might have slept quietly through the night were it not for two phone calls. At five in the morning Bo Sloan called to tell her that Sunshine had been born, and was healthy. Frances asked him if they could talk more in the morning, then fell back to sleep on my chest. At six thirty I gently pushed her off to take a call from Makkesh Makker.

"The deal has gone live, Tommy!" he shouted at the other end of the phone. "I need you at the office now! We need to get our presentation out today!"

Makkesh calmed down to explain how our deal had gone from an impossibility to an immediate reality. The Texas oil billionaires had met Tyler Russell, the Spenser managing director on the deal, at an outing in Napa Valley that weekend, and decided that they liked him a great deal, and that, just for him, they would take a closer look at the J. S. Spenser oil fields. All of the work that I had done so poorly in the weeks before now needed to be made perfect.

I pulled on a suit and rushed to the office, where Makkesh had me forward him the multibuttoned financial model I had built that past Friday. Makkesh fixed the formulas and checked my numbers and removed the big buttons that didn't do anything. Then he asked me very seriously to swear to him that I had at least entered the right data. I thought this was the one thing I had done correctly, and told him so. Makkesh then sent the model to Mathers, who got out of bed with his wife who hated him to give it a once-over, and then sent it to Ananias, who was in Rome attending a wine auction. Ananias took time away from his bidding to review the numbers himself, and then sent them to Robertson Petroleum, where an MBA just two weeks out of Stanford became the first person to actually look at what I had done. It was this man who discovered that the expert financial advisers at J. S. Spenser had converted the projected cash flows from their Canadian oil fields from Canadian dollars into U.S. dollars . . . after the Canadian accountants had already done so. As a result, our estimates of the oil fields' worth and profitability were about six hundred million dollars less than had been expected, and I broke new ground as a financial pioneer, the first and only man to ever successfully convert the U.S. dollar into itself. This I did at the rate of 1.58 U.S. dollars to the U.S. dollar.

Livid, Henry Wasserstein from J. S. Spenser Partners called Ananias, and there followed a torrent of abuse directed at Terence Mathers, in which Ananias demanded the head of whoever had sent the botched numbers. Mathers called Makkesh, wanting someone's head, and Makkesh managed to calm him down by convincing him that it was simply a computer glitch. Mathers then calmed Ananias down by convincing him that another vice president named Gary Evans was largely responsible for the error. So my head didn't roll, but all of my work had to be redone, and this in itself was suitable torture. Makkesh and I worked from early Monday morning straight through the week. We showered and changed in the J. S. Spenser gym, and it was Thursday before either of us was able to go home. Frances had been calling me the whole time, but I had never been able to talk to her for more than a few seconds. I had long since stopped expecting her to be enthusiastic about Sunshine, but never expected her to be genuinely disturbed by the little girl's birth. Her voice went dull when I told her that I had to go, and she grew angry when I didn't call her back, and she seemed incapable of understanding how anyone could be at work for so long unless they were launching a spaceship or rescuing a toddler from a well. I didn't think much of any of this until finally, after a week, I stole an hour from the bank to go back to the apartment.

She was lying on one of the old overstuffed sofas, her hair wrapped up in a lumpy, unwashed bun. She wore the same red kimono that she had surprised me with weeks before, but it too seemed different, and as I looked closer I saw that among its bright silken peacocks and dragons were burns from fallen cigarettes and stains from splashed sips of wine. The tulip-poplar chest was covered in books on Magritte, who had captured her interest after the eruption of Krakatoa. There was also a book on Warhol, opened to a color print of his Day-Glo frogs, which struck me as more beautiful than Magritte's gonad faces. I looked at the frogs and noted that the air in the apartment was nursing-home stale and that the windows had all been closed. Frances didn't move from the sofa but followed me with her eyes as I entered, then lazily crushed a Parliament Ultra Light in a Chinese vase turned ashtray.

"Where have you been?" she asked. "I keep calling your phone but you don't pick up. I haven't seen you in days."

"This is just how it is with a live deal," I told her, and pointed to the dark bags beneath my eyes. "I've slept five hours in the past three days."

"My father was on Wall Street for thirty years and I've never once seen him work like this," she said, gesturing up at me from the couch as if I were a stranger.

"This is what it takes," I said, sheepishly, and for the first time felt the strain of coming from a world just a shade different from hers. On the night that Frances said she hoped we would still be together in five years, I had looked at her mother's diamond, and realized that its two-carat stone more or less set a benchmark. I knew that supporting Frances would never be cheap, and I was fine with that. What I had not anticipated was the possibility that the job that allowed me to afford her might also cause her to resent me.

"Daddy sent pictures of the baby," Frances said sourly, and gestured to an opened envelope on the coffee table. "This kid's a real fucking bruiser."

"Did you have classes today?" I asked, hoping to get her to a happier topic. She told me that she was working on an independent study project, and wasn't attending regular lectures anymore. I believed her.

My cell phone rang, and it was Mathers, wondering where I had gone and when I would return. I kissed Frances and felt my lips slide across the oil of her forehead. She remained affixed to the couch, and raised her hand only to drape it through my hair.

"You know that it's late, because there are so many lies around," she said.

"Lies?" I asked.

"Everywhere."


STILL IN ROME, ANANIAS PULLED HIMSELF AWAY FROM BIDDING on wine long enough to talk with Tyler Russell and Robertson Petroleum every day, pitching them on sexy tax loopholes and capital structures for the deal, even though it was already more or less done. The real point was to somehow justify the twenty-million-dollar fee that we would make for doing next to nothing, so that the next time such a fee was paid to someone for doing nothing, it would be we who did the nothing.

But the universe is full of paradoxes, and somehow doing nothing created a ridiculous amount of work. Ananias would wake up in Rome at three in the morning and e-mail ten random questions to Tyler Russell. Russell would add a few of his own random questions, just to look as though he cared, and send them to Mathers. Mathers would hear his Blackberry rattle, lean over his wife who hated him, and forward Ananias's questions to Makkesh and me, usually adding ten of his own. We had long since stopped sleeping, and by the time we got the e-mails there could be as many as twenty useless assignments demanding immediate attention. I helped Makkesh where I could, but after the dollar-to-dollar conversion there was no more pretending that I was in any way competent. We couldn't afford mistakes, and there was no time for him to check my work. So he gave me little things to do that could not be screwed up, and I kept him abreast of developments in the world of reality television.

"Hey, Makkesh. Page Six says Kristin from *Laguna Beach* is going to be in a movie with Al Pacino . . ."

"As long as she wears a bathing suit! Now FedEx this to Dewey Ananias!"

We worked around the clock, and it was manageable for a while, but things grew insane as the weekend approached. Ananias thought he had found a way to dodge three million dollars in capital gains taxes, and as he explored this loophole his questions tripled in volume, with Makkesh bearing nearly the entire burden. I would bring him two venti-sized Starbucks mochas with skim milk in the morning and Diet Cokes in the afternoon. With dinner we would order a six-pack of Red Bull to drink through the night. Makkesh didn't do well with stimulants, though. Sweat saddlebags grew in wide arcs from beneath the arms of his shirt as he guzzled the unending flow of aorta-rotting drinks, munching all the while on low-cholesterol Cheez-Its. His cubicle became a graveyard of empty beverage containers, with encrusted Starbucks cups stacked atop sticky soda cans and half-empty Red Bulls. They grew throughout the weekend to the point that even the custodians began puzzling over Makkesh's many leaning towers of crap as they went about their rounds, and were soon avoiding his cube for fear that even the most delicate attempt at cleaning might precipitate a catastrophic structural failure. By Sunday night we had only two more days to complete the full presentation and Makkesh opened another Red Bull to fuel him through this final sprint.

He guzzled half of the iridescent beverage in a single swig. I watched as he proudly stacked it on top of Saturday afternoon's quarter-filled venti mocha cup, itself perched astride two of Friday morning's sticky Diet Coke cans, each of which was supported on its outer rim by ancient half-full Red Bulls. Sticky with sweat and sugar, Makkesh's fingers adhered to the edge of the Red Bull aluminum for just a quarter-second too long, and when he fully withdrew them the entire structure of half-consumed beverages gave way with a careening splatter. The topmost Red Bull splashed him in the face, which was in a way quite merciful, because his vision was clouded when the many Starbucks cups and Coke cans crashed across his laptop, cascading foul liquid across his open computer and covering the machine in a deadly bath that bubbled briefly in small pools upon the keyboard before disappearing down into its microprocessing bowels. There was a gurgle and then a failing groan as the screen went blank.

"Oh no! Oh, Vishnu!"

Makkesh's eyes began to tear as he looked at his ruined laptop and thought of all the work that had just been lost. I thought I had a solution, and I wanted quite badly to rescue him, as he had spent the last week covering for my many grotesque deficiencies. So I brought my computer around into his cubicle, and told him not to worry—we would plug it into the network, access our presentation on Spenser's shared drive, and all would be well.

"It will not work, Tommy! You have the Dell. I have top-of-line IBM!"

I might have paused to consider this observation, but did not. There were perhaps two hundred computers all around us on the M&A floor, each locked with a series of five-, six-, or seven-letter passwords that

Spenser had us shift about each month for "information security." We would have to wait until nine A.M. for the tech support staff to come in. Mathers would want to see something when he came in at eight, and I thought I could save us.

"Get up, you big Brahmin!" I told him, and looked again at the picture of a beautiful Indian girl, a Bollywood princess if ever there was, her body wrapped in saffron and purple robes, framed in engraved silver beside his computer.

"Is that your sister?"

"My old fiancée."

"The rubber heiress?"

"Yes."

"I thought that it was over."

He was beside himself, whether from the idea of imminent firing or homesickness I could not be sure, but he began to cry openly as he embarrassedly explained this Tiffany-framed shrine.

"That does not mean she is not still nice to look at."

At that moment I resolved to save our presentation, and that after that was done, I would find Makkesh a nice girl. I pulled back his Aeron chair so that he rolled out of his cubicle, and laptop in hand burrowed beneath his desk, Brailling about until I found the great and knotted artery of fiber-optic wires that connected man to corporation. The male ends of my computer's power cord and Ethernet cables did not quite match the many female receptacles beneath Makkesh's desk, but here I thought of nature. It is known that donkeys and horses do sometimes find each other and produce entirely functional if reproductively doomed offspring. Sometimes close enough is close enough. First I pushed the network connection in place, and it seemed to fit nicely, although there was a great deal of space around the wire. Next came the power cord, which presented a larger problem. I had a third prong on my cord; the one on Makkesh's computer evidently did not. I maneuvered the plug so that this third prong would thrust down the side of the outlet and not get in the way. I jammed the plug into its socket, which all too late I observed to glisten with a mixture of spilled Starbucks, Coca-Cola, and Red Bull. It didn't seem to matter. Nothing happened. Then more nothing. Then I heard the sound of the machine rebooting, and rose from beneath the desk, triumphant.

"There we are, my friend," I said, and placed a hand on his shoulder. "That is exactly what Alfred Chan would have done, and I've just saved us four hours . . ."

My victory speech turned into a funeral oratory as a plume of white smoke rose like a charmed snake from beneath the desk, making me think of papal elections. Then came the sparks. Not big or dangerous but fast and sprightly. For a moment it seemed as if a very small nation had achieved and then begun to celebrate its independence beneath Makkesh Makker's desk. He squealed and fled from his cubicle; I crouched down to witness the early stages of my most meaningful creation at J. S. Spenser to date: a modest electrical fire, which burnt the plastic casing of my laptop and melted the rubber housing of the misplaced power cord as it surged from the overloaded tree of outlets buried in the floor beneath Makkesh's desk. I believe that a few discarded napkins from Shun Lee Palace may have caught fire as well.

"Holy Jesus!" said Makkesh, which struck me as odd. Though perhaps he knew what was coming, because in time he would need help from all the deities he could beseech.

THE FOLLOWING DAY, TERENCE MATHERS TOLD US THAT A meeting with Jack Robertson had been scheduled at the Houston Petroleum Club for that Thursday. We told him that the people in printing were jammed and that he would have to wait to see our progress, but assured him that everything was fine. And then we proceeded to cram two weeks of work into two days. If being jilted by a beautiful rubber heiress had up until that point been the most challenging event of Makkesh's life, working with me on a live M&A deal now took its place.

Makkesh Makker's heart had been ticking for twenty-nine years. It had ticked its way through his small village in India, through sand-boxes, through chicken pox, and then across the Atlantic Ocean, where it ticked through Cornell with a 4.0 while on scholarship. After grad-uation, it ticked to J. S. Spenser Securities, into the Mergers & Acquisi-tions group, and eventually into the serene and significant favor of Terence Mathers, and therefore of Dewey Ananias. Now it was ticking at his desk. Forty-eight hours without sleep, with dozens of cans of Red Bull, quadruple-shot espressos, and cold sweats. Forty-eight hours of phone calls, sometimes from Ananias himself, as well as floods of e-mail demanding all sorts of analysis and detail for the client, the lawyers, Spenser Partners, the firm's own committees, and a thousand other entities quietly headquartered on various islands in the Atlantic and Caribbean. The torrents of work rained down on Makkesh as we toiled away in the empty office. Sweat poured down his face, and he was powerless to do anything but buckle and comply, pausing every now and again to wipe the sweat from his glasses.

Calls came each hour from Terence Mathers, who wanted progress reports in the morning, status updates in the afternoon, and where-do-we-stands? in the evening. It went on through the week, and by early Thursday morning, Makkesh had spent forty-eight straight hours in his cubicle. The gray carpet and oak surfaces were stained and scat-tered with fast-food wrappers, dead soda cans, and congealed blobs of cheese from the edges of the five Big Macs that I had watched him de-vour over the course of our misery. It had been forty-eight hours of the red digital clock at his desk changing each minute, as it did now to 3:21 A.M., forty-eight hours of his heart ticking alongside the clock, the blood vessels pumped and drenched and jammed and tired and bursting at their own protein seams. At 3:21:01, his left hand tingled, and a second later went fully numb, and at 3:21:01:05, in a moment which was to Makkesh Makker an entire lifetime but to Dewey Ananias asleep in Rome just a drop of drool, Makkesh's most sincere desire to move his right hand over to his left arm and find out what was wrong with it was vetoed by a strangely thick pulsing in his chest, which buckled like a suspension bridge in an earthquake. And now Makkesh Makker was doubled over on his own keyboard.

"A very bright bird is . . . ," I heard him say, and thought he was going to talk about his nephew again, but the sentence was never finished.

Makkesh's heart stopped, and then Makkesh stopped, loosing his considerable weight upon his chair. The Herman Miller Aeron cost a thousand dollars, and was the seat of choice for Wall Street firms. The Aeron had been expertly designed to deal with a full range of body curvatures and preferences, but it was entirely unprepared for the kinetic fallout of a dying overweight banker. The chair rolled back from the sudden shift of weight, and as it stole his last joules of energy, Makkesh slid to the floor in a lifeless bundle, his glasses smashing so that the broken shards drew drops of blood from his sightless eyes. His collar-stays turned inward on their owner and stuck him in the neck. Makkesh Makker tumbled with a dull thud onto the hard industrial carpet.

# 6

# AJATASHATR CHANDRASEKHARAN

My up-close-and-personal experience with death had heretofore been limited. When I was eleven my father saw a segment on *MacNeil-Lehrer* about the lack of proper living conditions and care for elderly priests in India. The church had spent half a century signing up Punjab padres on the willy-nilly, but gave no thought to setting up retirement plans for the men, who had taken vows of poverty but got squalor. The following week my father arranged to take in one of these neglected priests from a parish in Calcutta. As I told you, he always meant well. He had my mother's decorator completely renovate Alastair's old bedroom for the man. The room had been regarded as a cross between museum and shrine for years, but an impoverished priest allowed us to gut it free of guilt. Ajatashatr Chandrasekharan was kind enough to let us call him Father Gabriel.

"Boys, this man is a saint, he is going to heaven," my father told Mickey and me whenever the old priest was safely out of earshot. I don't know if the priest actually ended up in heaven or not, but he definitely didn't hang around on earth for much longer.

I remember the day he arrived. My father had feared that he had gotten lost after everyone on his flight had picked up their luggage from the carousels, and the old priest was still nowhere to be found. We were about to give up on him when he came down the escalator, mouth and hands filled with White Castle hamburgers. He smiled and ate the hamburgers all the way back to Rye, and when he entered our house, eagerly blessed anything he could get his hands on: Transformers, Tonka trucks, G.I. Joes, Koosh Balls, Big Wheels, baseball cards, dirt bikes, and without so much as pausing to consider the ramifications, Mickey's Super Soaker 100. Everything except for the family microwave, which he damned after it overcooked a pair of the miniature White Castle hamburgers that he had asked my mother to buy for him after deciding that his entire culinary existence had been but a prelude to wandering into the second-tier fast-food court at Newark Airport.

"Goddammit!" he had screamed, pressing every button on the microwave except the one that turned it off. He then watched, quite helplessly, as his beloved burgers sizzled. It was odd to hear a priest curse in this manner. Stranger still, our microwave broke shortly after the incident, for reasons unknown.

Beyond his clothes Father Gabriel owned a single set of dentures, which he often kept bobbing in a glass of Polident on his bedside table. Mickey discovered them one afternoon while exploring, and he claimed the teeth as a personal set of vampire fangs. The priest often woke to find my four-year-old brother jumping about his bed, pre-ADD diagnosis, hair slicked back with hand soap Eddie Munster style, arms held high and batlike, the dentures jutting from his mouth like fangs. And this went on every day when the priest woke up until the day when he did not.

"Wake up! Come on, wake up! Father Gabriel, wake up! Wake up!" Mickey yelled again and again. I ran downstairs to find my mother at the door to the room, aghast as the old priest's ashen limbs tossed about with Mickey's every jump.

She grabbed Mickey from the bed and carried him out of the room.

"Father Gabriel's gone to heaven," she assured him, but he remained unconvinced.

"Nuh-uh," said Mickey, pointing beyond the door, "I just saw him."

We watched from the hallway as the paramedics rolled the white cotton sheets from Father Gabriel's skin.

He was nude and worn and sagged into the bed linens.

His jaw fell open when they put him on the gurney.

We saw his mottled gums, and Mickey began to cry.

He had no family, and the Catholic Church had no money to spend on him, so my father arranged the burial. My mother vetoed Mickey's suggestion of stocking the casket with boxes of frozen White Castle hamburgers, but sat us down with a wicker box of thick Crayola crayons and a sheaf of multicolored construction paper to write cards to him, a bit of light reading to see Father Gabriel to wherever it is we end up after we end.

Which was where I knew that Makkesh was headed when they drove him off in the ambulance but did not turn on its siren. I stood alone outside J. S. Spenser and then walked home. I would have slept in the guest room but Frances had locked its door. In our bedroom I undressed, then came to bed and pressed myself to her. We had not had sex since my birthday, after which time she had become withdrawn. Still, I tried to platonically entwine, working my right arm beneath her torso so that she woke long enough to protest being woken.

"My associate had a heart attack. I watched and he died. Makkesh Makker . . . ," I whispered to her, and it was strange to say the name of a dead person. She opened her eyes halfway and cooed condolences.

"Oh, baby, that's terrible. Are you okay?"

"I don't know."

She held me. "Sleep now. Just sleep . . ."

She nestled her head on my shoulder, closed her eyes, kissed my neck, and fell back into the sleep she had not really left. It was more affection than I had seen in weeks. We lay together breathing. I held her closer and kissed her hair. The air was stale and still; the windows had not been opened in a month.

"I think you've got it wrong with the damn windows," I whispered again. "The really bad stuff seems to come through anyway."

She did not wake. It did not matter. The headlights of a car passing on the street below on Park stretched off the glass of the building across from ours, then into the room and over the bed.

THE NEXT DAY WAS SATURDAY, AND I SPENT IT ALONE IN BED, writing a letter to Makkesh's mother. It was a difficult thing to do, because I didn't know her, but I thought that as I had been there when her son died I really ought to send her my condolences. Also, there was something that I was hoping she might tell me. This is what I wrote her.

Dear Mrs. Makker,

My name is Thomas Quinn, and I worked with your son Makkesh at J. S. Spenser. I am writing to offer you my most sincere condolences on his death.

Makkesh once told me that in Hinduism very good people sometimes return in the forms of brightly colored birds after they are gone. I have found it very comforting to think about that these past few days, and I hope very much that it is true.

I will always remember Makkesh as a dear friend, and my thoughts are with you and your family in this difficult time.


Yours,

Thomas A. Quinn


I mailed it at the post office and walked around for a bit. I came back to the apartment in late afternoon to find Frances wrapped in a new yellow kimono, sitting on the couch with a picture of her new sister on the table, speaking in hushed tones on the phone to her father. I tried to listen in on the conversation, but then realized that I had calls of my own to deal with: on my phone were nine expletive-laced voicemail messages placed by Terence Mathers in two different time zones, which was sort of impressive. I listened to Mathers rant as Frances talked to her father. That night she stayed up reading *Vanity Fair* while I went to bed early.

I had left Mathers a message before going home, explaining that there would be no presentation waiting for him at Teterboro Airport in time for his Houston-bound flight on J. S. Spenser's private jet. He and Tyler Russell arrived empty-handed and over eighteen holes of golf and lunch at the Petroleum Club failed to interest Jack Robertson in our oil fields. Mathers got back from Texas the next Monday, and summoned me to his office that evening. He began typing on his computer when I entered and did not look at me or speak to me for the longest thirty seconds of my Wall Street career. Finally he turned his chair to face me.

"I've put off talking to you all day, Quinn. That's an anger management technique I've learned."

He kneaded furiously at a stress ball, then threw it in the trash.

"But can you tell me exactly what you were you thinking? We showed up in Houston with no presentation. What does that say about your commitment, that you would let that happen? You might be better off in Internal Credit, Tommy . . ."

I began to respond but was cut off.

"It's not that I think you are a bad team player, Tommy. I know that you would take a flying elbow to the groin for this team. But on Friday, you definitely let the team down."

Mathers had an amazing ability to say that he was not going to say something, right before going on to say that very thing. I didn't know whether to point this out to him as a kind of compliment or to protest the fact that nowhere in my employment contract was there a clause promising the willing absorption of gonad blows.

"Terence, I'm sorry, but you know that Makkesh died, and—"

"We know that, and that is awful, but it doesn't mean the deal stops. I missed my own honeymoon . . ."

I looked at the picture of him with Cheney and wished that Dick had been drinking that day too.

"The computers went down, and there just was no way that presentation was getting done. But do you really think Jack Robertson would have bought those oil fields anyway? These are some of the worst oil fields in Canada. Makkesh kept saying they were total crap."

"People buy crap all the time," Mathers shot back. "My wife buys me the crappiest ties from Ferragamo. Bright yellow with monkeys on them. She tells me they are very Palm Beach. I'm a cold-weather guy. Love Aspen. Hate Palm Beach. Plus, Ferragamo ties look like shit. Too flashy. But do you know what I do? I tell her I love the ties. And do you know why I tell her I love the ties?"

I was without response.

"Because before she gives me the ties she says so much stuff about her mother and her charity for kids with harelips in the Third World and her waxing appointment on Thursday that I can't even think straight. I'd take the tie if it had a big striped bass on it."

Perhaps Mathers had been seeing a shrink after all.

"So if the oil fields are crap, we don't stop. We throw farts and sunshine on them until they seem like the biggest gushers in Saudi. We use footnotes. We use italics. We make some things very big. We make other things very small. We use thick card stock, and lots of shiny logos . . ."

Mathers reached up to his bookshelf and pulled out a Goldman Sachs presentation bound in thick black paper with silver embossing. He treated it like a rare manuscript as he placed it on the desk, and pointed to its title: EMERGING OPPORTUNITIES IN THE GAMING SECTOR: A PRESENTATION TO PRINCE ALWALEED BIN TALAL.

"Look how well Goldman does it. Those guys sold a casino to a devout Muslim. Doesn't that kind of give you hope for the world?"

He pulled down another book, this one from Morgan Stanley. Again, he gestured to its title: SPICE NETWORKS AND THE FAMILY CHANNEL: CREATING VALUE THROUGH DEMOGRAPHIC DIVERSIFICATION: A PRESENTATION TO THOMAS H. LEE PARTNERS.

"Morgan Stanley got two billion dollars from Tommy Lee to merge Fred Rogers and Jenna Jameson. That's leadership."

Mathers carefully replaced his treasured, stolen pitch-books.

"So are the Spenser Partners' oil fields good? Maybe? Maybe not? I really don't know. Can we make them seem like they're good? Yes. That's what gets deals done. That's how careers are built. That's how wealth is built."

I looked past him to his duck-hunting photo with Dick Cheney. Both men wore green satin U.S. Marine Corps jackets and golden-winged hats from the USS *Theodore Roosevelt*. You would have thought that together they had raised the flag at Iwo Jima. Neither had ever seen a shot fired in anger.

Resting on this point Mathers checked his e-mail, which made him think of computers, which made him ask another question.

"And what happened to those computers? I have a fifty-thousand-dollar expense report for wiring and hardware replacement. That doesn't just 'sort of happen.' Your cubicle looks like the Sunni Triangle after the end of Ramadan. Quinn?"

I thought to play dumb, but ruled it out upon realizing that the entire floor still smelled of burnt plastic.

"I honestly don't know," I told him. "The laptops just started smoking, then they caught fire, and then they exploded. It struck me as very strange too . . ."

Mathers shook his head. I struggled to place the disaster in its proper context.

"A lot of things explode like that, you know, for no good reason at all . . ."

This was the most truthful thing said by either of us during the meeting. At Georgetown in The Earth and the Planets Today I learned that the entire universe owes its existence to a single unexplained explosion, a sort of anticataclysm that still puzzles minds greater than my own. Mathers was unmoved; Princeton evidently does not offer The Earth and the Planets Today.

"Don't you ever put me on a plane empty-handed again. That sort of thing ends you here. I've fired twelve people over the last three years. Neither of us wants to make that thirteen. Don't make me make you thirteen. Get it?"

I would actually have been amenable to a firing if it had come with a severance package of some sort, but there was no way of knowing that, and I thought it best not to find out by trial.

"Got it."

"Good. Ready for your next project?"

"Sure."

Mathers pushed two pieces of J. S. Spenser stationery across the desk. One read:

DEWEY ANANIAS JR.
Born December 18, 2001
Interests include video games

The other read:

THE BUCKLEY SCHOOL
212-983-7363

"The window to reserve interview dates for Buckley applications opens on Tuesday, November 15, at nine A.M. We need to be sure that Dewey Junior gets a shot. I suggest you start calling the switchboard at eight thirty."

I had been downgraded to getting Ananias's son into nursery school, and there was nothing to be done about it. Now that he had emasculated me, Mathers played the role of older brother.

"Are you coming to the offsite at Piping Rock next week?"

"I am."

"You'll love it. God, what a great course.

"You know, I've been asked to join Piping . . . but it's such a process." His voice wavered. "I mean, we know a lot of people out there. My wife's father knows a lot of members . . . I've played several times as a guest . . . It's not that I think it would be a problem . . ."

Terence had recently been accepted as a member at the Racquet & Tennis Club. I knew from Thorne that his admissions process had taken four years, but should have taken no more than two. The difference between what ought to have been and what was had scarred his ego.

Flora Fanatucci buzzed in over the intercom.

"Terence, your wife!" she screeched, announcing Mathers's wife who hated him.

"I'll call her back," he replied, most likely because she hated him.

Flora buzzed through again.

"Terence, it's your father-in-law!"

"Put him through," he said, and dismissed me with a curt nod of his head.

ROGER THORNE'S CORPORATE DESTINY WAS ENTIRELY THE IN-verse of my own. Great things began to happen for him from the very moment that he left Mathers's office to the magical jingling of his own Gucci buckles. The other analysts had never before seen a direct peer with such a gracefully receded hairline, a year-round tan, or a perfectly tied Windsor knot. They figured Thorne to be a new associate, and stood to greet him as he made his way about the office. The actual associates had not been notified of any new hire, and they assumed Roger to be more senior still, perhaps a vice president, a managing director, or even a special consultant. They too rose to introduce themselves, such that Roger amassed a small entourage as he took his maiden lap around the M&A floor.

"Where did you get your MBA?" asked Arnold Rosenbloom, who had opted not to get one, and was still unsure about the decision.

"My Major Babe Addiction? I was just born with it," replied Thorne, and snickered at his own joke.

"Where were you before you came to the bank?" asked Ding Ming, the thirty-one-year-old Harvard MBA who sometimes did calculus in her head, and had always intimidated Arnold Rosenbloom.

"I was down in Mexico," replied Thorne, who had indeed taken a surfing trip to Cabo San Lucas before training started.

"And what were you doing down there?" asked Elena Dementieva, the busty Wharton graduate who had just learned that she had a urinary tract infection, not syphilis, and already viewed Roger as the next person she would like to sleep with.

"I ripped it up! Now I'm just getting psyched to rock it up here!" replied Thorne, recalling the killer waves of Cabo San Lucas. "Do you guys surf at all?"

"No," answered Arnold Rosenbloom, who liked the idea of surfing, but could not bear to be seen with his shirt off.

"No," said Ding Ming, who fully understood how surfboards worked, but not how to swim.

"Yes," said Elena Dementieva, who had once gone water-skiing in Cancún.

"That's the only beat thing about working in New York," replied Thorne. "Great restaurants, great clubs, great babes; no waves. It might be cool to go out to L.A. at some point. I hear it's pretty chill out there. But whatever, mon chichis; I just try to keep my schedule as flexible as possible, and play the ball where it lies."

The associates nodded in agreement not only with Thorne's statement, but also with the conclusion that he was indeed someone of importance and a valuable corporate ally. The following week, Ding Ming placed Thorne's name on a two-billion-dollar syndicated loan for CNOOC, the Chinese state-owned oil concern. Spenser lost money on the deal, but Roger gained when the very next week a jealous Elena Dementieva wore a low-cut blouse and over a sushi lunch at Haru offered to include him on the deal team for IBM's one-billion-dollar convertible stock offering. The firm lost money on that deal too, but again Roger was a winner. Not only did he have sex with a syphilis-free Elena Dementieva, but when Arnold Rosenbloom saw that he had worked with her, he immediately put Thorne's name on a five-hundred-million-dollar bankruptcy restructuring for a failing American textile manufacturer. This transaction actually worked out well for both Roger Thorne and J. S. Spenser, though less so for the textile workers.

Announcements of Thorne's deals were e-mailed to the entire firm, and his name gathered such esteem that by the end of the month, when we went to Long Island for the M&A group's quarterly meeting at Piping Rock, he was well respected throughout the bank for the more than three billion dollars of transactions that he had not done. Senior and junior bankers alike pointed him out to one another as they stood on the bank's granite steps and pretended not to care who got the nicest of the limousines.

# 7

## SHOOTING WITH VEMA
## AND VANITA

The air in Manhattan was already crisp by late November.

"I love a blinged-out town car!" declared Thorne, as he ran past Arnold Rosenbloom and threw open the door of an idling Mercedes. "Dewey Ananias gets to take these hoopties to the bathroom!" The car had an entertainment system, and Thorne had brought movies. He pulled three DVDs from his bag: *Girls Gone Wild: Bad Girls, Girls Gone Wild: Girls Who Like Girls,* and *Gone With the Wind.*

"How did that last one get in there?" I asked.

"Shipping error. But I'll be damned if it didn't make me cry," he said, and loaded *Girls Who Like Girls.* An hour and a half later we approached the oak-lined entrance to Piping Rock. The limousines snaked up to the main clubhouse, a low-hung affair whose understatement might prevent you from deducing that the club was founded by the wealthiest men in America, circa 1917. The bankers filed in one by one, and most seemed disappointed that the club had not gone further out of its way to impress them. Inside we had a buffet breakfast in the main dining room. When it was over the attendants brought in a long table, and the men who ran the three global divisions of the group sat down behind it.

There was Robin Lord Peregrine, the English peer who ran Europe and Asia. He had ended Stephen Hoarey's career but could not operate his own microphone. Next to him was Manuel Oliveira Rodrigo Orjuela de Navarro, who oversaw Latin America, and whose need to have his full monogram of initials immediately removed from all of his shirts seemed obvious to everyone but him. And there was Tyler Russell, who ran North American M&A, but not very well. Each man had a placard, a microphone, a bottle of Dasani water, and a glass filled with ice. Dewey Ananias presided over them all. He could enrich or impoverish every banker in the room, but found himself powerless to make a single one of them quiet.

"Okay we're going to get started here. We have group heads from . . . Everyone, sit down . . . Can you hear me? Is this microphone on?" Ananias asked the front row.

"No, it's not on," drawled Robin Lord Peregrine. "Blasted devices never work properly."

Lord Peregrine brushed a shock of blond-gray hair from his high forehead, and began to adjust the volume control on his microphone, succeeding only in the creation of a loud screeching noise. Flora Fanatucci had spent the better part of the meeting doing the *Daily News* crossword puzzle, but upon hearing the feedback she dropped her paper and swished up to the dais to offer help.

"Whatcha doin', silly? You've got to adjust the treble on the receiver or you're gonna blow ever'body's eardrum!"

She bent down by his chair, and the old Etonian shifted his eyes in examination of her cleavage. The microphone feedback stopped.

"Why, thank you," said Lord Peregrine.

"Sure, honey," said Flora.

"And what is your name?" he asked her.

"I'm Flora!" She seemed offended that he didn't already know who she was.

"Robin Lord Peregrine," said Robin Lord Peregrine with a sigh, reaching for her hand and kissing the air just above it.

"Oh boy!" squealed Flora.

No one knew what to make of the encounter, but Flora had succeeded in fixing the microphones, and so Ananias began the meeting.

"This has been a challenging quarter for J. S. Spenser. In a moment I will walk you through our firm-wide results, but first we will hear from the heads of our various global divisions. We'll start with Tyler Russell, who as you know runs our North American practice."

Russell brushed back his chestnut hair, and leaned very gently into the microphone.

"It was a tough quarter. We issued a lot of paper, but . . ."

The room came alive with the ringing of a cell phone. Russell fished about his pockets, and took out his Motorola Razr. He placed his hand over his microphone, but everyone heard his conversation anyway.

"Hi honey . . . I can't talk now . . . We can't do it . . . Because we have to go to that benefit . . . For the little African kids with harelips . . . *harelips* . . . you know, sort of busted-up lips, harelips . . . Well we're both on the board and I promised we'd go . . ."

Russell begged the room's indulgence with a raised index finger; Ananias's neck bulged with rage, but his face betrayed only the slightest displeasure. While it was true that Tyler Russell worked for Dewey Ananias, at this moment in their respective corporate lives the relationship was inverted. It had everything to do with country clubs.

When Ananias had left Goldman Sachs for J. S. Spenser in 1995, the bank's president sponsored him for membership at the Round Hill Club in Greenwich. Problems arose when Ananias was taken to the club for dinner, and while there tipped a waitress with a fifty-dollar bill in plain view of a member of the silent admissions committee. This fifty-dollar bill made all of his millions worthless, and within weeks his social gaffe had derailed his candidacy. By 2000 he had recovered enough pride to undertake a similar campaign to join Winged Foot. A senile client had offered to sponsor him, but this man and Ananias's membership hopes were soon killed by the same brain aneurism. All seemed lost, until at long last Ananias's proctologist invited him to join Metropolis Country Club.

Here Ananias's lack of pedigree was never held against him, and he could relax as a self-made man among other men who, if not exactly self-made, liked to think they would have been if they'd had to be. He played happily there for two summers, and during this time left his second wife, Sharon, for his third wife, Deborah, a woman widely rumored to have started out life in New York as an actress in online porno videos. Ananias often told friends that she was the only person with whom he had ever felt entirely comfortable.

He covered this woman and her history in cash. A nose job made her look less trashy; charitable involvements gave her the appearance of a social conscience; a personal shopper erased any sartorial evocation of her online days; a psychiatrist worked her through the trauma of it all.

But money doesn't change you so much as it allows you to chase yourself around. Sooner or later you'll always pop out again. Late one August afternoon another member's wife found Deborah beneath the twelfth-hole lightning shelter, on her knees, with a caddy in her mouth. "What the hell are you doing?" the shocked woman had asked Deborah Ananias, who quite understandably had been unable to answer. The couple divorced that fall; Ananias was asked to leave Metropolis that winter. For a time it seemed that he was doomed to never again know the company of elitists, but now Tyler Russell was sponsoring Ananias and wife number four to join Piping Rock.

Tyler Russell's easy nature had made him the chair of the club's admissions committee, and his scratch handicap had made him its golf champion for two years running. So it was that he may have been the only man on the face of the earth at once enabled and inclined to get Dewey Ananias in anywhere. Still, the process had been grueling, such that both men understood that until Dewey Ananias was either accepted or rejected by Piping Rock, Tyler Russell could do no wrong. He went to finish his call outside of the clubhouse, and though Ananias's neck was a deep shade of purple, his voice was perfectly tranquil.

"Thank you, Tom," he said, "for all of your hard work this quarter. We know that the next quarter will be full of opportunities. So thank you for your strong leadership of the North American franchise. Now let's hear a bit out of Europe and Asia from Robin . . ."

I turned to find Thorne with a copy of the *Star* hidden inside a leather-bound portfolio. He had also worked his iPod earphones up through his blazer, and was half watching an episode of *24.* To the rest of the room he seemed to be taking notes; in fact he was entertaining personal fantasies of killing people on the behalf of the U.S. government and sleeping with Mary Kate and Ashley Olsen. With his Montblanc pen, Thorne added his own captions to a picture of the wraithlike twins at Fashion Week:

"I am a bone-smuggler and totally dig Roger Thorne and his huge hog," says Mary Kate to Ashley.

"I dig Roger Thorne and his huge dong too," replies Ashley to Mary Kate.

On the next page was a picture of Jessica Simpson in a string bikini licking an ice cream cone. She was similarly captioned, and Roger had her saying:

"I also dig Roger Thorne. Don't make me wrestle you girls naked for him. Because I will!"

"That is beautiful work you've done there, Rog," I said.

"Thanks *mon frère*. Totally untrained, it's all just very natural," Thorne replied. "How are things in the group going for you so far?" he asked me, and there was no sense in lying.

"Not good," I said. "I've converted the dollar into itself, blown up two computers, ruined a pitch to a Texas billionaire, and played a small role in a man's death."

Thorne paused, then used a chiaroscuro technique to accentuate what breasts could be seen on Mary Kate Olsen.

"I've done three deals so far and have another one cruising in this week," he said, and then assumed a rare tone of confession.

"Mostly I just talk on the phone, watch DVDs on my computer, hang out in the steam room at the Racquet, and cruise for pictures of nip-slips on the Internet. Yesterday I got so bored that I just closed the door and rubbed one out to this *Sports Illustrated* swimsuit babe, Isabella Ferraz Salles. Brazilian babe! I haven't had that much fun with a picture of a babe in a swimsuit ever! I generally need more hardcore porn. But this is the best part: I Googled her afterwards and found out she is dating a banker. Pretty exciting to know that we can take down babes like that, huh, *mon frère?* Anyway, I blasted my résumé out to some private equity shops this morning. Have you thought about hopping?"

"No, but I probably should. Mathers called me into his office last night. He talked about moving me to Internal Credit, and then asked me not to make him fire me."

Thorne looked concerned, and leaned in to speak but looked up at the dais as an exquisite English accent came across the speakers. Robin

Lord Peregrine seemed by far the most competent of Spenser's senior bankers, and was relating his observations of the latest fall of the West.

"It's been a very sluggish quarter for European M&A, no news there," he said. "Only true bright spot is China. Chinese are not only making everything, they're now buying everything. Steel companies, oil companies, textile manufacturers, and even a division from IBM . . ."

Thorne laughed audibly as a small helicopter blew up on his iPod.

"It's very important to remember that the Chinese own all of the American debt," continued Lord Peregrine. "They finance this country to the tune of several billion a day. They are like our national credit card company! And if ever they should decide to stop buying that debt, well, best not to think about that—"

Dewey Ananias interrupted. "I have a good friend on the Council on Foreign Relations . . ." Ananias was quite skilled as a name-dropper. "He assures me that the Chinese need us as a trading partner, and would never behave as you are describing."

Robin Lord Peregrine did not drop names on principle, but for his crass American boss he made an exception.

"I had lunch with Henry Kissinger last week, and he told me a story. When he visited China in the sixties, he had lunch with Chou En-lai, and they discussed the French Revolution—was it a good thing or a bad thing? That is what Kissinger asked. Do you know what Chou said?"

Ananias knew only accounting and finance. He shrugged.

"He said that it was too early to tell!"

Ananias didn't get the joke, but laughed as if he did.

"The Chinese take a big view of history that makes little sense to us. Don't *misunderestimate* them. We are seeing a lot of business from China, and look to see more in the future. They are already beating America out for energy, and are playing the Iran situation beautifully . . ."

I elbowed Roger, who removed his earphones.

"Did you hear that? In twenty years the Chinese are going to move into your family's beach house in Southampton . . ."

"Bring it! You know I love the Asian babes!" he said, and plugged his earpieces back in.

Lord Peregrine brought his comments to a close and Ananias introduced Manuel Oliveira Rodrigo Orjuela de Navarro. "Well now, let's hear from Manuel, who has led the Latin American team through twenty straight quarters of top-league table rankings. Manuel?"

Thorne and I had heard a great many legends about Manuel, about his affairs with young associates, about his apartment in the Carlyle Hotel, about his twenty-three-thousand-dollar watch. Roger paused his iPod and joined me in sizing him up. Some people's very manner is said to evoke money; Manuel made you think of rapidly mounting debt. He had his eyebrows waxed, his skin exfoliated, his teeth whitened, and his cuticles cut. He had four passports from three different countries. One, I'd heard, was from a place called Sealandia, which didn't even officially exist. By the time he got around to telling you that he had been conceived in a Champagne-filled Jacuzzi on a yacht sailing in international waters, you took him at his word; it was in fact the only way to really explain the man. It was said that as an associate Manuel had brought three lingerie models to the group's holiday party, that as a vice president he had been reprimanded for charging ten thousand dollars' worth of vodka to his corporate card, and that at last year's offsite he simply characterized his group's performance as *"muy magnífico,"* and then sat down. Thorne and I were looking forward to his speech.

"How do you make an Argentine?" he asked the room, his trim eyebrows shooting up like twin exclamation marks. "I'll tell you how! You start with a good amount of Spanish, pour that in there real good"— he began to stir an imaginary pot—"then you add in some German.

Then, some French. A dash of Italian. Maybe some Portuguese if you like. Stir it all in there, very nice. Now finally, you sprinkle in *just a little bit of shit.* But be *very careful* with the shit. Use just the *smallest amount of shit . . .*" He rubbed his thumb and index fingers together to demonstrate. "Just a touch! Because if you put in too much shit, you get a Brazilian!"

The two tables of Latin American bankers exploded into laughter. One man from the Brazilian team stood and held his arms up in a gesture of explanation. He wore engraved ivory cuff links and a suit so lustrous that it seemed to have been made from only the very softest hides of the very most endangered animals in the rain forest.

"It's funny because it's actually kind of true!" he said, and they all started laughing again.

"Well this past quarter in Latin America, we had a lot of shit! We lost money, even. But this group, this team of fine professionals, we overcame all that adversity to stay number one! And you can ask anyone on the street. Ask them: *This quarter, who were the Latin American All-Stars?* and they will tell you: *J. S. Spenser are the fucking All-Stars!*"

People might have been put off by the profanity, but soon they had a stranger offense to puzzle over. Manuel began to do a little dance behind the dais, in which he moved his head up and down to a silent salsa rhythm. As quickly as we had noticed his dancing, it stopped.

"Was it a tough quarter? You bet! But we remained number one in Latin American M&A! Which is *awesome*! And that is what matters!"

Manuel certainly knew what mattered. This quarter he had delivered the only bragging point for the entire firm. Ananias nodded in confident agreement, and I believe that I saw Manuel's teeth emit light as he launched into the final part of his speech.

"We have *amazing* things in the pipeline! In May we have an *incredible* conference in Cabo San Lucas! Carlos Slim will be there! Mario Dominguez will be there!"

The bankers wondered just who these people were. Thorne closed his copy of the *Star,* and put away his Montblanc.

"We are in the wrong fucking part of this bank," he said.

"I know it," I said.

"You are about to get canned, right?"

"I believe so."

"And I'm beginning to feel like I need to set new goals for myself, maybe branch out into international finance, merchant banking."

"Of course you are."

"Well, I think that working with this dude Miguel would help us both meet our respective career goals. All we have to do is party with babes and blow made cash in Cabo. And I love to party with babes and blow cash. So, yeah, I think we need to rock it with Miguel. In fact, I think we need to rock it with Miguel big time!"

"Big time. I think his name is Manuel," I said.

"Right. No reason why you and I shouldn't be in Cabo with Miguel."

"It's Manuel. His name is Manuel."

"Big time! God, I love Cabo! No reason not to kick it in Cabo with Miguel!"

"Manuel."

"Totally."

DEWEY ANANIAS HAD AN EVER-PRESENT FIVE-O'CLOCK SHADOW that made him seem dishonest and sinister even when he was not being dishonest or sinister. And when he was, well, he seemed especially so. "As a firm we will report earnings for the quarter of one cent per share," he announced gravely. "This will come mainly from syndicated loan revenues and trading operations, with M&A exerting a net drag.

So there will obviously be a reevaluation and rightsizing of head count going forward." A groan went out across the room, as one by one the Spenser bankers translated Ananias's words into plain English: There was going to be another round of firings.

"I don't know the specifics, or when it will happen. You can be assured that I will do my best to protect the people in this group, but sometimes these things are for the best."

Ananias grew pensive, as if turning something over in his mind, then continued with his speech.

"Just to put this in context for you, I collect BMWs. I like cars. But just this past month I had to sell one of my BMWs. Do you guys know why?" A strange and universal sympathy now filled the room; evidently things had gotten so bad that Ananias was liquidating his cars. Alas, this was not the case. "I sold them because I'm on the list for a new Ferrari. Do you see? Sometimes you need to make space to get what you want."

Peregrine gazed at Flora Fanatucci; Manuel contemplated his reflection in a window; Ananias brought it home. "Some firms on this street are not going to make it. Firms like Merrill, or Deutsche, or Citi. What you need to know is that J. S. Spenser will. We're a Ferrari. This is a rough patch, but we'll always be a Ferrari. And the guys who come out of this rough patch are going to be rewarded. So stick with it, and you can be a Ferrari too."

All across the room the bankers stared at Ananias in disbelief. Among the associates there were men in their early thirties with families. They made five hundred grand a year, yes, but spent most of this on private-school tuitions and mortgages and the sort of stultifying shopping sprees required to occupy a wife you never see. For them, getting fired was unthinkable. Their faces went gray as they pondered how Ananias could say such things, all the while struggling to decide what sort of European automobile they would ultimately come to embody. I did not have to think much on this last point, because Terence Mathers had already made it quite clear that I was a Yugo. Vema and Vanita's amazing competence would save them; Thorne's amazing incompetence would save him; I would be shown the door. For perhaps the only time in all of financial history, Latin America seemed by all accounts the safest, most stable place in the world.

"I've got a hard-on for the M8, but that new Ferrari is a hot machine," said Thorne. "You can see the engine through a glass plate on the back. Nice lines. Very sexy."

"Screw the Ferrari. Do you think we can get to Cabo with Manuel?" I said.

"Miguel?"

"Sorry."

*"Oui, oui, mon frère,"* said Roger in his best Spanish accent.


AFTER THE MEETING WE BROKE OUT INTO TEAM-BUILDING EXercises, then conflict-resolution workshops, and then finally we had our run of the club, which Ananias had rented for the day, using J. S. Spenser's fast dwindling cash to bolster his chances for admission. Ananias and Russell took a group golfing. Terence Mathers donned his Princeton Tennis Team uniform, which had been too tight in 1986 and was even more so now, and spent the afternoon emasculating poor Arnold Rosenbloom on the club's clay courts: 6–0, 6–0, 0–6, 6–0. Mathers had enjoyed himself so much during the first two sets that he had grown distracted during the third set, when the grandeur and exclusivity of Piping Rock made him recall with some horror his near–social death experience with the admissions committee at the Racquet Club.

Flora Fanatucci had been looking forward to the outing for six months, and it now became clear why. On tap for the afternoon was quail shooting, and I had overheard enough of her phone conversations to know that she was an active member of the Staten Island Gun Club. She spent most of her free time firing handguns, but she had won a shotgun in a competition and had learned how to use the thing.

Vema and Vanita had also been looking forward to hunting, mostly because they did not know how to play golf or tennis. From their frequent trips to the bathroom, it seemed they had even arranged with their underworld contacts for an eight ball of medium-grade cocaine to heighten the experience. So we set out for Piping Rock's polo fields, which had been left to overgrow all fall for hunting. Lord Peregrine stole glances at Flora, and Vanita began chatting with Manuel.

*"Usted necesita ayuda para su conferencia en Cabo, Manuel?"* Vanita inquired, in fluent Spanish.

*"Escribimos tesis de los honores en reformas de la privatización y de la pensión en Wharton, y amarriamos ayudar,"* added Vema, also fluent.

"Shit," said Thorne, who knew six words of Spanish but didn't need that many to understand that Vema and Vanita wanted to go to Cabo.

"We do need analysts for the meeting," said Manuel, licking his fingers and using them to style his eyebrows just so. "And not only do you speak beautiful Spanish, but I can tell just from talking to you that you are both All-Stars. Of course you can come to Cabo."

Vema and Vanita beamed in Manuel's praise, and in the glow of the early success that promised to make so many of their dreams come true. Thorne lamented his lost vacation, and I mourned my lost career as we walked to the shooting field, where a grizzled old man from the Watertown Game Ranch handed us shotguns, gave us a brief lesson in safety, and then stood atop a row of steel cages, each covered in burlap and filled with a furiously shitting, flapping brood of birds.

"I'm gonna open the cages and release these here grouse," said the man. "And they gonna fly every which way!"

We stood there before the great expanse of golden and gray fields where a century earlier Whitneys and Morgans had ridden polo ponies with bloodlines as pure as their own. A wind came in from the Atlantic and stirred the tall grass as we sat there, listening intently. Well, everyone except for Thorne, who began to explore the fantasy that his shotgun was not a shotgun at all but in fact a very large machine gun with which he mowed down all sorts of imaginary things. Many of them seemed to require multiple imaginary shootings before they imaginarily died. When they did, Roger cheered for himself.

"We gonna wait to let the grouse fly out in that field!" continued the old man. "Then we gonna walk out with the dogs, and they'll flush 'em out! Those birds come within thirty degrees of your line, and you've got the shot. You call for the shot before you take the shot. Do that, no problems. You all understand?"

All nodded, and the birds were released. They fluttered out and settled into the field, and the hunt began. A small hatchling was the first to rise out of the grass, and flew fast to the right.

"Shot!" cried Flora Fanatucci, as her gun popped and the bird dropped.

"Well done, Flora!" cheered Lord Peregrine.

"Geez! Thanks!" said Flora, whose running suit must have frightened the birds terribly as they flew out from the dried brush.

The dogs began pointing once more, and two grouse flew up from before a patch of brush.

"Shot!" cried Flora, and plucked a bird from the sky.

"Shot!" cried Lord Peregrine, as he did the same.

In all of his schooling and breeding, Lord Peregrine had never met a woman quite like Flora. Who really had? It was not just birdshot being discharged on that field; I believe that Cupid's arrows were flying about as well. The pink of Flora's attire became a kind of plumage in the eyes of the defenseless old peer, who was more accustomed to women in earth tones.

Both Flora and Lord Peregrine looked down at her fallen birds, and when they looked up again each embarrassingly found their eyes locked upon the other's.

"I daresay that I find you most beguiling!" said Lord Peregrine.

"Good lord, Lord!" squealed Flora, now blushing and equally enamored. "You're such a talker!"

Soon the dogs flushed out a group of ten birds that flew with a rush from the brush into the sky. There was a rolling blast as we all called shots, and thinned the flock. "Fuck, yeah!" said Thorne, because he had shot a bird, and also because he viewed the creation of such a big noise as an accomplishment unto itself.

"I made that bird like Pablo Escobar!" said Manuel, who had indeed blown the head off of a large male. The real champions of the hunt, however, were Vema and Vanita. Between the two of them they had managed to shoot seven birds. The dogs rushed over with the limp grouse in their mouths, and Lord Peregrine began to clap for the girls.

"You ladies have put these young men to shame!" he said, gesturing to Thorne and me.

"These are our new *All-Star analysts* for the *Cabo San Lucas* conference!" said Manuel, and Peregrine nodded in approval of his choice.

The sun began to fall in the sky, filtering bronze through the dried grass of the field and illuminating the figures of Vema and Vanita. They pulled back their obsidian hair as they talked about India with Lord Peregrine in perfect English and about Latin America with Manuel in perfect Spanish, the cocaine facilitating seamless transitions between the two tongues. Coveys of birds went up from the grass, and every animal seemed almost eager to receive his share of Vema and Vanita's shot.

Lord Peregrine proudly patted the girls on their backs as they walked back into the clubhouse and admired the feathery trophies that stuffed the pockets of their Barbour coats. Manuel made a great show of introducing them to the Latin Americans once we were inside. The girls shook hands and made jokes in Spanish. Far from not being able to believe their luck, they seemed to have long ago expected that all this was due them, and were only relieved that it had finally arrived.

I recall that they had an aura about them, that brilliant perfection of those who are excellent at what they do, and know it. I remember being absolutely sure that Vema and Vanita could do no wrong, that their future would simply be a great chain of triumph. I remember thinking that the universe was on their side, cheering them on as they hoarded handbags at Bendel's and snorted cocaine in bathrooms. And that was why I found it so terribly shocking the next day, when Terence Mathers sent out an e-mail saying that a drunk driver had plowed into the girls' limousine as it made its way home on I-495, and that they were both at Columbia Presbyterian Hospital, plugged into machines, badly injured.

# 8

## CUPID AND ROGER

Verna and Vanita spent several weeks in the hospital recovering from the accident. They were in braces and traction and physical therapy, but found time amid it all to initiate legal action against J. S. Spenser. By January the firm's lawyers, ever eager to manage headline risk, had settled with the girls for one million dollars each, and although at first I thought their absence might help my case with Mathers, it did not. The generosity of the settlement outraged certain of Spenser's shareholders, who now cried with renewed clamor for head count reductions and cost efficiency. I was elated and relieved when Thorne dropped by my desk to say that he had run into Miguel at Bungalow and over several rounds of Patron Silver shots shared with a group of Fashion Week models had convinced him to take us both into the Latin America group for the conference in Cabo San Lucas. "I told him you were an oil and gas expert," said Roger, with a satisfied smile. "Apparently a lot of these Mexican dudes want to get into the energy sector."

I figured that if Roger Thorne could be considered a vice president there was no reason why I couldn't be considered an oil and gas expert. I raised no objection when Thorne proposed that we get lunch at the Brasserie to celebrate.

We met at noon outside of the Spenser building. The Department of Homeland Security, whose mission statement rivaled only J. S. Spenser's as a tribute to vagueness, had raised their terror alert to amber that week. The government was by this point listening to just about everyone's phone calls, and apparently someone somewhere had said something about a bunch of Islamic terrorists blowing something up outside of our building in order to get in good with Allah. Had they known that I had already spent the better part of the last month blowing things up inside of J. S. Spenser while Roger Thorne climbed the corporate ladder with copies of *Star* and *People* tucked beneath his arms, they would have called off the whole thing and given us both matching turbans and mustache-grooming supplies. No matter. I spent the early days of the terror alert drawing pictures of Mohammed at my desk, and thought of it as a form of quiet defiance. But the gravity of the situation became clear to me that day, as a team of NYPD officers in navy blue riot gear lumbered about on the firm's smoker-filled black granite steps, fingers hovering just above the triggers of their machine guns, heads covered in ice blue combat helmets, eyes looking nervously up and down the street of banks with whom they enjoyed a peculiar relationship: the bankers had the money, the policeman had the guns. Each party puzzled over the other, not entirely sure who was, or would end up being, more powerful.

More puzzling still was that, as the weeks went on, the SWAT teams were there on Mondays, Wednesdays, and Fridays, but absent on Tuesdays and Thursdays. On these two days we didn't know whether we were safe or had simply been abandoned to face the terrorist threat on our own. The only person who seemed certain of anything was the long-haired schizophrenic man who liked to give incoherent speeches on the Park Avenue median strip. I couldn't really call him a bum, because he took his work so seriously and was always at his post well before I was at mine. Yet no one paid him much attention. Even the police officers ignored him, which was a bit of a surprise because he and they seemed in perfect accord on the topic of encroaching cataclysm. Perhaps they should have compared notes. But you had to appreciate this man. All religions will tell you in one sentence that God is infinite and unfathomable, then in the very next breath add that in addition to having him more or less completely figured out they have negotiated a unique deal in which he tells them all the good shit first. It's so confusing that every now and again you need a real nut job to come along and in his ranting let you know where everyone actually stands, which is never quite as far from old nutso as everyone would like to think.

"Do it up, you hairy bastard!" I thought as Thorne and I made our way across Park at Forty-seventh, reasoning that his apparent telepathy might be equipped with a call-waiting feature. "And if the Muslims are really gonna blow us all to paradise, just give me a wink and I'll be on the next Greyhound to Dubuque." Then, just in case he was actually listening, I filed additional requests: "Ask the big man to get me out of this exploding computer mess with Terence Mathers, and to make the Latin Americans like me. See if he can get Frances to change out of her kimonos and show me a bit of affection. And on the note of lost affection, see if you can get me a free pass on masturbation, because I've been doing a lot of it lately. . . ." The scraggly man never winked or nodded. He just ranted and raved and I thought that it would be okay if he was Jesus, Moses, and Buddha all rolled into one, just so long as he didn't turn out to be a Mohammed, a Cassandra, or a Pandora.

Thorne made a quick stop at the Racquet & Tennis Club to check on a squash match later that day—he and Big Larry were set to play a second-round match against two angioplasty candidates from the Union Club that afternoon—and we soon descended the clear plastic steps of Brasserie to sit in a corner booth. The restaurant had a French name and served French food, but for reasons unclear maintained a vaguely Asian aesthetic for its waiters, who had shaved heads and wore long black robes. You wondered if there wasn't some Master Po hiding in the kitchen, teaching them all levitation in between orders of sesame-encrusted, pan-seared tuna. At the table next to us, a thirty-something couple enjoyed each other's company.

"I just don't see why we should go into therapy, Abby. We're not even married yet," said the man, clearly a once great collegiate athlete whose muscle and will had softened at the same pace. He scratched his nose, which was just this side of bulbous, and wiped his already slick palm through his thinning black hair. His girlfriend and would-be fiancée/therapy partner had the look of a girl who had been voted best-looking in high school and perhaps taken it too much to heart. A diamond solitaire glistened on the grainy, matte skin between her clavicles. Her heavy makeup betrayed more than it concealed.

"We'll never get married if we don't go into therapy, because you don't understand me. And we don't do things together." She lowered her head to deliver the most damning charge, sotto voce. "Two years ago my mother put down a deposit at the Pierre for an April wedding in 2008. They called her yesterday and asked if she still wanted it. She had to explain that she wasn't sure. Do you have any idea how embarrassing this is for me, Martin!?!?"

Abby was smart. Before Martin could even get around to dissecting the logical errors in her statement, he had to exonerate himself from the allegation of cruelty to a would-be in-law, and the space of a weekday lunch simply did not allot time for such an undertaking. He found a stay of execution in a trip to the bathroom. Abby grunted as he left, and something about all of the marital bickering reminded Roger Thorne of his childhood.

"When I was a little kid," he began, "I had this pirate outfit, and a *Dukes of Hazzard* Big Wheel, and I'd ride around the neighborhood with my dog, getting into mud-ball fights with bigger kids, or playing in this stream behind my house that actually turned out to be a sewage pump but I thought was a river. My dad used to show me pictures of these crazy places in *National Geographic,* and read me books about badass explorers. I always wanted to·be just like them, you know, climbing Mount Everest like Ernest Shackleton, or sailing around the world like Christopher Columbus. But I always thought that I would settle for just being a pirate. Rocking it in pimped-out boats with other pirates, boozing and pillaging, taking down Spanish babes, having huge fights with other pirates! With swords! And if you lose your hand or something, well, you could just get a peg or a hook and smack it onto your stump, and then that just makes you an even cooler pirate, just sailing around, getting wasted, sharpening your hook, firing off your cannons! Boom!"

The silverware rattled as Thorne banged the table in time with his explosion. I had wanted to talk about other things, about Frances's strange withdrawal or Makkesh's death and the imminent firings at J. S. Spenser, but I had already lost Thorne to a magical land of historical inaccuracies, sword fights, and Spanish babes. He continued. "The buzzkill came when I was a sophomore at Choate, and we took this World History class, and I realized that all of the real 'exploring' exploring is done. Like finding new countries, or continents. Pretty much all of the really dank shit has been hit."

I had never considered that Thorne wanted to do anything beyond prosper and procreate, much less that he viewed our generation as having arrived at the blunt end of human discovery. Perhaps he was right.

Certainly there were people working all sorts of wonders with genetics and string theory, but you could only comprehend the impact of these fields in full when you saw your clone walking down Broadway with your girlfriend, which somehow seems infinitely less epiphanic (and exponentially more disturbing) than gazing upon a new ocean for the first time. You would run toward the ocean, but away from the clone. Had all that could be seen been seen? Alas, Thorne had found a single holdout.

"There is only one undiscovered place that I have been able to find. A mountain in . . ."

He paused, looked around for listening ears, and dropped his voice to a whisper.

*"Chilean Patagonia . . ."*

Thorne let the two words roll off of his tongue as one, all the better to impart to this place the full air of mystery that it deserved. He continued. "Now, you would think that you could just swoop in and name the place after yourself . . ."

This thought had in fact never crossed my mind, and yet it lived deep within Thorne's. Across his cerebral cortex blazed images of the highest peak in all of Chilean Patagonia: La Montaña de Roger Thorne. Soon I saw it too. Its snowy bowls buzzed with the unending vibrato of long-legged, thunder-tanned, turned-out babes all snowboarding to and fro in Day-Glo bikinis. They fawned over him with silver trays of his favorite things in the world: back copies of the *Star,* Grey Goose vodka, cocaine, and his holy trinity of hors d'oeuvres—prosciutto-wrapped asparagus, bacon-wrapped scallops, and Kobe beef carpaccio. His attendants fed him these while he recovered from a long day of snowboarding in a mountainside bungalow, soaking in a Jacuzzi with Gisele Bundchen, Lindsay Lohan, Jessica Simpson, and the Olsen twins.

"The only problem," he explained, signaling to the waiter that we were ready to order, "is that it never gets above zero degrees in Chilean Patagonia, and I am definitely more of a beach guy than a snow guy. So, no, I mean, effectively there is nothing left. And that bums me out, big time. But we are where we are, and what I have come to accept is that you don't have to necessarily find something new to explore. You can just have a new experience. Like railing a hot Asian babe, or dogging an Eastern European cream pie. Dude, there were periods of history when, if you were not an Asian dude or an Eastern European dude, you would just never meet those girls. My boy Trip Price was out in Thailand all fall, doinking Thai hookers. He said the body count was over sixty! Can you believe that, *mon chichi*? Just taking down that *poussoise*? Dude, I can't think of any better time for dogging exotic babes like those babes than right now!"

The immediacy of "right now" was made clear with the firm tapping of an index finger upon the table. The only problem was that, as quickly as "right now" is right now, it follows in the endless procession of right nows to become right thens. Which confused Roger. He paused for a moment, puzzling over his own finger and the inexorable passage of time. Then the moment passed, and Roger was back.

"So the deal is that I bring it like I swing it. Take, for example, hot older babes. There was a time when young guys like us didn't go near them. Then Ashton Kutcher and Demi Moore totally changed that. Just look at Cameron Diaz and Justin Timberlake. Or Maddox and Angelina Jolie. Dude, I was way out ahead of that one. People are just getting around to finding out something I knew, like, six years ago. In some ways I'm almost surprised that *Star* doesn't do some sort of story on me, because almost anyone will tell you that I was one of the first guys to rock out with my cock out while keeping it real dirty-something style. I mean, dude, I lost my virginity to Lauren's thirty-seven-year-old aunt when I was, like, sixteen. . . ."

I had not heard the story of Thorne's deflowering at the hands and loins of a woman more than twice his age, but would have to wait a bit longer. The waiter interrupted our conversation to take the order.

"Are you down for steak for two?" Thorne asked.

I nodded, and he ordered a bottle of St. Emilion.

"Where was I?" asked Roger.

"Losing your virginity," I offered.

"Right. It was spring semester of my sophomore year at Choate, and Lauren and I were down in Palm Beach staying with her Aunt Halsey for the three-day Easter weekend. Halsey was a hot red snapper. A total dirty bird. A pent-up libido babe with a fully waxed bunghole. A camel-toe rodeo. She had just finalized her second divorce from this big-time Goldman partner, John Decker, who made north of a hundred million on the IPO. He built this sick Spanish palace down there for tax purposes, until Aunt Halsey's super-shark lawyer alimony-snagged it as part of the divorce. I was fully pumped for a killer weekend, except that I had to write this term paper for my European Civilization class about the fall of the Roman Empire. Only, I had spent the semester drawing naked babes in my notebook, and didn't even know what I was supposed to be writing about. In fact, that paper still makes no sense to me because I studied abroad in Rome during my junior year at Princeton, and from what I could see the place was absolutely fine. Lauren kept nagging me, saying, 'Roger, read your books and write your paper, otherwise you have to do summer school.' And, I mean, I tried to do the paper, but it was impossible."

"Why?"

"I had crushed and snorted most of my Ritalin during the semester, and then they went and kicked me out of the library just for going into lewd chat rooms on the Internet. So I couldn't even borrow a book unless someone went with me. But even if I had had all of my books and my Ritalin, I'm not sure if I would have written that paper because from the moment we were down there Aunt Halsey was walking around in this space-age-silver, gun-toting, dental-floss bikini. People call her 'Cerebral Halsey,' but I swear to God, Tommy, if there was a Nobel Piece of Ass Prize, Aunt Halsey would win it every year. She is like the Stephen Hawking of ass. I had never even dogged a babe before, but it didn't matter. I decided from the first minute we were there that me and Aunt Halsey would hang out with my wang out before it was all over. A minx with nothing but time and money means constant plastic surgery, carrot and sesame body buffs, deep-sea detoxes, Pilates classes, a trainer-tight bod, full-on fake guns, and a well-maintained bikini line. I just started kicking back her vibes, Roger Thorne style. I would let her catch me looking at her, and then pretend to be all embarrassed about it, even though I was pumped. Then she would look over at me the same way, and I would smile like I was flattered because I had not expected her to look at me. Only really I totally knew she was going to look at me because I had been the one pretending not to look at her in the first place. Dig? Well, Saturday night Aunt Halsey had a big group of people over for dinner. She sat me right next to her and had Lauren all the way down at the end, and I think she must have planned it that way, because during dessert she reached under the table, grabbed my dong, and started working it. I was just like, 'Dude, it's on!'"

The conversation at the table next to ours was progressing on a sexual trajectory quite the opposite of the tale of Thorne's own formative coital encounter. Martin had ceded a great deal of the argument to his cognitively superior would-be fiancée, and she now bore into him with exponentially more potent material.

"And don't think I haven't noticed that you jerk off in the shower!"

Martin might have attempted some defense had he been given the time.

"We used to do it, like, three times a week! We've only done it twice this month! How is that supposed to make me feel? And I know you weren't like this with your other girlfriends . . ."

Poor Martin was done for, but Roger Thorne was just beginning.

"That Saturday by the pool Aunt Halsey took off the top of her bikini and started working on her tan lines right next to me and Lauren. Sure, she was on her stomach, but her implants just kept peeking out from under the sides of her body. After a few hours Lauren went for a swim, and Aunt Halsey pretended to reach over for my copy of *People* magazine. That's when I first saw those Tetons. She looked at me straight in the eyes and bit her lip; I almost blew a load right there. Lauren went inside the house to take a nap, but Aunt Halsey continued to kick it in her bikini. It was just the two of us lounging in these teak chairs by the pool, hanging out in our bathing suits. The energy was highly sexual, Quinn. Just a young buck and a hungry stone fox, ready to kick it. But even though she had felt my hog and I had seen her hogans, we really had nothing to talk about. So she was, like, 'How is your paper coming, Roger? What are you writing about again?' Which would have been a fine conversation starter, except that I didn't know anything about my paper, because I had spent the full semester blowing Riti lines, drawing naked babes, and talking dirty to babes on the Internet. And I had spent that whole weekend trying to bag Aunt Halsey. All I knew, and come to think of it, all I know about the fall of the Roman Empire, was the title of that paper, which Mr. Higginbotham had chosen for me after two months had passed and I hadn't chosen an 'area of inquiry' for myself. It was, 'The Role of the Boy Emperor Romulus Augustus in the Fall of the Western Empire.' So I was, like, 'You see, Halsey, my primary area of inquiry is the role of the boy emperor Romulus Augustus in the fall of the Western Empire. And you would not believe some of the ill shit that little Italian mofo let go down!' She was, like, 'Roger, Lauren is so lucky to be with such a smart young guy. Someone who really knows what he wants . . .'"

The wine presently arrived and was uncorked by our waiter, the Caucasian-Asian Shaolin monk. Thorne drank nearly half of his glass before continuing to recount playing Vili Fualaau to Aunt Halsey's Mary Kay Letourneau.

"I didn't know what to say, so just I flexed my guns a little bit. She reached over to get a glass of water from the table, and grazed my chest with her boobs. Then I went to give her the water, and intentionally spilled it all over my shorts and my abs. She started trying to dry me up with her hands, but hands aren't very absorbent so it was basically just like a happy-ending massage and obviously my dong got all excited. I was, like, 'Uh, Halsey? Who let my dong out?' She just kept pretending to dry me up until she wore me out! I mean, I busted it right there in my bathing suit! Then she patted my chest and said, 'Oh Roger, you are such a cutie.'"

"Then what happened?"

"Well, the next day was Easter Sunday. Most people think of Easter Sunday as a time to remember Jesus Christ, or rabbits. For me, it will always be the day that I lost my V to Aunt Halsey, the double-divorcée with a waxed bunghole. She had a bunch of people over for drinks and brunch after church, which we all slept through. So we just dressed like we had gone, and started drinking. They had this great raw bar, a full-on wet bar, and loads of hors d'oeuvres. They had salmon carpaccio, which I actually like even better than prosciutto-wrapped asparagus. It was, like, ninety degrees out so I was just throwing down oysters and Stoli tonics and probably would have passed out except there was this dude there who used to tag my sister at Princeton. Not Terence Mathers, Sam Ewing. Well, he had an eight ball on him and we just started ripping rails of Yay-Yo in the guesthouse. Pretty soon we were so Yayyed up that we figured we would go out to 251 and try to take down some babes, but that before we did we should smoke a joint, just to come down. But after we smoked the joint we got totally paranoid. I was, like, 'Dude, we can't drive! There are policemen everywhere!' And Sam totally agreed. So for most of the party we just hid underneath a blanket in the guesthouse with the lights off watching DVDs . . ."

"What about Aunt Halsey?"

"Well, finally that dude had to go home, and I went outside. It turned out we had been in there for like six hours! It was three in the morning! Lauren was peaced-out in her bedroom, and almost everyone had gone home. I started chilling by the pool with the bartender, Cesar, who it turned out was also a karate instructor. He was showing me how to break wood with my foot when Halsey came outside, ostensibly to turn the lights off. She threw Cesar three hundred bones, told him to adios, and soon it was just the two of us, all alone, outside, in the dark, by the pool, which was lit with those underwater floodlights, totally *Blue Lagoon*. I was, like, 'Yo, Aunt Halsey, this has been a great weekend, you're a total babe, I think I'll definitely send you a copy of my paper about that Italian mofo . . .'"

Thorne cleared his throat and then wet it with a long sip of red wine.

"The thing was that Aunt Halsey didn't want my paper. She wanted my dong. She walked up, grabbed it, and then dropped on me right there by the pool. I unbuttoned my shirt. She unzipped the back of her dress. And we took it down, bangbrothers-dot-com style, right there on the concrete. She got on top of me, and was, like, 'Roger, have you ever done this before? Do you do this with Lauren?' And I was, like, 'Uh, all the time, babe . . .' But she must have known, because she was, like, 'Just relax, cutie, and let me do the work.' Unreal! Her guns bouncing up and down! Her digits perfectly waxed! Top shelf! Bottom shelf! Pumping pistons of passion! The babe smelled like flowers. I was, like, 'Dude! I am getting rocked by a sex goddess with a perfect wax job and geared-up cans!' Finally I picked her up with her legs still wrapped around me, and we just stood there by the pool, rawdogging."

Thorne raised his arms just a bit above the table, and curled them as if he were supporting the weight of a phantom 110-pound double-divorcée, whose imaginary legs I could only assume were wrapped around his waist. Was Aunt Halsey a pedophile? A nymphomaniac? Perhaps some combination thereof? Whatever she was, the woman had made a lasting impact on Roger, who I would soon learn carried a soft spot for the dominant feminine beneath his alpha-male armor. This was his karmic inheritance from Aunt Halsey, the great Kamala who had converted her divorcée's fortune into a sexual force so potent that it still resonated a decade later. The young couple seated next to us had forgotten their would-be lovers' quarrel and were straining to listen to Thorne, whose perversions somehow met both of their needs.

"I think Lauren sensed that something went down because Halsey gave me long kisses on both cheeks when we left, and she sent me a picture of the two of us later that semester. Ever since that happened Lauren has never trusted me around older babes. That night when we had dinner with the midget and Big Larry at Cipriani? She was totally giving me death about looking at the old babe from Gastineau Girls, but I wasn't even trying to take that babe down; I was vibing Sophie Dvornik. We were talking about movies, and the possibility of me becoming an actor of sorts. I mean, I really dig Sophie. She is the sort of babe that I have never seen before. So I slipped her my number on a cocktail napkin, and you know what?"

"No, what?"

"She called me, like, fifteen minutes after we left! She was all, 'Hey, Jugsaw, why don't you come up for a drink?' So I told Lauren that I was going to the office to finish up a project and hopped a cab uptown to Sophie's pad in the Time Warner Center."

There was no way that Thorne could have known what lay in wait for him at the hands and home of Sophie Dvornik. The Dvorniks had a neo-Italianate mansion in Beverly Hills, an olive-oil-making estate in the hills of Tuscany, and had recently closed on a fifteen-million-dollar three-bedroom apartment in the Time Warner building. Sophie had moved there with her father after graduation, and only two weeks later had found him in bed with his twenty-eight-year-old assistant, an ambidextrous Stanford graduate named Lydia Schwartzman. Lydia was shown the door, and soon so was Mr. Dvornik. Father and daughter arrived at an unspoken deal whereby Sophie offered total silence in exchange for total use of the premises. Paramount Pictures was the only loser in the entire equation, and for the rest of that year paid for Mr. Dvornik to stay at the Four Seasons whenever he was in town.

Whether to eradicate the memory of her father's extramarital sex or to enhance the pleasure of her own premarital encounters I can't be sure, but Sophie had the place entirely remodeled. She ordered the walls knocked down and paid unknown artists a few hundred dollars each to paint pictures of her, then hung them about the apartment so that she could look at herself looking in on herself, and in this way feel at home. In time the apartment became like a very posh boardinghouse for emerging artists still awaiting their big sales. They slept sometimes on her floor and sometimes on her couches and sometimes in her bed, and often left her gifts. One Argentine photographer had given her a twenty-foot-long picture of a Mexican biker gang, arranged in the positions of Christ and the apostles at the last supper. It hung above her dining room table, and between this and the many nude paintings of Sophie herself, Thorne should have found some clue about what was in store for him. To be sure, he knew that sex and sin lay somewhere in his immediate future, but these were never truly far off for him. No, Thorne had no clue. After Sophie buzzed him in he walked quickly to the great bedroom, where he found her standing before the door in jeans and a T-shirt, a blindfold in her hand, paint on her lips, a command in her throat.

"She was, like, 'Roger, put this on.' I was just, like, 'Babe, I'm down for whatever if you smuggle my bone!' So I put on this blindfold, and took her hand, and she led me inside. She handed me this bottle of baby oil and said, 'I want you to rub my back. Standing at the bar before dinner made me so tired.' First I heard her unzip her jeans. Then I heard the snap of her bra. Then she went to her closet, and all I heard was this strange squeaking noise, followed by another long zipper. She came back, and started taking off my tie, my shirt, and my pants. She totally undressed me, and I just thought, 'Awesome, this is when I own her with my boner . . .'

"That's when she pushed me down on the bed. I reached up to grab my mask off, but the moment that I got my hands to my head I felt this stinging on my left butt-cheek. The babe started whipping me on the ass with her riding crop!"

The simple brilliance of this continent's design, with its two fallen coasts separated by three thousand miles of God-fearing hinterlands, had kept the magnificent forces of Roger Thorne and Sophie Dvornik from coalescing for more than two decades. In Sophie, Roger had found the apparent embodiment of the Hollywood that could and did exist only in his head, assembled over the years from the pages of supermarket tabloids. In Thorne the Spenser banker Sophie had found the very picture of East Coast propriety. They were drawn together like brightly colored moths with bad eyesight, each somehow mistaking the other for a flame. Thorne grew red in the face as he recounted his first encounter with S&M.

"It fucking hurt! I was, like, 'Yo! Don't whip me! I don't like getting whipped!' So she was, like, 'Fine.' And she stopped whipping me, but put these alligator clamps on my nipples. I was totally freaking out, not knowing whether to massage the sore spot on my butt, to free my nips from the clamps, or to tear off the blindfold. I was thinking about running the hell out of there when she grabbed my hands and cuffed them to the posts of her bed. We don't realize how fragile our freedom is, Tommy! This babe had blindfolded me, whipped me, clamped me, and bound me, and you know what the strangest thing was?"

"What?"

"I totally dug it! I mean, at first I panicked, but then I realized that I had in fact met a chick that was into this stuff in those chat rooms at the Choate library. That's when Sophie started to grind her latex bod up against me. I said, 'You're a little bit loco, whip-and-handcuff babe with a smoking bod and a killer pad. Bring it, biatch, these guns are for hire!" That's when she took off the blindfold, and pushed my face against her window. I totally thought I was falling. I looked out and all I saw was light! New York is like a big fucking casino, man! Blinking lights! Bad air! No clocks! You could see clear across the island, then lights for miles and miles, and beyond that just a big, black darkness. I was, like, 'Babe, what's that?' You know what she said?"

"No, what?"

"She said, 'That's the Atlantic Ocean, you moron.' And she was right. It was."

Sophie's apartment does have a magnificent view, and especially at night. The apartment looks out across Central Park, and beyond it a great yellow chasm shoots up from midtown, growing more faint beyond, then dwindling into the simple red twinkles of the freighters in the river, and beyond them the great negative space of the blue-black Atlantic. And at the whip-wielding hands of Sophie, Thorne had seen this ocean which he had swum in every summer since his boyhood, for the very first time. She had more firsts in store for him.

"When I looked away from the window she was straddling my back in this killer black bodysuit! I went to touch her guns through the suit, but she whipped me again! It was so kink. That's when I noticed all the plasma screens on her walls, and that she had set up about ten digital cameras and was recording the whole thing! She whipped me once, then grabbed this remote control from her bedside table. She pressed a few buttons, and all of a sudden we were all over the plasma screens! The room was so bright that I couldn't even see out the window anymore. We could see ourselves from every angle. I was, like, 'Babe, where did you get this shit?' She whipped me and said it all belonged to that dude Yves Grandchatte. She said she was storing them for him, but that he said she should use them, and told her they were the ultimate aphrodisiac. Then she unhooked my handcuffs, and we just took it down. I took her suit off and she was totally naked, and her bod rocked, and I couldn't even keep still! It was like, 'Whoa, there's a boob here! Whoops, there's a dong! Dig those legs!' Our bodies were everywhere! It was like being in a porno and watching a porno all at the same time. Dude, I didn't even mind it when she gave me the shocker, because when I looked at the screen it was just like, 'Whoa, look at that hot babe giving that buff dude the shocker.' Then I was, like, 'Wait! Wait one minute! That's me! And Sophie D is a high-definition multimedia sex goddess.' The only thing that could have made it better was a pair of 3-D glasses . . ."

The description of extended coitus, video equipment, baby oil, and riding crops seemed to have accomplished what an hour of haggling could not for the couple sitting opposite us. Martin rediscovered his libido and leaned over the table to give Abby a long kiss, pinching the flesh on her inner thigh with the fingers of one hand while signaling for the check with those on the other. He paid our bill and his with a platinum card; Abby shook Roger's hand and gave him a kiss on the cheek; and soon they were gone.

"I've been going over there every night this week. She ties me up, the cameras roll, then she whips me and we take it down. She even asked me to come with her to meet the artist who gave her the cameras and plasma screens. I guess they're honoring him at MoMA's winter party in two weeks. I told her I was down . . ."

I remembered that Frances had mentioned going to see Yves Grandchatte's gala at MoMA just out of curiosity. In fact, she had talked about it on the phone with Lauren Schuyler. "Roger, I think you're already going to that party with Lauren," I said.

His face was red, his shirt undone, his steak untouched. Sophie Dvornik had shown him the Atlantic Ocean and the joys of light bondage, and then taken him into realms of digital autoerotic voyeurism heretofore unfathomed. Was it any wonder that he had forgotten himself in her presence? This woman had made his dreams come true, and he was not about to let the matter of a girlfriend get in the way of that discovery. He approached the matter much as he had the issue of his 3.0 and inability to do addition at J. S. Spenser. It was not a problem, but a challenge. He shrugged.

"There will be enough of Roger Thorne for everyone!"

He was to be proven more correct than anyone could have imagined.

# 9

# Hang Gliders
## and Mars

From what I could tell Frances had stopped attending her classes at NYU entirely by the end of January. She said that she was pursuing an independent study, but this meant only that she read magazines, bought art books, spoke little, smoked a lot, and had no desire for sex. There had been no conflict between us, no falling out, but day by day we fell farther apart until it became difficult to recall what it had been like when we were close. Each time Wendy Sloan sent a new picture of her baby, Sunshine, Frances tore it up and threw it away, then with cold eyes dared me to ask her why. She went deeper into her reading, finding refuge in three millennia's worth of ruined cities. Still, I hoped that things would mend themselves and took it as a hopeful sign when one Saturday afternoon she began to air out the apartment

"They're almost sealed shut!" she groaned as she pushed to open the first pair of French windows. "This paint is old, old, old. Probably full of lead. Wendy should really get it stripped before Sunshine starts eating it. . . ."

She strained against the fused layers of paint, which creaked and then gave way with a resonant snap. The windows swung out and open, and the wind set the yellow toile draperies dancing. The silk of her kimono rippled and I surveyed the perfect disaster that she had made of the apartment. The paint had blistered on the tulip-poplar chest, the gears of the clocks had seized and stopped, and the old secretary now limped on its talon feet. There were wavering ziggurats of art books piled across the floor and atop the chest of drawers. The breeze now rushed through them, rustling open page after page, until they began to topple. Frances clapped as the towers crashed down onto the old oak floor, and I shook my head.

She had found the last of her mother's kimonos in a box of pink tissue paper at the top of her mother's closet. It was pristine, but did not stay that way for long. One evening she had declared herself inspired, and took to the guest bedroom with her laptop, an armful of art books, a sheaf of paper, a carton of Parliament Ultra Lights, and a case of Fiji water. She didn't come out but to respond to basic biological demands for seven days. I did not see the fruits of this mania until it was far too late; Frances never let me read her papers, and the few times that I stole glances I never understood them. But she was confident, this much I will give her. She canceled her appointments with her professors, and told me to let her be.

"I love you even more when you leave me alone!" she declared through the door each time that I knocked, until finally I stopped knocking.

When it was over, both she and her robe had suffered. Frances's eyes were dark and bagged, her knuckles cracked and red, her hair a puzzle of knots. The sleeves of the kimono and her forearms had been stained with spills and swirls of water and ink. She refused to shower, and I washed her face and arms in the sink, and it was beneath the running water of the faucet that I saw a fresh cut on her forearm. She winced as my fingers passed over the razor-thin slice, no deeper than a paper cut. She blamed it on Chairman Meow, and when I noted that the cat had not been in the room with her, she insisted that he had, and burst into tears, saying that I did not trust her, that no one trusted anyone. After this, language seemed to fail, and speaking only led to screaming. When we spoke again, we didn't mention the cut. It faded to a pink line, and slipped into view as she tightened the robe around her waist and hopped over to the next alcove. I cringed. The phone rang.

"Would you open the other windows, sweetie?" she asked me as she went to answer, pointing to the alcove to the left of the clocks and the fireplace.

The paint on the frames had indeed fused together, and the engraved brass knobs began to cut my hands so that I recoiled as a matter of reflex once they had opened. The windows met their own concrete settings with a crash. The old panes broke into jagged shards, and fell into the bushes below. I cursed out loud, and so did Frances.

"Oh please, Dad . . ."

Bo Sloan's booze-cured voice offered muffled appeasement on the other end of the line. For all of his many millions this poor man was always appeasing everyone, but could never say or give enough. Frances dug one hand on her hip and beat the air with the other.

"I'm sorry . . . I just worry about you . . . Dad, the baby . . . Well, did you really have to name the kid Sunshine? . . . You can't do that unless you are Paul McCartney or an Indian . . . I don't care if Wendy's one thirty-sixth Navajo . . ."

Bo Sloan slurred on about nothing, finally upsetting Frances so much that she cut him off.

"I feel so bad for you, Daddy . . . I just do . . . I'm only doing this for you, okay? . . . I'll ask Tommy now . . ."

She put her hand over the receiver.

"Sunshine is getting baptized in New York next week and she wants us to be the goddamn godparents," she said in a single breath.

"Isn't that a little strange?" I asked. "I mean, you are already her sister, and I'm not exactly close with Wendy . . ."

"It's some Navajo thing," Frances said with disbelief and revulsion.

"But isn't this an Episcopalian baptism? And aren't you an atheist?"

"I'm not an atheist, I'm agnostic. And it doesn't matter. Nothing has to make sense with Wendy. And Daddy wants us to do it. I have no choice. He's being awful and I have no choice. Please, Tommy, don't make it harder than it is."

Wendy had asked Bo to ask Frances to do this for him, but it was really for her. Now Bo had Frances ask me to do it for her, but really for him, which is really to say, really for Wendy. It was all very confusing. I shrugged.

"Fine," Frances told her father, most likely because "You've successful coerced me and I've now coerced my boyfriend in turn" doesn't have much of a ring to it. Though that is precisely what had happened.

And just like that, I became godfather of Sunshine. I carry the title to this day, and proudly. It sounds like it should come with a few magical powers, or at least a wand of some sort. I paused to consider just what these powers would be, and how I might use them, and was pretty deep into this daydream when I heard Frances ranting.

"I can't believe she did this. She came along and entirely took him over. New house. New life. New baby—and what a baby! She's got him with the baby. She knew that she would have him the moment he agreed to that awful little baby . . ."

Frances's breasts grew taut, her clavicles rippled, her cheekbones took on high relief. She was irresistible in moments like this, when she reduced all to nothing. The problem was that she was always left with nothing. Yet Frances had a point, and as she maligned Wendy I realized that I also had reservations about it all; reservations having to do with Bo Sloan's testicles.

At that moment, however, my primary concern was not Bo Sloan's sexual fitness, because—his brief career as a Bahamian cross-dresser notwithstanding—it was Frances Sloan, not Bo Sloan, with whom I lived in a state of estranged suspense, and with whom I went to sleep but did not sleep with at night. I told myself, and then her, that it was no big deal to simply dunk this little brat under water and say a few prayers. She told me that we had to do it but that it was just horrible, that she didn't want to discuss it, and that it had ruined her day.

"Why is the baby so awful?" I asked.

"Because it's a lie . . ." she managed to say through pursed lips, and stared into Wendy's framed portrait of her, Sunshine, and Bo Sloan.

"How is that?" I asked.

"In the most beautifully brutal ways," she said. "You'd never understand."

I looked at the portraits of the ancient Sloans and, beside them, at that new picture of Bo, Wendy, and Sunshine, and I realized that Frances was wrong about my not understanding. At that moment I absolutely did, and, frankly, should have all along.

MY FATHER HAD TAKEN A SPECIAL INTEREST IN WENDY SLOAN'S pregnancy from the moment I met Frances. One evening I returned from a day at the Sloans' to find my family sitting in the gray teakwood chairs on the patio for cocktails. My mother was busy fussing over a wicker tray of cheeses, intently placing small wedges of St. Andre on cracker after cracker. Mickey leaned back in his chair, murmuring softly to himself as he gazed first at a family of bright turquoise wrens in the trees above, and then at the faint red glow of Mars in the summer sky. We sat together as a family in total silence until my father finished his Stoli tonic and leaned across his armrest to ask what had seemed a very strange question.

"Does Bo seem at all, you know, ah . . . ," he began, but was soon overtaken by his often heard, never discussed, suckling sound. *"Tyut-tyut-tyut-tyut-tyut . . ."* I pretended to adjust my watch until he regained control of his voice.

"Is Bo excited about the pregnancy?" he finally managed to blurt.

"Is Wendy still, oh, you know, affectionate toward him?" he asked more loudly and fluidly, after a nerve-calming second cocktail. *"Tyut-tyut-tyut!* Quite a situation! *Tyut-tyut-tyut!* He's been in worse!" he unknowingly declared to the entire neighborhood midway through a third drink.

"Brian! Volume!" my mother scolded him, spilling her Chardonnay.

"Was I that loud?" he boomed, pushing the cocktail away.

"It would still be pretty awesome to be an astronaut," Mickey declared to no one at all, still looking at the sky. "I think what I want for graduation is a hang glider, and some climbing rope."

My mother tussled Mickey's dark brown Anglo-Afro with her St. Andre–caked fingers, happy to see the Ritalin finally working its way out of his system.

My father's curiosity about Bo Sloan, Wendy Sloan, and Fetus Sloan mounted throughout the summer. At the end of August he could resist himself no more, and asked me to play golf with him.

Owing to my involvement in a five-thousand-dollar golf cart disaster at Apawamis during the early 1990s—the wheelie was my idea, yes, but it was Jamie Kellogg's undiagnosed near-sightedness that landed us in that pond—my father had kept me clear of golf courses for some time. I agreed to join him today on the condition that, as stunt driving was out of the question, I would be allowed to fight the unbearable heat and boredom of his chosen pastime with a cooler and a bottle of Sancerre. He consented. We played.

I was drunk by the fourth hole, and began to lose golf balls at an alarming rate. Some dribbled off into the tall grass, others plunked down into the water. One went up into the sky and never came down. The late-summer sun had plunged blue and pink beyond the ocean when we reached the green of the eighteenth hole. Brian Quinn sank his final putt of the summer, and could contain himself no more.

"Tommy," he began, filling his voice with prefab pity, "I'm going to tell you something. You can't ever repeat this, okay?" I promised, several times, never to repeat what he was about to tell me. I repeat it to you now not out of any fault of character, but because when affluent middle-aged white men tell you not to repeat things, they never really mean it. We know this is true, because if all affluent middle-aged white men were to actually stop repeating all of the things that they tell one another not to repeat, they would never speak. We would have a population of affluent middle-aged white mutes on our hands. And with all of the ethos of a man who has been accepted to study medicine at the Universidad de Medicina de Santa Filomena, I can tell you that the healthcare system is in no position to deal with such a thing.

So this is what he said:

"I do estate work for the Robinsons, Frances's mother's family. And Mr. Robinson, Chance, is a very high-quality guy. You should meet him. I told him you're dating Frances, you know, *tyut-tyut-tyut* just because he asked about you . . ."

My father knew that I had never met Chance Robinson, and that he had never heard of me, and that the idea of him asking about me seemed less likely than my father telling him about me in order to tell him that I was dating Frances. I was about to point this out, but, like the Iraqi insurgents, my father was just a bit too fast.

"And he told me something that will make your jaw drop!" He raised his hands to the sky, not only to extend his moment of import, but also to congratulate and curse the cosmos for meting out Bo Sloan's soon-to-be-divulged and sure-to-be-tragic fate. A team of herons flew over-head, and I thought of my mornings with Frances and the flowers and Napoleon's son, and was in fact planning to stay with these thoughts, to tune my father out. But there was no ignoring him once he spoke.

"There's no way that baby is Bo's . . ."

His face broke out into a gleeful smile, which was soon tamed into a look of genuine concern.

"What?"

"The guy shoots blanks! Leslie miscarried after Frances. She had se-vere postpartum depression. That's when he had it . . ." He made a set of scissors with the pointer and middle fingers of his right hand, and began moving them through the air in a snipping motion. This I took to be the international sign for vasectomy.

"Just before they divorced, Tommy! And you can't tell anyone, but Wendy's walking around with someone else's bun in her oven! Bo's too ashamed to tell her it's not his! How's that for the old switcheroo, boy! *Tyut-tyut-tyut!*"

Sunburned and drunk, I called him a liar. "It's true, Tommy!" he in-sisted, and *tyutted* again. "He had it done!"

"So he had it reversed. Do you spend a lot of time thinking about Bo Sloan's testicles?"

The thing is, I didn't want my father anywhere near Frances or her family. He had spent the whole summer waiting for a cocktail invita-tion to the Sloans' house, and they had asked me to invite him, but I had always declined these invitations before ever delivering them. He was loud and excited and fumbling and bumbling and he embarrassed me and I didn't want him around for fear that he might break some-thing. Which was exactly what he seemed to be doing, hacking his way

into my bliss with a bit of thirdhand gossip. In the end I wouldn't have
believed him even if he had produced a full DNA analysis of Wendy's
fetus. This only made him want more desperately to be believed.

"He went around saying 'No kids! No kids!' for months. That baby
was a surprise, Tommy! Peter St. Clair, who is his lawyer and a gem of
a guy, told me the pre-nup had to be entirely reworked to even include
language about this kid!"

I was too drunk to argue.

"Why don't I just ask Frances? I'll say, 'Hey baby, tell me about your
dad's balls. I hear they're like big old watermelons, big old seedless
watermelons . . .'"

"*Tyut-tyut-tyut!*" he suckled on his anxieties. "Not a word, Tommy!
Not a word! When men get older they value companionship first. Those
other things matter . . . less. People's lives, you know? So not a word!"
There, upon the high altar of the eighteenth green, he made me swear
to uphold the very secret that he had betrayed. And when he was done
reveling in the imagined troubles of the Sloan family, he composed himself and remembered—who else?—God. "I thank God every night
that with your mother I don't have to worry about these things . . ."

I cursed him beneath my breath, threw my last golf ball into the
woods, and reached into my bag for the warm, nearly empty bottle of
wine.

Dehydrated and salty, I licked the last few traces of Sancerre from
beneath its neck, and pushed the entire day from memory.


I NOW LOOKED AT THE WALL OF SLOAN FAMILY PORTRAITS.
Had they not been so successful in business they might have founded a
circus act, the Flying Aryans, and done just fine. And on a table below
the wall of portraits, atop the pastel pink envelope in which Wendy

had sent it, was a picture of a blond-haired blue-eyed Wendy, blond-haired blue-eyed Bo, and in their arms, baby Sunshine, who looked . . . different.

She had black hair and olive skin and brown eyes and a flat nose, and these things made her, I realized with a hit of nausea and a sudden longing for Sancerre, at the very least, an extreme genetic improbability. Had Wendy Sloan been slightly more intelligent, she might have known not to send out so wildly and widely this portrait of fair parents and swarthy child. Or perhaps she might not have hung it so close to the gallery of other Sloans, who to anyone not afflicted with color blindness looked nothing like the newest addition to their line. She was far too smart and cunning, I felt, to do these things blindly. She almost dared you to say something, it seemed, and I wondered if that was perhaps the point.

"Have you noticed that Sunshine looks nothing like your father?" I asked.

Frances froze in the alcove.

"I mean, look at that picture. Or, look at all the pictures, really," I continued, knowing and malevolent, pure and innocent.

"What about them?" she wondered, and now we were both pretending.

"Well, Wendy is blond with blue eyes. And so is your dad. And, actually, so is everyone in your family. Which means that Sunshine should probably also be . . ."

"Tommy?" she warned.

"Sunshine should almost certainly have blond hair and blue eyes. Or at least one of each, but definitely not . . ."

"What?" And now we were both feigning ignorance.

"I mean, there is almost no way that she should look so, so, so . . ."

To say it or not to say it? To say it:

"So dark for her family."

I was being an ass on most levels, but on at least one I was betting that the truth would repair things between Frances and me. The problem, I learned, is that our lies can become more precious than our truths. I imagine this is why Frances threw the big Magritte book at me. You should have seen it soar through the apartment, a grand cascade of breasts, vaginas, apples, and top hats. I was so enchanted by its scenic passage that I forgot to duck, and took the book square in the eye.

"You've gone fucking crazy! You know that, right? Fucking crazy," I told her, pressing my palm against the cut.

"Stop it, you asshole." she said coldly, leering at me from the alcove.

"Stop it? You're not the one who just took a picture of a vagina in the face."

"Please, just don't," she said with a broken voice. Her lips began to quiver and her forehead became a mass of wrinkles. "You can't imagine . . . ," she managed, and began to cry.

A thin trail of mucus worked its way down from her nose and dripped off the line of her upper lip. She wiped it away but as she cried more came, and soon she was huffing and snorting quite violently to keep it from running out of her nose and onto her face. I had just thought to forgive her the book assault and comfort her when the blood started from her left nostril in a lacquered stream. For a moment, she thought it was just more tears. Then she wiped her face on the kimono, and looked down to see its silk heavy, stained, and shining, and this sight proved to be the first horror that Frances could not somehow sublimate.

She jumped back on the cushion, hitting her head on the rail of the window and causing some strained vessel in her right nostril to burst into hemorrhage as well. I walked forward from the fireplace to comfort her, but she held out her hands for me to keep away, gathering the ancient robe in handfuls and pressing it against her face until it sagged with blood and refused to take on any more. Frances sobbed uncontrollably as the blood flowed from her nostrils over layers of glistening mucus and onto her chest. She tried to wipe herself clean with her hands but succeeded only in smearing the mess across herself, like a great gash. This was when she decided that it was useless to resist.

Rolling breakers of sorrow came out in sets of three and four. She hid her face in her hands, and it grew wet and filthy, dark and bloody, worse each time she gasped for breath between her moans. She stood with her back to the open window, grabbed a twisted yellow drape, and leaned out against the railing.

"She's lost it," I thought. "She's going to throw herself out of that window, and she's going to crack her skull open on the pavement, and I'm going to have to explain it, and also why her nose was bleeding, and no one is going to believe me, and when it's all done I'm going to be a full-on leper . . ."

But that was not her plan. She tore the draperies from above the window, and they rattled to the floor. The wind flooded in behind her, lifting her hair in blood-matted tongues. Thick red drops fell from her nose to the floor, but she barely noticed. The soaked robe came undone of its own weight, and with her chest bare and foul Frances stepped down from the alcove, walked daintily over to Wendy's collection of antique grandfather clocks, and began kicking.

"Me!" she screamed, over and over, as she battered the old mahogany with a bare foot that bore through the wood until its flesh was torn by the timepiece's own brass innards.

Her torso naked, blood streaked, and twisted, her breasts stained, dangling, and bare, she cursed and bled and made her way to the Park Avenue side of the room, to the wall of family portraits and pictures of

Bo and Wendy and Sunshine that had started it all. I thought I saw her smile as she slid the miniature, ivory-backed paintings from their hangings, then zipped them like Frisbees through the open window. One by one they went, and she didn't stop until the entire family tree was defenestrated: the Sloan who sold opium; the Sloan who sold mustard gas; the Sloan who fucked his slaves; the Sloan who invaded Canada; the Sloan who died of syphilis; the Sloan who was shot in a duel. Even the Sloan who had shot himself now met his end again, sailing through the open French panels and down onto Sixty-fifth Street. She grabbed the framed picture of Bo and Wendy and the baby, and with all of her energy threw it outside as well.

Frances stared and sobbed at the empty wall. I took a step toward her, and when she didn't recoil I took another, and came to her and wrapped my arms around her from behind, feeling the weight of her little body slumping into my own. The sun dipped lower and lower until it was just a glow.

"I'm sorry," she said, and I started to offer my own apology, but she cut me off. "For the longest time after my mom left, I would come home, and he'd be passed out. He smelled like whiskey and ashtrays, but to me that was just how he smelled. I had to put him in bed. I had to put myself in bed. I had to put him to bed because he was a mess and he wasn't waking up. It was like I had a father but I didn't . . ."

She began to shake her head in disbelief.

"Wendy went around telling their friends he was going to marry her. Everyone said they heard he was getting married, so he decided it must be a good idea. Then came the baby. I asked him about the baby when the pictures came, and he said, 'If you're going to call here and say these things, I would prefer that you not call here.'"

Her voice crumbled as she quoted her father. She wrapped her arms around my neck, and I felt the striation on her forearm pass against my shirt, grazing the old chicken pox scars on my back.

"I think in this world there is only truth and lies, Tommy. They'll baptize the baby free from one lie just as they saddle her with another. It's so late in things. What better way to enter this world than under false pretense? Who will know? Who will care? Not the priest. No one will ever be able to find that lie in ten years. Even your father will forget, or act like he has. There are just too many lies to keep track of."

Frances tightened the filthy kimono about her waist, and closed her eyes. She spoke to herself, out loud.

"It's a fog of fogs. That's why we expect so much of God, and so little of ourselves. You know in the paintings at the Met, how Jesus looked like those Greek gods? We did that to him. We're so desperate that we always need saving, so we're always busy manufacturing saviors. We just change the façades every couple of hundred years, then fight about them. It's everywhere. And for every Yves Grandchatte there's another Yves Grandchatte. And for every Mohammed there's another Mohammed . . ."

She stopped to breathe. I wiped the blood from her chin as she continued.

"I once thought you could read and think your way to the place where things started. But you can't excavate down that far. The world as cities built on cities built on cities. I think that's why the world feels so cluttered, Tommy. It's so late in the play and the stage is filled with dead bodies and old props and fallen lights and bloody glass. You just want the stage to fill with water. Or fire. The endings beat the lies."

I thought of Sunshine's baptism, and how Eden had ended with the first lie. I suppose you don't need God for that story to be true. I held Frances and she breathed softly against my neck. I brushed her hair back, and tried to quiet her.

"We're trapped," she whispered. "In saviors and bodies and families and lives."

"You can't even see to cut your way out," she told me.

I kissed her gently on the forehead.

I carried her to the bathroom, and together we washed.

I carried her to the bedroom, and entwined, we slept.

# 10

## LA MACHINE ÉTONNANTE

By the night of MoMA's winter ball in honor of Sophie Dvornik's star client, the self-educated sculptor and painter Yves Grand-chatte, Frances and I had put things back together, both in the apartment and between us. Of course Wendy and Bo were verboten as a topic of conversation, as was Frances's cut. So to look back it was a Pyrrhic bliss. At the time it felt quite real.

I felt as if I now knew her, like I understood what all the books and the gloom had been about. One day after work I went to the Howard Rose Gallery, from whose catalog Frances had taught me so much the month before. I had not really planned on finding anything to buy, but amid the many antiquities there was a pair of turquoise-and-gold Mayan earrings that, compared to the gallery's grander offerings, seemed relatively cheap at thirty-five hundred. I only had about fifteen hundred in my checking account, but told myself that I would get at least a small bonus at the end of the year, and that there was at least an even chance I would make it that far without getting fired. So I charged the earrings to my Amex, and had a jeweler fit them with clips, because Frances's ears had never been pierced. I gave them to her just days after the fight, and she smiled the way she had among the lilacs that past summer, and though in time Amex would be calling me at all hours to demand payment for the purchase, I have never once regretted buying those earrings.

On the night of the party Frances wore them with a tea green silk Chloe dress, and kissed me on the back of the neck after perfecting the bow tie of my tuxedo. We met CeCe and Phoebe and their new boyfriends for dinner at Le Bilboquet. The restaurant's single cramped room was in prime form, every table brimming with tuxedoed men and brilliantly colored silken women looking to thin the blood and warm the senses before heading to the MoMA party. CeCe wore a tiered silk chiffon dress whose black-and-white pattern seemed to have been inspired by Yasser Arafat's head rag. Phoebe was aflame in a satin tube that had been done up in Armageddon camouflage of bright reds, yellows, and oranges.

"I had them custom-made in China! It was super cheap! I'm leaving Carolina Herrera in a month to open up a boutique in NoLiTa!" said CeCe, stealing a glance at the reflection of the reflection of her ass in the mirrored wall behind her from the mirrored wall in front of her.

"It's to raise awareness for the war!" gushed Phoebe.

"See, I'm like a Pakilstanian," said CeCe, running her hands down her silhouette.

"You mean a Palestinian?" asked Frances.

"Yeah, you totally look like a Princetonian," said Phoebe.

"And I'm . . ." Phoebe stared down at her own dress. "CeCe? What am I?"

"You're just like a big explosion, Pheebs!" said CeCe, waving her fingers wildly, and adding expertly: "War has lots of explosions."

I shall never forget CeCe and Phoebe, who brought together Chinese prison labor and Middle Eastern imagery to produce cleavage-enhancing, couture testimony to the downy oblivion of American wealth. But we lolled in the feathers together, and it was around this time that I realized that the most attractive aspect of wealth was its role as insulator. In my day-to-day worries about employment and the dwindling level of my checking account I came to understand the power of millions of dollars quietly at work. Money is like matter, and exerts a potent gravity when you get enough of it together. It's irresistible, and magnetic, even. You had to be jealous of the way these girls viewed the world. How they thought not, and how they worried not, and how blissfully they had created—and worn—two of the more damning relics of a generation.

"I'm so glad that you're doing this," I said to them. "I feel like, if we can just get enough people to wear your dresses, these poor kids from Arkansas will stop getting blown up by roadside bombs."

Frances cracked a smile.

"I know, it's really amazing," said CeCe, and looked at her own reflected ass in awe.

"Wow," said Phoebe, also looking at CeCe's reflected ass in awe. "So amazing."

We walked to a table in the corner of the small, bustling restaurant, and it was here, beneath a painting of a bleeding horse, that I met the girls' new boyfriends. CeCe had broken up with John the midget, and was now dating Prince Fahad, a minor Saudi royal. Everyone says that nearly all of the 9/11 hijackers were Saudi, that these people hate America. But unless driving around New York in a chauffeured Bentley with half-naked women and eight balls of blow counts as anti-

American activity, Prince Fahad had registered few visible grievances against the Great Satan. He stood only about five and a half feet tall, with a small head that surged up from his tight collar with a certain amount of repressed violence that I wrongly ascribed to basic princeliness. Fahad wore several medals on the lapel of his tuxedo, slick silk ribbons of red and green and purple and yellow and blue, with intricately etched circles of gold and silver attached. What he had done to earn them was never made clear. But I remember being quite impressed by the sight of him, even as he looked at me with disdain. I had lost the Blueberry competition at Cipriani with Big Larry, and I was not about to get into a contest of comparing decorations with Prince Fahad.

"Those are very impressive, Prince," I said. "How did you get them?"

Frances looked on in amusement as the prince struggled to explain the origin of his many valors. Then the waiter came, and we ordered dinner. Phoebe and CeCe had steak tartare. Frances had Chilean sea bass, and the rest of us ordered steak au poivre. We finished our cocktails and ordered wine and the food arrived. CeCe cracked two small, speckled quail eggs atop her tartare, and with a lazy motion spread the raw egg over the raw meat. Phoebe studied how she did this, and followed suit, but whatever anxiety suppressants she was on must have interfered with her motor functions, because she dropped the eggs on the floor.

"I dropped my quail eggs," she announced, sadly.

"You dropped your Quaalude?" CeCe asked, concerned.

"No, my quail eggs," said Phoebe, then checked her purse, just to be sure.

We spoke about people who had gained weight. About people who had lost weight. About Frances's cousin William, who was in the middle of his seventh year at Dartmouth. And about how no one we knew

knew anyone fighting in Iraq, although Phoebe expressed her hope that CeCe's evening wear might soon change that. Soon the table fell silent but for the grating of steel on porcelain.

Phoebe had broken up with Big Larry and now dated another Larry who was not a Lawrence but a Laurance, and a not just any Laurance but a Laurance Whistlestopper. He had not said anything all night, and it now became clear why. In a state of extreme focus, this man had cut his steak into small pieces and now cut it into smaller pieces still. I learned only later that Laurance Whistlestopper was a fifth-generation Rockefeller, and that he was by most estimates at least mildly retarded, and that these attributes made him, in the opinion of some women, one of the very most eligible men in Manhattan. He looked like a Labrador puppy, with big white cheeks and a head of thinning blond hair that flopped lazily over his brow. His face was dominated by a set of sad brown eyes whose dull resignation revealed that the brain behind them had stopped trying to make sense of most things long ago. These eyes now lit up with a memory.

"One summer in Bar Harbor, I held my breath underwater for three whole minutes!" he bragged excitedly. No one knew quite what to make of the statement.

We smiled blankly at Laurance and Laurance smiled blankly at us. Suddenly he looked to Fahad.

"Hey, Fahad? How long can you hold your breath for?"

"I do not know," said Prince Fahad, who wanted to compare medals, not lung capacity.

"Well, you wanna have a contest? Because I bet I'd win it! Oh, I bet I would!" Laurance beamed.

Owing to language and cultural barriers, Prince Fahad was only partially aware of the extent to which Laurance Whistlestopper was special. Fahad knew that Laurance had gone to Brown, and was a Rockefeller. Fahad further knew that he himself had gone to Sand-hurst, and was a prince. And knowing these things was all Fahad needed to know to know that he knew that he would never back down from any challenge issued by Laurance Whistlestopper.

The medals on Prince Fahad's tuxedo jingled as he took a deep breath, and held it.

The knot on Laurance Whistlestopper's tie came loose as he followed suit.

And two scions of the world's greatest oil families glared at each other in choking silence as I counted off the seconds on my watch.

"Come on, boys! You can do it!" I cheered them on, and thought fondly of Charles Darwin.

Fahad turned blue in the face after forty-five seconds, but Laurance seemed just fine. After a minute, veins began to bulge from Fahad's neck, but Laurance was Zen-like and tranquil. Fahad clenched his fists and began to shake after ninety seconds, but Laurance focused only on his plate of little steak pieces, and I believed hatched plans to cut them even smaller once the breath-holding contest was over. It was just after the two-minute mark that Fahad exhaled in defeat, and Laurance began waving his hands in celebration, but continued to hold his breath.

"Honey, it's over! It's over and you won!" said Phoebe, her modest bosom surging proudly in the Armageddon print dress as she rubbed his forearm with maternal care.

He let out a surprised gasp.

"I did? I did! I won!" he cheered, bouncing up and down in the banquette.

"Yes, you won," said Fahad, spilling a glass of red wine that soaked into the white tablecloth as he leaned across the table and into Laurance's face. "But tell me, Laurance Whistlestopper, have you ever had a man killed?"

Laurence Whistlestopper looked first confused, then frightened, and finally dejected as he shook his head sadly to admit that he had never been an accomplice to murder.

"Well, well . . . ," said Fahad, and crossed his delicate arms across his decorated chest.

WE TOOK CABS FROM LE BILBOQUET ACROSS TOWN TO MOMA. The museum had been lit in shades of pink and green and blue for the evening, and men and women in black tie and evening gowns pulled up in town cars and milled about Fifty-third Street, then walked onto a short red carpet leading to a broad white backdrop where two banks of cameras burst in a continuous volley of light. CeCe and Phoebe grabbed their dates and ran toward the cameras.

"I totally hate these paparazzi," said CeCe, obscuring Prince Fahad as she turned her bronzed shoulder back a bit to appear thinner, and tossed up her mane of a thousand highlights in case anyone wanted an action shot.

"It is really annoying,"said Phoebe, looking at Laurance Whistlestopper with just a hint of disgust, because there were other things that she also found annoying.

"I hate that I have to *tell* people he is a Rockefeller," she would later say to Frances in soon-violated total confidence. "Whistlestopper is such a funny name. Phoebe Whistlestopper? I don't know. Do you think he can change his name back to Rockefeller? Phoebe Rockefeller. Don't you love that?"

Right now she just had a vague feeling of being somehow lesser beneath the klieg lights, and made it go away by studying and imitating CeCe's many manipulations of shoulders, heels, and hair. The two girls hated having their pictures taken so much that they cycled through a range of poses and pouts for the better part of two minutes. Finally the experience became so unbearable that they discarded their dates altogether, posed back to back, and began blowing air kisses.

Shortly after dating the petite movie star CeCe had begun to view herself as possessing a certain level of discreet fame. It started by accident, when a picture of her at a reception following a screening of the midget's movie, *Lilliput Revisited,* was published in *W.* Owing to John's shortness, and no flaw in his character, he had been lost from the image during cropping. As a result only CeCe made it onto the page of photos that also included Jennifer Aniston, Kirsten Dunst, and Heidi Klum. CeCe was beautiful, and on this page of celebrity party pictures struck no one as out of place, least of all herself. Which may have been the problem.

CeCe began to refer to Jennifer and Kirsten and Heidi in casual conversation. And she began to lament that the paparazzi—singular, relentless, entirely imagined—*was absolutely everywhere.* These ruthless phantoms, the same people who killed Lady Diana, soon became the central feature of her life. She would often roll her eyes in ecstatic disgust and curse the cost of her own sudden and self-conceived fame, then pray silently for more of it. Someone might have said something, but increasingly the only person whom CeCe talked to was Phoebe, who might have been the only person to find the fantasy of CeCe's fame and following more genuinely exciting than CeCe herself did. Phoebe had always loved famous people, and now she got to feel as if she was hanging out with one all the time.

I had begun to fill my long days of doing nothing at J. S. Spenser with extensive Internet searches. I read about a great many things, but mainly medicine, and in a British medical journal I found an article about this incredibly rare condition called *fetus in fetu.* It happens with twins in the womb, in the early days of pregnancy. For whatever reason, one fetus becomes so dependent on the other that it allows itself to be swallowed up by it. The consuming fetus develops and is born as a single child. Decades later, some X-ray uncovers the homunculus of their long-forgotten sibling, their first friend, still in its arrested state, still inside of them. I thought of this condition as I stood watching the girls stand outside the museum, the shutters and bulbs flashing and releasing, loud and blinding, over and again. Soon there was no more CeCe, no more Phoebe. Conjoined in Palestinian silk and fiery camouflage satin, they smiled not out on the world but in on themselves. I suppose that they needed each other, and that by that point there was no hope in excavating one from the other, and that such a relationship is a sort of love, and pure, if not entirely noble. Phoebe reached down and took CeCe's bronzed, glittery hand, and she held it in her own for some time, like a very rare and special object. A pair of puzzled publicists finally had to usher the girls away from the cameras so that Chloe Sevigny could make an entrance.

CeCe and Phoebe rejoined their dates and found Frances and me in the sleek granite lobby of the museum. The two rooms spilled out into the sculpture garden, although you could not see beyond the open doors, so thick was the crowd of young men and women, none more than two or three degrees removed from any other. The ticket counters and information desks had been covered in pink silk bunting and turned into bars behind which struggling actors in white tie poured pink and purple martinis and rosé Champagne. More waiters circulated with gleaming silver trays filled with small parmesan risotto cakes, smaller blintzes with smoked salmon and caviar, and even smaller pieces of sushi.

Over the course of that year everything seemed to get smaller, and indeed the hors d'oeuvres shrank from party to party. Chicken satay with Thai peanut sauce, quite popular only months earlier, now seemed embarrassingly mammoth and socially unthinkable. And I can tell you that, at least in certain circles on the island of Manhattan, life does imitate hors d'oeuvres. The parties themselves were also shrinking. As if choreographed, the anointed sons and daughters of Late America bobbed and hovered about the room, that vast light box of tanned flesh, watercolored silk, black satin, and white cotton. Each man and woman actively reduced his world as he went, so that third-degree associations became second-degree acquaintances, second-degree acquaintances became first-degree friends, and first-degree friends became intimate relations. The entire process emitted a low, consenting sound, a buzz of agreement that our boozy beatification was good and natural and even written in the stars. Standing like the sun in the center of this collapsing universe was Roger Thorne.

He wore a single-button Armani tuxedo, had his hair slicked back, and stood in place with the charged look of a man who has a thousand social algorithms finding speedy solution in his mind. He held Lauren Schuyler and she played with the champagne flute in his hand. Her golden hair was pulled back into a bun, and her sun-damaged décolletage was jeweled and taut in a black strapless grown, a thin crescent of pale pink areola peeking curiously out at the party. Thorne seemed unsure just how he felt about this nip-slip, which was so close to home. Lauren Schuyler's nipples had lost their power over him a long time ago, but that they should be seen in a place where they should not be seen made them somewhat exciting. He looked warmly at the exposed flesh before tapping Lauren on the arm and indicating that she should adjust herself. Once she did, he looked across the way at Sophie Dvornik, who had dressed herself like a Bollywood sex goddess in a blue-and-pink sari. She had henna tattoos running up her left arm and a red Brahmin dot on the middle of her head, but had omitted the obligatory undershirt. As she approached to say hello her ruby-bearing cleavage parted the crowd like the prow of a great ocean liner.

"Frances! How are things at NYU?" she asked with a sadistic smile.

Frances squeezed my hand tightly, and I winced as I again felt the sharp edges of her pear-shaped diamond against my palm.

"Good."

"That's great. I have a friend who teaches there." Sophie rubbed her nose, which was just out of bandages from the third of her rhinoplasties.

"Um, do you remember CeCe and Phoebe?" Frances cut her off, and pushed the sleeve of her dress down.

Sophie reintroduced herself to CeCe, who introduced her to Prince Fahad, and then to Phoebe, who introduced her to Laurance, whose last name she incorrectly stated as Rockefeller. And when all of this introducing and reintroducing was over, Sophie re-re-introduced herself to Roger Thorne as though she only barely knew him.

"Sophie, I think you know Lauren from that night at Cipriani," said Thorne, introducing his girlfriend and life partner to his dominatrix and porno partner.

The two girls shook hands, and I had to believe that even if she did not permit herself full awareness, Lauren suspected something. Roger and Sophie, were, after all, linked by a pungent, powerful pornographic karma. The air grew thick with pheromones as they stood next to each other that night in the warm pink lighting of the museum.

"Are you from Bangladesh or something?" asked Lauren cattily, looking at Sophie's dress.

"No," said Sophie. "It's just that my latex bodysuit was at the dry cleaners, and this was all I had."

Lauren laughed painfully, Thorne smiled fondly, and Sophie gestured for Yves Grandchatte to come over and say hello.

The party was strictly black tie, but the fact that he had been on the cover of *New York* magazine and was being honored by MoMA exempted Yves Grandchatte from any dress code. He wore his hair in a close faux-hawk, and covered his chest with a tight black T-shirt that read NAMBLA in cracked white iron-on letters. On one forearm he had a tattoo of a naked woman, and on the other a large hand extending an even larger middle finger. On one set of knuckles he had tattooed the word SHIT, and on the other its cousin FUCK. The faded do-it-yourself tattoo ink was green and violent against his pale olive skin. Shadows accentuated the flattening of his nose, which seemed to have been broken several times. He smelled of Versace cologne and motor oil.

"I bought zees glasses from ze eBay, from ze widow of pilot of ze *Enola Gay*," he explained, and his muscles spasmed in frenetic jerks as he took off his aviator sunglasses.

"Yves's work is all about a new understanding of history, and the systemic reinterpretation of . . ." Sophie set about explaining her gallery's star client, and was visibly impressed by the beauty of the jargon dreamed up by her bosses to market the man.

"What she means is zat I've never been, uh, how do you say? Educated? I was, a, how do you say, drug addict? Yes, but even then, I rejected ze twelve steps. I did keep zem from getting, uh, inside of my head?"

His breath smelled like truffles.

"Who?" I asked, because I was by that point quite unhappy with my life and thought it comforting to consider that my many mounting problems might be attributed to a cabal of people living inside of my head.

"Who what?" he replied angrily in a gust of truffle breath.

"Who did you keep from getting inside of your head?"

Grandchatte scanned around the room nervously, and whispered,

"Who do you think? Zees, how do you say, *player haters*? Yes? Zey are, uh, always *crushing* on a *nigger*?" He said this in his thick French accent.

CeCe and Phoebe gasped at the sound of the word *nigger*. Privately each girl would rather kiss a cousin than a black man, but that didn't mean that they couldn't view themselves as entirely progressive. In fact, it only made it more important for them to publicly register offense in moments like this. Yves Grandchatte received an icy glare from the girls, but was forgiven as he continued, and it became evident that he was, at least in his own mind, not white.

"But zey never got close to me! Because in Paris I am known to be very tough. I fuck zem up, no?"

"Really?" said Phoebe, who now found a thrill in being so close to someone so vulgar.

"Yes, zees is true," said Grandchatte, shifting his hands through his faux-hawk. "I was a, you know, a *drug dealer*? Does that *freak you out*? Oui? Does that *get you hard*?"

Sophie took Yves's FUCK-tattooed knuckles, and showed them off as further proof of enlightenment.

"Yves's total lack of education is precisely the reason why we all have so much to learn from him. His art is intuitive. He is not bound by any one culture, and identifies as much with the French aristocracy as with the American inner city. We could never understand the world like he does, because unlike us, his development has been entirely *sui generis.*" Sophie had forgotten that she had used that word before, but Frances had not, and knowingly rolled her eyes. She began to laugh outright when Yves Grandchatte inserted a tattooed finger up his nose, and started digging.

"I think that after you see his sculpture tonight, you'll agree with me that he sees things more clearly than we ever could. I think you'll especially like it, Roger. . . ."

Sophie introduced Roger to Grandchatte. The artist had already viewed each of the Dvornik-Thorne porno tapes several times, but failed to remember that he was never supposed to have seen them at all. He grabbed excitedly at Thorne's crotch.

"I am a great, uh, *admirer*? Yes, I do admire very much this man! I put him, how do you say, in my sculpture?"

Sophie elbowed Yves in the ribs and he suddenly fell silent.

Roger Thorne seemed strangely distressed.

Lauren Schuyler seemed typically confused.

CeCe admired her own fingernails.

Phoebe admired CeCe admiring her own fingernails.

And soon Prince Fahad was the only one talking.

"Later that week his motorcycle skidded off the road," he said to Laurance Whistlestopper with extreme self-satisfaction. "And that was one less cousin in my way . . ."

Laurance seemed more afraid than usual, and grabbed for Phoebe's hand. She held him close. Then a brilliant white glow came from the sculpture garden, overwhelming the lobby. Everyone turned to see it, straining against the blinding light with their hands held over their eyes.

"Oh! Let's go to the sculpture garden! I think it's starting!" said Sophie, adjusting her sari.

"Follow me!" said Yves Grandchatte, who led us all from the lobby and into the now phosphorescent sculpture garden.

The small enclosure was not up to the task of holding the more than thousand young art patrons who had come to see Yves Grandchatte's sculpture. We all jammed into the farthest corners of its marble walkways and, from the loftiest Band-Aid heiress to the lowliest plus-one, stood on tiptoes and sat on shoulders and leaned on priceless sculptures to watch as Yves Grandchatte made his way to the center of the yard and stood beneath the brilliantly glowing mountain of plasma screens installed atop a system of pumping hydraulics and rising scaffolds in the center of the garden. He raised his SHIT fist into the air. We called to him and whistled and clapped. CeCe and Phoebe climbed atop a Miro sculpture, the better to see and be seen. Grandchatte took a microphone, and began to delight the crowd by way of insulting them.

"I am not like you, uh, how do you say? *Chickenheads bitches*? No. You see, I cannot read? No. And I cannot spell? No. I am, uh, *colorblind*? Oui? I am, ah, you know, *dyslexic*, oui? I have STDs. Oui? I used to mug young women, yes, and huff glue . . . *with Algerians*!"

Everyone but Frances clapped as he enumerated his deficiencies, and there was a cheer as he raised his fist to the air and summed himself up in a single sentence.

"I am a *criminal*! An *alcoholique*! And a *drug addicté*!"

Amid the applause Yves Grandchatte, the hottest artist in New York, assumed a karate position and, pointing to the letters of his NAMBLA T-shirt, kicked his leg out at the crowd.

"I know karate! Does that freak you out?" he asked hopefully, and we cheered for him again until he held up his hands for silence.

"Wiz a lifetime of pain and a grant from ze Guggenheim Foundation, I have created zees! *La Machine Étonnante! The Amazing Machine!* You may ask me, 'Yves, what does it do?' I tell you! It is *artificial intelligence*! It is *perpetual motion*! It is a cure for, how do you say? *Herpes*?"

People were with Yves until his last claim, at which they shook their heads in disbelief. We were more than willing to accept that Grandchatte had simultaneously achieved a thinking computer and a source of infinite energy, but a cure for herpes seemed simply too good to be true. Perhaps sensing that he had gone too far, Grandchatte shook his head to say that, yes, it was true, and then instructed his assistants to turn on the machine. We all cheered more loudly and struggled to touch him as he stepped back and into the crowd. The lights in the garden flickered, and in a singular eruption of light and sound Yves Grandchatte's perpetual-motion, artificial-intelligence, herpes-curing machine came to life.

The hydraulic pistons began pumping, lifting the rigging up and up and up so that over a period of ten minutes the full mess of plasma screens and computers sorted itself into three distinct tiers. These in turn began to spin, powered, I can only assume, by Yves Grandchatte's perpetual-motion machine. And as each tier revolved, its screens played feeds of images of all sorts. On the lowest level there were bloody Iraqi beheadings and fiery precision bombings and terrified Columbine students and towns leveled by tsunamis and stranded New Orleans families and smoky World Trade Center suicides of beautifully attired bankers who looked no different from you or me as they fell like dead pigeons from the first tower, their bodies inverted, their ties sailing up as they plummeted down. The second tier moved faster, and across its screens flashed clips from episodes of every sitcom of the modern era. The screens raced from *The Andy Griffith Show* to *Charlie's Angels* to *The Golden Girls* to *Buffy the Vampire Slayer* and then began to cut faster and faster still, through the millions of hours of proliferated reality viewing. And on the third wheel of screens, atop the rest, were Yves Grandchatte's favorite porno flicks. The images jumped as the screens whirled, and the air filled with the flesh and moans of every man or woman to ever document their own faked orgasm. As the three tiers of the structure spun it became difficult to make out any distinct images of entities at all. There was just an irresistible blur of greenish light, and the rhythmic pulsing of so many sounds already heard.

The machine was loved at once.

"They should have one of these at Marquee!" said Phoebe, as she wrapped her arms around CeCe high atop the Miró statue.

"It's a dazzling deconstruction of worldview," said Chloe Sevigny to her agent.

"That's the green I'm gonna use for my spring collection!" said Zac Posen.

"When does it cure herpes?" wondered Phoebe, who then looked ashamed and covered her mouth.

Even I was in awe, and hardly noticed Sophie Dvornik bent down to her knees, laughing hysterically, trying in vain to cover her face with her handbag.

"What is it?" I asked her.

She threw a Parliament Ultra Light onto the base of a nearby Rodin, and reveled in ironic and post-ironic delight as she parodied the explanation of Yves Grandchatte's work that her gallery had been sincerely selling to every art collector on the island for the past two months.

"The sculptor Yves Grandchatte has created an algorithm capable of accurately predicting to one thousandth of one percent the content of the television viewing and Internet search habits of the American public . . . ," she began, soon laughing too hard to continue, and requiring a moment to compose herself.

"Mr. Grandchatte credits his near total lack of education,"—she had to gasp for breath amid her own laughter—"his battle with addiction, and his associations with Parisian street gangs as inspirations for this work. The machine has also achieved perpetual motion, and is capable of curing her . . ." Sophie was finally in tears, and had to stop.

"He's full of shit, isn't he?" I said.

"His grandfather is a *duc,* and I'm pretty sure he graduated from the Sorbonne in 1999," she said, wiping tears of laughter from her eyes. "I tell you because I love you. Repeat that and I kill you."

Frances had been right all along.

Sophie looked about with a malevolent smile. "Now, where is your well-endowed friend Mr. Thorne?"

And to find the answer to this question, she did not need to look very far at all.

The tiers of screens now began to spin faster and faster, like some rickety carnival ride. Through some trick of computer programming, Yves Grandchatte had managed to coordinate the blurring of the three spheres to play a single moving picture, and this picture, the crowning event of the evening's display, was of Sophie Dvornik, fully spirited in her crotchless latex bodysuit, straddling a man who looked very much like Roger Thorne, and seemed to have given himself most fully over to the throes of a new and wild ecstasy.

Just a few feet away from Sophie the corporeal Roger Thorne stood beside Lauren Schuyler, staring nervously at the ground, fidgeting with his cuff links as the digital titan of his image thrust away to the delight of the awestruck crowd. There was broad fascination and shock-arrested stares from the men and women around Roger, who all seemed possessed of a sudden suspicion that the six-foot-two man in their midst was also the sixty-two-foot man being ridden by a woman in latex on the screens above them. The real Roger Thorne kept staring at the ground and fidgeting with his cuff links as all around him people looked up at the screen, then at his profile, again and again, trying to decide if the august young banker in the tuxedo beside them was the same man being ridden by the latex-suited woman on the screen up above. And no one tried harder to make this connection than Lauren Schuyler.

"Roger, that guy looks just like you!" she squealed, and began to clap.

"Oh my God! It does look like Roger!" said CeCe.

"Roger the porn star! Roger Jeremy!" said Phoebe, and began clapping too.

"Tommy, is that really him?" whispered Frances in my ear.

I didn't have to answer. The truth is that Roger Thorne the M&A banker might have gotten off the hook had Roger Thorne the S&M enthusiast not decided to throw his trademark 1980s heavy-metal hand signs to the cameras in Sophie Dvornik's bedroom. It was only when this happened that CeCe and Phoebe gasped, and Lauren Schuyler fell silent. We stood and watched the thrusting and the pumping and the whipping and the licking and the spinning and the money shots, one after another. It made you dizzy and hot just to look at the rotating screens and to hear the amplified sounds of the Thorne-Dvornik passion.

"Oh stop, it's not Roger," said Lauren Schuyler at long last, nervously scratching at a dark mole on her shoulder. "Roger's *you-know-what* doesn't look a thing like that!"

The girls took Lauren at her word, and she seemed to believe herself too.

Thorne merely nodded in agreement, unable to take his eyes off of himself.

As the screens continued in their centrifuge of sex the faintest scent of burning rubber spiked the air of the gardens. We all sniffed about for its origin, but the guessing stopped as a curtain of black smoke fell down from the scaffolds and across the crowd. Soon the fiber-optic cables were aflame, hissing and spitting sparks through the darkening gaze. Then the garden went black save for this frenzied spark-light, which illuminated the twisted shadow of Yves Grandchatte as he raced about his *Amazing Machine,* tearing at its wires and drivers in a hopeless attempt at artistic abortion. He cursed and screamed at us, but as he had been cursing and screaming at us all night, most took the frenzy as proof that all of this had been planned, that everything was well. CeCe even started to clap.

"It died of its own vibrant life," observed Chloe Sevigny, wistfully, to her agent.

"We all do that, don't we?" he replied.

"I think I like this color red for fall!" said Zac Posen.

"Oh, I love it, it's like a burnt umber almost . . . ," replied the woman he was with.

Frances saw that it had all gone quite wrong. She pulled me by the hand, away from the machine and into the crowd whose admiration turned to fright when the highest tier of plasma screens melted from its hinges and crashed to the ground. The mass of revelers buckled, then moved in a screaming crush back to the safety of the museum lobby.

Inside we stood in the twin stenches of burnt hair and rubber, and stared out through the vast window as Yves Grandchatte's *Amazing Machine* preformed its last feat, tumbling to the ground to form its own funeral pyre. It simmered dull red in the garden, now dark and empty save for the glowing mound of plastic. It was announced that the party would continue and there was applause and people spoke only of having escaped this conflagration and the horrible stench of it all. Forgotten entirely was Roger Thorne's resemblance to the man on the screens. More Champagne was poured, and the party picked itself back up quite nicely.

Frances alone was unsurprised; she had seen it coming all along. In fact, the only thing that came as a shock to her happened much later that night. By one in the morning it was time to go, and no one could find CeCe or Phoebe anywhere. Laurance and Fahad searched the upstairs galleries, and then waited impatiently by the street. Frances was the only one who thought to look outside the big window, and saw them both still in the garden, holding hands, their dresses all aflutter, as they danced for each other among the glowing remains of the self-destructing machine.

# 11

## Oscar de la Hoya

A great many people at Sunshine Sloan's baptism suspected that the baby had not been fathered by Bo Sloan, but only two people knew for certain who her real father was. I wasn't one of them. I didn't know it at the time, but the story was far more complicated than I could ever have imagined, and began long before I even had the capacity to understand it.

Wendy Sloan was born to schoolteachers living in West Texas, and from a very early age she resolved that she would not grow up to be a schoolteacher in West Texas. God had made her for greater things, she knew, because everyone at Baptist Youth Organization prayer retreats told her so. Often while staring at her breasts.

She had never regarded these prolonged takes at her budding rack as at all strange. In many ways the breasts themselves seemed to have come from heaven: one day they had not been there, and the next they were. Further, in combination with Wendy's fine skin and golden hair, they seemed entirely capable of miracles.

First came a cheerleading scholarship to UCLA. Then a part-time job as a model. And finally, genuine love with a UCLA offensive linesman named Cesar Munoz. He was Mexican and from San Antonio, and Wendy's parents hated him. She loved him anyway, and she married him the year before graduation. He might have been drafted by the NFL, and Wendy might have been a perfectly happy pro athlete's wife, but the poor man died of a heart attack during a training camp workout held in ninety-five-degree heat, three months after their wedding.

A widow at twenty-six, Wendy came to Manhattan.

She took a job as a business reporter with New York 1. Her salary was minimal, but Wendy soon came to realize that this job, which allowed her to call up any Wall Street titan and arrange dinner under the pretense of journalism, was as direct a path to riches as she was likely to find. Bo Sloan thought that he had asked Wendy out on their first date, but in fact this was not true: she had begun courting him on the morning that he was named trustee at the Metropolitan Museum of Art, when she arranged for a lunch to begin researching a segment on museum patrons that was never aired, and was never intended to be. Before Bo, Wendy had dated Teddy Coleman, a junior partner at pre-IPO Goldman Sachs. She had found him boring but indulgent. He had found her beautiful and accepting of a pre-nuptial agreement. He had been ready to propose when Wendy fell for another man.

His name was Oscar de la Hoya.

Yes, the Mexican lightweight boxer.

Teddy Coleman had bought two front-row seats to take Wendy to see Mike Tyson's 2002 rematch against Lennox Lewis in Memphis, Tennessee, and had flown her down to the fight on a chartered Citation. Teddy planned most everything in his life, and planned on asking Wendy to marry him after the fight. Apparently he went into a major depression after what Wendy did to him that night, and not even the

Goldman IPO and fifty million dollars in stock was enough to pull him out of it fully.

Personally, I think that he was way too hard on himself.

How could Teddy Coleman have ever known that his front-row seats would plant Wendy right next to Oscar de la Hoya? Or that Oscar de la Hoya's face and name would remind Wendy of her dead husband? Or that Oscar de la Hoya wore Drakkar? Or that the combination of these factors would cause Wendy to work her hand beneath the jacket on Oscar de la Hoya's lap and against the soft wool of Oscar de la Hoya's pants, and that she would begin caressing him gently until she broke into a full massage, then would rub him closer and closer, faster and faster, so that although Tyson didn't go down until the eighth round, Oscar de la Hoya went bust in the fourth.

Poor, rich Teddy Coleman could never have known these things.

He had to see them out of the corner of his eye, which is exactly what he did before going to the bathroom and not returning, leaving Wendy to find her own way back to Manhattan.

She didn't care. At thirty-one she was nearing her sexual peak and all she could think about was Oscar de la Hoya. Oscar de la Hoya, who reminded her of things she thought were dead. Oscar de la Hoya, who might have been a lightweight boxer but was a heavyweight lover.

Oscar de la Hoya, who over the course of one torrid year flew Wendy to his bouts and sat her ten rows back in the stands so that she could join the Mexican flag–waving crowds as they chanted for him: *"Oscar de la Hoya! Oscar de la Hoya! Oscar de la Hoya!"*

Oscar de la Hoya, who sat his wife in the front row, so that when he kissed his glove and waved it to Wendy in the tenth row both women felt that they owned his heart.

Oscar de la Hoya, who eventually told Wendy that he loved her deeply, but that for the sake of his children and his fortune, he could not leave his wife.

Still she continued to love him and to see him, guiltily, greedily, and when they were apart she dreamed his name: Oscar de la Hoya.

Oscar de la Hoya, who stood in the back of St. Bartholomew's church on Park Avenue on the morning of Sunshine Sloan's baptism, mistaken by most for a custodian amid a sea of finely bred white faces.

There were the Sloan cousins from Locust Valley and the Sloan cousins from San Francisco who had not spoken in a decade because of an argument that apparently began between two alcoholic cousins over one sober nephew's right to take a mulligan. They did a good job of seeming to say hello to one another without actually saying hello.

There were lawyers and accountants and bankers with whom Bo had made a lot of money. There were other people with whom Bo Sloan had lost lots of money: Archie Mueller from Yale, who had founded www.freestuff.com without realizing that giving things away was not really a way to make money; Gifford FitzSimmons from St. Paul's, whose electric cocktail shaker seemed to be the next big thing in 1982, just before it electrocuted all of those people in 1983; David Mullins, from Long Term Capital Management.

We had all arrived at the church vaguely drunk from the pre-baptism brunch at the Four Seasons, where the Jamaican au pair, Eunice, had dealt with baby Sunshine, freeing Wendy to mingle with Bo on her arm, talking to his friends as if they were her own.

Over the course of the morning Bo had disappeared only five faintly Bloody Marys.

Frances had gone to the bathroom and stayed there for more than an hour.

I had occupied myself by building a small house out of sugar cubes, and drinking the better part of a bottle of Haut-Brion blanc.

Wendy had flown in five Navajo tribal singers to perform for the ceremony. They stood to the side of the altar in their turquoise ponchos and began to sing just as the red-faced priest tottered up the aisle behind a pair of altar boys and a man holding the Bible.

The old priest stopped to adjust his hearing aid to the frequency of the Navajo birth song. Evidently the Episcopalian church had provided him with only a bottom-of-the-line hearing aid, because he soon gave up, and continued walking.

Wendy Sloan wore a cleavage-baring black suit jacket and a pair of white cashmere pants that prominently displayed the ass and legs that, after giving birth, she had beaten back into shape with six-hour days of Pilates and elliptical training. In this outfit she began to move her hips and bob her head ever so faintly to the Navajo drums.

"Doesn't the Navajo music sort of defeat the purpose?" Frances asked, more curious than scandalized.

"No, no!" said Wendy, and dipped her hip just a bit. "It all comes *together*, Frances. When you get older you'll see that."

Frances was horrified, and not alone. There were Jews and Catholics and Protestants in attendance, and although they had many differences when it came to God, and had distant ancestors who had tried to kill one another over these differences, they all seemed to realize that this was not appropriate music for a christening.

The only person who took no notice was Bo Sloan.

He stood to my right in the velvet-cushioned pew. I turned to see his reaction to Wendy's direction of the tribal singers, but found him pretty much checked out. He had dipped his big head of gray-blond hair back, and his jowls sagged as he looked up at the ceiling of the church, filled with glittering mosaics of people who were saints, staring down at the pews filled with people who were not.

"*I just don't know,*" Bo mouthed, and then burped softly to himself as he stared at the mosaics, shaking his head. "*I just don't know,*" he repeated, this time aloud.

"Why are you saying that?" I whispered, leaning in against the soft cashmere of his navy blazer.

"Saying what?" he replied, quite unaware that he had said anything, his hair shifting as he looked down from the ceiling.

"'I don't know . . .'" I told him, because that was what he had been saying.

"You don't know?" he whispered back, perplexed.

"No, 'I don't know . . . ,'" I said.

"Then I guess there's no way for me to tell you," he shrugged.

I tried once more. "I asked why you said 'I don't know.'"

"I know," he said.

"Good. What?" I asked.

"How could I tell you when you don't know?" said Bo, and with this sentence plunged us both into a state of extreme confusion that lasted for several seconds.

Several pews behind us, Sunshine burped.

We forgot the odd conversation and were left with only a sense of boozy familiarity.

"Have you ever been to Bermuda, Tommy?" Bo slurred.

"I haven't," I replied.

He seemed a bit stunned, and shook his head.

"God, I used to love mascara when I was your age," he said, as if he were still talking about Bermuda.

"Mascara?" I asked.

"Bermuda?" he asked.

"I have nothing against Bermuda," I told him. "It's just that I've never been there."

He opened his big mouth in a big yawn.

"What were we just now talking about?" he wondered upon recovery, and stared around as if he had just materialized in the front pew.

"Bermuda. And mascara," I told him.

The mention of these two things caused him to smile warmly.

"Good man, good man," he said, placing his big hand on my shoulder.

We looked at the altar where the white-haired priest filled a deep golden bowl with water for the baptism. It seemed to take forever, and Bo stared at the shining bowl and squinted his eyes tighter and tighter with the quickening sound of the water.

"You could drown in that thing," he said, wincing when finally it was full.

"What?" I said.

"You could drown in that thing," he said once more, and, staring at the bowl with a mixture of shame and fascination, nodded in agreement with himself.

The priest then called for the parents and godparents to approach the altar. I went to take Frances by the arm; she gave me only the pale white scalloped cuff of the long-sleeve peasant dress that she had bought for the day. We walked to the altar, but halfway there realized that no one had Sunshine Sloan, and that, as this was her baptism, she was of some importance.

Eunice the au pair stood from the third pew where she had spent the service burping Sunshine. Wendy turned and took the baby from her. Then she noticed the rag speckled with regurgitated baby food that hung from the au pair's shoulder, and passed the baby to Bo, who held his daughter who was not his daughter for just a moment before developing a cramp somewhere in his lower back.

He passed the baby to Frances.

We walked up to the golden bowl and Frances held her sister who was not her sister in her arms and saw what a beautiful little girl she was, and without thinking began to rock her gently back and forth.

It was then that I heard the first little poot.

*Pfft!*

It was soft but loud enough, like the opening of a very small parachute. It was the first in a series of protest farts that Sunshine Sloan would issue throughout her own baptism.

The baby evidently found the sound of her own flatus delightful, because she was giggling to herself like mad well before a charmingly pungent scent overtook the altar. Frances and I had to struggle to maintain straight faces as we stared down at this little person who had made such a big noise.

The sound of Sunshine was in fact so distinct that the old priest broke from the ceremony, and began to look around for the source of the noise. He bit his lip with intent as he adjusted his hearing aid once more, this time in search of the exact frequency of baby farts.

He found it just in time.

*Pfft!* went Sunshine again, squealing with laughter as her latest salvo concussed across the altar.

I realized that though adults know that mouths are for talking and bottoms for other things, babies very well may not. It further occurred to me that this infant, still many months away from her first words, was using the only really powerful means of communication at her disposal to protest her own baptism. The noise of the farts had indeed succeeded in halting the ceremony, and did so far more gracefully than any string of sentences.

I am unsure if it was part of the ceremony, or simply an attempt to deodorize his workspace, but the priest summoned an altar boy who took a smoking silver incense burner on a long chain and with it began to fumigate the four corners of the altar.

*Clink!* went the chain against the censer as the blond-headed kid swung it back and forth, watching in awe as little clouds of scented smoke rose up to the frescoes.

*Pfft!* went Sunshine, now with a faintly wet signature. This new aroma was more powerful than the others and soon joined and finally overtook the burning incense. The altar began to smell of pureed peas.

Sunshine cooed happily; Frances pushed back her own golden hair and gave the baby her pinkie. Sunshine took it in her small fist and stared back at Frances with her vast eyes that saw everything for the first time. The baby's lips puckered and pleaded to suckle and Frances made a face that said she had no milk to give, but raised Sunshine to her chest and carefully kissed her soft head.

The old priest now shuffled toward us. His face was not uniformly red but only seemed so because of the thousand burst capillaries that covered it. He took Frances and me by the hands and led us down from the altar to the gold baptismal font set on steel prongs bolted into the cool slate of the church floor.

"As godparents you will guide Sunshine throughout her life as a Christian woman," said the priest. To avoid laughing I looked down into the golden dish and on the dimpled surface of the water found Frances gazing dolefully back at me. Our reflected eyes bled into one another until Sunshine decided to test her suspicion that Frances's hair was edible. The baby had settled her toothless gums around a dark fistful of blond bangs when the priest indicated that it was time to make her a Christian.

He gestured for me to take off my jacket, and to roll up my sleeves. I put my battered cuff links in the coat's breast pocket, and tried to keep its torn lining from view as I hung it over the edge of the front pew. The priest then turned to Frances.

"You'll want to roll up your sleeves as well, young lady," he told her.

"It's okay," she said in a stern tone that I had heard before and knew to respect. And I believe that he would have respected it too, but his hearing aid was tuned to the wavelength of baby farts, not of human speech.

"What?" he asked, quite frustrated to live in a world of mumblers.

"Pardon?" she said, hoping that he suffered from Alzheimer's in addition to deafness, and would forget the entire matter.

"The water is very wet!" he yelled, as if he was the first person to discover this, and I realized at once how he had gone so far in the church. He instructed again: "Roll up your shirt sleeves!"

Frances looked at me in terror as he took the baby from her, gave it to me and began to undo the pearl buttons that fastened the cuffs of her peasant dress. His hands trembled with Parkinson's and hers trembled with fear as in one brutal motion he yanked up her sleeves. A pair of Band-Aids fell to the floor.

I watched them float down to the cold slate and wondered where they had come from, and then I looked up and saw that Frances's old scar had been joined by a pair of small jagged cuts, still oozing, only freshly clotted, the result of an act perhaps committed in the bathroom of the Four Seasons during brunch.

She looked away from me and reached for the baby, whom she cradled in her sliced arms. The priest forced the innocent girl down just above the shallow basin of water and began his incantation.

"You are sealed by the Holy Spirit in baptism," he said, pushing Frances's arms down so that Sunshine was partially submerged. The water took on a faint pink tincture as Frances's open wounds corrupted the clear, cool holy water. The priest's hands shook violently as he dipped them into this water and made the sign of the cross on the baby's forehead.

"You are marked as Christ's own forever," he said.

A series of small bubbles came up from the water and the baby squirmed in her dress, whose cotton rubbed up and down against Frances's open scabs, further opening them so that the water took on a more undeniably sanguineous hue. Sunshine began to cry, and squirmed about uncomfortably in the golden font. Frances winced, and pulled the infant up to her chest.

The priest raised his hands to indicate that it was done, and as no one in attendance knew quite what to do, they all began to clap.

Wendy and Bo came up behind us, blind to the growing discoloration of Frances's dress as we all followed the priest from the church outside into the the early spring sun. I looked down Park toward Grand Central for the ranting schizophrenic, but he was nowhere to be found. It was Wendy who had drawn a crowd. "And we didn't want to tell anyone until three months in, because you know all sorts of things can go wrong," she said, holding Sunshine in her arms for the first time all day. "But Bo and I found out last week that Sunshine has a brother on the way!"

Frances fell against my chest. I pressed my hands against her arms, and held them there tightly as Wendy and Bo accepted congratulations for the baptism just passed, and the one yet to come.

WHEN I ASKED ABOUT HER CUTS FRANCES AGAIN BLAMED THEM on the cat. During the weeks that followed I spent my days alone at my desk worrying about my impending performance review at J. S. Spenser, and my nights beside Frances, worrying about what might befall her next. Something had to change and I took it as a measure of the desperation of things that my last and best hope seemed to lie with Manuel and the Latin American economic conference in Cabo San Lucas.

Mathers didn't need to tell me that the conference was in every way my last chance at Spenser, and that even if things went well, I still might get the ax during reviews. Everyone in the office seemed aware of my straits. Vice presidents whispered about me as I walked the halls, and the other analysts asked me whether I was thinking of leaving. They all knew I was doomed, but Frances did not, because it was my secret, and I had never told her.

So she was puzzled at the sudden business trip, and begged me not to go. She told me that after the christening and Wendy's new pregnancy she needed me to be with her. She would never leave me when I needed her, she told me, and could not understand how I could leave her now. Like a bastard, I used this as an opportunity to reopen the topic of her cuts, and told her that as she had merely been scratched by a cat I could not see why her needs were so pressing.

Frances didn't want to tell me about the cuts, and I could not blame her. I was also keeping secrets: that I was the worst young banker on Wall Street; that there was no pot of money with my name on it; that a woman named Indira had started calling from American Express about my overdue balance; that I needed every penny of my salary to maintain the lifestyle into which she had been born.

So together we guarded these secrets with a perfect silence broken only by Frances's sobs when the limousine pulled up in front of the building to take me to the airport.

Morning-eyed, Frances made me promise to call her as soon as I had arrived, and to come back safely, as if I were leaving for some voyage on perilous seas. I kissed her. She rubbed the scabs on her cuts, as if trying to reawaken the wounds themselves.

I pretended not to hear her sobs as I broke from our embrace, and walked to the waiting car. The limousine pulled from the curb and drove out onto Park. Frances followed behind me, to the sidewalk, a flush of angry red against the cool gray morning. I watched her wilt onto the stoop and felt myself swell with emotion as I had not known since the summer.

Pity, for yourself and another, can be taken as a fitting substitute for love.

# 12

# THE GREATEST DANCER
# IN ALL OF LATIN AMERICA

Even at the very end, with the snubbed nose of an Uzi jammed into his side, Manuel Oliveira Rodrigo Orjuela de Navarro was in love with the world. He claimed to have been conceived aboard a yacht in a Champagne-filled Jacuzzi, and to have eaten salmon tartare from the bottom of the Czech model who took his virginity, and to have once hallucinated after consuming several pounds of caviar. No one doubted him. All he wanted from life was to live at the Carlyle, to eat fine foods, to drink excellent wines, and to make love to beautiful women. Since he frequently did each of these things, and sometimes did them all at once, he was in a fixed state of bliss. Still, it may have run deeper than that.

As a young man Manuel had watched his family squander a fortune of just under a billion dollars in just over a decade. His grandfather was José López Portillo, the Mexican president who impoverished his country but enriched his family during what was until very recently

considered the most inept and financially irresponsible presidency anywhere, ever. Manuel had been raised in Manhattan until 1980, when
his grandfather made his father minister of the interior, a position with
an official salary of fifty thousand dollars and an unofficial salary of
twenty-five million. The family moved back to Mexico City, so Manuel's
knowledge of American politics and culture after the seventies was
spotty. Decades later he maintained an avid interest in disco and
blamed Jimmy Carter for much of what was wrong in the world.

In Mexico City, Manuel came of age amidst million-dollar, limited-
edition Porsches, ten-million-dollar Picassos, and twenty-million-dollar
yachts. Blowing through cash was for him never regrettable in the least,
but just another leisure activity. So when the 1994 peso devaluation
leveled his family's finances, Manuel's general affinity for life was un-
affected. He just blamed Jimmy Carter, and went on. There remained
enough clout and wealth to get him into and out of Harvard, and into
J. S. Spenser, where he never quite fit in. Terence Mathers kept a picture
of Dick Cheney in his office; Manuel kept a faded Polaroid of his bank-
rupt father dancing on a conga line with Bianca Jagger in Mustique. The
American prosperity rests on thin vapors of security and stability that
Manuel had simply never breathed. I sensed this about him even then,
and wasn't surprised when the town car that picked me up at Frances's
door took me not to LaGuardia, but to the private airport at Teterboro,
where a chartered twelve-seat Citation waited to take us to Cabo.

When I arrived, Manuel was in a state of high exaltation beside our
fueling jet, admiring its red and green stripes as he described to the
other Latin American bankers the differences between his tan Ferragamo driving shoes and Thorne's black Belgian loafers. Beside him
stood a beautiful woman whom I recognized as the Brazilian model
to whose *Sports Illustrated* swimsuit photo Roger Thorne had mas-
turbated in his office. We had known that Isabella Ferraz Salles was
dating a Wall Street banker, but had never guessed that banker to be

Manuel Oliveira Rodrigo Orjuela de Navarro. Isabella Ferraz Salles was beautiful. In fact, she was so beautiful that just the sight of her made Roger Thorne remember something that he had been trying to forget all morning.

"Holy shit!" he said, as if realizing that he had lost his passport. "I got engaged last night!"

"Bullshit," I said, because marriage seemed mildly at odds with Thorne's burgeoning career in porn.

"She told me that if I didn't, someone else would . . . ," Roger continued in a tone of puzzled defeat that raised a hint of empathy on the fiercely expressionless face of Isabella Ferraz Salles.

"I am sure she is special girl," said Isabella, squeezing Roger's arm at first to show empathy, and then again because she liked what she had felt.

"Yes," said Roger, mesmerized.

All of this made Manuel understandably nervous. He ran his hands down Isabella's back as if she were a prize pony, and hastened to introduce me to the other Latin American bankers, all of whom shared his unfortunate love of monogramming.

"This is Héctor Esteban Raúl Padrón Enrique de Stefano," said Manuel, introducing me to Héctor, who scratched uncomfortably at his crotch with one hand, and ran another through his elaborately groomed black hair.

"Carlos Ungaro Núñez de Talarico," Manuel continued, as I took the limp hand of a spindly man, the only member of the group to have his initials stitched into the tongue of his belt. He was about to say something when the last banker rudely cut him off.

"Antonio Suárez Sánchez," said the man, swelling his chest with pride.

Finally I was introduced to Isabella Ferraz Salles, who leaned forward, kissed me first on one cheek, then on the other, and then on the first once more. The whole experience made me dizzy, and I was happy to hear Thorne speak to her before I had to.

"Babe, you have an excellent tan," he said.

Isabella shifted uncomfortably beneath his glare, and although her nipples did not escape from her blouse, they did stiffen and shift within it, and this caused Roger to ejaculate. Verbally.

"You're a killer babe from the fourth dimension! A babe with perfect bone structure!" he blurted, and might have gone on had Isabella Ferraz Salles not been distracted.

Her buttocks tightened as she looked and lusted down the runway where a Gulfstream V dropped its landing gear and hit the tarmac with an extended screech. She turned back in a state of excitement, and as she did I believe I witnessed some of the thrill of the descending Gulfstream transfer itself onto Roger Thorne. Isabella stared at him with conflicted intent, kneading her hands; Roger sensed that this was his moment.

"Ciao, mama," said Roger, popping his collar.

"Ciao, Roger," she whispered back in her soft Brazilian accent.

The stairs extended from the forty-five-million-dollar airplane, and three uniformed stewards emerged with two sets of bagggage. One bore the mark of Louis Vuitton, and the other the insignia of the Staten Island Gun Club. From the cabin emerged a woman in a Sergio Tacchini running suit, and behind her came a man in a double-breasted, gold-buttoned navy blazer.

We watched in aspiration and awe as the woman's bright red hair danced in the exhaust of the jet engines. "Who is she?" wondered Isabella Ferraz Salles. As the couple came down the stairs to their waiting town car, I realized that I knew.

"It's Flora Fanatucci," I said, though I wasn't quite sure that I believed it.

"Who?"

"Flora Fanatucci. She's an online Tetris champion . . ."

"Ah, Tetris, I play in Monte Carlo," said Héctor, who gazed on as Flora Fanatucci, international Tetris champion, held onto the arm of J. S. Spenser's chief of European and Asian M&A, Lord Robin Peregrine. When Flora saw us watching she began giggling and waved excitedly.

"He's such a romantic!" she squealed of her new beau, and began to dance so that her breasts bounced. Lord Peregrine blushed as he had not since his days in the showers at Eton.

"She is the Orient of my Occident!" he quoted to Manuel.

"Oh lord, Lord!" squealed Flora.

"A most beguiling creature!" he giddily declared, then helped Flora into the waiting town car whose driver took them away into the Manhattan morning.

"I love her running suit," said Iséabella Ferraz Salles.

"It's Sergio Tacchini," I told her.

"I must have one," she declared.

Soon our pilots arrived and we boarded the Citation.

THE JET WAS UPHOLSTERED IN WHITE LEATHER, WITH A central table covered in white linen decked with trays of champagne flutes and tiered porcelain platters of Manuel's favorite foods. There were toasted blintzes, Astara Persicus caviar, jumbo shrimp, cold filet mignon, chilled Maine lobster tails, smoked Irish salmon, artisanal cheese, chocolate-dipped strawberries, *bloc de foie gras,* white truffles, black truffles, truffle oil, truffle paste, Serrano ham, and sliced melon. Manuel reached into a built-in refrigerator below his seat, removed one of twelve bottles of Perrier Jouët Champagne, and, in an expert motion, filled our flutes. We drank to the beauty of Isabella Ferraz Salles as the Citation mounted the sky, and the jet's cabin filled with

Spanish chatter until Manuel gestured for silence so that he could give Roger and me a brief lesson in gastronomy.

"Irish smoked salmon is much saltier and smokier than Scottish," he explained, gesturing for us to try the fish. "I find it to be especially palatable when combined with a touch of goat cheese, on a toasted blintz, like we have here."

We ate the salmon, which tasted not unlike salmon.

"It is definitely saltier and richer in flavor than Scottish salmon," lied Thorne.

"Of course! Don't be ridiculous!" said Manuel, who then reached across the table and opened a large metal tub filled with thousands of blackish-gray eggs that glistened in the cabin's light. He let their thick scent waft up to his nose and sighed.

"Amazing," he said upon recovery, and anointed each blintz using a small gold spoon, explaining that caviar did not react well with silver.

"The only good caviar is Iranian caviar," he continued. "Everyone is worried about these Taliban bastards in Iran cutting off our *oil*. But what about *good caviar*? What would we do if we couldn't get *good caviar*?"

We laughed, but he was not joking.

"*What would we do*? We would have to be tough! Not like that turkey *Jimmy Carter*! We would have to *take back this caviar from these Taliban bastards*!"

My head hurt as I wondered: Who did he mean by "we?" Mexico? America? A Caviar Coalition of the Willing? I was about to ask, as well as to point out that the Taliban was in Afghanistan and not Iran, when Manuel's perfectly manicured fingers forced a caviar-covered blintz into my mouth. The sturgeon eggs were warm, salty, and intoxicating. Thorne stared at the big metal tub, and his eyes fixed on a price sticker that read five thousand dollars.

"Manuel, how do you expense all of this stuff?" asked Roger, who had recently tried to hide a three-hundred-dollar bill from Bungalow on his corporate card, only to receive an angry call from auditing.

"I bill it all to an internal project that I've had set up for years!"

"What's the name of the project?" asked Thorne.

"Project Awesome!" said Manuel, licking his fingers, slicking his eyebrows, and doing a celebratory dance in his seat.

When done dancing Manuel began to shave a single black truffle over the foie gras. The commingled aromas of truffle and goose liver filled the cabin of the Citation, and unleashed hidden forces. Tightly tailored to begin with, Manuel's pants simply could not contain the more extreme erotic effects of the foie gras and truffles upon his person. A long bulge developed in his pants, growing until it ran eight or nine inches down his thigh. I struggled against laughter, but need not have. High above the earth in a private jet with a Brazilian model and truffled foie gras, Manuel had attained materialist bliss. He sat still for a few moments like a bourgeois Buddha. When he returned to consciousness he showed no memory of our conversation, and quietly set about eating the entire *bloc de foie gras* with a knife and fork. When he finished, he placed his hands above his crocodile-skin belt and below his small belly, then leaned back in the white leather armchair, spent.

Héctor removed a plastic squeeze tube from his briefcase, and began to rub a dark orange cream over his face. Antonio and Carlos soon joined him, and the tube was passed to me when they were done.

"It is prescription bronzer! From Geneva! Illegal in America, because it is so good! Try! You look like a ghost!"

I wanted to believe these men, so I told myself that if I just applied a bit of this stuff I might achieve the mocha tones of my new Latin American colleagues. I took just a dab and rubbed it over my face, unbuttoning my shirt and being sure to get it down into my chest as well.

It began to burn, and the sting woke me from the Champagne stupor. I looked about the cabin in high alert, wondering exactly what this illegal Swiss bronzer would do to me as Héctor, Antonio, and Carlos debated the question, Who provides the best service for Patek Philippe watches in all of Buenos Aires?

Owing to my distress and lack of knowledge of Patek Philippe, I was the only one who noticed as Isabella Ferraz Salles cast a disdainful glance at the drunken, stuffed, sleeping Manuel. Snarling in disgust, she put her flute of Champagne down by her side, and did not move her hand when it touched the edge of Roger Thorne's thigh. Thorne looked down at her delicate fingers, then up at her face. Isabella pressed a bleached white tooth against her painted lower lip, which seemed ripe to explode. The pilot announced that the Pacific Ocean was in view on the starboard side of the plane. Thorne stared dreamily at the great body of water, and something about its sight gave him the courage to let his pinkie slide across Isabella's, and then settle down atop it, and finally entwine with it. She did not resist him.

"Ciao, mama," whispered Roger Thorne to Isabella Ferraz Salles.

"Ciao, Roger," she returned, then closed her eyes and let her body shiver amidst the vibrations of the Citation lowering its landing gear to touch down in Cabo.

J. S. SPENSER'S LATIN AMERICA GROUP PAID JUST A BIT UNDER A million dollars to rent Las Ventanas al Paraiso for the week of the conference. The resort lies on a three-hundred-yard stretch of white beach dotted at intervals by Thai palm trees and thatched cabanas. An extended horizon pool sits just above the breaking waves, and just above this pool a succession of serrated white stucco bungalows provides the promised view of paradise for just under two thousand dollars a night.

The front lobby was a Marxist's nightmare. There were sheiks from Dubai, commodity traders from London, oilmen from Texas, and underworld kingpins from Russia. There were deposed dukes from Paris, Manhattan hedge fund millionaires, and ill-enriched Indonesian timber barons. Among them but above them were early-arrived representatives of the families invited by J. S. Spenser: Slims from Mexico, Mendozas from Venezuela, Santo Domingos from Colombia, and others from the handful of oligarch families that control Latin America. They brought women with them: blondes and brunettes and chocolate-carved Latin princesses who fought for their beauty as their husbands and lovers fought for their wealth. Manuel completely ignored Isabella Ferraz Salles as he filled his lungs with the scents of these people, their colognes, their sweat, their cigarettes, their prosperity. It was good to be home.

"Manuel! We have not seen you since . . . ," began the concierge, who stopped in mid-sentence as Manuel frenetically flicked his eyes in the direction of Isabella Ferraz Salles.

"Since last year?" guessed the concierge at last.

"Yes!" said Manuel with relief. "And it is amazing how quickly the year has gone by! It feels like no more than two or three weeks!"

He had just dodged one bullet of infidelity when two more were fired. A pair of women began to wave at Manuel from the hotel bar.

"Manuel! Manuel! *Ay,* Manuel!" shouted the leggier of the two in a cigarette-cured voice. Her silicone chest bounced behind the strained silk of a red and gold Hermès top as she waved.

"Is it *him*? Is it *Manuel Oliveira Rodrigo Orjuela de Navarro*? Fuck me! It is! *Bueno! Bueno!*" cheered her friend, the more voluptuous of the two.

"Holy Toledo!" exclaimed Manuel, with the thrill of a biologist encountering a species once thought extinct. "It's Lilliana and Silvana!"

The women abandoned their Caipirinhas and in matching white slingbacks shuffled over to say hello. As they approached it became clear that at some earlier point in their lives they had sealed their friendship by hiring a middling plastic surgeon to send them forward in life with the same shrunken pyramid of a nose.

"Manuel! How come you never called us after the weekend in Ibitha last month!" asked Lilliana, the tendons of her thigh rippling like plucked harp strings as she battled the booze for balance.

"You are very bad, Manuel!" said Silvana, adjusting her enormous breasts. "But in Ibitha you were being very good!"

"Ladies! Don't be ridiculous!" said Manuel, his smile growing in proportion to his lie. "What's this about Ibiza?"

"Ibitha," corrected Lilliana. "And it was you and me and the Silvana in the bed with the girl from Madrid and the Algerian pool boy and the wheel of manchego and a bottle of . . ." She might have continued but was silenced by Silvana, who noticed Manuel's companion just a bit too late.

Isabella Ferraz Salles slapped Manuel clear across the face, called a bellhop to take her Ghurka duffle bags and steamer trunks, and turned to Thorne. "Roger," she said. "Please help me to my room."

Thorne looked up to find Manuel resigned to the loss of his Brazilian model, but quite enraptured by the prospect of completing whatever business had been left unfinished in Ibiza with Lilliana and Silvana.

"It's okay, Roger," said Manuel, who would not be made to look bitter in the presence of a young associate. "Help her to her room."

Roger shrugged and took Isabella's luggage.

"You are such a strong boy, Roger," she said with a sigh, and placed her hand on his bicep.

"You're such a fine babe, babe," replied Thorne. And off they went.

THE PUZZLED STARES OF HOTEL STAFF AND GUESTS PROVIDED A clue that my experiment with the bronzer had not been a great success.

But I didn't realize the extent of the disaster until I arrived in my room and looked in the mirror. Parts of my face did look genuinely Latin American, and were as dark and sun-appointed as the fairest stretches of Isabella Ferraz Salles. However, there were sickly ochre streaks between these stretches that were more akin to desert camouflage than perfect Latin skin.

"Serves you right!" I thought to myself as I scrubbed in vain. "You should have gotten past this vanity thing long ago, but no, you're twenty-four and still hooked like a lab rat! Like a rust-colored, streaky lab rat! And it serves you right, motherfucker!"

This botched tan was not the most inauthentic aspect of my Latin American banker persona. I did not speak a lick of Spanish, did not recognize a single face, and the full extent of my knowledge of Latin America was that the place was south of North America and contained Thorne's Chilean Patagonia. As a result I proved glaringly useless even by J. S. Spenser's standards, unable to answer the most basic questions for the invited guests at the twice-daily economic conferences. I was listed in the conference materials as an oil and gas specialist, and daily found myself besieged by Latin Americans eager to benefit from my thoughts on Saudi Arabia's inclination to increase its output of light sweet crude in the next sixth months.

"It's difficult to say," I told them. "But I'll tell you this much: as go the Saudis, so go the Dubaians . . ."

I had furrowed my brow and nodded my head philosophically to try to impart an air of profundity to this bit of nonsense. No one was impressed, and after the incident Carlos Ungaro Núñez de Talarico asked me to avoid one-on-ones with clients for the remainder of the trip. I continued attending, sitting in the back of the room in the hope of salvaging at least some goodwill from the Latin Americans—my last and most pathetic chance at salvaging something from the wreckage of my early career. Thorne was equally useless, but entirely unconcerned. Faced with the prospect of looming marriage, he took refuge in Isabella Ferraz Salles, and by Tuesday had stopped turning up for meetings altogether. The two lovers spent mornings by the pool, and by mid-afternoon the sun would warm their affections to full-blown passion, causing playful giggles and joyous moans to effuse from within Isabella's bedchamber. Yet I did not guess the extent of things between Roger and Isabella until that Saturday, when Manuel asked me to meet him in his room with Thorne. I knocked on the door of Isabella's suite. Roger answered with familiar whip marks across his cheek, his face slick with honey and saliva, and a digital camera in his hand.

"How did you get such big jars of honey?" I asked him.

"Room service," he said.

"And the swing above the bed?"

"Isabella flirted with the janitor and got him to drill it up there today!" Thorne said proudly.

"Ciao, Roger! More honey! Spin me!" moaned Isabella from within the room. As Thorne turned to leave I told him that Manuel wanted to see us that night.

MANUEL HAD INSTALLED HIMSELF IN HIS USUAL SUITE ATOP the resort. The quarters included a formal drawing room, a wraparound terrace, a remote-controlled fireplace, and a gurgling jade fountain. We entered to find him on a divan wearing a monogrammed blue silk robe with matching monogrammed slippers. Outside on the terrace Lilliana and Silvana drank Bellinis and chain-smoked Capri cigarettes, sunning themselves in matching white bikinis. Inside, the sheets were dark with spilled Champagne and, presumably, many other fluids. He removed a pair of cucumber slices from his eyes and informed us of his latest triumph as head of J. S. Spenser Latin America.

"Carlos Slim is worth thirty billion dollars, and wants to divest three billion dollars of his holdings in Mexican telecoms," he began. We were all distracted by Silvana removing her bikini top on the terrace and caressing herself with coconut oil.

"We have been invited to a party on his yacht tomorrow night," Manuel continued. "I want you both to come. The boat is very famous. You may have heard of it, *El Saudade*." He pronounced the name of the boat with reverence, and reminded us that since he had been conceived in a Jacuzzi on a yacht, he always felt at home on the sea. We agreed to meet outside of the resort late the next afternoon, and then turned to leave him to Lilliana and Silvana.

"Roger!" said Manuel as we left. "Please feel free to bring Isabella. I'm not jealous! And I didn't mean to hurt her! It's just that . . . I have so much love to give!" He gestured helplessly to the terrace where Lilliana and Silvana fed each other slices of fresh mango, and in their Donatella Versace voices called for Manuel to remove his robe and join them. "Manuel! Take that silly *cock and balls I don't know what thing* off!" groaned Lilliana.

"*Ay, cock-and-balls!*" laughed Silvana. "Take it off!"

It was not hard to understand how Manuel could be so selfless about the loss of Isabella Ferraz Salles. He even gave Thorne a bit of advice. "She *loves* it when you bite her ear, *just a little bit*!"

"I know!" said Thorne, with excitement. "And naked honey fights!"

"Naked honey fights?" mused Manuel, then called room service, ordered three jars of honey, bid us *buenas noches,* dropped his robe to the floor, and in a bulging cheetah-print thong joined Lilliana and Silvana on the terrace in the fading Mexican sun.

LOTS OF PEOPLE CALLED ME DURING THAT WEEK IN CABO. There was Indira from American Express, who again inquired as to the whereabouts of the three thousand six hundred twenty-one dollars and thirteen cents I owed to her company; there was my father, who wanted to talk about Mickey's failure to get accepted to a single college; there was Mickey, who wanted to know if my father had called to talk about his failure to get into a single college; there was my mother, who wanted to talk about how my father and Mickey were not talking; and there was Terence Mathers, asking why I had never called the Buckley School to reserve a spot for Dewey Ananias Jr. I sent them all to voicemail. The only person I called was Frances, who sent me to voicemail. When finally she called on Saturday night I felt a great rush of homesickness and loneliness and guilt. In the background there was a crash.

"What's that noise?" I asked.

"Meow Zedong," she said. "He just fell off the bookshelf."

"Is he okay?" I asked, wanting to talk about the cat for as long as possible.

"I think he's maybe down to his last life," she said, and there followed a silence, which I broke with gossip.

"Did you hear that Roger and Lauren got engaged?"

"I did," she said. "Phoebe told me that Lauren's dermatologist found a melanoma, and after they took it out her parents told her to stop wasting her time." Frances's voice turned vindictive at the mention of girls wasting their time. She asked me if Roger seemed happy, and I was honestly able to tell her that I had never seen him happier.

"You left me on the street," she hissed, conveniently omitting that in this case the street was six feet from her front door.

"I had to get to the airport. I had to come here," I told her in appeasement.

"It's a stupid trip," she said. "You told me the Latin Americans never do *anything*. You're just there for a *fucking vacation,* and God knows *what else you're doing* . . ."

"God knows what I'm doing? God knows what you're doing in your three-hour private art theory sessions."

I heard the familiar sound of her voice breaking. "Don't say that. Please don't say that. Please just come home. Why can't you just *leave?*"

"We're coming home Monday. It's a private plane. I can't control it."

"You love it. You love all of this shit. I hate it. I hate it all, and I hate this stupid trip," she spat.

"It's more than that. I need this. We need to talk about some things, Frances," I said.

"I have so much I need to tell you," she said and her voice broke again. "I'm not okay right now, Tommy."

"I know, I'll be back on Monday," I told her.

"I hate you," she whimpered.

"Please don't do that," I said.

"I love you," she said, relenting. "I have to go now. Monday . . . ," she said distantly, vaguely, weakly. And I heard another crash as Chairman Meow worked through his last life.


MUCH LIKE MY FACE, THE SKY WAS STREAKED ORANGE AND amber when we met outside of the hotel late in the afternoon that next day. A pair of armored black Lincoln Navigators picked us up, and we set out on a twenty-mile drive up the coast.

"What happened to your face, meng?" asked Carlos, who had been looking at me with concern all week.

"Your illegal tanning cream, asshole," I thought.

"Just a bit of a rash," I said.

"These windows could stop anything but an AK-47!" said Manuel, tapping the inch-thick glass.

"What happens if they shoot us with an AK-47?" asked Thorne, who was sleeping with Isabella Ferraz Salles, and did not want to die.

"Well, if someone comes after you with an AK-47, chances are they are Zapatistas! Or revolutionaries! Or Taliban-Jimmy Carter-cockroaches! Or something like that! So you're fucked!" burst Manuel. "They will kidnap you! And beat you! And torture you! And make your family pay millions of dollars just to get a piece of your earlobe in the post!"

"Really?" asked Thorne.

"That's if you're lucky!" said Manuel.

"Whoa," said Roger, looking out the back window to be sure that we were not being followed.

"It happens all the time in Mexico," explained Manuel. "It happened last Christmas to my cousin, Fabian Aguilar Gonzalez, the greatest dancer in all of Mexico! Those Communist Taliban turkeys kidnapped him on his way to see Enrique Iglesias in Acapulco!"

"Ay, Fabian with his bright Pucci scarves! He loved Enrique Iglesias! And his go-go dancing was *cock-and-balls-I-don't-know-what*!" said Lilliana.

"Ay, *cock-and-balls*!" laughed Silvana. "I will never forget how he freaked me in San Tropez at Les Caves du Roi!"

"What happened to him?" asked Roger.

"No one knows," intoned Manuel. "But wherever he is, he's missing an earlobe."

We came to a private road guarded by a pair of armed men who waved us through upon recognizing the Slim family crest on the Navigators.

"When you are worth thirty billion dollars in Mexico, you have many enemies," explained Manuel.

At the end of this road was a sprawling hacienda whose lawn stretched clear down to the water and served as an impromptu helipad for a large black chopper that now readied its turbines. Guards opened the doors of the Navigators, and after checking our passports walked us to the waiting helicopter. One by one we climbed aboard: Manuel, Lilliana, Silvana, Thorne, Isabella, Carlos, Antonio, myself—everyone except for Héctor, who complained that the tropical heat made it too painful for him to do much beyond lie in bed and regret the past.

The blades cut into the humid day again and again, razing gravity until we rose up and pitched out across the ocean. Soon the coast faded from view, and there was only the pink twilit sky above, the glassy turquoise ocean below, and the lot of us, somewhere between. The newly betrothed Roger Thorne held Isabella closely, pressed his face against the window, and stared in awe at the beautiful ocean. Dolphins breached from the water in sprays of blood and oxygen with doomed tuna writhing in their jaws.

"When I was a little kid I loved dolphins," said Thorne to Isabella Ferraz Salles. "One year I was a dolphin for Halloween, and I used to beg my mom, 'Yo, babe, send me to dolphin camp!'"

"Do they have dolphin camps?" asked Isabella.

"No," said Thorne sadly. "That was the problem."

He closed his eyes and offered a silent prayer to whatever force had placed him here. His contentment only intensified twenty miles out into the Pacific Ocean when Carlos Slim's yacht rose from the horizon. It was not the monstrosity that you might have expected, but still impressive in every way: one hundred and fifty feet long and three stories high with strobe lights that shot up from the helipad near the prow. At the rear of the ship more than a hundred of the luckier people alive mingled around a covered pool turned dance floor. The staff readied the boat to receive the helicopter and stood at attention as we touched down.

The yacht was captained by an amiable Argentine named Gustavo. He greeted us at the helipad and explained that it was Carlos Slim's daughter's sixteenth birthday, and that since the girl was in love with

Johnny Depp, her father was throwing her a masquerade party with a *Pirates of the Caribbean* theme. Captain Gustavo acknowledged that we were in the Pacific, not the Caribbean, but asked us not to mention this to Carlos's daughter, whose poor sense of geography was on this night a source of much joy. Porters took our bags; we followed them to our rooms, where we found our costumes, and after getting settled and changed, joined the party on the rear deck.

It was quite something.

A brigade of hefty, black-suited bodyguards with Aztec features lined the perimeter of the ship; shirtless black men dressed like slaves carried huge wooden canoes filled with oysters and sushi and pyramids of caviar; costumed stilt-walkers toppled across the deck in brilliantly colored silk pants; torch-bearing Moroccan acrobats did jumps across the aft decks, blowing fire from their mouths; baby Bengal tigers play-fought with one another in bamboo cages; and parrots flapped flightlessly from perches high above it all. Carlos Slim's sons, Ricardo and Juan Cristobal, had flown in a team of Eastern European escorts for the night. The women vied with one another for the attentions of the two scions of Latin America's greatest fortune, and drew nasty glares from the aging Latin wives, who struggled against time with frozen brows, plumped lips, and bony mud-tanned frames. And everyone was dressed like a pirate.

"Arghh!" said Thorne, adjusting his long black pirate wig and carrying a giggling, kicking Isabella Ferraz Salles over his shoulder with one arm as though she was a captured princess and waving his plastic sword with the other. His pirate fantasy had now been fulfilled along with so many others, and something about his general glee touched Manuel.

"Tommy!" he screamed above the piratical din of the party. "I know that Terence Mathers is a tough guy to work for. I want you to know that you two always have a home in the Latin America group!

You can see quite well that you don't really even need to know a lot of Spanish. You just need to know a lot of Latin Americans!"

"It really feels like home here," I lied.

"Doesn't it?" he said, and I fought to suppress both delight and laughter as he guided me through the crowd.

"Look!" he said. "Over there by the ice sculptures is Mario Dominguez, the most famous racecar driver in all of Mexico! And that woman by the baby tiger cage is Paulina Velázquez, the greatest soap opera actress in all of Ecuador! And that man there by the big Champagne bottles, the Nebuchadnezzars, that is Roberto Alvarez! He was on the Mexican Olympic cross-country skiing team in 1988!"

I had not known that Mexico even had a winter Olympic team.

"How did he do?" I asked.

"Not so good," said Manuel. "He got lost."

Silvana and Lilliana emerged from the cabin and jiggled over to Manuel. They must have known in advance about the pirate theme, because they were the only women on the boat wearing chain-mail bikinis.

"Do you know how I attract such elegant, refined women?" Manuel asked, quite sincerely.

"I've been wondering that the whole trip," I told him.

"I may not be some great Olympian or racecar driver or actor, but I have a talent that those guys can only dream of. I am the Greatest Dancer in All of Latin America!"

"No! There is no better dancer in all of Latin America than Fabian!" groaned Lilliana. "He freaked my thong into a sailor's knot in Marbella! I love his Pucci scarves and his *cock-and-balls-I-don't-know-what* go-go dancing!"

"*Ay! Pucci scarves! Cock-and-balls!*" laughed Silvana. "Fabian's moves were genius!"

"Perhaps," said Manuel. "But Fabian is gone . . . and I am alive!"

I walked to the second-tier deck to get Champagne, and from there watched with the waitstaff as Manuel took to the middle of the dance floor and shouted to the deejay in Spanish. The man cut from a salsa remix of "The Milkshake Song" to pay homage to the memory of Manuel's cousin Fabian: a disco remix of Enrique Iglesias's "Escape." Everyone cleared the floor and all eyes were on Manuel. As the beat kicked in he began gyrating his pelvis suggestively and strutting like a ripe-for-mating peacock around Lilliana and Silvana, who pressed their bare inner thighs together and began to grind. Manuel now launched into a flamenco-inspired Running Man, inching closer and closer to the girls. He finally joined them, and as a trio they moved their bodies in a single humping rhythm. They ran their hands up one another's torsos and through one another's hair, sweating and heaving until it was too much for anyone to bear. Several of the older women had to ask the waiters for water as things progressed.

The girls bared their cleavage to all by leaning backward like champion limbo dancers, and they began to caress themselves. Manuel jumped up from between them and soared six feet above the dance floor, turned a backflip in midair, and landed in a perfect split between Lilliana and Silvana. They caressed his body with their hands and breasts and began to spin in X-rated pirouettes as Manuel got down on all fours, and after drawing applause with a series of one-armed pushups, did the worm across the deck. Lilliana and Silvana joined him in these perfect undulations and they wormed clear across the boat, then flipped to their feet and began to robot.

"I have not seen anything like this since the days of Fabian Aguilar Gonzalez!" said the directionally challenged cross-country skier.

No one disagreed. The Russian girls and Latin princesses breathed heavily for Manuel, the stilt-walkers whistled from atop their wobbling perches, and the fire-breathing acrobats lit the night in celebration. But Manuel was out to surpass Fabian, not merely to equal him. He helped Lilliana climb atop Silvana's shoulders, and then bent down so that Silvana could climb atop his, and then, with Lilliana standing atop Silvana and Silvana standing on him, Manuel moonwalked backward across the deck. Even up on the second deck, I had to raise my head to see Lilliana, some eighteen feet above the ground. The stilt-walkers looked on in admiration as Manuel glided seamlessly across the dance floor, then began to spin in place, and not stopping until Lilliana and Silvana had jumped from his shoulders and somersaulted down to the deck, each wrapping her legs around Manuel's still-gyrating waist.

There was nothing for any of the partygoers to do but shout and clap, and nothing for Manuel and Lilliana and Silvana to do but beam and bow, and amid all of this shouting and clapping and beaming and bowing not even the Slim family's bodyguards noticed as the first of a dozen grappling hooks was launched onto the prow of the ship from below, and up from a flotilla of rubber rafts climbed the first of the many gunmen who had set out earlier that night to make an example—and a prisoner—of Carlos Slim. In a letter to Mexican authorities taking credit for the assault they would later identify themselves as Zapatistas—poor farmers from the jungle who had been driven to kidnapping and drug trafficking by the cold indifference of the Mexican system—but as they climbed aboard the ship, heads wrapped in bandanas, chests glistening in coarse cotton shirts, loose black pants blowing in the evening breeze, these men in their humble poverty looked not unlike the rest of us in our costumed debauchery. Indeed, to the pirate-costumed partygoers the grizzled Zapatistas looked a lot like pirate-costumed partygoers, and to the grizzled Zapatistas the pirate-costumed partygoers looked a lot like grizzled Zapatistas. Manuel's applause stopped and the deck grew silent as each party stared at the other. One of the men wore a silk scarf with brilliant turquoise and magenta swirls, and something about it endeared him to Manuel.

"You turkeys!" he said, welcoming the new guests to the ship. "Those costumes are *amazing*! I was almost going to board the boat with a grappling hook myself! I mean, *holy Toledo*! You guys *really* look like pirates!"

Manuel's sentence was still fresh when he realized what it was about the scarf that had made him think these men familiar. He froze as Lilliana and Silvana shouted in horror, "Ay! *Cock-and-balls,* this is the very scarf that Fabian Aguilar Gonzalez wore on the night he was kidnapped!"

"Long live the people of Mexico!" said the Pucci-scarved Zapatista, shaking his Uzi in the air, and all at once we realized that these newest partygoers were not partygoers at all.

"You Taliban bastards!" Manuel screamed, trembling with the realization that his cousin was most likely dead, and that he might soon be too.

Men trembled. Women cried. The Zapatistas threw off their shirts, wincing as they tore free the Uzis earlier duct-taped to their hairy backs. The bodyguards drew their guns as reflex and in a lifetime of thirty seconds members of both parties fanned out across the dance floor, berating one another in terrified Spanish to drop their weapons. The only thing between them was Manuel Oliveira Rodrigo Orjuela de Navarro.

The bodyguards might have gunned down the Zapatistas on the spot had they not feared spilling Manuel's presidential blood. Sensing this, the Pucci-scarved Zapatista leader pointed his Uzi at Manuel and motioned for him to come across the dance floor; Manuel had no choice, but resolved to surrender on his own terms. He moonwalked into captivity, clear across the deck, and before handing himself over twisted into a blurring 360-degree spin that would have been the envy of any figure-skating champion. It was to be his last dance move, and with it he saved a great many lives.

The Zapatistas stared at Manuel in awe, unable to figure out how any man could spin so quickly for so long, and in their distraction the Slim family's bodyguards opened fire. I ducked at the sound of the shots and picked up my head to see a gunfight raging below. The Zapatista leader grabbed Manuel and with his Uzi at his back made a human shield of him, then looked on in panic as his band of peasant commandos buckled under the stress of combat, and for good reason. Several of the Zapatistas were heavy smokers, ill suited to the cardiovascular demands of kidnapping. Others were mere children, untrained in the firing of guns. One particularly ineffectual man seemed to be mildly inbred, an Aztec Laurance Whistlestopper. Sensing this disorganization and afraid for their lives, the partygoers joined the fight to save themselves and rescue Manuel. The Eastern European escorts made daggers of their fingernails; the Latin American princesses made missiles of champagne flutes; Carlos Slim's sons fired their bodyguards' guns wildly across the deck.

Deep in the fray was Roger Thorne. With reflexes made razor sharp by countless hours on the Racquet Club's squash courts, Thorne did not pause or flinch as he punched one Zapatista in the face, kicked another in the groin, and bitch-slapped a third into submission. He soon began to exert such gravity on the fight that the Pucci-scarved Zapatista leader cried for someone, anyone, to take him out. I looked on in horror as down below me the inbred Zapatista, evidently desperate to distinguish himself in some small way, shakily trained his Uzi on Roger Thorne.

"Thorne!" I screamed from the top deck, because I had already been part of one colleague's death at J. S. Spenser, and could not bear another.

But he was busy grappling with a man who had attacked Isabella

Ferraz Salles and could not hear me as the inbred Zapatista prepared to fire. I could not fail him as I had failed Makkesh, and I looked about in a panic for a weapon, settling finally on one of the six-foot-tall bottles of Cristal. The staff had fled, so all alone I wrapped my arms around the thick base of the bottle and planted the seeds of future hernias as I strained to raise it just a millimeter off the ground. I paused in exhaustion but had no time to rest and felt tears of anger stream down my face, as with atrophied muscles and clogged veins I lifted it a foot, then two feet, then three, up in the air, against the rail. For a moment I thought I might drop it, but I managed to lock my knees. It was then that I heard a great clap of thunder in the sky, and in a glorious moment felt the tears on my face cooled by a rush of rain. Down below, the baby Bengal tigers broke free from their cages and pounced on the old, fat Zapatista as the inbred Zapatista looked up to see what was making him wet. His face glowed broad and confused in a single flash of lightning. I'll never forget that poor, poor Marxist staring up me and the teetering twenty-thousand-dollar bottle of Champagne that would spell his doom.

"Sometimes we come back as birds!" I screamed down to him. I didn't say it because I had any clear idea of what it meant, but rather because Makkesh had thought it important, and I had imagined that it brought him comfort as he died. That seemed the least I owed this poor retarded farmer; I didn't really want to kill him, but we had been set against each other by the nature of things. There was no malice, but there was no choice.

The Cristal crashed down on him, leaving only a mangled corpse and bloody bubbles that surged across the deck in a red tide. Thorne saw what I had done and that I would need more than his gratitude; in killing their mildly retarded friend I had made myself a target for three of the remaining Zapatistas. Their fat and fatigue were negated by a rush of adrenaline and they ran toward the stairs to seek vengeance. Ever loyal, Thorne left Isabella's side to stop them, and might have succeeded had he not tried to roundhouse kick all three at once. Never one for yoga, Roger pulled his groin. His pain intensified as the Zapatistas pistol-whipped him into a stunned state, then pushed him like a rag doll from their path as they charged up the gangplank. Roger staggered for a moment on the edge of the ship, and it was all that he could do to cast a final look at Isabella Ferraz Salles and grab hold of a life preserver before falling down into the black ocean, where I would soon join him. The Zapatistas came toward me with full guns blazing. Their bullets ricocheted off the brass rails of the yacht turned battle scene, and I had not the luxury of thought as I jumped forty feet down into the sea. The yacht cascaded above me in a flash, and the last thing I saw before crashing into the waves was the Zapatista kidnappers rallying to their Pucci-scarved leader, who with Manuel still at gunpoint had commandeered one of the yacht's lifeboats, and now readied its engines for escape. Resigned to his fate, Manuel cast one final, fond glance at the big bottles of Champagne, and thought that his life had been good, and smiled.

# 13

# In Iesu Spes Nostra Est

The next thing I knew, I was staring up at Jesus. He had a dark, beautiful face and a long, flowing beard. Around his head glowed a light nearly as bright as the sun. He looked down at me, and then he kicked me. Jesus Gonzalez, Thorne and I would learn at great cost, was among the more corrupt rangers of the Mexican National Parks Service. His name was written in black Magic Marker across the breast pocket of his sweat-stained olive uniform, and he wasted no time in extorting us.

"*No te mubes!*" Jesus boomed, then put his hand on his gun and demanded money from us for violating the beach, which was apparently an endangered-species sanctuary. We actually believed him, because he was wearing a Mexican park ranger's uniform and drove a Mexican park ranger's car. Indeed, the kicking and extorting aside, we were happy to see Jesus, because this man and his busted-up VW bug were our best hope for salvation on that barren beach. Frances was right,

I've realized, when she said that in our desperation we mint saviors. It didn't matter that this man wanted our money, or that he wouldn't let us talk. When you're sunburned and homesick and penniless, a guy like Jesus can be the only hope you have. All had been lost during an evening of drifting in the sea: passports, cell phones, wallets, credit cards. We were left with only our soaking loafers, our pirate costumes, and our watches. Though I am not sure that even Thorne's Amex platinum card and all of its customer-care services could have helped us. Once Amex heard I was with him, they would have put Indira on the line, and the old battle ax would have demanded repayment of my three thousand six hundred twenty-one dollars of debt before authorizing any rescue operation.

Whether it was from too much caviar or too much salt water or the jarring sight of Jesus, I do not know, but I felt very low indeed as we sat there on the beach, trying to communicate with the man. We all have thoughts that we fight to keep at bay, and mine now gang-banged me: my mounting debt to Indira; my poor brother, ruled a failure by the world at age seventeen; my only corporate protector, now having his earlobes cut off by leftists. Frances would wait up all night for me, alone but for Meow Zedong the cat, and I would not come home. I could see her seething in the apartment, and the fear of her anger and its likely outlets weakened my wrists and kneaded at my insides. I vomited in the sand.

Jesus looked down on me with disgust, and explained to Thorne in pidgin Spanglish that for a hundred dollars he would be happy to forgive us our trespass. Thorne told him that we had no cash on hand, but plenty at Las Ventanas al Paraiso, back in Cabo. Jesus considered our shared predicament, and with a definitive swatting of the flies from his mustache offered to drive us the sixty miles back to the hotel in exchange for the sworn promise of three hundred dollars upon arrival, and Roger Thorne's Rolex as temporary collateral.

We were in no position to disagree, though I now realize that Jesus liked Roger's watch just a bit too much from the start. He sang to it and he shined it from the moment that Thorne handed it to him, and as soon as we had piled into his foul car and set off back to town he listened to it and he stared at it and finally so lost himself in its sapphire crystal that he landed the VW in the ruts of the jagged jungle road. As the car creaked to a stop, Jesus raised his hands to show them bandaged and bloodied from a morning of clearing trails. He explained that if we wanted to keep going Thorne and I would have to push the car from the ditch.

"Poor Jesus, with no healthcare and gashed hands," I thought, and forgave him even his extortion as we pushed the car out of this ditch.

We arrived at Las Ventanas al Paraiso a bit after midnight. Jesus drew whispers and stares from the staff in the lobby, who didn't know whether to get him medical attention for his hands or call security to escort him out. As it was he didn't stick around long enough for them to make either decision. I walked to the concierge to see if Frances had called; Roger went back to his room to get the money, and in the space of just a few unsupervised seconds, Jesus disappeared, and Roger Thorne's Rolex with him. I was stunned not so much by the man's theft, but rather by the mysteries of physics that had allowed him to vanish so quietly and quickly.

"Jesus!" screamed Thorne when he returned to find him gone along with his ten-thousand-dollar Choate graduation gift.

"Indeed," I said, still mystified.

"You didn't try to stop him, Tommy?" Roger was bereft.

"I, uh, well . . ." I struggled to describe it. "He was just awfully quick . . ." I shook my head in disbelief. "Just supernaturally fast."

"Whatever," said Thorne, resigned. "It's insured. And I'm pretty sure that Lauren's getting me this killer ice blue Sub Mariner for an engagement present anyway."

The great swirl of newspapers and magazines arranged in the hotel lobby showed that news of the attack on the yacht had swept Mexico, and told the story of how the wounded vessel had been rescued by the Mexican Coast Guard and towed back to Cabo that morning. *Quién* magazine published pictures of Manuel as a young boy with his pet puma and all but pronounced him dead; *Chilango* expressed hope that he and Fabian were together in captivity, and that in time they would escape with a full repertoire of new dance moves; *¡Hola!* ran as its cover a grainy cell phone picture of Roger Thorne head-butting one leftist while karate-chopping another. Its headline read: EL GRINGO MISTERIOSO.

Perched at the hotel bar, chain-smoking and wistfully staring at this picture of *el gringo misterioso,* were Lilliana and Silvana. Like many of the guests they had stayed on for an extra day to let their nerves settle after the attack. They wore no makeup, and their small noses were swollen, their eyes red and puffy. They gave us each four kisses on our cheeks and told us how happy they were that we were not dead. I thought that Lilliana and Silvana were the saddest people I had ever seen until Thorne learned about Isabella Ferraz Salles.

"She thought you were being so dead, Roger!" said Lilliana.

"She crying all the way back to the hotel!" added Silvana.

"Is she here now?" asked Roger, excitedly.

"No," said Lilliana. "She feel much better today and fly to *Majorca* on *Gulfstream* with *Juan Cristobal Slim*!"

Isabella, it seemed, had grieved Roger's passing for just shy of a day, and then learned to love again with the son of a multibillionaire.

"Oh," said Roger, stunned. "I guess that's just how it goes when you rock it with these swimsuit babes."

He looked down at his watch, but it, like his love, was nowhere to be found. It is no easy thing for a man to lose his watch and his love in the space of a single day. Thorne's eyes grew moist as he stammered to excuse himself, explaining that he was exhausted and ought to be getting to bed. Isabella Ferraz Salles had managed what a thousand Ivy League graduates and prep school princesses had not. She had hurt Roger Thorne. Stung, the great WASP grabbed several copies of *¡Hola!* and was gone.

The night was a torture of sweats and loneliness and nausea. From the very moment that I got to my room I began calling Frances. I called her cell phone. I called the apartment. I even called her beach house, not because I thought she was there, but because it felt good to know that I was sending a ringtone across the lawn and the pool, and that at least these things retained traces of perfection. I called and called, but no ring would turn into that most rare of sounds, a soft and familiar voice. I called until I was desolate. I called until my fingers hurt from dialing. I called until I fell asleep, and then I woke on Tuesday and called again. I was still praying for an answer when the concierge broke through with Roger Thorne and Terence Mathers on the line.

Mathers explained that he had new J. S. Spenser Amex cards couriered to our hotel from Spenser's office in Mexico City; that Flora Fanatucci's replacement had booked us a return flight the next morning on AeroMexico, the only carrier that would accept passengers with less than twenty-four hours' notice; and that Spenser's global security office had arranged for Roger and me to receive new passports from the U.S. Consulate in Cabo the very next morning. He then addressed the matter of the most recent thing that I had failed to do for him.

"Quinn, do you know what didn't happen yesterday?" he asked, and then proceeded to tell me. "Yesterday the Buckley School announced next year's kindergarten class. Guess who isn't on their list?"

"Who?"

"Dewey Ananias Junior," said Mathers.

"Oh shit," I said.

"Damn right 'Oh shit,'" fumed Terence. "That little thumbsucker's gonna wind up at P.S. 141 with motherfucking Latrell Phelps!"

This seemed unlikely.

"Aren't there a lot of other private schools in Manhattan?" I began, but was cut off.

"Do you know how angry Ananias was? Do you know that he entrusted this to me, and that I entrusted it to you? That's not high-level accounting, Tommy. That's basic responsibility. Do you know what Latrell Phelps is going to do to Dewey Junior in the fall?"

"Can't they just—"

"He is going to make him his animal cracker-ass bitch. Yes, he is going to make little Dewey Junior suck his shit. They do that up there. You know . . . Harlem . . ."

"I thought you found Latrell Phelps inspiring?"

"I do. He inspires me to reform the legal system and start treating juveniles as adults," said Terence. "Oh, I really thought I had gotten through to him in those first three mentoring sessions. Then we got together for hot dogs and basketball again last weekend. The little shit threatened to cut me. He was wearing all red, with a do-rag. I think he's joined the Bloods. I can tell you for damn sure that he stole my cell phone. I've been getting voicemails all week from a guy named Jerome looking for weed—"

"I've actually got a pretty good weed hook-up," offered Thorne, who had been on the call for the duration of my emasculation.

"Good for you, Roger. Now hang up the phone," said Terence.

"I'm so sorry," I said, acutely aware that my last corporate protector had been kidnapped, and resigned myself to failure on most of life's major fronts. "Just tell Ananias that it's my fault, and that—"

"You'll tell him yourself," Mathers interrupted. "He wants to see you and Cheech Thorne when you get back in the office on Thursday. I'd be shocked if this didn't come up. Quite a year you've had—"

"You've no idea—"

"Don't miss your flight."

He hung up.

IT GOES WITHOUT SAYING THAT WE MISSED OUR FLIGHT. THE people in the consulate made us each tell our story seven times, tweaking it until it fit their vision of events. Then a dyslexic cabby took us to the airport, driving us to the Delta and Continental terminals before finally getting us to AeroMexico, just in time to see our plane taxi down the runway and lift off into the sky. The terminal air was thick with cigarette smoke and thin with oxygen. I stood in line, exhausted, covering my mouth, retching in place. At long last Thorne and I approached the ticket agent and asked her to please help us leave her country as quickly as possible.

"Is there anything leaving for New York tonight?" Roger asked, and the woman told us that all was booked for two days straight.

"Do you have anything in the region?" I asked, and she said that there was a flight to Chicago, and that from there we could get to a great many lower-tier American cities.

"Philadelphia, Raleigh-Durham, Providence . . ."

"Philadelphia!" said Roger, as if he were a Diasporic Jew and it were Jerusalem. "My cousin's at Penn and he's a member of The Owl and they've got crazy babes and ill blow. Rebound! We'll take it down."

Under different circumstances I might have gone to Philadelphia with Roger, just to help him mend his wounded heart. The thing was that somewhere within the list of second-tier cities I thought I had found an opportunity to start making things right.

"Can I get on the flight to Providence?" I asked, realizing that Frances in Manhattan was only three hours away, and Mickey in Portsmouth Abbey's dorms and Alastair in Portsmouth Abbey's grave-yard only forty-five minutes. It seemed a rare opportunity to mend things with the people closest to me, with whom things in a thousand unintended ways had gone wrong. If I had known how it would all play out, I wouldn't have worried about Mickey a bit. I would have bought the most expensive ticket to Manhattan from any airline will-ing to sell, just to be with Frances that evening. But Mickey's string of college rejections had made me realize just how badly I had neglected my younger brother, and I felt I needed to see him. "At least I've been there for Frances," I thought, like an absolute fool.

THE AEROMEXICO PLANE WAS SIMILAR TO THE CITATION THAT had brought us to Mexico in that it also had wings and an engine. I was seated in the middle aisle, crushed between a row of seven unbeliev-ably thin UVA sorority girls heading to a beach house in Cape Cod af-ter a coitus-filled post-graduation celebration at a Sandals resort. The sight of their emaciated frames woke my appetite, and I found myself famished after twenty-four hours of nausea-induced fasting. When the stewardess came around offering AeroMexico peanuts I greedily grabbed a fistful of bags, and dared her to protest with a death stare. I had, after all, recently killed a man. I feasted on these peanuts, bag af-ter bag, as happily as Manuel on his *bloc de foie gras*. I closed my eyes, reclined the seat, and fell asleep.

I switched at O'Hare, and after a short hop landed in Providence at four thirty. I rented the last car available at Avis, a burgundy Kia Sportage, and in this triumph of Korean engineering headed to Ports-mouth Abbey. On talk radio I listened to enraged conservatives dis-cussing illegal immigration, and I thought how amazing it was that in the modern era a man could go from an old German car in a Mexican rain forest to a new Korean car on a New England highway, all in the space of forty-eight hours. Soon I pulled into the craggy, shaded lane leading to the school, feeling overwhelmed by the intense beauty of the campus in late spring.

The sun ignited the garnets in the stones of the campus's gothic buildings, and made the copper roofs of newer structures unbearably bright. Were it not for its Catholicism, Portsmouth Abbey might have been one of the nation's great prep schools. Many Kennedys had attended—Bobby for a year before switching to Choate, Teddy for several years before being expelled for hanging his roommate from his window by the poor man's feet. Somewhere along the way the place had slipped, but it was still gorgeous. Between the dormitories and the academic buildings stretched great grassy quads, all on anabolic fertilizers, glowing unnatural shades of green. In the middle of the campus, off the holy lawn that Mickey had once made his personal snow-based sex museum, a large tent had been pitched. Inside it a brass band played, their bouncy beats mixing with the happy conversation of young men and women and the breaking of the waves on Narragansett Bay.

It seemed my lot to be forever wandering, uninvited but well received, into other people's parties. Every year at Portsmouth the faculty gave a clambake to honor the class of graduating seniors, to thank them for the one hundred and twenty thousand dollars that their parents had spent on a third-rate prep school diploma, and to wish them luck wherever it was said diploma was taking them. I walked along the garish green lawn, and joined the newly graduated young men who seemed, and in some cases may have been, quite refined, and the newly graduated young girls who seemed, and in some cases may have been, quite virginal.

The chapel bells began to toll "Amazing Grace," and I began to look around for Mickey. My plan was to find him and use my total lack of association with or regard for his school to pull him away for the night. As the only non-college-bound senior in his class he would probably want to leave anyway. We would have dinner in Newport and bill it to J. S. Spenser. I would tell him everything, and ask him to tell me the secret of not being so broken by it all. Across the tent I saw a young girl whom I recognized from a picture in Thorne's office. She didn't seem broken in any way, and reminded me of how Frances might have been in the time before I knew her.

Lilly Schuyler had just recently become beautiful and was not yet aware of it. Her plain brown eyes simply beheld the world, and so by default were great wonders. Her entire being seemed made for the warm evening light that illuminated the wisps of honey that slipped from her hair as she talked. Perhaps in time she too would know the ghastly terrors of marriage-inducing melanomas. Right now it was I who felt ugly and old, then bathed in a great many shades of shame as the young girl recognized my stare.

"It's Mickey's brother!" she said, and once she fell silent I longed to hear her lips make music again. "I'm Lilly," she went on to say. "I know you from the picture on Mickey's desk."

We both knew each other from pictures. And though it felt quite sordid for me to have picked her out in Thorne's office, she was unashamed to know me from Mickey's desk. This, I realized, was because I was by that point indeed quite sordid, and she was, and I imagine always had been, unashamed.

"It's so nice to meet you," I said, deciding against telling her how I already knew her. "Is Mickey here?"

"That's actually what everyone keeps asking," she said, as if the sum total of human curiosity were contained beneath the tent. "He didn't show up this morning at assembly, though that's sort of normal for Mick. He set the record for taking blue cards this semester."

"Blue cards?" I cringed to ask this question, which revealed me as a product of public schools.

"The infirmary gives you red cards for sickness, and blue cards for being crazy," she explained. "Well, Mickey used all his red cards last semester, so he had to move on to blue cards. I don't think there's any limit for blue cards."

Mickey had gone from sick to crazy. I looked around the tent at the college-bound men and women with plastic plates of salad and hamburgers, all celebrating and discussing their admissions to Rollins and Saint Lawrence and Duke and Bates and Bowdoin and Trinity and Yale. It was a masturbatory affair, and Mickey had always preferred actual masturbation to socialized masturbation. I would have bet the full available line of credit on my J. S. Spenser Amex card that he was in his room using the school's Internet connection to subvert its moral ideals.

"Where is his room?" I asked.

"Well, they just kicked him out of St. Hugh's for stocking the fountain with tropical fish," she explained. "I think now he's over in Benet." Lilly pointed to an old gothic building that rose across the quad, overlooking the bay.

"You'll need a card to get in," she said, brushing back the strand of divine hair once more. "Come, I'll take you."

She walked uncertainly on a pair of long legs only very recently transmuted from genetic code to flesh. She told me about Mickey's failed tenure on the student council, from which he was dismissed for lack of attendance after an initial failure to get hang gliding funded and approved as a varsity sport. She told me about his performance on last semester's French oral exam, for which he had failed to memorize any of the prescribed vocabulary, but received a mercy C-minus by spewing perfectly accented, perfectly meaningless dialogue. She told me how strange it was that although he could not remember a single word in French, he knew the exact species of every bird on campus.

Lilly told me these things as we walked around the dorm, and I looked out at the big ocean which had long ago become mere backdrop for her. I followed her inside Mickey's dorm, through the 1970s-era common room of foosball and Ping-Pong tables. We walked down a stale-smelling, soft-green brick hallway until we came to a door from whose knob dangled half a dozen pieces of navy blue cardboard.

"I told you he has the record for blue cards," said Lilly, admiring the certifications of self-declared insanity.

The door was locked, but the lock was old and soon broken. The door swung open, and Lilly and I beheld Mickey's empty single, which looked less like an idyllic vision of Americana than like a very preppy section of downtown Beirut. A stale air of vice swept over us, equal parts tobacco juice, pubescent sweat, cigarettes, marijuana, Febreze, stale beer, and, most strangely, sulfur. The very noxiousness of these fumes seemed to have scared away any lingering oxygen long ago. On the floor was an outcropping of blue and pink and white oxford cloth, the several dozen filthy shirts that my mother had bought for Mickey in the hope that wearing them might make him less himself. The pile bled strands of Hermès silk out onto the stained industrial carpeting in whose gray synthetic fibers were nestled fine sediments of grime: yellowed cigarette filters, crushed orange Adderall tablets, pulverized white Ritalin powder, sticky splotches of spilled soda and plasticized gum. The sight and smell reawakened my nausea. I began to regret my feast of AeroMexico peanuts.

Mickey's bed was a demonstration of frustrated eros: His sheets had not been washed since he left Rye with them that summer. Then they had been off-white, but now they were light brown and peppered with innumerable gym socks that had been used for more than gym. Amid these sheets and socks was a modest trove of soft-core pornography: copies of *Maxim* and *FHM* turned to airbrushed pictorials of Sarah

Michelle Gellar and Tara Reid. I wondered only that Mickey had not found better material with which to pleasure himself but wondered no more as I looked above the bed to find a poster of Jenna Jameson, which, for all of his distractions and disorganization, Mickey had made time and arrangements to have autographed by the woman herself. On a faux mahogany desk in the corner of the room was a pile of papers that I walked toward and sorted through, finding a library of failed and incomplete academic work. Its wonders included but were not limited to: a three-paragraph paper on the apparently not-so-complicated French Revolution; a proposal for a science project in which Mickey Quinn would "gain deeper understanding of our planet" by "simulating a live volcanic eruption" using "only baking soda and vinegar"; and a math quiz whose very staggering wrongness was itself a bold refutation of the Newtonian universe. Atop all of these papers were their ugly children, letters of rejection from the colleges that had once presented his best hopes: Saint Lawrence regretted that their class was filled with an unexpected number of early applicants. Hobart acknowledged Mickey's many fine achievements, but lamented the competitiveness of this year's crop. The president of Holy Cross wrote personally to acknowledge the many calls he had received from my father's social betters, and to regretfully explain the utter impossibility of matriculating Mickey Quinn. Nearly overwhelmed by the piles of detritus was a framed picture of me and Mickey in our blazers, taken the previous Fourth of July before heading out to the club. I thought with pain of Frances and the year gone by. Lilly's voice only made it worse.

"I'm not sure that I've ever seen a room of Mickey's this bad," she said in astonishment. Her eyes settled on the picture of Jenna Jameson, then looked down in embarrassment at her own beautiful feet. She kicked at Mickey's pile of laundry with the turquoise leather flower at the tip of her sandal, and as the pile spilled, Lilly recoiled as if it might attack her, a fear that was entirely justified. Between the semen-soaked socks and the amphetamine-laced carpet it seemed hardly unreasonable to think that somewhere in his primordial mess Mickey might have stumbled upon the building blocks of life. As it was, the pile merely toppled over, and as the shirts and ties spread out they revealed themselves to have concealed a hastily torn-open box from Amazon.com, from which now slid several titles, including *Flying by the Seat of Your Pants: A Hang Glider Pilot's View of Life* and *Hang Gliding Training Manual: Learning Hang Gliding Skills for Beginner to Intermediate Pilots.* Finally I noticed the one book that Mickey may have managed to read in full: *The Ewoks' Hang Gliding Adventure.*

I picked up his copy of *The Ewoks' Hang Gliding Adventure* and stepped over the clothes and the other books to Mickey's desk, where I noticed one thing that was not like the other ones; a printed acknowledgment from American Airlines showing that Mickey's debit card had been accepted for a charge of thirteen hundred twenty-one dollars and twenty-two cents to fly from Providence to San José, Costa Rica, that morning. Rejected from every school in the entire country that might take him, my brother had simply rejected the entire country. Mickey had flown from Providence to the jungle that morning, just as I was headed from the jungle to Providence. I couldn't even claim surprise. He had declared his intention to the entire family that summer, and we had ignored him, because we were drunk and babbling about bastard babies. My only real wonder was how he had paid for it. I pulled open his desk drawer, and within its plywood confines rolled several dozen empty, amber prescription bottles, all made out to Mickey Quinn.

"It's funny, right?" said Lilly, who had assumed the existence of this drawer long before ever seeing it. "They give this stuff to the kids with D's, and they sell it to the kids who are getting A's."

"I'm sorry?" I asked, unfamiliar with the workings of the boarding school Ritalin black market.

"He's the biggest Ritalin dealer on campus," said Lilly, now embarrassed to learn that I didn't know that Mickey Quinn had established himself as the Pablo Escobar of Portsmouth Abbey.

I thought first of how my father would react. A freckly knot would consume his face, and he would grow deeply ashamed, not for Mickey but for himself. I hated him for this, and in that moment of hatred I reveled in the cosmic elegance that, after Alastair's peanut oil–fried egg roll and Mickey's Costa Rican hang gliders, I should be the last of my father's sons standing at his beloved Portsmouth Abbey school. Brian Quinn would never learn of the Ritalin dealership; Lilly and I would gather the bottles and throw them away in the dumpster behind the dorm. But the beautiful thing was that, even if he had known, it would not have mattered. Mickey was in Costa Rica, with thousands of dollars of his classmates' parents' money, swooping up and down, high above the jungle canopy, a great bird among other great birds. I had wanted him to tell me the secret of not being so broken by the world, and in absentia he had revealed the secret to be just that: absentia. The only way to avoid the bastards? Flee. Fake sick, fake crazy, sell your meds, book a flight, do whatever, don't think twice. Flee. Because once you set foot in the amazing machine, the world of fanged stepmothers and suffering lovers and melanoma marriages, it's all over. You'll be hooked. You'll never get out. I had been on a stretch of virgin beach just two days earlier, miles away from my troubles, sick to my stomach just to get back to it all.

I stood looking at the flight receipt and shook my head at Mickey, who would not stick around to suffer. Marvelous little shit, my brother. I let out a small laugh that must have sounded like a whimper, because Lilly stepped around the pile on the floor and placed her hand on my back. I turned around with the Ewok book still in my hand and thought how uncannily she resembled a young Frances, and how beautiful she was. I felt so ashamed for finding her so beautiful that I almost didn't hear when she said that she had been dating Mickey all semester. She could not believe that he would leave without telling her.

"Are you all right?" I asked.

"He kept talking about it," she said. "I just never thought he'd do it."

Mickey Quinn had left behind the prettiest girl at prep school for a jungle that existed only in my mind. Right then and there, I knew that he had surpassed Alastair as the greater of my brothers.

WE DISPOSED OF MY BROTHER'S SMALL DRUG OPERATION, AND returned to the tent just in time to see the clambake dispersing. The faculty remained as the girls walked back to their dorms, careful not to stain their shoes on the grass, and a group of boys skulked down to the shore for an illicit cigarette. Members of both groups looked at Lilly in the way that semi-attractive people look at stunning people, and they whispered to one another.

As it has always been my dream to impress a sixteen-year-old girl by showing her my burgundy Kia Sportage, I didn't decline Lilly's offer to walk me back to my car. I knew that there was one place left that I needed to go, and somehow I wanted her there with me. We started slowly around the holy lawn, bidding farewell to the second graduating class in the school's history to begin with a Quinn and end without him. Oh, Alastair.

Lilly talked about her cousin in New York who had just gotten engaged, and though I knew a great deal about Lauren Schuyler and Roger Thorne, I took care not to ask any questions that might reveal this fact. I wanted to know her only as I knew her.

"She's so gorgeous and sweet and she used to baby-sit me in the summer at Fishers," she explained. "She's been dating the greatest guy and it's just amazing. I mean, they are so, so happy together."

"It is amazing. I'm not sure I know anyone like that," I said, because it was true, and because I wanted for her to stay beneath the cool shade of delusion for a very long time.

At the far end of the holy lawn a team of migrant Latino laborers with gasoline-fueled Toro weed whackers and bottles of insecticide tended to a slightly smaller lawn. I knew why they moved about so gently, and what they were taking such care to avoid stepping on, although I wasn't going to mention a thing until Lilly did.

"That's the graveyard," she said guilelessly, and I assumed that she knew of Alastair and the egg roll.

"I've only been there once," I told her, and without a word we walked off the pebble path, toward the small plot.

The cemetery was perhaps ten dead people wide and twelve dead people deep. Its one hundred and twenty dead residents were afforded a bit of privacy in which to enjoy eternity by a perimeter of Japanese dogwoods. Fully bloomed, their petals glowed pink and white in the waning day's sun. It had been a decade since my father had taken me here to see the school, though he had really brought me here to see the grave. I realized with some satisfaction that I no longer remembered where Alastair was. Lilly smiled warmly as I meandered around the headstones, finding this one too old, and that one too new, to be Alastair. Finally, four rows in, beneath the shade of a leaning dogwood, I found him, somewhere in the middle of receiving a nice chemical spray and a light trimming from a stout middle-aged Guatemalan. His name, Cesar Augusto, had been embroidered by an unsteady hand across the breast of his stained green jumpsuit. Cesar Augusto seemed a very pleasant man. I say this because he turned off his weed whacker and hung his head solemnly when he saw that Lilly and I had come to see the grave. Gasoline fumes overwhelmed the scent of the freshly cut grass as he cut the machine's small engine. The smell mixed with the deadly sweetness of the pesticides made my stomach feel as if it were being massaged by a very small hand. I tried not to breathe as I read the inscription on the stone, whose once flawless Florentine marble had been chipped and greened by weather and moss over the past eighteen years.

ALASTAIR WALSH QUINN, 1973–1989, *IN IESU SPES NOSTRA EST*, it read.

*"In Jesus is our hope,"* translated Lilly, in an attempt to demonstrate her mastery of Latin, and offer comfort.

"Do you really think so?" I asked her.

"I like to think so," she said.

I stood there looking at the tombstone, knowing that the bones of my brother were just a few feet beneath my feet. I wondered whether he was the only person in the entire graveyard not dressed in a robe. I wondered what state his last blazer and pair of loafers were in. Could you take off his tie and wear it new as the day they had put it on him? Or do these things rot too? I wondered if the worms had eaten him and his clothes, or if caskets were too advanced to let that happen these days. I wondered if there was any truth at all in the inscription, and since Lilly seemed convinced by it I sought the only other opinion immediately available.

"What do you think, Cesar Augusto?" I asked the Guatemalan gardener, gesturing toward the inscription at the base of the grave. "Any truth to it?"

As it happened, Cesar Augusto's language skills had not developed in step with his gardening skills. He followed my hand not to the Latin quote, but to several angry tufts of crabgrass that had made their home atop Alastair. He nodded his head in acknowledgment and apology, and with his squirt bottle doused the weeds with fresh poison. Wanting so badly to be understood I now gestured more emphatically toward the tombstone, curious for this man's thoughts on Jesus and hope. But nowhere is it written that we get to be understood. Perceiving my expression as conveying only further dissatisfaction with his gardening, Cesar Augusto blasted the crabgrass once more, and reflected on its tenacity.

"I spray, yes. It go away, yes. But always, come right back," he struggled to explain, then shrugged, started his weed whacker again, and with it trimmed the grass behind Alastair's headstone.

# 14

## FLOOD ON PARK,
## PARK ON LEXINGTON

I got back to Manhattan at seven minutes to midnight. I parted with the Kia at an Avis in midtown, and then completed the last leg of my return to Frances on foot, because I had no cash for a cab. The city streets re-radiated the day's heat, which seemed to fuel the hatching of insects into the early-summer air. So it was through the buzz of a living haze of mosquitoes and gnatlings that I made out the sirens of police cars and then saw the small crowd gathered at Park and Sixty-fifth Street. As I approached the scene it became clear that it was that most spectacular of urban marvels, the broken water main. Plumes of water went ten, eleven, twelve feet into the air. A team of city workers sweated and strained with steel braces and magnesium torches, but the water only came stronger, lilting up against the streetlights before pounding down atop an unfortunate Mercedes.

The wheels of the Mercedes were engulfed by a brackish puddle fast spreading across the intersection, and on its shore I joined the gathered residents of Frances's co-op. I pretended to share their concerns but did not. Spending an evening adrift in the Pacific makes it hard to really fear puddles. The next day's *Times* would report that the pipe was laid in 1903, but to me it seemed much older. The crowd groaned as its rust-eaten surface crumbled under the weight of the men and equipment intended to fix it, then fully disintegrated. The water shot up bits of asphalt shrapnel. The workers covered their faces, and the foreman declared that no one should expect much progress before the morning. I waded downstream to Frances's door, where a light shone from the second-floor window.

I took the extra key from the carriage light, then opened the door and stepped into the foyer. As I walked slowly up the stairs I thought of how I would tell her about the Zapatistas and the big bottle of Champagne and Jesus, and how she would love these stories even more than the story of Chaim Spero, and how, if I told them just right, she would forgive my long absence. There was a light on in the living room, and it glowed on a Sloan, but not the one I was looking for. Slumped over the arm of the overstuffed sofa where she had smoked away her year was not my Frances, but Bo. He had been dressed quite nattily for something—a hastily arranged birthday dinner at the Brook Club, I would learn—but as the universe grows messier by the hour, so do its occupants. His tie looked like one I owned, but was spotted with drool. His soft blue shirt might have cost him three hundred and fifty dollars, but was now a rag of sweat. His initialed Tiffany belt buckle dangled unclasped above his unzipped pants and, opened to a nude pictorial of Scarlett Johansson and Keira Knightley on the cushion beside him, the February issue of *Vanity Fair* told the rest of the story. I too had been in this position, and I can tell you that even though masturbation ranks among life's most inconsequential endeavors, failure at it is significant beyond measure. But this was not the first thing to cross my mind.

"Why is Bo here and, why is Frances not?" I wondered.

"Why not wake him up and ask?" I wondered further.

"How can I do that when he is passed out with his pants undone?" I wondered finally, and there followed an epiphany.

I knew that much of being polite lies in minding the boundaries between what you know about other people, and what they know you know about them. But this took me only so far. To really succeed, I had to do more than mind these boundaries. I had to actively build them. So I crossed the floorboards, tightrope style, and from Bo's side removed the too-lurid but not-lurid-enough issue of *Vanity Fair,* then gifted him an alibi with the only other reading material available: Mickey Quinn's copy of *The Ewoks' Hang Gliding Adventure.*

I slapped Bo gently across the face. He stirred and stared, first blankly at me, then around the room, and finally with some concern at the book that had just materialized beside him.

"Mr. Sloan, what are you doing here? Where's Frances?" I managed to ask. He gave a drunken sneer, as if I ought to know the answers to both of these questions. Then he picked up Mickey's book.

"I must have taken this from the club," he said. "I don't remember doing that, though . . ."

Bo's past troubles now made way for new concerns: Had he stolen anything else? Had anyone witnessed his theft? And what had he been doing reading a *Star Wars: Return of the Jedi* book with his pants undone?

"Where is Frances?" I asked him again.

Bo ascribed the book to the great mass of human mystery, then birthed an ursine yawn that caused his eyes to tear, and perhaps allowed him to access a deeper grief. He stared at me through twin wounds, and struggled to make it all clear.

"Frances is . . . *tired? Tommy?*" he said. "She's just *so very tired.* She's away. And she'll rest for a while."

He nodded to approve this condensed version of events. I considered what being *so very tired* might mean for a girl accustomed to slicing her arms, and I realized what in truth I already knew. The blood rushed to my head just as two days earlier it had rushed from her wrist.

Bo nodded softly, and in this single motion acknowledged all that we both understood, and also another truth: Artful arrangement of words can turn a lunatic to an eccentric, an addict to a connoisseur, a lecher to a bon vivant, but every now and again language refuses to be so whored. It abandons us to our rancid selves. Bo could call Frances "tired" all he wanted, but that wouldn't make it right. So he jerked his arm up from the couch, and held it out like a zombie. Gold blazer buttons fell to the floor and cotton tore as in a single motion Bo ripped bare his forearm, and twisted it to show the soft white skin of his wrists. Then, in morbid pantomime, he slashed himself with two shaking fingers, making clear a painful truth as painlessly as possible. There was only one thing to be said.

"I know," I said.

"I know you know," he said.

His face fell into his hands, and he was no longer so big or noble. The clanking of the workmen outside was now drowned out by pained whimpers that I had heard only once, long before. I sat just an inch from Bo's curdled figure, then placed my hand on his shoulder and left it there to be smacked away by the gold of his wedding ring. But Bo was unlike my father. He leaned into me, and I into him. Not because we could make things better for each other, but because we could not. Because we now each knew the same dreadful things, and through them, at least for a while, knew each other. Bo lifted his head, raised himself an inch from the couch, and looked out the window where the men continued battle against the fast growing puddle.

"You could drown in that thing," said Bo. "You could drown anywhere, and there's nothing to be done about it."

He was right, that you could drown anywhere, that there was nothing you could do about it, that it was now perhaps too late to seek a newer world. Hadn't Frances gone under in a perfectly arid living room? And what could I offer him beyond the shared absorption of the blow? Where would I find hope for us? In the Bible that baptized Sunshine? In Frances's book-projectile about Magritte? Or perhaps in a nice rehab memoir. No, there was nothing to be done about it. Except flee, and I thought of flight as Bo tucked Mickey's book into his jacket pocket, and hauled himself up from the sofa on a second attempt. I rose with him, and he turned to me.

"I borrowed a tie," he said, looking apologetically at the filthy strip of silk.

"It's all right," I said.

He then raised an aged hand to my face, and slapped me lightly on the cheek, then felt the whiskers of my juvenile beard. And in this way we said good night.

Bo went to Frances's bed, and I to the guestroom where my thoughts turned to The Earth and the Planets Today. At the end of that class we watched Stephen Hawking deliver a speech in which he argued that humanity's best hope for survival lay in making good on Mars. I spent the better part of that class teaching myself origami with notebook paper, but a year later I thought how Hawking had probably been right. You might expect a robot man to be just a step ahead of the rest of the species.


BO SLOAN WOKE ME AT SIX THE NEXT MORNING, AND WE LEFT the apartment to play squash at the Racquet Club. On the hardwood courts you would never have guessed that the man had been drinking the night before, or for that matter, for the better part of the last forty years. He pirouetted like a ballerina to return some balls, rushed low to the ground for others, and sweating from his nostrils like some Pamplona bull smashed against walls again and again without so much as a grimace. I looked at him with some awe on that court, thinking that for all of his messes and pain Frances loved him dearly, and that he somehow made more sense than my own mystery of a father. In the steam room we sat naked, and Bo added to our body of shared knowledge: Anyone who asked was to be told that Frances was receiving spa treatments at Canyon Ranch, the resort in Arizona. He, Frances, and I would alone know the truth, that she was receiving treatment of a different sort at Silver Hill, the genteel . . . well, I guess it is a mental hospital, up in New Canaan.

"She's allowed visits in two weeks," Bo told me, as we settled into a long green leather couch and wrapped towels about our torsos to effect terry-cloth togas. "I know she wants to see you, Tommy."

"I'll be with her as soon as I can," I told him, knowing that there was most likely quite a bit of free time ahead of me.

We walked in towels to the club's green-carpeted, mahogany-paneled changing room. Bo took the book I had planted on him the night before from his duffle bag and, swaddled in terry cloth, settled into a leather couch. He flipped knowingly to the inside back cover, and began chuckling as he happened upon a nametag that Mickey had stuck there during a model-UN conference at Harvard. They always assign the worst students the least important countries at these things, so it was no real surprise that Mickey had been made a delegate from Equatorial Guinea. Still, he had made the best of it. His nametag read:

MR. MICKEY QUINN

AMBASSADOR OF PRESIDENT TEODORO OBIANG NGUEMA MBASOGO

WHO IS ONE CRAZY MOTHERFUCKER

"I'm keeping this book," said Bo with a smile, then settled back into the green leather sofa to read about the Ewoks and their hang gliding adventure.

AT MY DESK AT J. S. SPENSER WERE DESPERATE VOICEMAILS from Frances, angry e-mails from my father, and a sheaf of letters from American Express, who really, really, really wanted their money. The only bright spot was a letter postmarked from Jaipur. This I tucked into my blazer pocket as Monica Speer, Dewey Ananias's executive assistant, came down the aisles of cubicles to my desk. I was almost happy to see her. I was ready to get it over with.

"Dewey has to cancel his three-fifteen with you," she said.

I pretended first to have known about the meeting, and then to seem upset by its cancellation.

"He'd like you to come by his apartment, tonight at eight," she continued, handing me Ananias's engraved calling card.

The white card stock felt like a baby's skin. Engraved atop it in royal blue was a coat of arms that looked strangely English for a man from upstate New York. Below, hand-painted in letters almost too faint to read, was Ananias's address.

DEWEY & ZOYA ANANIAS

740 PARK AVENUE

NEW YORK, NY 10028

"He and his wife just moved into *Seven-Forty Park*," said Monica, seeming to extract physical pleasure from the mere pronunciation of the city's most vaunted address.

"Doesn't LaToya Jackson own in that building?" I asked, just to piss her off.

"I don't think so," she said after a moment's thought, and then marched off.

I HAD A J. S. SPENCER TOWN CAR DROP ME OFF AT THE FAMOUS 740 Park Avenue just a bit before eight. From John D. Rockefeller to Steve Schwartzman, 740 Park Avenue had housed most of Manhattan's potentates. It seemed that, having been rejected from so many elite establishments, Ananias had finally been accepted somewhere. I buttoned my blazer, walked inside the gleaming granite lobby, and told the doorman that Dewey Ananias and his wife, Zoya, were expecting me. He could not have looked more surprised had I told him that I had come to see LaToya Jackson.

"There's no one in this building with that name," he said, and when I asked if he was sure, he said that he was, and suggested that I leave.

I walked back onto Park. I looked down at Ananias's card, which still read 740 PARK AVENUE. I then looked up at the numbers on the building, which also read 740 PARK AVENUE. I was by this point entirely used to things not going my way, and numbers have never been good friends of mine, but this seemed entirely preposterous. Was the doorman out to get me? Was this an aptitude test of some sort? Or was I hallucinating, like Manuel, from all of the caviar down in Cabo? I tried to think things through, and then, far down Seventy-first Street, I noticed a huge yellow cement truck.

I have loved trucks like this since I was a little kid. It just seemed very cool to think that they could show up anywhere, turn on that big cylinder in the back, and—presto!—build anything you wanted. Operating a cement mixer was one of those jobs that every kid back in kindergarten said he wanted to have one day, before it all got confused. So I walked down the block, almost to Lexington Avenue, and I watched this big truck closing up work for the day. The guys in hard helmets had just laid new sidewalk and were washing out the combine in the back, and I nodded to them and they nodded back and it made me feel not so old just to see this truck. I waved as they pulled away, and as the truck left the curb I noticed that it had been obscuring a long, green awning, and that this awning was just feet away from Lexington Avenue, and that upon it was the number 740.

"Could anyone possibly be so deluded as to live ten yards away from Lexington Avenue, but insist they live on Park?"

This I wondered as I stared up at the building which rose to hover above Lexington Avenue in thirty stories of white brick and tiered verandas. It was a lovely building, to be sure, but seemed to have been built only recently, and had nothing in common with the foreboding limestone façade of the famous 740 Park Avenue. Still, I approached the doorman, a Haitian immigrant dressed to resemble an English nobleman.

"Does Dewey Ananias live here?" I asked him.

"He do, sah," said the man.

I explained myself and he picked up a beige phone with his white gloved hand. Someone in the Ananias apartment acknowledged my invitation, and the doorman waved me to a shiny brass elevator, which quickly rose up to the nineteenth floor of a building that, although most aptly described as 740 Lexington Avenue, seemed to have supplied all that Dewey and Zoya Ananias needed to realize their dream of living at 740 Park. The elevator opened into a foyer, and I was met by a bowlegged Filipino maid. She smiled politely, her dark head floating above the white linen of her uniform.

"Come in!" she said, and bowed. "So happy! So welcome!"

She began to walk backward, then stopped sharply and grimaced. At first I feared a stroke, but soon saw the real cause of her discomfort. Behind her five-foot frame was the young Dewey Ananias Jr., fat and happy on a neon-green Big Wheel, water-balloon hand grenades bulging from his pockets. I parted with any guilt for botching his Buckley candidacy as he shot the little woman in the back with a pink plastic Super Soaker.

"Latrell Phelps is gonna love you," I said to myself, and he must have heard because he raised the gun and squirted my face.

"I own you, fucker," he giggled in his castrato-like voice, and I realized that, despite his frenetic schedule at work, Dewey Ananias had made time for his son.

"You what?" I asked.

"I own you, fucker!" he sang, then threw a water-balloon that missed me but soaked the elevator and Big-Wheeled off down the hallway.

"So sorry!" said the maid as she mopped up the water-balloon shrapnel.

"*Dewey Junior funny boy!* Big Dewey, by piano with guests. I take you now!"

THE WHITE STONE FLOOR OF THE FOYER OPENED ONTO A hallway the size of Frances's living room. Life-sized nude portraits of a woman who seemed not too distantly related to Melania Knauss hung in recessed panels on the walls. Whoever this woman was, she had recently mastered a look of feral surprise, and carried it through each of the pictures even as her poses changed. In the first portrait her right forearm covered her breasts, and she straddled a chained tiger. In the second she raised a knee to preserve modesty, and held a blowtorch. In the third her torso was turned to betray just the curvature of her oiled buttocks, and her face was streaked with grease. In the final portrait she was fully pregnant, and exposed. I wondered why Ananias's wife would choose to decorate in this manner, but soon wondered no more.

Standing before a white grand piano in a midnight blue satin evening gown was the woman from the pictures, and she was Zoya Ananias,

Mistress of Park-on-Lexington. Seated at the piano was a man in his thirties who endeavored to look like a man in his fifties with a shaved head and a pair of thick metal-rimmed eyeglasses. Beside Zoya stood an androgynous Hispanic teen. He chewed nervously at his purple-painted fingernails and wore more foundation than any woman present. Zoya raised a delicate arm at my arrival.

"Dewey," she lazed in an Eastern European accent. "Is boy from bank."

Guests arranged on white silk sofas across the room turned from Zoya and momentarily stopped sipping from glasses of white wine to greet me. I noticed Tyler Russell and his wife, Sadie, who looked exactly like him, with the small exception of a small pair of breasts. Opposite the Russells was a young blond couple. The man seemed to have a permanently raised eyebrow; the woman seemed to be eternally smelling something foul. They nodded lame hellos, then stared at an orchid-filled vase on the glass table in front of them. Presiding over the entire room was Dewey Ananias, seated on a divan like some ancient conqueror. For the first time I noticed the unnaturally dark color of his hair. It was not too far from the midnight blue of his wife's dress, but somehow worked well with the unnatural tan of his face. He attempted a smile, but succeeded only in baring a set of yellowed teeth.

"You cancelled on me today! Don't do it twice! You're here just in time for the music! Sit, sit!"

This warm reception made me suspect from the start that Ananias had confused me with Thorne. There was no time to correct him, though, and his evident pleasure at my arrival made the orchid-staring couple on the near sofa rethink their disdain. They shifted to accommodate me, and introduced themselves.

"Ashley Aitken," said the young man in an exquisite Kensington accent, and gestured to the woman beside him. "My wife, Stephanie."

*Institutional Investor* had profiled Ashley Aitken after he made managing director at J. S. Spenser as a twenty-six-year-old. Ananias had been instrumental in his rise, and in securing an investment of two hundred million dollars from Spenser Partners when Ashley left the firm to start Pax Partners, a defense-sector private equity fund. Donald Rumsfeld did the rest, and by his thirty-second birthday Ashley was worth sixty million dollars. The fortune had qualified him to marry the former Stephanie Thayer, a Diane von Furstenberg publicist who had gained social mastery of Manhattan at Spence, and never let go. I had no idea where to begin with this pair, and, perhaps sensing my discomfort, Ananias asked me a question.

"Do you like Lindsay Lohan?"

"Do you want to fire me, or chat about teenage coke addicts?" I wondered.

"I think my brother is a fan of hers," I said.

"She's very big with young people," informed Ananias. "Zoya is going to be playing her in a musical! I'm producing. Ashley and Tyler are investing."

The other men nodded to acknowledge their participation, and that they possessed wealth enough to throw away. Ananias gestured to the bald, bespectacled man at the piano.

"Bernard wrote the thing. He directed *Rent*. Have you seen *Rent*? Of course you have. Bernard's a genius. A real genius!"

An article in *New York Magazine* would reveal that Bernard Kauffman had indeed directed *Rent,* yes, but only for Carnival Cruise Lines. Right now he was putting his oceangoing days behind him, and rose from the piano bench to discuss his new work.

"I've been working on *Lohan: The Musical* for two years," he said. "Act One is performed entirely on roller skates, like *Starlight Express*. It conveys the frenzied rush of Lindsay's rise from Disney's *The Parent*

*Trap* to mainstream stardom. Act Two goes on to explore the emergence of Lindsay's sexuality in her *Mean Girls* years. It's told entirely from the perspective of her hoo-ha, like *The Vagina Monologues*. Act Three grapples with the tabloid-devoured Lohan of today, drowning in her own fame until the character of Karl Lagerfeld rescues her with his solo, 'I'll Protect You from Yourself.' It takes place entirely underwater, just like—"

"Like *The Little Mermaid*!" interjected Ananias.

"Yes, like *The Little Mermaid*," said Kauffman, eyes twinkling from behind his thick plastic frames. He nodded to the fey young man beside Zoya.

"Esteban Villegas was my Angel when I did *Rent*. For *Lohan: The Musical* I've cast him in the role of Wilmer Valderrama. Zoya will play Lindsay. We've got great makeup people, and they'll freckle her up. But tonight I thought we would do a number from Act Two. Zoya? Esteban? Are we ready?"

Zoya and Esteban took deep breaths, and nodded yes.

"The song is called 'Come Inside,'" said Kauffman, trilling gently on the piano. It was an age of plagiarism, and no grievances were registered as he played a song that sounded an awful lot like "On My Own" from *Les Miserables*. But once Zoya and Esteban began to sing I realized I had never heard music quite like this. The Russells and Aitkens hung somewhere between speechlessness and offense. Bernard Kauffman gloried in the song, though, and in his starlet too, as Zoya traced Esteban's cheek with her painted fingernails and explored the top of her register:

*No one else,*
*Can me shake and quiver!*
*So what is love?*
*If not Lohan, and Wilmer?*

These lyrics and the sight of his happy wife were enough to convince Dewey Ananias that *Lohan: The Musical* would be worth every dollar. He cut short the recital with applause and looked at his fourth wife as if she were his first.

"I met Zoya five years ago," he bellowed from the sofa. I noticed his gray belly peeking out from between the buttons of his shirt, and holes bored into his beard by adolescent acne. Suddenly he seemed quite old.

"I was staying at Le Richmond in Geneva for an oil conference," he continued. "They've got girls from all over the place at these things. Romanian girls, Estonian girls, Slovakian girls. But I knew from the moment I saw her that Zoya was different! Look at her!"

He gestured with his glass up and down her body.

"Who knew she was so talented? I had to donate twenty-five grand to Chuck Schumer just to get her a visa. Was it worth it? Stop. It was the best twenty-five grand I ever spent. I always wanted to marry rich and beautiful. Zoya taught me that sometimes getting half of what you want isn't bad."

Ananias thought this a high compliment, and so was a bit taken aback by Zoya's suddenly wounded face. He resolved to do better.

"She's gonna be even bigger than Lindsay Lohan!" he said, and bade us raise our glasses to the entwined futures of Zoya Ananias and *Lohan: The Musical.*

"I'm famished, darling," said Stephanie Aitken to Ashley Aitken.

"Yes, quite," said Ashley to the room.

"Maria! We'll have dinner now! Maria!" shouted Ananias, and the little Filipino woman appeared, and we proceeded through another Zoya-portrait-covered hallway, past a sweeping beige staircase and an empty-shelved library, until finally we came to the dining room.

The room was dominated by a titanium-legged mother-of-pearl

table. The floors were made of soft-white glass tiles; a supernova-inspired chandelier dangled from the high ceiling, and its translucent crystal panels chimed as our entrance stirred the air of the room. Ananias sat at one head of the table, Zoya at the other, and the rest of us settled between them in places dictated by cards in brushed-metal holders. Stephanie and Ashley Aitken sat across from me; Bernard and Esteban were beside them. I had Sadie Russell on my right, and Ananias to my left. He sprayed my cheek with saliva as he ordered Maria to adjust the lighting.

"Maria! Get us lighting setting four!" he said, and she punched away at a digital console in the corner of the room. The chandelier woke to a vague glimmer and all around us green, pink, and blue murals of a sprawling Southampton estate glowed to life.

Ananias clapped at the wonders of lighting setting four.

"Maria!" he shouted. "We'll have the first course! And three bottles of the 2006 Falernian! This is Zoya's night! We'll have only the best!"

He smiled happily at his wife and guests.

"I bought the seeds for these grapes at Christie's in London, and we got our people growing them at our estate," he explained. "They're ancient. Roman. Cost me almost a million, but so good that it's all worth it. Bordeaux? Napa? Stop. Tonight it's my million-dollar wine."

Ananias inspected his guests' faces, and stopped at Stephanie Aitken, who was looking lustily at the murals of the grand Southampton house. She had long ago been conditioned to court the company of anyone who owned such a place.

"Ashley and I just returned from France, visiting a friend of his from Cambridge," she said. "The family has an old château in St. Emilion and makes lovely Bordeaux. But I agree with you, wines from the Hamptons are just as good. . . ."

She craned her neck to better see the mural on the wall behind me.

"What a fabulous place. Is it turn of the century? I feel like I've seen it before."

"Isn't it big?" said Ananias. "We finished it last year. The vineyard is on three hundred acres."

"Three hundred acres in Southampton?" said an amazed Ashley Aitken.

"Southampton?" responded Ananias, incredulously. "I owned out there for a while, but in the end I couldn't stand it. So I had an architect copy one of the old Duke family places. Then I had it rebuilt. Except, obviously, a lot bigger. Now I've got the biggest house in Garrison, New York!"

I was at this point fully in awe of Ananias, who managed to live on Park Avenue while on Lexington, and in Southampton while in Garrison.

"We hear it's very nice up there," said the Aitkens, who had never heard of Garrison, New York, before that moment.

Ananias smiled to acknowledge their compliment, and his grin only grew as Maria entered with the bottles of his million-dollar wine, an amber liquid with the consistency of motor oil that actually did taste lovely. Stephanie Aitken noted hints of flowers and honey. From her place beside me Sadie Russell agreed. The first glass of the stuff hit me like Prozac, and as my fears of firing faded I joined Tyler Russell and Ashley Aitken in a second glass, then a third. Maria emerged from the kitchen and served porcelain bowls filled with vichyssoise. Zoya's name had been glazed upon the bowls in a continuous script, and upon noticing this Esteban complimented her on her taste. Soon their conversation was joined by soft chatter and the delicate clanking of silver on bone china. Had I not been drunk I might have winced as Ananias jutted a stout forefinger into my arm.

"You've had a good year with us, right?" he said.

"I'm sorry?" I slurred.

"You've done a billion-dollar deal and you're only just out of school. That's a pretty good year," he said.

It was true; Ananias thought I was Roger Thorne.

"I'm Tom Quinn," I explained, hoping to end the poor man's confusion. "*Tommy Quinn. I worked with you on the Spenser Partners oil fields. With Terence Mathers?* Do you remember that?"

It was out, and soon it would be over.

"Of course I do," said Ananias. "We sold the oil fields last week. For three billion."

I couldn't have been more shocked had Elvis, Hitler, and Mata Hari conga-lined into the room. Ananias was proud as a king. I stared at him in disbelief.

"Who bought the oil fields?" I asked.

"J. S. Spenser Asset Management," he said. "They manage five hundred billion for pensions, retirement funds, nothing big. But money is money. I told the head of Asset Management that if he didn't buy those oil fields, we might have to find a new head of Asset Management."

So this was how you made a fortune. Ananias had somehow coerced J. S. Spenser to pay J. S. Spenser a multimillion-dollar fee to sell J. S. Spenser oil fields that J. S. Spenser already owned. It was dizzying just to process such advanced inanity, and things grew stranger still.

"Bonuses are off the charts this year," continued Ananias. "You're years away from the real money, but I've got you down for eighty grand. And next year we'll get you more."

His tie was iridescent in the chandelier light. Sweat rolled across his hyper-tan face and pooled in his acne scars. He looked at me with some concern, and asked a very important question.

"You're not thinking of suing anybody over this Mexico conference, are you?"

I had neither the money nor the will to sue, and shook my head no.

"Good. You're smart. Those Indian girls were stupid. What did they get? A few million? And they'll never work on Wall Street again. At least not as long as I'm around. All for a couple of million. Do you know how many people have a couple of million?"

He gestured greedily about the table.

"Russell? He's a fifty-million-dollar guy. Ashley? He's a hundred-million-dollar guy. Me? I'm a two-hundred-million-dollar guy. You? You could be a thirty- or forty-million-dollar guy if you play it right. But can you imagine being just a million-dollar guy? Could you live with that? Of course not."

"Why not?" I asked, and thought of Bo Sloan's vast wealth, and the happiness it had evidently brought him.

"Because then you'd only be a million-dollar guy!" said Ananias, and looked at me as if to say, Aha! Bet you didn't think of that!

That Spenser would not be firing me, but paying me eighty thousand dollars not to litigate against them, was a powerful revelation. I could now stay in Manhattan with Frances. I could stop the calls from American Express. Or I could simply flee. I could go to medical school, and even if it was an awful Costa Rican medical school, who cared? I'd be the happiest student at El Universidad de Medicina de Santa Filomena. Frances would come and Mickey would visit and we would live on the beach and no one would drown.

I dreamed of all these things, and was drawn back to the dinner party only when Maria reemerged from the kitchen struggling beneath a huge white ceramic platter bearing two whole Chilean sea bass. Each fish had been glazed a dark brown and given a head sculpted from mashed potatoes. The mashed-potato faces smiled at each other as Maria served our plates, and then vanished from the room. The fish was roundly praised, and just when it seemed that no higher compliments could be offered, Ananias offered his own perspective on things.

"These things are endangered, you know," he said through a mouth of sea bass. "In ten or twenty years, they'll all be gone. So eat up while you can!"

Ananias's guests rushed to show expertise in sea bass, and his appetite seemed to grow with each bit of piscene trivia. He shoveled the fish from his plate, drained one glass of wine and then another, and finally burst with excitement.

"We ate these things to extinction!" he said, scraping the last of the fish from his plate and eyeing what remained on the platter. "Can you believe it? How amazing is . . ."

Ananias's voice trailed off. His face grew red, his mouth hung open, and his eyes bulged as somewhere within his esophagus, the endangered sea bass took a stand. It took a few seconds for us to realize he was choking. And even then, no one knew quite what to do.

"Dewey choking!" screamed Zoya at last, and rushed to her husband.

We watched as she wrapped her fine arms around his rough gut and thrust. I backed away as she rocked him in his big chair like an overstuffed rag doll, failing again and again to clear his throat. She was just high this time, just low that time, and as she kept missing the spot Ananias's body went limp and his face turned blue and his guests gawked, poorly passing off fascination as concern. Say what you like about these bankers' wives. Laugh about how they use their husbands' cash to pursue useless careers. Whisper that they are just prostitutes with long-term contracts. Feign shock at all these things, which might all be true. I can only tell you what I saw. Zoya Ananias fought like hell to save her husband from choking on his fish.

"That's it. That's it!" I cheered, when finally she found the rhythm of the Heimlich.

Ananias's eyes had by now rolled fully back, but Zoya was no quitter. She kicked off her heels and shot out her giraffe's legs to brace herself as she pulled her double-fist eight inches into her husband's vast gut, and with this final rush against the diaphragm sent an inch-long, bloody sea bass bone up from Ananias's mouth, through the air, then clanking through the panes of the hanging chandelier, and onto the table.

"Oh my Dewey! Oh my Dewey!" Zoya cried, as he regained consciousness.

"Holy shit! Holy fuckin' shit!" wheezed Ananias, and although his life had been saved and the man ought to have been thankful, the outrage of being so close to expiration kept him from displaying any gratitude.

"I almost died!" he screamed, then leaned forward, and in a gurgling rasp filled his plate with a fetid bouillabaisse of esophageal blood, partially digested fish, and foamy saliva. A few drops of this mixture made their way to Stephanie Aitken's cleavage. She recoiled, and Ashley rushed to attend his debutante-bride with a concern far greater than anything shown throughout his mentor's brush with death.

This annoyed Ananias greatly.

"Fuck you people!" he said. "I feel this fucking bone go down and it cuts into my windpipe and everything goes black. What do you do? Huh? You just sit there?"

We stared blankly at our plates.

"I come and give you Heimlich," whimpered Zoya, who alone had acted. "I am thinking you were dead . . ."

"*You* did!" said Ananias, his strength turning to anger as quickly as it returned. "But what about the rest of them? I was almost dead! I almost died!"

He leered at Ashley Aitken, who had shown more concern for his wife's décolletage than Ananias's life. Even the typically sedate Tyler Russell cringed as he lashed out at him.

"What would you have said about me if I died?" Ananias sneered, wiping his face with a napkin that I alone observed to grow a dark shade of copper by the self-tanning ointment.

"Dewey, please," pleaded Ashley, embarrassed for himself.

"Tell me," commanded Ananias, numbing the cuts in his throat with a quick glass of million-dollar wine. "What would you say about me?"

"Please, Dewey," said Zoya, now as embarrassed for herself as her guest, "now let's be relaxed and eat."

"You shut up!" He spat at her, soft gray patches now visible beneath his dyed, disheveled hair.

"You tell me what you would say if I died," he demanded of Ashley Aitken, then threatened, "or I swear to God I'll pull every cent of J. S. Spenser money from your fund."

Ashley Aitken placed his hand on Ananias's arm in hope of making things better. Ananias cast him a look of venom.

"Don't you touch me!" he snarled at his old protégé. "I'll pull us from your fund faster than you can say *shit*. You know that? I own you, fucker!"

Zoya decided that she would have to calm him down, and began to recite what she would have said at her husband's funeral had he died.

"I would say that you brought me to New York City and gave me Park Avenue house," she said. "I say that you gave me very beautiful things. Beautiful boy. Beautiful clothes. Beautiful musical. I would say you die too soon, eating sea bass. Eating favorite food. I would say you are good man, and that—"

"*Was* a good man!" corrected Ananias.

"Was good man," continued Zoya, eviscerated, "and I would say I loved you very much. Miss you very much . . ."

Ananias took Zoya's hand, and stroked her flesh to comfort her imagined mourning. The blood drained from his pale, pitted skin. He fixed his dyed hair. Then, still holding his wife's hand, he leaned back, laid his arm across his chest, and closed his eyes as if the sea bass had done him in. Zoya wiped her nose with her hand and smeared the mucus against the back of her chair.

That year I had seen exploding machines, farting babies, a spitting midget, angry leftists, homemade porn, psychopathic Saudis, inbred Rockefellers, and a great deal more. Still, nothing could have prepared anyone for Zoya's odd funeral oration. Expert as she was at affecting the right poses and phrases at the right places and moments, not even Stephanie Aitken knew what to say. Maria served cake, then coffee. We ate and drank in silence. In time Ananias had sufficiently recovered to offer wisdom gleaned from his proximity to death.

"People say life isn't about money," he intoned, with an apologetic glance to his newly broken wife. "They're wrong. Life is entirely about money. It's death that has nothing to do with it."

He paused to let his hard-won revelation sink in.

"Death has nothing to do with money at all," he said once more.

"And that's the very worst part of it."

# 15

## THE RACQUET &
## TENNIS CLUB

The elderly, ashen black man wore trash bags for shoes and took swigs from a warm forty of Miller Genuine Draft as he made his speech to the crowded 6 train of Upper East Siders. From the way he moved his hands as he talked it felt as if he had to be making pretty important points, but as I entered the subway at Seventy-seventh Street to ride down to Grand Central it seemed no one much wanted to hear him. The riders buried themselves in magazines, inspected their feet, and turned up their iPods as he went on with a strange intensity.

"I mean, it turn out, human beings always trying to create life itself, right?" he said, and looked about the car to see who was with him.

No one was, but he continued anyway.

"Human beings have always contemplated the creation of life itself. Because human beings, homo sapiens, have always wondered: *Where do I come from? How was life created?* You know why? Because

if it's within the realm of human understanding, we could do it ourselves!"

I leaned in to hear him better. He caught my eye and went on, now
emboldened by an audience of one.

"But if it is within us to create, why is it that we cannot create it?" he
asked, and paused to let the question sink in.

At Grand Central I would catch a 3:40 train to New Canaan to see
Frances. I had no idea what we could reasonably say to each other that
could get everything back where it should be. I didn't so much fear as
expect disaster. Oh, I was tired and morbid and generally in need of
some wisdom, some big epiphany, one of those glowing keys that turns
all the question marks to exclamations. I was in no position to be
choosy about where it came from.

"You tell me," I asked him. "How come we can't do it?"

My fellow riders let out a collective groan as he raised his leathery
brow and went on: "I'm sayin' this doctor, okay? His name be Franken-
stein! Doctor Frankenstein! Now he says, *Go get some bodies! Dead
bodies! I'm gonna bring 'em back to life! I'm gonna bring that—I'm gonna
bring that back to life! 'Cause ain't no reason why a person can't create or,
or, or . . .*"

He nailed it on the fourth try: *"Organic life!"*

He looked mournfully around the car, unable to accept that all of
this should be wasted on just my set of ears. The thing is, though, you
can't make anyone learn anything. So I admired him, but I knew that
he was hopeless when he looked at the young woman seated next to me.
She was tall and surrounded by Bergdorf bags, and with her strained,
plain looks bore a strong resemblance to Phoebe.

"Miss! Miss!" he asked. "You sense my question?"

She ignored him, and buried her face in the week's *Time,* an issue
exploring stem cell research. The other passengers rallied to her aid
with pissed-off leers, but the man was undeterred.

"Fuck those bitches!" he said, and waved off the Phoebe doppel-gänger and the rest of them as he continued: "This Doctor Franken-stein, he said, *If life has been created, why is it that homo sapiens cannot create life?* Homo sapiens, man! He said, *I got some genius! No reason I can't do it! I'm intelligent enough!* 'Cause when he was in school, he was an honor student . . ."

I wanted to know where he going with it all, but as the man ram-bled on, the train came to a stop. I rose from my seat, and he dismissed me with a nod that made me think of my old college professors. I nod-ded back, then ran to make the train to New Canaan.


THERE IS SO MUCH THERAPY DOLED OUT DAILY AT THESE country club mental hospitals that just by showing up and wearing a blazer you are bound to get a dose. Silver Hill's campus was dotted with big white country homes and might easily have been confused by the uninitiated for a luxury real estate development, or at least a day school. I had not been there for twenty minutes when I found myself in the place's main house, trying very hard not to watch a mating pair of red cardinals flying about beyond the window as I spoke with Frances's psychologist. Dr. Phillip McCarthy was built like a troll, short and stout. In his late thirties, he seemed to have received just about every degree that NYU and Columbia could confer. I don't know much about the insanity industry, but I imagine it has the same hierarchies as the finan-cial world, both of them being, after all, money-making endeavors. Whatever his position, Dr. McCarthy was at least doing well enough to pay another doctor several thousand dollars to harvest hairs from his ass and back and replant them in neat rows across his scalp. He screened me before I could see Frances, then set the terms for the visit.

"We'll keep it to fifteen minutes. This is all very stressful for everyone, as you well know. She's waiting for us over in Grey House now . . ."

———

THE EDGES OF FRANCES'S CUT WERE KEPT TOGETHER BY A lacing of purple sutures. They had been processed to extreme fluorescence and glowed from beneath a bandage of translucent silicone. Dr. McCarthy sat on a sofa in the far corner of Grey House's living room, happily reading a copy of *Cosmopolitan* with Jessica Simpson on the cover, whose brightest headline read HOW TO SET HIS THIGHS ON FIRE! He looked up at us occasionally, though for the longest time we didn't even look at each other. I thought of telling Frances that her bandage reminded me of her picture of Andy Warhol's Day-Glo frogs, and that I had not known that bandages could be beautiful, and that wounds could be made to look like works of art. I looked at her wrist and the slash, which started in a straight line, then slid into a curve, so that each Day-Glo stitch could be seen as a single star in the Little Dipper. I looked down at this very odd constellation and tried to decide whether it was a good or a bad thing, and I remained mesmerized even as the hand attached to the wound rose from the table and whirred through the damp country air on its way to my face. I caught it before impact. Frances stared at me in rage as I held her by the cut.

"You never came home," she said weakly. "I waited up for you. I didn't leave the house for two days. And I needed you. And you never came."

"On the last night of the trip we went out on a yacht," I told her. "There was a kidnapping, and Thorne and I were thrown overboard. I've been trying to get to you since I hit the water. You were right, Frances. Thorne and I met Jesus, and you were right about the saviors. He robbed us and disappeared without a trace."

She searched my eyes for some sign of a lie, and when she found none could only shake her head.

"Pirates," she said, in disbelief.

"Zapatistas," I corrected.

"No difference," she concluded. "Not for you. Not for me."

"Not for we," I said, and she smiled a weak smile.

"I've lied to you," she told me, and brushed her hand across the bandaged cut.

"I know," I said. "And I've lied to you. I am a disaster at work. They've been trying to fire me all year."

She took my hand and held it in her own.

"Let's leave," I said. "I'll enroll at the Universidad, and we can go to Costa Rica, and we can watch it end from there. An escape act. I can't promise the singing monkeys, but it will be beautiful, and no drowning Frances. No drowning."

I was so happy to feel her again that I didn't notice how her face dropped at the mention of flight.

"It's too late for escapes," she said, taking her hand away from mine and shaking her head, as if to rid it of this foul notion. "Don't you see how it's far too late? And what's in Costa Rica? There's nothing in Costa Rica. We'd only come back."

With nothing to say I looked down at Frances's hands, and found them somewhat different.

"Where is your mother's ring?" I asked her.

"They took it," she said weakly.

"Why?"

"It was too sharp," she said, and her voice broke, and she began to cry.

Dr. McCarthy looked up from his magazine and tapped at his watch to signal that the meeting was entering the realm of failure, and ought to end.

"You're wrong," I said to Frances, sensing our last moments. "Let's leave."

*"There is no leaving,"* she said, sad and impatient. "It's too late for escapes."

"My brother left," I said hopefully.

"He'll be back," she said dolefully.

"You don't understand," she added. "It's only we that matters, not where."

I went to touch her hair but she recoiled at my hand. Dr. McCarthy stood above the table as we sat across from each other, old strangers.

"I think that this is over," he said, and he was right.

I moved my things from Frances's apartment that evening.

She got back from Silver Hill that Sunday. I know because she called to ask why my things were gone from the apartment. She was surprisingly even for someone who had just spent a month under the care of Dr. Phillip McCarthy. Maybe it was the medication. Maybe she was just exhausted. Maybe there was nothing left to be said.

"Is that it for us?" she asked.

"It doesn't have to be," I replied. "Please come. If it is all so bad, why can't you just come?"

"It is brutal," she said. "But jungles are places we came from, not places to go to. Don't you understand?"

"I'm not quite sure I do," I told her, because I wasn't.

She was right, things didn't go as planned for Mickey in Costa Rica. Hang gliding as a sport requires intense concentration and great attention to detail. For all of his many gifts, Mickey comes up awfully short in both of these areas, and so he was ill suited from the start for his chosen pastime. Within a few months he would crash his hang glider into a eucalyptus tree, and run out of money. But that all came later, and in my mind, during the waning days of June, I saw him swooping up and down over the rain forest canopy, darting about with all the other brilliant creatures of flight. I was tired of the city. Tired of the streets and buildings and people, all kept just a few degrees below combustion to slow-cook into deformity. Tired of the SWAT teams and the United Nations and George W. Bush staying at the Waldorf and his daughters grinding at Bungalow, and tired of Park Avenue spreads overlooking Lexington and pockmarked priests and . . . tired of it all.

"I don't want you to leave," said Frances.

"I know you don't," I said.

"I know," she said.

The days passed and through e-mail I received word from El Universidad de Medicina de Santa Filomena that my acceptance was still good, and that I had a place in their class for the next fall. I took fifteen hundred dollars from my bonus and bought a ticket to San José on the eve of Thorne's engagement party. I felt the sharp edges of its paper as I leaned against the railing, and looked in at Frances. I wondered what to do.

THE SUN HAD JUST LEFT US, AND THE TWILIT SKY WAS DARK against a pink moon. Sophie hung over the rail of the balcony and ashed her cigarette down onto Park and declared it all *breathtaking*. Inside the ballroom the Hispanic porters rang silver bells, and so well-conditioned were the men and women of the evening that they did not even break from their conversations as they floated, in pairs and threes and fours and fives, down the hallway and into the vast reading room, which had been set for dinner. There is a gravity to so many people moving at once, and you're powerless against it. We hung on outside for a bit, but soon the novelty of our transgression wore off, and we rejoined the party.

The dining room was dark save for a gleaming white-clothed table that ran for most of the room's considerable length. There was glistening silver and glossy china and perhaps fifteen perfectly polished candelabras, each twinkling with dozens of ivory candles. The diminished visibility caused distant faces to fade into the rugs and paneling, and kept me from seeing that I was seated next to Frances until I had made my way around that table in search of my own name, and found it on an ivory card on the plate just beside hers. I sat there for a while, feeling the ticket in my pocket, and noticing as I did another piece of paper there as well. I had put the letter from Makkesh's mother in my pocket before the dinner with Ananias, and been so taken with the spectacle of his near death that I forgot it altogether. I took it out now, and held the thin paper envelope to the candlelight, and with my butter knife slit it open. Inside was a news clipping, and atop it, a letter.

Dear Thomas Quinn,

Thank you so very much for your very kind note. I can see that you cared very much for Makkesh. Please know that Makkesh was given a beautiful funeral, and that his favorite prayer songs were sung, and that we spread his ashes in a knoll not far from our home, where he played as a boy.

It is true that Makkesh had a nephew, and that many believe he returned as a bird. They say this because this bird came to his mother's window each day until she spoke to him, and when the bird saw that she knew it was fine, it flew away. So I do believe that yes, it is true, and this sometimes does happen.

I am sending you an article from the BBC. Scientists from the University of Delhi have discovered a new species of sparrow, not far from the place where we spread Makkesh's ashes. I would not send this to you ordinarily, but the bird is very pudgy indeed, and has a thick stripe of black feathers on its head, and does look like Makkesh. It has not visited my window, but makes me feel happy indeed.

I wish you happiness and joy,
Aparna Makker

I unclipped her letter from the article, and although I'm not religious, as I've said, I can only tell you what I've seen, and that bird looked exactly like Makkesh. It had his dark eyes and his little nose and his big belly and his thick black hair. Its chest was purple and blue, like his favorite gingham shirt. Its talons were dark brown, like his best pair of Cole Haan loafers. The article went on about the rarity of the discovery, and how people had thought that every bird species in India had been found, but that this one had somehow eluded everyone. I've talked to you about those epiphanies, but will tell you plainly that I didn't know what to make of this. I knew one thing, though, that if someone like Makkesh had opted out of another go-round of this human-being business, there was scant hope for the rest of us. And even though I didn't know where I stood on the whole reincarnation thing, I felt that I could understand how, assuming it was true and there was no escape, you might elect to trade all of your thought and reason for a brilliant set of feathers and a strong pair of wings. I thought of Mickey, and how he had done just that. I held the picture up, and examined every bit of that bird, and couldn't believe my eyes. I was so in awe that I didn't notice Frances until she sat down right next to me.

She looked beautiful as ever, and as I pulled out my chair looked at me with eyes that now seemed a bit dimmer than when we first met. She did not speak but smiled warmly as she extended her dainty hand, and as I looked down at her fine fingers I saw that she had gotten her mother's ring back, that things were better. The glowing sutures and silicone bandage had disappeared, and left behind only a faint pink swoop that would soon fade to nothing. Frances did not mind as I inspected the scar. She smiled at me with saddened eyes and held her battered wrist in the space between us, wanting me to do more than just look at it. I thought of Makkesh and Mickey, and how perhaps there was no escaping the rot of this human-being business, and that it was neither her fault nor mine. I only wanted very badly to take her hand, and this is what I did.

She smiled at me, and we sat there with the picture of the Makkesh bird between us, and looked at it and each other as the room filled with pre-dinner chatter. Thorne had seated Sophie Dvornik next to him at the head of the table, but was so excited as he spoke to her about his newest idea for a film that everyone heard him.

"I feel, like, the scene where I fight all of the Zapatista pirates is definitely the pivotal moment in this movie," he said.

"What about the honey and the sex swing?" asked Sophie.

"That's all fun stuff, but totally secondary," explained Thorne. "Because you have to ask yourself, 'Why is this guy fighting these pirates?' And of course the answer is: babes. But if you ask yourself, 'Why is this guy rocking all these babes?' the answer is not pirates. Dig?"

"Dig," said Sophie, and though she laughed she seemed to take this idea of Roger's more seriously than the rest.

"I'll set up a meeting with my father," she said with a resigned shrug.

"Thanks, babe," said Thorne, and beaming, imagined himself in the lead role.

At the other end of the table a hired photographer took a picture of Lauren Schuyler and her mother. As his flash rippled across the many place settings CeCe leaned across Laurance Whistlestopper, who had fallen asleep, and spoke to Phoebe.

"You know, Pheebs, I'm just used to it by now," she said, nodding to the photographer. "I don't let it bother me anymore."

"That's a really mature way to deal," said Phoebe, and followed CeCe's hand with all that remained of herself as her famous friend tossed her long, naturally blond hair.

"Where's Fahad tonight?" Phoebe asked, when CeCe's hair had settled.

"It's so sad, but his older brother died last weekend scuba diving in

Dubai," she said. "Something went wrong with his equipment, I guess. So Fahad's in Riyadh for the funeral."

"Oh, that's too bad," said Phoebe, rolling her eyes at the sleeping Rockefeller. "Do you want to go to Bungalow after?"

"Totally," said CeCe, and dropped her shoulder back as the photographer took another picture.

Frances squeezed my hand just a bit as the familiar strains of conversation filled the room, and I felt the diamond of her mother's engagement ring against my flesh. I wanted to tell her about the bird, but I knew by then that nothing is taught, only learned. We entwined our fingers and I almost lost track of where mine ended and hers began as two candelabras down from us, Terence Mathers fought with his wife who hated him, who now evidently hated him more.

"We had three more people call the apartment today looking for crack," she spat.

"I told you I don't do crack, honey," pleaded Terence.

"How would I know? I never see you," his wife retorted.

*"It's that little shit from Harlem who stole my cell phone!"* burst Mathers.

"Always someone else, isn't it?" exclaimed his exasperated wife, and Mathers resigned himself to the fact that he wasn't winning any arguments that night.

There was one story about Chaim Spero that I had never told Frances, not for any particular reason, but just because I had forgotten it. Between the birds and the chatter and the feeling of her hand again in mine this memory somehow came back to me, and I leaned in to whisper in her ear, and share it with her.

After Chaim and I failed first grade the first time, our parents had signed us up for summer school at Rye Country Day. Chaim made loud noises, yes, and fine, I couldn't subtract, but we didn't really belong in this class. It takes a real moron to fail first grade, is what I mean, and that class was filled with every hopeless case in Westchester. There were paste eaters and kids who pissed themselves and kids with incredibly thick glasses and kids who bit other kids. There were kids who had been born weighing too little, and kids who had been born too early. We spent that full summer with them, and let me tell you, it was no place to be.

Chaim and I stuck together, though, and one day thought that we had found our plan for escape. The teacher had gotten the idea to march us in Rye's Fourth of July parade, and promised that if we spent a week filling old toilet paper rolls with gravel to make noisemakers and twisting big sheets of construction paper into hats and painting others to be American flags, we'd get a day off from all the subtraction and the addition and vowels and consonants. It would be like a regular summer, and as this was all we had really wanted, we agreed. We painted the toilet paper tubes to look very American. We made big flags and small flags. We dressed in red, white, and blue. And then the Fourth of July rolled around, and the teacher brought out a long rope with multicolored hoops in it, and stood before that group of dimwits and sold it off as a toy. She told us to pick our favorite colored loop and not to let go of it for the whole parade, and everyone thought that being tied up like this was pretty exciting indeed. Chaim and I stood there and watched as they all fought for their favorite spots, unable to believe that we had spent a week stuffing toilet paper tubes with gravel for this, eyeing the rope like it was some giant turd. By the time it was ready to go there were two loops left, at the end of the rope, and these were given to Chaim and me.

We marched out from the school, all the little kids going crazy with their noisemakers and flags and their big pointy paper hats. The July sun bore down on us and the rope dug up under our arms and the teacher kept yelling at us *do not let go of the rope,* as she led us from the school, and onto the main street of town, where we joined a larger parade of Girl Scouts and Boy Scouts and Rotarians and PTA mothers, all dressed up and marching. People lined the sidewalks and shouted to us as we passed, and the other flunkee first-graders all waved back with their flags and their toilet-paper-tube noisemakers. I even got in on the action too, I'll admit. Chaim was beside himself, however. He was short and the rope dug into his arm, and as it chafed at his skin he began to *eep,* and in *eep*ing drew puzzled looks from the stroller-pushing mothers on the street, which only made him *eep* more. He tried to turn his face away so that the *eep*ing wouldn't be so easily pinned on him, but this only caused greater problems with the rope, which tore against his underarm each time he shifted against the momentum of the other summer school first-graders.

It was right at the train station when Chaim had had enough. He tried to wiggle out of the loop, but a sudden shift knocked it against his little body, and he fell to the ground. His noisemaker broke and the gravel went spraying. I leaned down to help him but got dragged along too. Chaim *eep*ed like mad and I yelled as loud as I could, but there was a brass band and a lot of people singing "America the Beautiful," and for an endless period of thirty seconds we were towed by the big chain of idiots, the gravel from the noisemakers tearing the skin from our knees, the bright red, white, and blue hats falling down and blinding us, the sun burning against the back of our necks, the rope digging into our arms, me crying and Chaim *eep*ing and no one doing anything. No one stopping the whole mad line, or getting up to lift us from the asphalt. The whole stupid process just went on until finally someone noted the tension on the damn rope, and brought it to a stop, and we were dusted off. But not for our sake. For theirs.

I told this story to Frances, and felt her hand grow tighter around mine with each word. I thought of how I felt that day, and of the burning of the gravel against my palms, and I swore that I could now feel the very same burning, the very same pain. When I was done with the story Frances stared at me blankly, and then at the picture of Makkesh's bird, and then I realized that although the story was done, the pain had not gone away. It didn't hurt so much as it released, and this it did better than Xanax. For a moment I thought that the story had just been particularly cathartic, but then I felt the warm liquid on my hand, and looked down upon the table, and first noticed the thin trail of dark red trickling from our hands down into a crimson stain growing fast on the tablecloth.

At first I thought one of the waiters had spilled wine, and gently touched Frances's arm to show that we ought to clean things up. It wasn't until she loosened her grip that I saw how her mother's diamond had gouged a pock-sized chunk from my hand, and how the blood had pooled within the vacuum of Frances's grip, and how it came now more quickly, in pulses, rushing down my palm, through her fingers, and how, in the space of a final epiphany, I understood it all.

# ACKNOWLEDGMENTS

My deep gratitude is to the many in whose debt I happily stand. Anthony Balbona, friend and mentor, Francophile and Hellenist, who introduced me to Frances; Bob Bliwise, who always believed in me; Sarah Bowlin, who was always just very lovely to me; Alex Hurst, who shared my dream and threw himself behind it; Rob Kindler, who keeps a picture of Abraham Lincoln in his office, and gave me my Trimalchio along with so much else; Billy Kingsland, who offered a road map to the finish; Geoff Kloske, a godsend in whom I could place my trust; David Kuhn, a modern-day Prospero whom I treasure, and who has worked so much magic on my behalf; Megan Lynch, whose steady hand, endless patience, and dependable brilliance I happily count among my blessings; William Meyer, who once got a black eye for me in Mexico City and who lent his many gifts to this writing; Professor Stanley, my greatest teacher, whose love and mastery of the ancient novel inspired me to attempt a modern one. Finally to my family, without whom I would be nothing.

# ABOUT THE AUTHOR

Dana Vachon was born in Greenwich, Connecticut, and raised in Chappaqua, New York. He attended Duke University, and graduated, as he claims, *"cum nihilo"* in 2002. After graduation, Vachon landed a job as an analyst at JPMorgan and began work on this novel. His writing has appeared in the *International Herald Tribune, Men's Vogue, The New York Times,* and *Salon.* He lives in New York City.